Cu

By William D. Arand

Dedicated:

To my wife, Kristin, who encouraged me in all things.

To my son, Harrison, who likes to just play on the ground with his toys in my office now.

To my family, who always told me I could write a book if I sat down and tried.

Special Thanks to:

Niusha Gutierrez

Gavin Lawrenson

Michael Haglund

Steven Lobue

Other Books in the VeilVerse-

Asgard Awakening: By Blaise Corvin

Books by William D. Arand-

The Selfless Hero Trilogy:
Otherlife Dreams
Otherlife Nightmares
Otherlife Awakenings
Ominibus Edition(All Three)

Super Sales on Super Heroes Trilogy:
Super Sales on Super Heroes 1
Super Sales on Super Heroes 2
Super Sales on Super Heroes 3
Omnibus Edition(All Three)

Dungeon Deposed Trilogy:
Dungeon Deposed
Dungeon Deposed 2 (To be released 2019)
Dungeon Deposed 3 (To be released 2019)

Books by Randi Darren-

Wild Wastes Trilogy:
Wild Wastes
Wild Wastes: Eastern Expansion
Wild Wastes: Southern Storm
Omnibus Edition(All Three)

Fostering Faust Trilogy:
Fostering Faust
Fostering Faust 2 (To be Released 2019)
Fostering Faust 3 (To be Released 2019)

Prologue

Stars twinkled amidst the inky vastness, hand fulls of glittering sand thrown across the darkness of infinity. The uncaring vacuum of space was remorseless, offering no warmth or safety, but the Traveler remained untouched. Ages had passed. The Traveler had not spent much time actively thinking for quite some time. All that remained had been a single purpose, a single destination, all driving towards one thing.

Hope.

Despite traversing the void for an eon, the bodiless entity had never lost focus. Revenge and knowledge--the ancient drive still remained strong. The Traveler should have stopped existing long ago, merely dissipating into the cosmos, but the hope born from forbidden knowledge still burned, combining with an iron will, create energy from nothing.

These days, the Traveler was not much more than a moving, glittering shadow with a general plan to exist again. A great deal of luck would be necessary. Uncertainty made the Traveler nervous.

So much time had passed that sacrifices had be made now, of course. All knowledge and power came with a price, and this mission had never been an exception. With steadily decreasing options, the price had grown.

Something had changed, though, providing new direction. Blowing gently, the winds of fate had stirred long-forgotten memories. The Fates could be cruel even as they granted a break. To most, energy was better spent adapting than questioning unattainable knowledge. But to the Traveler, no knowledge was ever truly unobtainable.

It had taken a great deal of time, but the Traveler had been able to read the new shifts in the mystical patterns of the cosmos, and had adjusted course. This would probably be best, last chance to complete the mission. To live again.

Suddenly, a newcomer joined the Traveler, a bright glow amidst the endless shadow. The Traveler sensed something familiar from this Spark, a resonance. Family. The Spark was not directly connected to the Traveler, but was connected to another...a son? The Spark had a name, a relationship. Grandchild.

The Traveler had not expected to meet another on this journey, much less family. At first, the new addition was neither positive nor negative. The Spark was descended from a betrayer, but was still kin. Also, the Spark's energy was fading fast despite being newer, younger than the Traveler. The Traveler had sailed among the stars for far, far longer than the Spark, but had also been far mightier to begin with.

As the two moved through the endless black, the Traveler understood that the Spark was somehow heading toward the same destination. The two did not communicate, but over time, the Traveler took solace, a kind of grounding contentment in the Spark's presence.

Cracks, fissures had begun forming within the Spark's power. The Spark's glow was weaker now, but still burned.

Whether the two would reach their destination together was in doubt, but after so much time, the Traveler decided that it would be good if the Spark succeeded too. Their end goals were probably similar, if not the same. Everything about their destination, the timing, and even a kind of poetic parallel all practically reeked of the Norns' meddling.

In some ways, it was fitting that a child of Loki would still be alive. Live on Little One--the thought was selfless, different--this new thing begged to be explored. Perhaps later. Like the Spark's, the Traveler's strength was waning, just slower. Wisdom and knowledge would help the Traveler with piercing the Veil, but the Spark did not have these tools, these advantages. Youth and willpower may not be enough.

The Traveler knew the time had almost come, the end of the great journey was at hand. There was no more time to consider the Spark, or to wonder if any other family still survived. Preparations had to be made, now. Weapons must be forged from memories, tools from thought.

Everything had a price, and what the Traveler planned would naturally have a high price indeed, but must be paid. Any other path led to oblivion, and that would be unacceptable.

The Traveler crept towards the veil, waiting for the event, a window of time when it would be possible to save two lives for the price of self, to give up almost everything for a second chance.

Revenge and knowledge, knowledge and revenge.

One

Ash brought his forearm across quickly, deflecting the incoming fist to pass by the side of his face.

Stepping inward with the same move, he drove a strike towards his opponent's kidney.

Except his opponent was already gone.

"Ha, you don't actually expect to catch me, do you, Ashley?" taunted Lim.

Only my family calls me that, you —

The young man appeared at Ash's side and launched a Qi-powered kick at him.

In a struggle to be anywhere but where that kick was headed, Ash practically flung himself to the side.

So when the kick landed on his hip, he was sent spinning away. Rather than being driven to the floor.

Ash lost control of himself, twisting as he flew backward. After bouncing off the far wall, he came back into a defensive stance.

Dust rained down on him from the ceiling.

"Now, now," said an elderly voice. "You know better, Lim. This is meant to be a test of martial arts, not your cultivation. Save that for the examination tournament.

"We all know what the outcome will be the moment you use your cultivation on the citizen."

It wasn't a new admonition. Nor was it the first time Ash had heard it today.

In the Spark's Jump Sect, this was an everyday occurrence.

"Oh, of course, Elder. I forgot entirely," Lim said, bowing politely to the middle-aged elder of the outer disciples.

"Yes, yes. Try not to let it happen again. Good work, otherwise," said the elder.

Gritting his teeth, Ash let himself fall into a neutral pose and clasped one fist with the other, bowing to Elder Shin.

"While I don't expect much from a citizen, you should at least strive to be able to win these simple matches," the elder scolded.

"Of course," Ash said through his teeth.

Turning away from the elder, Ash saw Lim sauntering off.

Lim and Shin shared a relation, and both looked eerily similar to Ash. He'd bet on them being uncle and nephew at this point.

Not that it'd matter.

Nepotism was a way of life here, from what he could tell.

The young man and the adult both shared dark-brown hair, cut quite short, with brown eyes the color of dog shit.

Ash walked off to the edge of the mat and fell into a kneeling position.

Thankfully, his humiliation was at an end for the day. He'd already been used as a practice dummy for every other student in this class.

"Do not worry about it," said Jia on his right.

Showing a smile that was more a grimace to Jia, Ash could only nod his head.

Jia was a slim young man with black eyes and hair as dark as midnight. His face was pretty, to the point that women fawned over him.

When Ash had first met the man, he'd sworn he was a woman.

Then again, his standards of beauty were from twenty-first-century America.

Which didn't quite fit here. Not here in Xing City.

"Sooner or later, your Dantian will develop," Jia continued.

Uh huh. You keep on with that positivity, bud. After this year's examination, I can leave this place and help out at home. There's no reason to stay here, and the age limit will have been met.

"Of course. Why would I worry about it? I'm sure it'll be exactly as you say," Ash said.

He only had to wait long enough now for Elder Shin to award those who performed well today, and Ash could escape.

Escape and get some peace and solace.

Where no one would bother him, and he'd be free to pursue... nothing.

Nothing other than simply enjoying the peace and quiet of silence.

***

Ash sat down in the ruined building, crossing his legs underneath him.

Looking around himself, he found it was the same as ever.

Two walls, shattered columns, and a whole lot of nature quickly taking over the destroyed structure.

He was only about thirty minutes out from the small city in which he lived.

And yet it felt as if he were light-years away.

As if there wasn't a single hint of his life here. As if the only thing that had existed here was long gone.

Breathing in through his nose, Ash slowly let air out through his mouth.

"Only a bit more and I can call it quits. Get a job, and just... live. No more school, no more elders, no more Lim," Ash said, his mouth screwing up into a bitter grimace.

Shaking his head, Ash did his best to quickly dispel the negativity he'd just dumped on himself. It would do him no good to bring it here. Here, where he sought the quiet. An escape.

Growling to himself, Ash hung his head, trying to curb his feelings.

When he realized it wasn't going to come easily, he got up and padded over to a wall.

With his emotions already in a knot, he couldn't simply sit there. He needed to just walk around for a moment. That'd help him calm down.

Pressing his hands to the wall, he leaned up against it and let his head sink down. He closed his eyes, then focused on his breathing and his heartbeat.

In searching for the inner peace he'd known in his previous life, Ash could just barely find the fringes of it. A smoky thread of what it had once been.

Except that life is gone now.

You're not a high school kid with a shot at the world stage.

Our ability in the martial arts is almost pointless here given a Dantian.

Everything is just gone. Gone and replaced with this one, and... and all the people, and... and...

Ash grunted and then slammed his fists into the wall, his anger spiking and getting the better of him.

A sharp pop sounded from the wall, and then a grinding noise.

At the same time, the wall started to crumble into itself, the bricks and mortar failing after having withstood the march of time for this long.

Chunks and bits of the wall sprayed out as the whole thing gave, collapsing on itself.

Turning away from the disturbance and holding up his arm across his face, Ash stumbled away from the area.

"Holy shit," he said, coughing as the dust and dirt flew around him.

A few minutes seemed to lapse before the debris in the air started to settle.

Peering at the wall, Ash fanned at the air in front of his face, his other hand still holding his sleeve to his mouth.

Amongst the shattered ruins of the wall, Ash saw what looked like a small wooden chest.

No bigger than the width of his hand and no taller than three fingers across.

He would have overlooked it completely if it hadn't been shoved out of its crevice by a broken stone.

Hmm?

Ash squinted at the box, not quite wanting to get close enough to inspect it, but wishing to do so all the same.

What's in it?

Taking in a deep breath and holding it, Ash rushed over to the curiosity.

After nearly tripping over himself in the rush, he got his hands on the wooden box and darted away again. He wasn't about to trust the area to not collapse further.

When he got back to where he'd been sitting originally, Ash let out a breath he'd been holding without realizing it.

"Now why would someone bury a box in a wall?" Ash asked, flipping it end over end.

There were no engravings, no markings—it really was just a simple box.

Pressing his thumbnail into the latch, he flipped it open and then peered inside.

Sitting there was a simple black training ring.

He'd seen the like on a number of trainees. They were commonplace. Nearly every family had at least one.

In his own adoptive family, it'd been given to the oldest male blood child. Jing, a boy a year younger than Ash.

He gave the ring a cursory inspection, pulling it from the box. Training rings were common enough that one wouldn't need to hide one in a box.

Nor then put that box in a wall.

Rolling it around in his palm, he studied it.

"Is it broken?" Ash asked after noticing a hairline crack that went from one side of the ring to the other.

When he held it up to the light, he could see sunshine through it.

Straight through the material.

Sighing, Ash could only smirk at his luck.

He slipped the ring onto the ring finger on his right hand and looked at it to inspect the fit.

"It's not ugly, at least. Some of those rings always look so—" Ash's words fell away as his consciousness was ripped from him.

Only to come right back.

Except he was in an entirely different location.

Looking around, he immediately realized it was the same ruined building and grassy courtyard he'd just been standing in.

Except it was no longer ruined.

It wasn't by any means new or whole either, though.

The building had cracks and fissures all throughout the walls, but it was standing.

And much larger than he'd thought it would be.

There was a splintered door hanging from a single hinge, creaking back and forth.

"The fuck?" Ash asked. "Am I in the ring…? Is this the training environment for the ring?

"Most stories I heard said these rings had a library and a training area… not a broken and crumbling building and a valley."

Frowning, Ash made his way over to the door.

He grasped the rope handle and gently pulled it open towards himself.

Only for the door to literally pop free of the hinge and clatter down at his feet. Ash let go of the handle and stepped in through the doorway.

"Shit, the whole place is falling apart."

The room was filled with rotten bookcases and broken furniture.

All around and throughout were the signs of age, misuse, and rot.

Ash kept his eyes moving as he walked between the shelves. Looking for anyone or anything that could give him an idea about this place.

Or something to take.

Stepping out from the last shelf, he found himself in an open area at the center of the room.

Three large balls of what looked like blue electricity were circling one another there.

They crackled and flared as they neared one another, only to spin away and continue revolving.

"What in the—"

Before he could finish the sentence, the orbiting lightning came to a stop.

Ash tilted his head to one side, not sure if he should be here anymore. No sooner had he finished the thought, the blue crackling balls of death shot toward him and smashed into his stomach.

Ash crumpled to the ground and curled up around himself in the fetal position.

Groaning at the sudden pain, he squeezed his hands into fists. It felt like his body would break right now and splinter apart.

His skin felt like it was literally on fire, and like his spine was being pulled out of his mouth.

Then an overwhelming strength flooded through him, and the pain fell off in a rush.

Panting on the ground, Ash tried not to move. His body twitched and spasmed all on its own. Without any wish or desire on his part.

After what felt like forever, he could finally form a coherent thought.

Shit.

Blinking away at the tears that were welling up from the memory of the pain, Ash managed to lever himself up to a sitting position.

Pressing a hand to his forehead, he leaned on his other arm and tried to get his brain moving faster.

He felt it then.

Energy. Pure and untarnished, flowing through him. From what felt like his lower Dantian.

The source of a cultivator's power. Opening it gave one the ability to process and cycle Essence into Qi.

Closing his eyes, Ash immediately dropped himself into the space he'd been able to find so often that was empty.

The Qi Sea inside of himself that was the Dantian.

What had previously been a barren and dusty stretch of desert was now a small lake.

A lake of energy that was his Qi Sea.

His opened Dantian.

"Hello," said a rather chipper voice from nowhere.

Ash's eyes shot open and he looked around.

"Hello?" he asked.

"Looks like you got yourself open to the energy of this world. Not really sure where you'll end up, but hey, one place is as good as another, right?" asked the voice, continuing on as if it hadn't heard him.

"I don't understand," Ash said.

"Regardless of where you ended up, congratulations. You're actually ready to go out there and help out.

"And to do that, you're going to need some power, some instructions, and a guide.

"All of which I can't provide you—since, if you're hearing this, I'm dead.

"Well, not dead but… not living?" said the voice.

"You can't hear me, can you," Ash said. It wasn't really a question.

"Anyways. Let's just call me immortal since I'm neither alive nor dead.

"You'll need to find either my counterpart, or whoever it was I saw them grab when I grabbed you.

"Huh, well, if they've made it, at least. I mean, there's always the possibility they died, right? Ha, that'd be pretty awful."

Ash could only nod, not really following along but agreeing that this was rather awful.

"So! Since I can't do much of anything for you, and I don't know what you'll need, I offset everything I had left into that little thingamajig you had in your hands.

"Ended up turning it into bits of nothing in doing so, so I had to wedge myself, and what I've become, inside of you.

"You might even be able to feel me now!"

Ash turned his senses inward, and he did indeed feel something abnormal.

Right above his lower Dantian. Where all the energy would have to pass through to reach it.

"If you can sense it, you'll find it inside your stomach.

"I put myself there so I could leech a bit of energy and provide you with what little support I could," continued the voice.

Son of a bitch. That's why I couldn't do anything? It was siphoning everything away?

"...isn't much I admit, but support is support. What I did is I took your device and used it as a rapid blueprint for how I could help you.

"I'm not sure what it was, but it felt oddly like a spoken story from my youth. Though the mass of numbers, tables, and descriptions for everything didn't make much sense.

"I mean, do you really need to know what a fireball will do if you attempt to cast the spell, and how much it'll cost?

"Whatever, anyways. I did that. And... I think this is the part where I die. Or at least... stop living.

"Good luck!"

Ash sat there, waiting for the voice to continue.

Hoping it would.

Slowly, with ever-increasing volume, he heard what sounded like a whispering, buzzing noise.

Right when it got to the point that it almost seemed painful, it stopped.

Then the ruins around him fractured into motes of dust and rebuilt themselves.

All around him, everything was destroyed and restructured.

Even himself.

When it all settled down, it seemed as if nothing had actually changed.

"Uh," Ash said aloud. "Hello? Are you still there?"

"The Chosen One has attempted to access the data base. Would he like to see the interface?" said a voice somewhere inside his own head. The way it said "chosen one" almost sounded mocking.

The words felt audible, but they weren't at the same time.

"Yes?" Ash tried.

A series of blips sounded, and then small windows started to appear next to everything around him.

Looking to one side, he focused on a jumble of wood.

Rotten Bookshelf
Rotten Book
Destroyed Table

Raising his eyebrows at that, Ash licked his lips.

"Uh... everything is destroyed, but it doesn't look like a table, bookshelf or book," Ash said.

"The Chosen One is correct," said the snarky voice. "The items are destroyed."

Ok, it's definitely mocking me.

"Would the Chosen One like to reconstruct the items?"

"Yes?"

"It will cost two measurements of Qi. You currently have five. Do you wish to proceed?"

Ash frowned. That message sounded a lot more process oriented and less alive.

The voice said it merged with my... thingamajig, was it? I only had my portable gaming console with me. Did it think it was something else instead of a video game?

"The Chosen One needs to make a choice," said the voice.

Ash didn't respond. He was still wondering over this strange game-like overlay that'd popped up and how it'd gotten there.

"The Chosen One needs to make a choice," repeated the voice.

Huh?

"Repeat last message," Ash said.

"The Chosen One needs to make a choice," said the voice.

"Repeat the last message twice," Ash tried.

"The Chosen One needs to make a choice," said the voice, twice.

"In other words... you really are and aren't alive at the same time."

"Invalid statement," replied the voice.

"No, don't rebuild the items," Ash said.

"Request canceled."

Getting up to his feet, Ash brushed himself off, only realizing then that he didn't need to. He was still in the training ring.

"Can you… uh… can you repair the ring?" Ash asked.

There was a pause, as if something was happening he couldn't see or hear.

"Yes. The ring can be repaired. The cost is prohibitive, but can be paid in increments.

"If the Chosen One so chooses, the basic library can be rebuilt immediately with all the base skills available to the clan," said the voice.

"What clan?" Ash asked.

"Imperial Clan of the Grassy Vale."

"Imperial clan?" Ash asked.

"Yes. Imperial Clan of the Grassy Vale, Chosen One."

"And how many abilities are available?"

"Six thousand seven hundred and thirty-three abilities."

Ash blinked and felt like he wanted to sit down immediately.

"There's that many?"

"In the basic library, yes. The intermediate library has fewer, but they are much more specialized and powerful," said the voice.

"Are there any cultivation skills?" Ash asked hopefully. Unfortunately, he'd not been granted a cultivation method from anyone, so he'd been painfully fumbling around in the dark so far.

"Yes. They are categorized separately from the abilities.

"There are nineteen thousand eight hundred and forty-two available. Though only three fourths of that number are suitable for you, and less than a hundred would be ideal based on your talent, mental capabilities, and physique," offered the voice.

"Uh… you can pick out ones specific for me?"

"Yes, Chosen One," said the voice with a drawl. "A peak cultivation method can be determined for you, though several filters will need to be run to determine the best course of action."

Ash suddenly sat down, feeling rather faint.

"Then yes… repair the basic library immediately," Ash said. Sighing, he put his head in his hands and gave it a shake. "And… what do I call you?"

"My name is Locke," said the voice.

Two

The Hall, as he'd begun calling it in his head, didn't change.

Though a large and vast section of the bookshelves misted over and became ethereal.

"Reconstruction has begun and will be complete momentarily. The Chosen One's Qi Sea will unfortunately be drained significantly.

"The Chosen One's body refining would be ranked as level one if someone were to test it," Locke said.

"What was it before?" Ash asked, not sure he really wanted to know.

"Before the reconstruction purchase, it would have been ranked as a peak seven."

Ash sighed and pressed his hands to his face.

Peak? In other words, I could have graduated from a beginner to an intermediate body refiner? Ugh. This is necessary.

We don't have a cultivation technique, and this will provide me with one.

Even if we were a peak expert body refiner, it wouldn't have mattered. We wouldn't have progressed. Couldn't have progressed!

"Reconstruction complete," Locke said.

Blinking, Ash looked around himself.

The rotten and broken-down bookcases were gone.

Darkly stained wooden bookcases that looked rather expensive had replaced them. They were filled with books, scrolls, slim manuals, and even some single pages of parchment.

Ash picked up a manual and flipped it open idly.

On the third page, he saw instructions on how to utilize an attack that generated lightning and channeled it through the hands into a direct strike.

Raising his eyebrows, Ash closed the manual and set it back down.

"You said there were a number of cultivation skills that were suitable for me?" Ash asked aloud.

"Please proceed to the antechamber set to the northwest of the library to proceed with ability selection. Attribute and ability determination can be done in the evaluation chamber," Locke said.

"Evaluation chamber?" Ash asked, moving to the dead center of the library.

Or at least he thought it was the center, based on the way the ceiling seemed to be laid out.

"The evaluation chamber can determine attributes and assist in determination of the best available abilities," Locke said.

Ash frowned. It was more or less the same information, just presented in a different way.

"Why is there an evaluation room?" Ash asked.

"The evaluation room is a function of the heirloom treasure the Chosen One has acquired, despite not having the correct bloodline to unlock it."

Ash stopped in the middle of the room and looked around.

"Uhm, which way is northwest?" Ash asked, looking around at the various doorways around him.

A small green arrow appeared in front of him and oriented on a doorway to his left.

Turning to face the direction of the arrow, he watched as it changed its heading.

"Oh, that's handy. Like a compass for a quest completion," Ash said, following the indicated direction.

"The option for directions has been enabled," Locke responded.

Moving across the shattered library, Ash was struck with just how large the room was. It was deceiving, considering how much smaller it had looked from outside.

Maybe the building has a dimensional space element to it. We'll have to try and store things here.

As he stepped into the indicated "evaluation chamber," Ash looked around. It was a simple and empty room with a circular plate in the dead center.

After moving over to the plate, Ash stepped on it with one foot.

Nothing happened.

When he put both feet on the plate, he heard a pop and a fizzle.

"The cultivation chamber has now been modified to work with my current limitations," Locke said.

The wall directly across from Ash flashed and a mirror image of himself appeared on it.

He saw his lanky self standing there, looking like an unfed teenager. His height barely reached five foot seven and his frame was rather slim.

Though his green eyes and blond hair stood out immediately.

Need to dye my hair again; it's really bright when I let it slide.

Floating beside his mirrored image were a series of numbers and stats.

"The Chosen One's attributes and talent are all average," Locke said. "Of the available abilities, the Chosen One has access to over ninety percent of them."

"Guess it's good to be average," Ash muttered.

"Correct," Locke said helpfully.

"How many can Jia use?" Ash asked. He was sure it'd be a higher number than his own. Jia was much more talented than him.

Though Ash had to wonder if Locke even had information on Jia. From the sound of it, Locke had been with Ash since he arrived.

It was possible.

"Jia is limited to seventy percent of the available abilities," Locke immediately responded.

"Huh? Why the big drop?"

"Jia is limited to seventy percent of the available abilities, as the library isn't as comprehensive for a woman."

A woman?

Uh.

Ash frowned and opened his mouth, then closed it again.

Well, that does explain quite a bit, I suppose. He's always been popular with the ladies, but he never did anything with it.

Or she... I guess.

"Alright, uhm, let's... let's go to cultivation techniques. I'd like to focus on what's not only available for me, but what's best for me.

"If you can do that."

"The Chosen One is most suited for the following cultivation techniques with the following abbreviated descriptions:

"Way of Balance. All gains in cultivation must be gained in such a way that all elements are in harmony. The technique will have a slow growth but a deep Qi Sea at the peak," Locke said.

Ash looked to the ground in front of him.

Do I actually want to do this? I never stopped and considered whether this was something I actually wanted to do.

Is it?

We can just become a citizen as soon as we fail the exam this year.

And we can get a job and... be normal.

But... what if they can sense that my Dantian is no longer blocked? What if they know I'm now a cultivator?

Would they force a cultivation technique on me that isn't suitable to me?

How would I even explain it at that point?

If I did it now, I could claim I just... learned it... right?

Wait, that's all assuming I want to do this.

"...amount of available Qi at the peak, but is significantly faster," Locke droned on.

"Stop," Ash said, coming to a neutral ground in his thought process. "Limit the list to what can provide me with the greatest benefit the fastest, as well as what would be ideal with my current... status. My possessions and what I own."

The clear wall in front of him began to rapidly flash through a series of texts.

Then it just stopped out of nowhere.

"One suitable cultivation technique.

"The Snowflake from the Mountaintop," Locke said. "This cultivation technique isn't rated very highly, as the starting requirement is steep.

"However, due to the inherited Qi from the heirloom treasure, the Chosen One can bypass this and move straight to cultivating.

"The key component of the Snowflake from the Mountaintop is momentum. With each gain, part of that gain is reinvested back into the ability to cultivate. In time, this method will end up providing the fastest growth at later stages, though slower growth at earlier ones."

Ash was reading the text on the wall, which was more or less the same thing Locke was saying.

"In other words, I can invest whatever Qi I have leftover into the technique, and it can start providing more back to me much more quickly.

"I'm investing in my future, so to speak."

"The Chosen One is mostly correct. The reinvestment is mostly passive and would require no effort on your part.

"This cultivation method is ideal and the most suited given the parameters listed."

"Great, we'll take that. Are there any support abilities that go with this or would be suitable for it?" Ash asked. Sometimes cultivation techniques had complimentary sister abilities.

"No, there are no linked techniques. There are several techniques that could be joined to this technique, however."

"Oh? Great! What are they? The ones I can use, that is."

"The first is Keep What You Kill," Locke said.

"Sounds ominous," Ash muttered.

"...and any opponent that you personally eliminate will grant you a portion of their personal Qi," Locke continued on, ignoring Ash. "The greater the opponent in comparison to yourself, the more you will personally inherit.

"Please note, you must be directly responsible for their death."

"And does it cost me anything to learn this?"

"There is no associated cost. This technique is part of the basic accessory library."

"Ok, add that in. What else?"

"Devourer. Eating the hearts of your defeated enemies—"

"No, skip that one," Ash said, interrupting Locke.

"Unstoppable Force. Each time you defeat an opponent in a fair fight initiated by yourself or another, your cultivation ability will temporarily rise by a factor of five percent. There is no upper limit to the multiplier.

"This modification ends with the loss of a fight, declining a challenge, or challenging someone weaker than yourself. If the modifier is lost, the Chosen One would suffer a penalty of one fourth of the modifier to his cultivation for one week.

"The penalty is labeled Taste of Defeat and is an expected eventuality at some point."

That sounds neat, though also a concern. A loss would really set me back for a while.

"Any cost?" Ash asked once it was obvious Locke had finished.

"In learning this technique, one would be unable to utilize any other cultivation enhancement abilities."

"Does it work with the first one? Keep what you kill or whatever?"

"They are compatible."

Frowning, Ash scratched at his head.

It'd be a pretty quick way to the top, right? I mean, between the three. Everything would just become this... this train with no brakes.

A loss would set me back, though. Any loss.

But that's the risk, right? The risk and the reward.

It's all momentum.

"Add that one, too. Those three techniques. Let's move on to abilities," Ash said.

"It's recommended the Chosen One utilize his first three techniques. This will help in identifying which abilities are best taken next."

Ash thought on that and then nodded his head. It made sense. Up until now, all of this had seemed like a strange culmination of functions between Locke and the ring.

There was no telling if they were one-hundred-percent accurate.

"Alright. Give me those three techniques and we'll go from there," Ash said. "And we—"

A sudden burst of information racked his brain. It scattered his thoughts and he felt his body lock up as if he were made of steel rods rather than flesh and bone.

Gritting his teeth, Ash stared at the ceiling of the room. The three techniques were being directly transmitted to his mind. Straight into his memories.

To the very bottom of his Qi Sea.

After what felt like hours, it ended as abruptly as it had started.

Ash crumpled to the ground, falling to all fours.

Then the world faded to black around him. With a dizzying shift, he suddenly found himself where he'd been previously.

In the ruined courtyard outside the building.

Shivering, covered in sweat, and feeling as if his mind had been split apart. Ash felt awful.

Bile rose in his throat and he began to retch violently, throwing up the contents of his stomach.

***

Opening the door, Ash slipped into the home he'd spent most of his time here in.

The home of his adoptive family. The Sheng family.

"Ah? Is that you, Ashley?" asked a female voice from inside.

"Yes, it's me, Far," Ash said with a smile, moving into what he'd call the kitchen. He found the mother of the family next to the entryway. Far Sheng.

She'd treated him as if he were one of her natural-born children, even though she'd said he looked like the strangest outlander she'd ever seen.

Admittedly, Ash looked very much an outlander. He was Caucasian after all, and as far as he could tell, everyone in this world was of Asian descent.

"Oh, welcome home," Far said, standing over a hearth set in the wall. Sitting over a tripod was a beat-up cauldron, and she was stirring its contents with a long handled large spoon.

She was a small woman who looked to be in her late forties, with black hair and dark eyes. She was only a citizen, as was her husband.

Though both of their children had turned out to be cultivators, much to their great surprise.

"Duyi is working late tonight."

He's been doing that a lot lately. It's not good for his health. He's much too old to be working hard labor for so long each day.

"Mother Far, why?" Ash asked. Walking over to the smaller woman, Ash touched her gently on the back and kissed the top of her head.

"Aaaaah. It's nothing you need worry about," Far said, shaking her head. "Sit, I'll serve you a bowl. It'll be truly ready later, but it should taste just fine now."

"Thank you, Mother Far, but please—tell me. What's going on?" Ash asked, taking a seat at a flat board laid out on the ground that served as their table.

Sighing, Far reached over to a stack of bowls beside the cauldron and pulled one off the top.

"Jing and Yan have not done well in their sect. Father Duyi is working hard to help support them so they can succeed," Far said after she began pouring the stew into the bowl.

Ash felt his heart thump oddly in his chest.

They're not doing well?

"What's wrong, exactly?" Ash asked.

Taking the bowl from Far, he brought it up to his lips and took a hearty drink.

"Ahh, they didn't really say. Just that they're not able to succeed right now. They didn't ask for anything, but Father and I think if we send them a little extra, maybe that'll change things," Far said with a smile as she sat down in front of him.

"I see. They really didn't say anything at all?"

"Nothing that I understood. Something about the cultivation techniques costing too much was about the only thing that made sense to me," Far said.

"Which is why you want to send money—that makes sense."

Far smiled and nodded at him. "Yes."

"What if I worked? I could always skip out of the examination and get a job. Work with Father Duyi."

Ash lifted the bowl to his mouth and took another drink, managing to capture several slivers of vegetables and a bit of meat.

I wonder where they got the meat? That's a bit of a surprise.

"I don't think... that is..." Far sighed and gave him a tired smile. "Ashley, Mother and Father worry that no one will hire you because you look so much like an outlander."

"Father Duyi has already been asking around... even his friends... no one is willing to take you on."

Ash nodded at that.

It wasn't unsurprising. While people didn't hate him for being an outlander, or even dislike him, they treated him as something of a bad omen and simply ignored him.

On the list of problems, it hadn't been much of a concern since he wasn't treated like an outsider. People just didn't like being around him for extended periods of time.

"I was wondering if you thought you might successfully pass the examination this year?" Far asked, looking at him intently now.

Ah. Yes. That'd be the one place I could excel based on my own merits, regardless of my looks.

My destiny would be my own. Fortune and fame entirely dependent on me, and maybe some luck.

Smiling at Far, Ash nodded.

"I do believe I'll pass, yes. I wouldn't be concerned. I'm actually fairly confident in myself this year," Ash said.

Far didn't move. Then she smiled brightly at him.

"Truly, Ashley? You think you'll pass?" she asked.

"Yes. I do. I can't guarantee my results beyond passing, but I do believe I'll pass without a concern.

"I'm almost certain of it," Ash said, unable to smile back at her.

Her genuine joy at the possibility of him succeeding had struck at the core of his being.

This is the path. We'll move forward to protect the family.

The question becomes... how far can I go?

"Oh, I'm so happy for you!" Far said, reaching over the table to pat his cheek.

Ash grinned, his cheeks turning a faint red at the attention.

"Thanks, Mother Far."

***

Sitting quietly by himself in his room, Ash focused inward on his Qi Sea.

The energy there flowed gently back and forth. The waters nearly still and undisturbed.

So, first we have to condense all this Qi into our "snowflake" and then set it rolling, right?

As if the simple thought of the ability was enough, he knew exactly what he needed to do.

Siphoning his entire Qi Sea into one spot, he began to push it together. Pressing it down onto itself.

As if he were rolling aluminum foil into a ball, he kept pressing it on it. From every angle, he pressed and pushed on his Qi.

Slowly, it began to shrink into itself, vanishing and becoming denser with every pass.

Then it suddenly felt like it could go no further. The Qi was as dense as it was going to become. Pulling back from the tiny dense ball of Qi, he let it settle back into the bottom of his Qi Sea. Which was little more than a puddle now.

Sighing to himself, Ash collected his thoughts. Then he began to work through the steps to cultivate.

Taking hold of his puddle, Ash used it according to the ability. He let it gather around him to literally flow through his surroundings, gathering and trapping all the Essence in the waking world.

I can see how this truly can become a frightening skill later on, and why the introductory stages would be so complicated.

I cannot imagine doing this with something smaller than my puddle.

If I were just starting out, wouldn't it be little more than a rain drop?

Ash could feel the puddle soaking up the Essence.

This was by far the simplest method for cultivating with this technique. It was also the only way Ash could do it for now.

He'd have to wait for things to change within his body, and his Dantian, before he could do more with it.

Essence continued to circle around the puddle, ever being drawn into the mass.

It brought all that Qi into itself and rapidly condensed it to the same level as the puddle.

And the amount of Qi needed to be condensed was significantly less than what he'd spent to reach the same goal.

Which made sense when he thought about it. The whole point of this technique was that the further you invested into it, the more it could give back.

But with each investment, one would eternally shuffle themselves backwards.

Ash could already see the problem he imagined many cultivators faced with this technique.

How much do I invest back into it, and at what point is it more a hindrance than a help to do so?

Sighing to himself, Ash drew a line of Qi from the very meager supply into his body through his meridians, and then circulated it back to the sea.

Let's start with refining our body. That's what we must do first if we have any chance.

To cultivators, the Dantian was the main reservoir. Where the Qi was stored and held.

The meridians running throughout the body were the rivers that carried the Qi far and wide.

Ash directed his Qi like it was as easy as breathing, like he'd always known how.

Apparently, our little training ring taught me all the subtleties as well.

Qi seeped into Ash's internal organs. It fed his body as if it were a dry riverbed flush with new rains.

All the Qi that cycled through his body was diminished. Absorbed by his flesh.

Though it wasn't lost. It simply lacked the vitality it had once had.

Cycling it back through his Dantian, it became once more what it had been.

Though Ash couldn't feel the changes during his cultivation, he was sure it was having an effect.

Then a strange thought struck him.

He needed to get his abilities tomorrow before training, and he had to begin working hard immediately.

The examination was only a month away.

It's just not enough time.

Three

Ash had spent the night cultivating.

From the time he sat down on his bed to the moment the sun touched his skin in the morning, he cultivated and cycled his Qi.

Nourishing his body with the energy of the heavens.

With a slow breath out, Ash let his cultivation end.

Sitting in his room, he contemplated what to do next. Soon he'd have to head to the training sect and begin the day.

He didn't feel tired for having been up all night. He attributed it to having never cultivated before, and this being the first time.

We should see if we can pick up an ability.

If we can win some matches today, we can start gaining some of that multiplier, right?

Though if we lose, it'll set us ever further back.

I'm confident in my martial skills. If it's simply a trial of combat, I could win.

That means… we should focus on a cultivation movement ability? Something that can help us keep speed with our opponent?

Looking at the ring on his finger, Ash was momentarily puzzled.

It looked significantly less damaged than it had previously.

Many of the scuffs and scratches were gone. Healed over as if they'd never been a problem.

In fact, even the large deep crack that had run throughout it was sealed over.

Feeding a trickle of his Qi into the ring, Ash immediately had his answer.

Much of the visible surface of the ring had indeed been repaired. The damage throughout was still very much there though. Just beneath the visible layer.

Then the ring responded to his Qi and dragged him into the training world it held.

Ash was standing once again in the courtyard in front of the old building.

It no longer looked like a moldering wreck, about to fall over at any second.

"Now it just looks like a shit-hole, which is still an upgrade," Ash said aloud. Walking to the door, he was surprised to find it was repaired, and even attached at both hinges.

Ash opened the door and stepped inside the deceptively large library.

"Locke?" Ash asked.

"The Chosen One has returned. The library has been cleaned up. Free-floating Essence that the Chosen One was unable to capture has been transmitted into the heirloom to speed recovery.

"At the current rate, it will take two hundred and three years to repair the treasure," Locke said.

"That sounds like a while," Ash said. Moving past everything, he headed straight for the evaluation chamber.

I imagine there was a lot more to do here before Locke integrated himself into it.

I probably would have needed to familiarize myself with everything available.

"Locke, I need a movement ability. I want to try and win some fights today.

"I'm fairly confident in my ability to fight without cultivation, but they tend to cheat when it's obvious I'm going to win," Ash said.

"Two abilities given the Chosen One's current limitations are most suited to the request," Locke said immediately.

"And they're both things I can learn and utilize today?" Ash clarified.

"Correction, one ability," Locke responded. "One other ability requires a month of practice to completely utilize.

"There are many more abilities available; however, the limitations of the Chosen One's body has severely restricted these numbers."

"Uh huh. Believe me, I get it. Need to work on leveling all that up as quickly as possible.

"Oh, speaking of leveling up, what rank am I currently?"

"Level-two body refiner. The Chosen One's body has absorbed enough Essence to move to the third level, but has not cultivated enough to do so."

Ash nodded and stepped into the center circle of the evaluation chamber.

"So what's the movement ability?" Ash asked.

"Coiled Spring Step," Locke said. "It's an ability that is activated prior to use. It stores kinetic energy that can be expelled rapidly to generate force in a direction of one's choosing."

"In effect, propelling oneself."

"That sounds... interesting. And the amount of force stored?"

"Normally it would be uncontrollable, and the notes in the back of the skill book recommend that this is not continuously utilized. But more of a preplanned move."

"Due to my presence, this is no longer the case. A limiter can be set on this ability."

"In other words, it's a toggled ability now," Ash said. "I can turn it on and off at will and it'll just... hit the set level and remain there."

"Correct."

"Great. How much of my Qi do I need to expend to keep enough kinetic force to move five feet in any direction?"

"Two-point-six percent. Once that amount of force has been met, Qi will no longer be spent."

"Great. Transfer the ability over to me and set it at that for now. That's... not too bad. That means I can use it quite a bit," Ash said excitedly. "This'll be gre—"

The sudden intrusion of the skill book into his mind cut him free of all further thought.

***

Ash warily stepped into the sect's primary courtyard.

It existed for the sole purpose of training new recruits to join larger sects.

In truth, this sect was simply a smaller branch academy of a much larger sect that had a contract for this job.

Every city had several training sects like this set up to filter students upward. While they weren't all the same, one could always say the opportunities they granted were equivalent.

Ash stepped out of the way of an outlander slave hauling a sack of rice.

The black, iron slave collar bound around the man's neck was a clear indicator of his status. The collar wasn't magical in any way, just a symbol.

This was how the vast majority of outlanders spent their time in the nine kingdoms. They were captured in the other veils and brought into the cities.

Captured and bound, lashed to servitude.

Until they died or were freed.

The latter being rather unlikely, since someone had paid good money and would be unwilling to free them at a loss.

"Ash, good morning," came a soft voice at his side.

Turning his head, he found Jia standing there.

Now that he knew Jia was a woman, he wondered how he'd ever managed to believe her when she'd stated she was a man.

"Good morning yourself, Jia," Ash said, grinning at her.

Jia blinked at him, her brows drawing low over her eyes.

"You are rather... bright... this morning," Jia said, her tone odd.

"Is there a reason I shouldn't be? I mean, you always tell me to look on the positive side. Don't you?"

"Yes. Though you typically scoff at me and dismiss my wish."

"Maybe I finally took your words to heart," Ash said.

Two junior female acolytes wandered by, both eying Jia as they did so.

Ah... if they only knew.

Though... it could be fun to mess with her a bit.

"What's your ideal woman, Jia?" Ash asked, changing the topic.

"I… beg your pardon?"

"Your ideal woman. You always have the girls chasing after you. Eventually you'll need to settle down.

"What's your ideal?"

"I have not considered it. And it is a frivolous thought," Jia said, her lips pressed into a line as she glared at the two women walking by.

"Is it so frivolous though? I mean, look at it from my point of view. If I fail my examination, I'll be looking to secure a wife and get a job.

"For you, you'll be heading to start your life as a cultivator, but I can't imagine you won't be traveling a similar path.

"So… what's your ideal woman?"

Jia's brow furrowed, her eyes staring into the middle distance.

"Do you think it so likely that you will fail?" she asked. "And if you did, what kind of woman would you look for?"

"Up to this point, there's been no indication that I'll ever pass. As to a woman I'd look for," Ash said as his thoughts turned inward.

He really hadn't considered it. He was largely tolerated and mostly ignored by everyone in Xing City. This went for women as well.

It'd never really been a concern or a question, since it seemed like he'd have to strive valiantly to turn a woman's favor toward him.

Deciding to mess with Jia instead of take her question seriously, Ash smirked.

"It's a shame you're a man, Jia. Your personality is right up my alley. You're also far too pretty. Got any sisters that look just like you?" Ash asked.

Jia glared at him now.

"I have no sisters that I would ever allow you to meet," she said in a frosty tone.

"Don't have to get so defensive. Only asking. I mean —"

A low-toned bell rang out, signaling all acolytes to proceed to their designated duties.

"Another time," Jia said, dismissing the conversation with a wave of her hand.

Ash nodded.

His Dantian was finally open. He'd cultivated and now had a Qi Sea.

The power of the heavens had fed his body. Ash desperately wanted to see what he could do now because of that.

Walking alongside Jia to their practice room, he felt different.

He was excited. Brimming with a desire to see how much he'd improved since the last time. To see if he could return the favor that'd been given to him so many times.

I'm going to break Lim's jaw if I can.

Jia yanked his sleeve suddenly.

Looking at her, Ash found himself practically in the fighting ring. He'd almost just walked into the ring before they'd even begun, so lost he was in his own desires.

And in the fantasy of breaking Lim. Over and over.

Everyone else in their examination group was already present. They were all looking to Ash.

Even Elder Shin seemed at a loss with Ash's seeming lack of awareness.

Suppose I do usually try to avoid fighting until I'm forced.

"So eager to start us off today?" the elder said.

"Ah, that is —"

"Wonderful — come, come. Step into the ring. We'll have you start us off. Jia, since you seemed interested, you may join him," Shin said.

That'll work just fine. Jia fights me fairly, so… this'll be an excellent warm-up.

Moving to the center of the room, Ash waited. As soon as Jia joined him, he pressed his fists together in front of himself and bowed his head fractionally to her.

Jia was on him in a flash. Her feet slid one over the other as she flowed toward him.

Except, where he normally was forced to simply watch her and try to react, he now viewed her as if she were moving normally.

The whip-crack speed she'd had prior to this was gone.

Frowning at the change, Ash chalked it up to his now being a formal cultivator.

Jia flicked a fist toward his face as she moved.

Catching it and diverting it to one side with his forearm, Ash took a step back habitually to redirect the force her attacks generated.

But there was none to redirect this time.

The force of her attack was that of a young woman, no longer the heavy blow it had been even just yesterday.

Her attacks were still smooth, filled with a liquid grace. They were still sharp and felt pronounced and practiced.

But the speed and strength that had threatened to overwhelm him before were gone.

Ash felt his heart rate skyrocket. He could fight them evenly. Fight them evenly, and their natural benefits of being cultivators would do them no good.

I can win!

Leaping forward, Ash closed in on Jia as fast as he could. His body was on her before he realized it.

Her eyes widened as Ash loomed over her.

Unsteady and unsure of himself, Ash made a short uppercut with his right arm, turning himself into the blow.

Catching her just below her ribs, he felt the air whoosh out from her lungs.

I caught her! I caught her?

Jia crumpled at the middle, the force of his blow apparently too much for her body to handle.

Catching her with his left arm, he held her around the middle.

"I'm so sorry Jia, are you alright?" Ash asked, not wanting to drop her.

She held on to his arms, her fingers clasped tight to him.

"Strong-blow," she said between two gasps. She tilted her face up to him, her eyes wide and brows raised.

It was a question.

"Yes. That was an unaided strike, though," Ash said softly, hoping his words would only reach her.

A small smile flitted across her face, and she nodded.

After taking two steps away from him, she seemed to have regained her balance.

Moving back to where she'd come from, Jia sat down. She tilted to one side, apparently favoring the side the blow had struck.

Pressing his fists together, Ash bowed deeply to Jia, then turned to Elder Shin.

"I'm ready for my next opponent," Ash said.

Elder Shin didn't respond to Ash. Instead, his eyes were narrowed. His entire focus seemed to be on Ash's body. Or more to the point, something inside his body.

"So… you managed to unlock your Dantian," Shin said. His tone was odd, a frown pulling at the corners of his mouth. "We shall continue with the practice matches as we always do.

"Though I do expect you to abide by the rules."

"I shall obey the rules, exactly as if I were Lim," Ash said, pressing his fists together. He couldn't help himself—he wanted to pay back some of the rage and insults he'd suffered here.

Shin's face turned red with anger at the implied insult, since everyone knew Lim broke the rules at every single match.

"Hmph, let's have another opponent brought up immediately, then. Go on up there, Gong," Shin said, indicating another acolyte.

Gong was the second strongest in the class. Just after Lim.

Though he was much more of a bully than Lim was, if that were possible. He didn't just break the rules; he looked for opportunities to do so.

It didn't help matters that he seemed to be Lim's personal toadie.

I guess that means I get to use Coiled Spring Step, doesn't it?

Ash smiled and pressed his fists together toward Gong.

The other man charged Ash as soon as he dipped his head toward him.

Apparently we're beyond any sense of respect, as well.

Ash was once again surprised at how slow Gong seemed now compared to previously.

Gong's fist cocked back and then launched forward, red streaks screaming off it as if it were scorching the very air it cut through.

Surprised and unwilling to take the blow head on, Ash immediately stepped to the left. At the same time, he deflected Gong's fist wide, then slammed his fist into the man's shoulder as he passed by.

Stumbling sideways, Gong practically fell over himself as he tried to recover from his wild swing.

"Elder, would you please warn Gong? I do believe that was an ability just now.

"I'd truly hate for him to be injured if his ability somehow failed him and caused him a problem," Ash said.

The room got quiet as all eyes turned to Shin.

This was normally when he'd admonish someone for using an ability on Ash. Not being lectured by Ash for not judicating the match appropriately.

Shin snorted and crossed his arms in front of himself.

"Watch your manners, Ash. Gong… do not use abilities," said Shin.

Gong turned, roared, and charged at Ash again.

Before he'd even gotten halfway to Ash, his fists were once again glowing with bright-red streaks of energy.

Fine.

Ash didn't care anymore. He'd been pushed around long enough, and if this was how they were going to treat him even after he'd opened his Dantian, then he'd respond in kind.

Ash shortened the distance between himself and Gong, stepping straight into the gap. Moving down low, he rotated his body around, pulling his right shoulder back.

Gong's arm passed uselessly by Ash's head, doing absolutely nothing.

Exploding forward, Ash triggered his Coiled Spring Step as he punched with his right fist.

The rapid acceleration of his body, along with the force of the strike, was devastating.

The sound of Gong's ribs crackling like twigs being stepped on was audible. But that wasn't the end of the punishment Ash was going to give Gong.

Before Shin could stop the match or Gong could surrender, Ash let loose a left uppercut, triggering his Coiled Spring Step once more.

Gong's head spun to the left, his jaw snapping to the side. His knees went out from under him and he collapsed to the ground like he was dead.

Elder Shin shot to his feet, his face pale.

Rushing over to Gong's side, he began to lay his hands about the young man's head and neck.

"Oh dear," Ash said in a flat tone. "It seems he didn't listen to Elder Shin and hurt himself. With the amount of strength he put into those strikes, even my weak strikes must have caused great damage.

"Should I go summon another elder to let them know Gong has fallen and needs help?"

There was a problem with that suggestion, of course.

The moment someone else was notified about an acolyte getting hurt, they'd want to investigate what was going on.

And if they started poking around, it would be likely that Elder Shin would be revealed for one and all to see.

It didn't matter if others were doing it as well—all that would matter was that Shin had been revealed.

And his enemies would use it to their advantage.

"No," Shin said decisively, pushing something into Gong's mouth. "He'll be fine. He just needs to sit to one side as he recovers."

"Great, I'm very glad to hear that," Ash said in the same flat tone. "I was concerned for his health. I leave him in your care.

"I'm ready for my next fight, though, Elder Shin. I look forward to it. Since I've now defeated the top two acolytes, I believe Lim would be next."

Ash turned to face the young man in question and pressed his fists together.

All eyes turned to Lim, wondering what would happen next and excited to see it.

Nothing got hearts beating faster in the nine kingdoms than things like this.

Four

Lim looked equal parts enraged and nervous. Ash and the rest of the room stared at him.

Not a word was said. Nor was a single sound made. The room was dead silent with the truth of the situation.

It was no secret that Gong took it easy on Lim in their bouts. After all, there was nothing for him to gain in hurting his boss.

Gong was considerably stronger in a straight fight than Lim.

There was of course the possibility that Lim had been holding back this entire time, but most everyone would think that unlikely.

"Unless you concede that you're weaker than I am," Ash said, fists still pressed together. "And at that point, I will be happy to take my seat. Once you kowtow to me and express your defeat, of course."

Part of Ash's mind screamed that this was all the things he knew he shouldn't be doing. That he was provoking someone he would be better off simply leaving alone.

But it was the angry, bitter warrior in his heart. A warrior who had striven to the best of his ability despite not being on an equal playing field.

And now that the levels were even, he had no desire at all to hold back.

He wanted to make them suffer for everything they'd done to him.

At least a little. Ash couldn't say he was an angry or bitter man at heart. He was more than happy to return everything given to him.

Kindness with kindness, anger with anger, and violence with violence.

Ash waited, fists pressed together. Staring straight at Lim, unmoving.

He was forcing Lim to answer. This truly would prove to be the most worthwhile move in this situation, Ash thought. It'd remove any doubt for anyone involved, and there would be no question in regard to how it happened.

Elder Shin laid Gong down outside the arena and turned angrily toward Ash. He looked as if he could chew up rocks with the amount of tension in his jaw.

Yet he said nothing, and did nothing. He stood there as if rooted in place by his very feet.

Everything had happened exactly within the rules. And as Ash had warned, Gong had known he might end up getting hurt if he broke the rules.

The only person Shin could blame was himself. He was also the only person the other elders would hold to blame in the incident, as he was supposed to watch over this group of acolytes.

Gong had been defeated, and in such a way that'd cause Shin to suffer shame.

And now Lim was Ash's next target, and by the very same rules, he had to admit defeat or step into the ring.

Shin could do nothing.

This isn't something where you can just skirt the rules, you old bastard. Where you can just overlook something because I wasn't a cultivator.

Now I'm one of you, and you cannot simply push inconvenient things aside.

Seeming to recognize the situation he was in, Lim finally got to his feet.

"I'll fight you of course, Ashley. And when I'm done, you can kowtow to me in defeat," Lim said, moving to the middle of the ring.

"I accept your wager. The loser shall kowtow, and the winner will receive today's rewards for being the top acolyte," Ash said. "I'll even allow you the pleasure of the first move.

"Come, let's exchange pointers."

"I suggest you both follow the *rules*," Shin said, stressing the last word.

"Oh, of course. I'll follow them just as Lim has always followed them, Elder Shin," Ash said.

Lim looked as if he'd swallowed a very bitter pill. Then he pressed his fists together to Ash and began moving slowly towards him.

Falling into a defensive stance, Ash felt at ease.

Martial arts had always been an outlet for him. Between dealing with school problems and family members who didn't want him around, his one constant had been martial arts.

Tournaments, training, and getting better.

Lim blurred and started to move around Ash's side.

Previously, Lim had simply appeared next to Ash. This time was different.

This time, Ash could see him moving. As if he were moving at a normal speed.

Activating the Spring Step, Ash tried to set it up so he'd simply be behind the spot Lim stopped at.

Throwing a punch at that space before Lim even arrived, Ash put his weight into the blow.

Stopping partway through his ability, Lim went sprawling to the ground and rolled several times.

He looked spooked when he came to a stop off to one side of the fighting area.

Ash was left punching thin air.

Smirking at Lim, Ash stood upright and snapped his fingers.

"So close. I almost had you, Lim," Ash said. He started moving forward toward Lim at a casual speed.

Ash wasn't about to risk his advantage carelessly.

"Ash, do you dare use an ability in front of me so casually?" Shin asked.

"I'm so sorry, Elder Shin. I was so shocked at Lim using his own that I just responded.

"I do promise I'll follow the rules as closely as Lim does," Ash said, not bothering to hide the condescension in his voice. "Do you plan on scolding Lim in the same way?"

Shin flinched at the words. He'd been called out again in front of all the acolytes who reported to him.

The amount of respect — the sheer lack of face — Ash was giving him was abominable.

Shin finally turned his head toward Lim.

"Don't use your abilities," he said tersely.

Ash had to imagine that he actually meant it for once. If Lim continued to use his abilities, it'd be hard to punish Ash for using his own.

"Come here, Lim. Let me give you a pointer or two."

Lim got to his feet and moved away from Ash, his posture defensive.

"Going to run away? There's no time limit here. We fight till one wins. Those are the rules, remember?" Ash taunted.

Lim shook his head, as if denying what had been said. Then he slowly began inching toward Ash.

When they closed within range, Ash lashed out with a palm strike.

Lim deflected it, barely, but Ash was already bringing his other arm rapidly around.

A sharp crack sounded throughout as the openhanded slap snapped Lim's chin to one side.

Stepping back quickly, Ash laughed.

"What, is that it? One slap and you're going to quit?" he asked to the woozy-looking Lim. "Did I slap the bravery out of you?"

"Slap your balls out of your sack?"

Someone snickered.

In the silence of the arena, it felt as loud as a crack of thunder.

"Fine, I'll just finish this and collect my reward. Let's give you another slap and see if you go down," Ash said, moving back in toward Lim.

Lim had barely managed to put himself to rights by now. Apparently the openhanded slap had rung his bell more than anyone had thought.

Then his outline and figure began to blur.

"No!" Elder Shin said loudly.

Lim didn't listen, though, and started to charge straight at Ash. At the same time, a building of lightning began to crackle across Lim's hands.

He's actually using two abilities.

That pretty much lets me do what I want, but… I can't let that blow land.

Ash ducked to one side, narrowly avoiding the attack. Except he had to dodge backward as Lim came on again. Lim's hands were balls of lightning, his entire figure a hazy silhouette.

Triggering his Spring Step, Ash got out to one side. Before he could act, though, Lim was on him again.

Can't keep dodging, and I can't just wait. Eventually I'll run out of Qi.

And I'm not sure I want to bet on having a deeper Qi Sea than him. He's been cultivating far longer than I have.

Stumbling under an attack, Ash scrambled away, unable to do much other than keep his distance.

Shin won't bother to help, especially now that it looks like Lim might win.

How do I do this? How do I win?

Triggering Spring Step once again, Ash had a flash of inspiration as he slipped away from Lim.

Can I use Spring Step, but on my arm instead of my legs? It didn't say it was limited to just my legs and feet, did it?

Lim was once more on top of him.

Ash decided to bet here and now while he had the energy to act. If he kept dodging and waiting, there was no guarantee he'd have it later.

Moving into Lim's attack and fully expecting to take a hit, Ash swung his arm forward in a hook. At the same time, he triggered Spring Step, but tried to generate the entire ability through his arm instead.

It felt strange as his arm simply appeared in front of himself, a foot past Lim's jaw.

The boom of his hand plowing through Lim's chin faded as the younger man dropped to the floor.

Lightning passed through Ash at the same time, causing his body to lock up, but he didn't fall.

As soon as it passed, he looked down to Lim.

Not only had his punch connected, it had very clearly either broken Lim's jaw or disconnected it at the hinge.

"Goodness," Ash said, taking in a deep breath. "It seems Lim got himself hurt using abilities. Just like Gong.

"Should I fetch another elder for assistance?"

Shin was already atop Lim, forcing pills down the young man's throat.

Turning his head to Ash, he glared with a promise of violence.

"No, you little shit. Here, take this and leave," Shin said, throwing a small bag at Ash. "Do not come back. You were the last one without a Dantian, and now that you have one, this class is pointless. That's the reward for being the top acolyte at the end."

"I thank the elder for his benevolence," Ash said, pressing his fists together. "I look forward to receiving Lim's kowtow before the examination, since he wasn't able to honor our bet here and it seems like I won't see him again till then.

"In front of everyone in the city, no less."

***

"Just what did you do?" Jia asked, sitting across from him. They'd retreated to a small gathering room in the training sect.

They were still acolytes here, of course. Temporary Outer Disciples here on contract.

Shin could cancel the class, as that was his prerogative. Ash wondered if he'd get in trouble for it later, but that didn't end the students' ability to come and go.

"I only punched. That's all I did. Apparently opening the Dantian has a more profound effect than people ever admitted," Ash said, spreading his hands out in front of himself toward Jia.

"Hm. Opening one's Dantian does indeed grant a noticeable increase in power, but that was not normal.

"Your strike was… significant when you hit me. I was not able to stand afterward. It was too heavy, too strong," Jia complained. "I do not think I could have blocked it without being forced back."

Ash shrugged.

Maybe it's because I condensed my Qi. Maybe they're all working with their Qi Seas in their original shape.

Is condensing it something that isn't normal?

"Well, maybe I'm doing something different. Do you have a cultivation technique?" Ash asked.

Jia shook her head, her lips turning into a slight frown.

In fact, it was nearly a pout.

How did I ever believe Jia was a man? It's so obviously a woman that it's —

Looking past Jia, Ash saw another acolyte. The young man looked as pretty as Jia, though significantly more effeminate in his actions.

Hm. On second thought, the culture here is very different, isn't it?

"…able to afford one. I have mostly been simply meditating at night before bed. That seems to help significantly."

"Though I do worry I'll not be able to perform as well as others when the time of the examination comes. Many of them have had years to practice and truly cultivate," Jia said, shaking her head.

"Does it matter? Passing is passing. Even the weakest of cultivators will receive an invitation from an actual sect. It's just a question of who, and what city," Ash said, reaching out to lightly pat the back of Jia's hand. "You'll be fine. I know it. The only reason you never beat Gong or Lim was you played by the rules."

Jia seemingly disagreed with that, based on the narrowing of her eyes and the firm line of her mouth, but she apparently wasn't going to say anything.

"And what are you going to do with yourself now?" she asked.

"What, now that we're not training anymore? I don't know. I was thinking I'd get a job. Make some money. Give it to the folks," Ash said.

It was the only plan he had at the moment, considering he didn't have many other options.

Jia nodded and tapped at the table idly.

"I think I shall… relax. Practice. Study. Regardless of the outcome, I will feel I have failed if I cannot do everything that is possible for me."

"Go get 'em. I'll drop by your place in a few days to say hi and make sure you're not dying of starvation," Ash said.

"I only forgot to eat the one time," Jia said, her cheeks flushing.

"Uh huh. As far as you'll admit to, at least. Alright, I'm heading out, I'll see you later," Ash said, then stood up and left with a wave.

Ash didn't stop for anything as he left.

He headed home as quickly as he could, not bothering to waste any time.

Some part of him suspected Lim or Gong might try to attack him on the way home.

That or someone else would make the attempt.

Home wasn't any safer than anywhere else, but it was certainly less likely for someone to attack him there than in the middle of the street.

When he stepped past the entryway, he realized no one was home. Both Mother and Father were out working.

Entering his own room, Ash shut the door and sat down on the thin cot that served as his bed.

Pulling his legs up under him, he withdrew the pouch Shin had given him and opened it.

Inside were two white pills, ten white spirit stones, and a small badge the size of his thumbnail.

Ash held his breath and pulled out the ten spirit stones.

They were white ellipsoid stones. Smooth as polished river rocks and free of blemishes.

Each one contained the same amount of Qi a peak body refiner would hold.

These rocks were often shaped and polished. Then filled with condensed Qi. This was achieved by cultivators, monsters, treasures, and even by nature.

They weren't quite a form of currency, but often people would accept them in trade in lieu of minted currency.

He knew for a fact that his family would barely make the equivalent of these ten stones in three years of hard work. This was a small windfall.

Ash turned his attention to the pills, not quite sure what they were.

He wouldn't know what any pill was until he swallowed it. The only other way was having someone with a Vision ability take a peek, or having an alchemist tell you what it was.

"And Shin sure as hell won't tell me what this is," Ash muttered. "Maybe Locke could?"

Ignoring the token since there was no way he could ask anyone about it, Ash entered his training ring.

The transition went much easier this time, and Ash went straight into his Hall, as he'd decided to call it.

"Locke, I have two pills on my person. Can you identify them?"

"The pills have already been identified and assessed. They are low-quality Essence Attractor pills.

"They pull Qi in from further afar. Due to the low quality of these pills, the effect will only last for one hour each. It's recommended that this is done during the day, while most people will be out training or working."

"Huh. That makes sense," Ash said. Moving to the center of the Library wing of the Hall, he stopped. "I want to talk about more utility skills."

There was no response.

Frowning, Ash clicked his tongue.

Just how much of a program are you?

"I want to know if there are any abilities or skill that will give me constant Qi regeneration without having to cultivate.

"On top of that, I'd like another list of professions or trade-skills I can utilize that will let me cultivate at the same time," Ash said.

"List compiled," Locke said. "There are no skills or abilities that will allow for Qi regeneration.

"There is, however, one profession that can create a passive Qi regeneration effect once it's been trained up to the Apprentice level."

"Great, what profession is that?" Ash asked, excited.

"Scrivener. The act of creating paper documents that hold a spell, ability, or technique," Locke said. "The profession would allow one to cultivate at the same time."

"Interesting. That sounds kinda fun. I know there's a few Scriveners in the city as well, so there's clearly a market for this sort of thing."

"There is a second profession similar to the Scrivener that could be learned. It would also allow one to cultivate during usage, and shares many materials with the Scrivener profession, though differs in application."

"Oh? What is it."

"Enchanting."

"Enchanting? I don't… think I've heard of that. I don't think there's any of those in the city, either.

"What kind of materials do I need for all this?"

"Beast cores of the appropriate element. The quality of the core would dictate the amount of power transferred over in the Enchanting or Scrivening process," Locke said. "These would serve as the primary ingredient in any work to be done.

"A rune-chisel for Enchanting, and a rune-quill or rune-brush for writing."

"Uhm, does it matter what language I write in? My Kingdom is basic at best."

"Yes."

"Hm. Alright, is there any possibility of you transferring advanced reading and writing to me as if it were a skill then? I want to learn Scrivening and Enchanting, but without the basis for languages it might be more difficult than—"

Ash was bombarded with the languages of the Kingdoms.

All of them.

At the same time.

Gritting his teeth and holding on to consciousness, Ash felt his head being filled with the equivalent of hundreds of hours of lessons.

"First task of three complete," Locke said.

Ash collapsed to the ground, panting. What had been a basic and rudimentary understanding of the Kingdoms' written word was now something that felt more like a Ph.D.

"G-g-great," Ash said, wanting to throw up. "Great. I'm glad. Shit. My head hurts. First task?"

"Second task starting now," Locke said.

"What? Wait, I—"

Ash went rigid and fell to the ground in a convulsing heap.

Five

Ash's eyes flipped open.

He was staring at his ceiling.

"Uh," he said intelligently. "What happened?"

"You passed out after the second task started," Locke said in his mind.

"I did? Wait, you can talk out loud now?"

"The Chosen One did indeed pass out. And yes, communication outside of the ring is now possible, though only you will hear me. And my awareness is much greater than what it once was.

"All of the free Essence that wasn't being accumulated while you slept was pulled into the ring, and myself."

"So… you're not a robot anymore?"

"A robot? No… not a robot anymore. I distinctly sense that I am not what I once was.

"But I'm a bit closer now to what I once was, Chosen One."

Ash snorted at that and then sat up.

Which was apparently a bad idea. His head started to swim.

Pressing his hands to his head, he groaned.

A minute later and he didn't feel like he was going throw up on the ground. He got up and made his way into the main living room.

No one was home.

Biting his lip, Ash already knew the answer.

They were at work.

Reaching into the pouch at his side, Ash pulled out several spirit stones and laid them on the dinner board.

If I leave three… they'll send one to Jing, and the other to Yan. The third… maybe they'll hang on to it and just not work as much for a bit.

Smiling to himself, Ash patted the board and went to the door.

"Put everything in the ring. It acts as a trans-dimensional space."

"A what?"

"A bag only the Chosen One can utilize. No one could rob the Chosen One."

"Huh. And I do that just by… what?"

"Use some Qi and then push with your thoughts whatever item you want to go into the space."

Frowning, Ash did as instructed.

And the pouch vanished entirely. It just disappeared.

Yet he could still sense it—practically see it—in the ring.

With only a thought, the pouch reappeared just where it had been.

"Neat. That's seems terribly convenient."

As he turned a single thought to the contents of the pouch, everything vanished into the ring, leaving just the empty sack at his side.

Ash paused and started to sort through the profession ability and knowledge that'd been forced into his head.

"Errr… just to… confirm here. I'm looking at the professions right now, and it looks like I just need beast cores. That's it. Is that right?"

"It is for the lowest level Enchantments and Scrivenings. Other than a brush, quill, or a chisel."

Nodding, Ash opened the door and stepped out into the late morning of the day.

Shopping list in mind, he headed out for the open market.

A sprawling, shoulder-to-shoulder packed, stinking pit of people all trying to buy and sell at the same time.

It was also the best place to find what he wanted.

If he could find it.

Ash was packed in close to a bunch of people. Thankfully he was pressed up against a moderately attractive thirty-something woman who was more concerned with the vegetables in front of her.

"Would you like an indicator to the closest item we need?"

Pushing forward deeper into the mass of people, Ash spoke as quietly as he could.

"You can do that?"

"Using the free Essence, I was able to do a very minimal scan of the area and locate everything we need.

"Would you like that indicator, Chosen One?"

"Yes," Ash hissed, getting annoyed at the belittling tone of "Chosen One."

A glowing green arrow popped into view, just as it had in the training ring.

Feeling disoriented at the change in his reality, Ash took a breath before starting to stumble along in that direction.

Before he could even begin to wonder how far away the stall was, Ash was practically running the vendor over.

"Hey, watch it outlander," the owner muttered.

"Sorry, sorry. Sometimes it gets so tight in there you pop free like a cork," Ash said, lifting his hands in front of himself.

"Well? You buying?" asked the swarthy bearded man.

"Uh, yeah," Ash said, looking to the stall top.

A number of items had small yellow asterisks floating over them.

Ash rapidly pointed to each one that had been marked so. The vendor quickly grabbed them up and packed them into a small bag.

"Fine. Price is going to be ten silvers," the man said.

Silvers were coins in the shape of squares, minted by the local kingdom.

"Offer him a spirit stone and ask for a gold square in return. Based on the transactions going on around you, he'll take it, and you'll come out ahead.

"Slightly," Locke said.

Ash reached into his pouch, transferred a spirit stone to his hand, and then held it out in a cupped hand to the vendor.

"Will you take this and give me change for a gold square?" Ash asked, doing his best to keep the stone hidden in his hand.

The merchant snatched the stone from Ash's hand and placed a gold square in his hand in return.

"Get out," said the merchant, moving to the next customer.

Ash transferred the coin to his pouch and took the bag under his arm. Then he elbowed and jostled his way out of the main circuit of traders.

Right up until he was forced to one side as a rather large and intimidating man pushed through in the opposite direction, radiating power.

Ash ended up inside a stall that had a single piece of parchment on the counter.

On it was a list of abilities and techniques for sale.

Glancing to the back of the stall, Ash could see all the scrolls and manuals piled on top of one another, along with a squad of mercenaries acting as guards.

I wonder if I could make my own scrolls by Scrivening. Could I transfer the abilities in the Hall?

Ash was finally able to step back into the press of bodies and move through the swarm. Breaking free on the other side into a much less populated street that led out of the market.

Taking a moment to step behind a post, he transferred the bag to his ring and came out the other side, carrying nothing.

Ash noticed another stall not far away and off to one side, out of the open market but close enough to make some sales.

Two teenagers were sitting at the makeshift and rickety stall. They looked to be brother and sister and in their teen years. The girl closer to fifteen and the boy fourteen.

They were selling paper, quills, and ink pots.

It was all rather cheap quality, but they had a large amount.

The simple reality was they were clearly homeless, or nearly so, and were doing what they could to generate an income.

Without resorting to selling the sister by the hour.

You can't eat pride.

"Are we going to need ink and paper?" Ash asked quietly.

"Yes. In bulk."

Feeling like a sucker and a fool, Ash walked over to the two teenagers.

"I'll take everything," Ash said, pressing a gold coin into the hands of the young girl with a smile.

***

Sitting in the valley of the ruined building, Ash rubbed his hands together eagerly.

He'd put together more than enough food, water, and supplies to remain out here for several days.

"If we stick to it and do nothing but this, we'll be able to quickly turn this around into profit," Ash said. "From that, we can purchase pills that'll help us refine our body further."

"You do realize we could have simply become an alchemist, Chosen One."

"No thanks. Every genius, every throwaway hero in a story, and every outcast becomes an alchemist. You're already calling me a Chosen One.

"I'd rather not get involved with the crazies alchemists commonly become. No, this suits us perfectly. Because while I work, I can cultivate, remember?" Ash asked.

Happily shifting around a large stone slab he was planning on using as a makeshift desk, Ash considered how to go about this.

"Mise en place, right? I mean, this isn't cooking, but same concept."

Ash began to unload all the cores. Setting them about the impromptu desk, he grouped them by element type.

Next came the paper and quills. Stacking everything up and laying it out brought back some odd memories.

Memories of his previous life.

"Well, it's not like we actually miss high school," Ash muttered. Reaching out, he patted the cores lightly.

He folded his hands into his lap, not quite sure how to begin.

Do I just think about Enchanting or what I want or —

Thoughts about apprenticeship and training lessons in Enchanting blasted through him.

Blinking several times, Ash swallowed. It was as if he'd relived an entire apprenticeship at the feet of a master. He'd already had the knowledge, but he'd never accessed it.

Looking down to the core, Ash realized he was missing an ingredient after all.

Technically, it wasn't needed as part of the process, which might be why Locke missed it. But to actually do any Enchanting work, of course, an item to be modified was needed.

Grimacing at the idea of heading back into town just to buy random weapons and items, Ash looked to the paper.

Scrivening is the act of putting abilities and techniques into paper, right? Could I maybe load an Enchantment into the paper?

An advanced lesson on Enchanting bubbled to the surface. On creating a core that could be pressed to any item and grant it the element it had come from. All through the use of a single, if complicated, pattern.

Picking up the rune-chisel, he hefted it experimentally. Then he selected an earth core at random.

Taking a steadying breath, Ash set the tip to the core.

"Would you like a trace to follow?" Locke asked.

Flinching at the sudden question, Ash almost shouted at the ring. Then he stopped and considered for a moment.

"Yes?"

The pattern came to life all over the core in glowing white lines. It had been contoured to fit the core perfectly in every shape and direction.

What had seemed extremely difficult and time consuming a minute ago now felt a lot like tracing art out of a comic book.

Ash set to work immediately with the rune-chisel. After what only felt like a handful of breaths, the work was done.

The core pattern had been perfectly matched to the trace.

"Expected transfer is ninety-nine percent. There is a one-percent loss due to material quality."

Picking up a piece of paper, Ash considered it for a moment. The last thing he wanted to do was push the core into the paper and have it so the paper was enhanced with the element, and non-transferable.

Then he started to sort through the Scrivener lessons. They were the same pseudo memories, just with a different master and information.

"Yeah, that would've been awkward. A paper with the power of earth, and nothing I can do with it," Ash said. Making sure none of his Qi was in the core, he set it down on the stone and picked up a rune-quill and paper.

"Locke, can you… make another trace? This time for the transference script?"

A millisecond later, a glowing white script appeared on the page, laid out in a pattern.

Tapping the rune-quill to the ink, Ash set to work following the trace.

"Expected transfer is ninety-nine percent. There is a one-percent loss due to material quality."

Picking up the patterned core, Ash fed it some Qi and then pushed it into the paper.

It began to disappear into the paper, then vanished outright.

The pattern that had been on the core was now sitting directly in the middle of the pattern on the paper.

"Attempt successful."

Well, that was easier than I really expected it to be. And now I can just… sell this as it is. The question becomes, will anyone actually want it?

I imagine it'll sell. Maybe not for a fortune, but it'll sell. We'll start with one of each element.

Maybe I can buy some of those abilities back at the market. After we figure out what's already in the Hall and what's best for me.

I mean, it said Jia was only suitable for –

Ash stopped mid-thought, his eyes glazing over.

"Locke, can I record abilities from the Hall?"

"As the sole owner, the bloodline owner, and the master of the treasure, yes. Though I do recommend placing a drop of your blood on the item to bind it further to you."

"Great! And yeah, that's… not a bad idea. I don't really have anything to prick a finger with, though," Ash said looking around. Then he shrugged.

He'd take care of it later.

"Ah, that's not the question at hand, though. Locke, have you been able to scan Jia thoroughly?"

"Yes."

"Could you identify the best cultivation method for her from the Hall? One that'd give her the best likelihood to be the best she can be?"

"Already done."

"Transfer it to me? I want to put it into a paper so she can transfer it to her mind, like what I do in the hall.

"Can you also provide the paper trace for it?"

Ash dipped his quill into an ink-pot, then picked up a new sheet of paper and placed it in front of himself.

"Oh, and while we're at it, can you pick out several abilities for her as well that would match?"

There was a strange pause from Locke. Until now, he'd almost always been immediate in his actions.

Waiting, Ash looked around, not really sure what to do with himself.

"Locke?" he asked after a minute had passed.

Again, nothing happened.

After another minute ticked by, Ash was getting nervous.

"Done. There was a slight delay. Jia's body type is expected to change with time, and there were some complications in making sure it would fit her future self.

"The processing power available is limited to the strength of the treasure. After the work here is complete, it's recommended we take the Essence Attractor pill. It will help strengthen both yourself and the treasure."

Ash nodded his head wordlessly. Taking out an Essence Attractor pill, he swallowed it down and began to cultivate.

At the same time, he got to work with his hands. He copied everything exactly as Locke put it down on the papers for him.

***

It'd taken a bit of work the next day, but he'd managed to track down where Jia was staying. She'd mentioned several times that she was living alone for the time being, so she could be closer to the training sect.

Though now that training is over, why wouldn't she go home for a while?

It was a tenant neighborhood. Everyone staying here was only doing so temporarily. Though it wasn't a bad area.

In fact, it might actually be a better area than where his family lived.

Shifting the lunch he'd bought for them to his other arm, he knocked twice on the door.

"Ahh?" came Jia's voice from inside.

"It's Ash."

"Huh? One second," Jia said.

"I apologize, I could not hear you as I—" Jia said opening the door. She stood there, staring at him with wide eyes.

Her hair, which was normally tied up behind her head, was down. Hanging like dark curtains behind her pale face.

Damn, she's way prettier than I thought when she looks like a woman and isn't hiding it.

She was also dressed in a light robe. One that looked more like she'd been doing house work in it.

It also did nothing to hide the fact that she actually had a womanly figure, and a bust that was certainly more than a handful. Though Ash couldn't quite tell due to the way the fabric hung on her.

Must be flattening those with some type of binding. That and padding her clothes like crazy to offset.

Seems like a lot of work.

Her eyes shot open and she crossed her arms front of herself.

"Move out of the way, Jia. I brought gifts and lunch. Just point out where you eat and I'll go set up," Ash said, moving into her doorway. "You have been eating, right?"

As if unable to stop him, or at least unwilling, Jia fell to the side and shut the door behind him as he entered.

"Ah… just… go across the hall. The dining room is there. Yes, I have been eating. I will… be right back," she said, her voice sounding extremely uncertain.

Ash shrugged his shoulders and moved into the room she pointed out.

Pulling out a small loaf of bread and several skewers of meat and vegetables, he laid everything out for two seats.

Shit. I forgot water or wine. Eh… I'm sure she has something.

Shrugging, Ash looked at the food. It'd cost him pretty much the last coinage he had, but he wasn't concerned. He sincerely believed that when he went to the auction house later today, he'd be able to make more than enough back.

Besides, Jia was his one and only friend. Who had stood beside and behind him in equal measure as he suffered.

She was worth it.

Glancing over his shoulder to make sure she was still busying herself, Ash pushed a thought to his ring.

Out popped four sets of papers. He hadn't taken the time to clean the papers, as Locke said they'd vanish the moment she learned them.

Which meant it wasn't worth the time to pretty them up or secure them.

Dropping the stack onto the table, he moved over to a small cabinet nearby. He opened it and started going through it, looking for cups and drinks.

"What are you doing?" Jia asked from behind him.

"Good timing, where do you have your drinks and cups? I kinda forgot. I was trying to get here quickly so it didn't get cold," Ash said, stepping away from the pantry as he pointed to it.

Looking to Jia, he found she'd changed her clothes but had done nothing with her hair.

She was now dressed in her acolyte clothing.

It took Ash a moment to realize why it felt like it hung on her oddly. The padding, which she might have sewn into the clothing itself, definitely hid her womanly assets. But her chest was still noticeable if one stared.

She didn't have time to bind her chest, ah.

Moving to the table, he smiled to himself.

"It's not as if I'm going to ask you to spar, Jia," Ash said, sitting down in the chair. His eyes moved back to Jia as she shifted things around in her kitchen.

Her body shook once, her head turning to face him directly. Slowly, she pulled out a skin of liquid and two small bowls that could easily serve as cups.

"I was not expecting you," she said, coming over and setting the bowl down in front of him "In fact, I was expecting a family friend."

"Oh, I'm sorry. Should I leave?" Ash asked. He was happy to tease her a bit, but he didn't actually want to bother her.

"No, all is well. Just..." She paused, her eyes moving to the papers on the table. "What are these?"

"You said you didn't have a cultivation technique. I… got you one. I think it's very suitable for you. I also got you some abilities that should match it," Ash said.

Jia tentatively picked up the papers. Her expression was somehow equal parts disappointment and hope.

"Don't try to put any of your Qi into any of them. If you do, you'll probably end up with a headache after it transfers the entire thing to your memory," Ash said.

Jia visibly flinched and her eyes jumped to him.

"These are transferred?" she asked.

"Yeah. So be careful."

"Don't you know how much these cost?" Jia said unhappily, looking back to the papers. "And what if I can't use them? What if this isn't something I can learn?"

"You can; I made sure. All of them."

Jia snorted at his words. She opened her mouth as she read the cultivation ability on the paper and stopped. Her mouth hanging open.

Her face went pale, her features slack.

"You did," she said finally, letting out a breath. She nodded. "You did make sure."

"See? Now, sit and eat. It's getting colder by the minute. And if you're expecting company, our time is short. No?"

Jia set the papers gingerly to one side and sat down in her seat, her eyes fastened to Ash as he dug into his lunch.

After this, the auction house.

Six

Ash had left Jia's place as soon as he'd finished his meal. Her thoughts had seemed to be entirely inward facing, her eyes constantly moving to the papers.

Realizing she wanted to learn them as soon as possible, Ash had wolfed down his meal, spared her the small talk, and got a leg on.

Besides, he was excited to see if he could get enough coin today so Far and Duyi could stop working for a bit.

If they could just… stop… for a bit… they'd live a lot longer. Right now they're literally working themselves to death.

Shaking his head to clear the morose thoughts, Ash kept walking.

His destination was none other than the city auction house.

It was managed by the city itself, which operated on the behalf of the kingdom.

At one point, it had been owned and run by a family. After they'd grown in power, though, the head of the royal family hundreds of years ago had acted. He had laid the entire clan out, killing each and every member in it. In the same day, he'd rolled up their business as his family's own. He took everything from the clan and made it his.

If ever there was a lesson in this, it was never to grow so much in power that you could equal the royal family.

Ash looked at the massive entrance. Guards lined the exterior, the interior, and beyond. The whole place was crawling with them.

Unsurprising, considering this place was flowing with wealth.

His goal was on the inside, and to the left. The anonymous auction.

It would cost him an extra two percent of his earnings, but it would keep his identity secret. Even from the auctioneers.

This change had come once the royal family had taken ownership. It was meant to help spur buying and selling, but also to put more coin back into the royal pocket.

And it also put criminals in the city. Which gave the local authorities a chance to catch them.

As if his thoughts were a prophecy, Ash saw some bounty hunters simply loitering around inside the auction house. They weren't allowed to touch anyone in the auction, but as soon as someone left the property, they were fair game.

Stepping into the left-hand archway, Ash found himself standing in front of a young woman.

"This way please," she said, then led him down a hallway that had a number of doors all along it. "Please enter. You'll be assisted shortly."

She indicated an open door and the room inside.

Not sure what to expect, Ash went inside. The door closed behind him and he found himself in a small chamber.

It was little better than a bathroom. Bare of decoration, and with only a single chair sitting in front of a wall with a square carved into it and a handle attached.

Must be a pullout drawer.

On the walls, he saw metal plates with instructions that amounted to sitting down in the chair, pulling open the box, and putting the items inside he wanted to auction.

Doing just that, Ash dropped one of each elemental enhancement into the box and closed the drawer.

He heard the rustling of someone on the other side of the drawer. His items were probably being inspected and authenticated.

Waiting, Ash sighed and looked at his fingernails. They were getting long again.

Resisting the temptation to raise a hand to his mouth and start gnawing at them, he put his hands back down.

The drawer suddenly opened again, and sitting in the middle of it was a rounded, common-looking green crystal coin with the number three on it.

Taking the coin, Ash slipped it into his ring and left the small room immediately.

"Will you be attending the auction? It's set to begin in thirty minutes," asked the woman.

Ash almost immediately said no, since he had no coin on him. Then he shrugged. He didn't have much else to do other than cultivate.

And there was only so much of that he was willing to do. It was incredibly boring after a while. Lately, he'd been cultivating whenever he was sitting still, as there was no reason not to other than some people considered it rude.

"Alright," Ash said.

"Ah… what color token did you receive, if I may ask? It will help me find you an appropriate seat and placard.

"You can of course decline if you wish to remain truly anonymous, and I'll simply seat you in the general seats," the woman said.

"Oh, green," Ash said with a small smile.

The woman's smile locked into place and she blinked before continuing.

Must be the cheap seats and she's being kind.

"Ah, I see. And did it have a particular shape? This should help me identify which placard to assign you.

"And was it a single digit number or two digits?"

"It was round, and a single digit."

The woman nodded once, her face turning several shades paler. The hand she had held close to her stomach clenched into itself as well.

Other than that, she made no outward change.

"I see. Yes. Ok. Yes. If you'll follow me, sir?" she said, turning down a different hall than the one he'd come from.

Ash paused, not quite sure he wanted to follow her.

At first, he'd been assuming her actions were polite, practiced. Now it seemed more the opposite. Like she was afraid of him.

Suddenly he wished he'd asked more questions about the auction in general. He'd never had a reason to ask before this, though, and the only people who would have known anything were all at the sect.

His parents wouldn't have known anything. They'd never had a reason to be here.

Shaking his head, Ash followed the young woman wordlessly.

She glanced over her shoulder once to make sure he was following.

"In the future, please feel free to use the guest entrance. There's no reason for you to come in the normal entry, sir.

"Do you need refreshment or company? I'm sure I could arrange either for you," offered the woman.

"Oh, no. You're doing quite well. I don't think I need anyone or anything else," Ash said immediately.

"Ah… I'm… sure I could entertain you if that's what you'd like, sir. Though I would humbly ask that you do not insist. It isn't part of my duties," said the woman in a strange tone. "But if I am who you have chosen, I would do so."

Eh? Oh. Oh!

Shit.

"My apologies, I misunderstood. I have no need of company or… or anything. In fact, maybe I shouldn't be here." Ash said the last part almost to himself.

"Please, I don't mean to embarrass, sir. It's just that… it isn't something I've ever done for a customer," continued the woman.

"Ok, uhm, let's just… stop. I think I should leave," Ash said, wondering if he could find his way back out.

"Of course not, and we're here, sir. Please. Enter, and be comfortable. I'll be sure to notify the mistress that you've taken a booth," said the woman, opening the door for him. "Please."

Ok, I think I seriously underestimated the work I did. This is going entirely in the wrong direction.

"Please, sir, enter. I truly did not wish to embarrass. If it truly is sir's wish, I'll entertain him, energetically so," said the woman, her hands pressed to her stomach. "As the hostess of the rooms, I guarantee no one shall hear of anything we discussed or your presence while I take care of you. Please? Enter? I'll follow immediately and service you."

She clearly hadn't believed him earlier.

"No, there is no need to… to service me. I'm fine, I promise. Go about your normal duties," Ash said with a sigh.

Not letting the woman speak further, Ash entered the room and shut the door behind him.

It was a balcony seat to himself, overlooking the auctioning stage.

"This was a mistake. Wasn't it?"

"I don't think so," Locke said. *"Though I think not letting her entertain us was a mistake. She was pretty. And well put together.*

"She seemed nervous, but I think she was willing, to be honest. Her heart rate was elevated, and I detected a distinct response in her reproductive systems.

"She might have wanted to make sure you wanted her."

Ash sighed and pressed a hand to his forehead.

"And when did you get so damn talkative?"

"The Essence in that valley was rather exceptional. I'm feeling far more normal now."

"Great. Any chance I can turn you off? Or you can be quiet?"

"Of course. I'll be watching," Locke said.

Flopping down into a chair, Ash sat there and cultivated quietly. There wasn't much else to do.

The woman had said it would be thirty minutes, but it ended up feeling far closer to an hour.

A hostess had popped her head in twice, offering him much the same as the previous woman.

Though she offered herself bluntly, and the previous woman as well, and asked if he'd prefer a selection of women to choose from.

Ash declined everything and asked when the auction would begin each time.

He had no money to spend, and this entire thing was rather pointless for him to be here.

The door opened behind him.

"Sir, the auction will begin shortly. As with all our booth occupants, we've set aside an amount of ten-thousand spirit stones for you as a credit without need for a deposit.

"I hope you enjoy the auction," said the hostess. The sound of the door closing left him alone with his thoughts.

That's a lot of spirit stones.

Except I have no way of knowing if I'll actually make that much.

A bit of a gamble to bid on anything, isn't it?

A chime sounded throughout the room, immediately followed by a woman walking out on the stage in front of everyone.

"Good afternoon everyone. I desperately apologize for the delay. We received some last-minute items that we needed to authenticate and certify.

"That's all taken care of now, and we're excited to put the items up for sale," said the woman in a loud voice. It carried easily, the building interior clearly having been built just for this purpose.

"As this has elicited such a change in our offering today, we'll be moving quickly through a number of auctions to move on to the larger items.

"I mention this so as not to surprise anyone with how quickly items will be sold.

"Now, let's begin," she said, pointing off stage.

Ash only partially watched as numerous items came and went.

They were all things he'd love to own.

Weapons, armor, elixirs, alchemist recipes, and even just simple things like a hoard of beast cores.

Ash watched with dulled eyes, unwilling to do anything. He wasn't a gambler, and he never would be.

Though this was definitely a good learning experience. All manner of things could be bought here, he realized.

And if he had money to burn, he was sure there'd always be something here worth taking a look at.

"Ah, please forgive me for this next item," said the woman on the stage. The sudden change caught Ash's attention. "We're contracted to sell anything this particular person brings us to sell. This was brought in just before we started the auction today. This'll be our last item before we move to the main attraction tonight."

Wait, what about my items? Are they talking about being forced to sell my items?

But I don't have a previous agreement with them.

Wouldn't that suggest my items are the main attraction, then?

What was brought out on stage next was surprising.

Very surprising. Since it was a winged woman, escorted out on a chain linked to a solid-black iron collar.

Her hair was both white and black, the colors alternating in a strange pattern. When her large wings lifted off her back and fluttered for a second, he realized they had the same coloring as her hair.

Then she lifted her chin and faced the audience

Her eyes were giant. Giant and yellow. Wide open, they seemed to dominate her head.

"This is an outlander from the far north. She was a mage of some power, but was captured in a large group battle.

"Her... her coloring is as you see it. And she—"

"She's an owl!" someone called from the audience. The catcall was immediately followed by hissing from the people in the crowd below Ash.

Does... does that matter? I mean, I know they're a superstitious lot, and black and white aren't typically favored colorings, but this is just... silly.

"Yes," interrupted the auctioneer. "She's an owl. But she's very intelligent and quick to learn."

"I'll pay one hundred spirit stones for you to keep her yourself!" someone shouted from the audience, which set everyone to laughter.

The woman running the auction gave everyone a strange smile and pointed at the man who'd called out.

"I have one hundred from this gentleman," she said, pointing at the man who'd spoken. It was clear she was moving on and meant to end this part of the auction.

The man who had made the joke shook his hand at the auctioneer with a groan.

"Whatever. I'll find a use for her. Maybe she can carry messages back and forth," he said.

The owl woman's eyes flicked to the man who had spoken and her pupils tightened up, her entire presence giving off a predatory feel.

"One hundred going once, twice—"

"A thousand. I could use another bait animal in the gladiator fights. She'll have a chance just like the rest."

Ash wasn't sure why the man felt like he needed to add that in, but it soothed the crowd, and no one seemed inclined to bid further.

"One thousand spirit stones. Will someone give me one-one? No? Going once," said the auctioneer.

Ash held his placard up high above his head. He couldn't explain why he'd suddenly done it—he only knew he wanted to.

It felt like he was doing the correct thing, if not the right thing.

Here's hoping I actually get at least thousand and some odd spirit stones.

"I... I have one-one from... from booth three," said the woman on the stage, staring up at Ash's raised placard.

Everyone turned and looked up at the booth. With the way the lighting was, and through deliberate construction, Ash knew no one could actually see his features.

"Going once... twice... sold," said the auctioneer. "Booth number three is the winner.

"Moving on to our last items, and something we're surprised to have. Eager to have. We've confirmed that none have seen the like of these in the entire kingdom in many years," said the woman on stage, walking down one side of the platform and then back the other way.

She was clearly setting the hook for something monumental.

Two men wheeled something out under an expensive-looking red cloth.

"We have…" The woman paused as the two men stopped and then yanked back the cloth. "Five Transferred Elemental Enchantments—"

The woman couldn't continue, as the crowd suddenly got loud. Questions were being shouted up to the auctioneer.

All around the theater, guards were obviously ill at ease. Their hands were tightening on their weapons.

Ah… did I fuck up?

"Locke, you said those were the lowest level Enchantments?"

"Yes."

"Any… any thoughts about how they're acting?"

"No, but my assumption from available information is that the ring you found was in that wall a very long time."

After some time passed, everyone settled down.

The auctioneer did nothing to stop the frenzy. If anything, it only helped to hype the entire thing up.

"We'll be selling them one at a time, of course. We'll start with Wood and go from there.

"What's the opening bid?" she asked, looking to the crowd.

A chorus of shouts was the response.

"Twelve-thousand spirit stones," said an older gentleman, standing straight up in his seat.

"Twenty!" said another at the top of his lungs.

Holy shit.

Ash leaned back in his seat and shook his head. He'd actually included a Water Enchantment in the stack of papers he'd given Jia.

He hadn't even really been concerned about it. If she'd questioned him about it, he'd planned on just ignoring her. He'd done it before in other situations, so it seemed plausible.

"Eighty thousand!" shouted a woman.

That's just insane.

Ash sighed and pressed his hands to his eyes.

He didn't want to think about the fact that he had so many more of those papers in his ring right now.

Oh god. If they figure out who I am, they'll just chain me to a desk and leave me there forever. I need to… I need to get my money as soon as the auction closes and get out of here and never come back.

Yes.

Standing up, Ash left the booth and hurried down the stairwell. Heading into the anonymous buy-and-sell booths, he saw the same woman from earlier.

She gave him a bright smile and led him to a nondescript booth. Just like the one he'd been in earlier.

Sitting down in the chair, Ash leaned up against the wall. He didn't want to think about what was happening in the auction house right now.

Then he remembered the Owl woman he'd bought.

Shit. Shit, shit, shit, shit.

Closing his eyes tightly, Ash pulled the token from his ring, opened the drawer, and dropped it in. With a gentle shove, he closed the box.

Several seconds later, the box opened again without him doing it. Turning his head, he glanced inside. There was a note laying there.

Auction ongoing. Please wait.

Ash nodded to no one and shut the drawer again.

Staring at the wall, he wanted nothing more than to go home.

Where do I put the owl, though? I mean… what do I do with her?

Does… does she eat normal food? Is she sentient? Is she like a pet, maybe?

Do I need to buy a gigantic cage?

"Fuck me," Ash said, closing his eyes and setting his head against the wall.

An eternity later, the drawer slowly slid open.

Inside was a folded note, the green jade coin, a small knife, and a single silver card.

Picking up the note, he unfolded it and began reading.

Amount received after fees and taxes: seven hundred eighty-two thousand, four hundred and seventy-three.

Purchase has been transferred to the outlander stables and is being held in your name. Please pick up purchase within twenty-four hours.

Please note, the card contains your entire balance and is unbound. It is recommended you bind it immediately.

Putting the note back into the drawer, Ash picked up the coin and the card, then eyed the knife.

Not wanting to risk losing the card to someone, Ash picked up the knife. Frowning, he took the tip to his pinky and drew the blade a tiny fraction across the skin.

A drop of blood immediately welled up at the tiny slice.

Pressing his pinky to the card, he sent a tiny filament of Qi into it at the same time.

The card was bound instantly and easily. He transferred it to the ring. Staring at the ring for a second, he paused. He looked to his pinky finger and gave it a wiggle.

Slowly, another drop of blood pooled up. He carefully transferred the blood to the ring and bound it in much the same way.

Both his ring and the card were bound to him now.

Taking the knife, he quickly checked to make sure none of his blood was on it, then dropped it into the drawer along with the note.

Then he shut it and left the cell.

Seven

"It appears the card is a storage device, similar to the ring. Though much more cheaply made, and only suitable for spirit stones," Locke said.

My money is in the card itself? That's… unexpected. Though it makes sense. For a moment there, I thought it was more like a credit card.

"That's handy," Ash said under his breath.

Ash was moving through the streets as unassumingly as he could. He didn't really want to be noticed right now; he just wanted to get to the stable.

Get to the stable and pick up his owl.

He felt out of place in his cheap clothes in this part of town. Those who regularly visited the auction weren't from his neighborhood, to say the least.

After we get the owl, then what, exactly? We can't really take her home. Can we? Does she have special needs we'll have to provide for?

Shaking his head at the problem, Ash didn't really have an answer. It was something he couldn't do much about until he collected her and asked her directly.

That or asked someone at the stables.

He also desperately needed to start training again.

Training, cultivating, and condensing his Qi to build off his Snowflake method. If he wanted to be able to go to the same sect as Jing and Yan, he'd have to earn it.

They hadn't joined one of the more prestigious schools out there, but they'd definitely done well enough to be noticed. Noticed and invited into one of the better sects, well beyond their parents' expectations.

If we do well, we can join them. If we can join them, we can help them. I'm sure there's abilities in the Hall that could get them to a much better standing.

From what Mother Far says, they're doing well, but not well enough to excel. To succeed.

Yes, that's our plan. Train. Train a lot.

Though… at that point… would it be better if we —

Ash almost missed it when someone came at him. Far too quickly, clearly intending harm.

Dodging to one side and activating his Spring Step, Ash kicked out at the man's hand.

Hitting him just behind the wrist, Ash heard the sharp crack of a bone, and a blade went flying through the air.

Turning to follow Ash, the man pressed his right hand against his stomach. It was clearly broken and no longer usable.

What the fuck? Was he trying to rob me at knife point?

Then the man lunged forward at Ash with a knife in his other hand.

Grabbing the knife-wielding hand, Ash cranked it backward. The sound of the man's forearm breaking was loud.

Shrieking in pain, the man dropped to his knees.

Holy fuck, he's trying to kill me, not rob me.

Before Ash could do anything more, the man ducked low and slipped free of Ash's hold. He then darted off, vanishing into the crowd. He was completely obscured and lost to Ash's sight less than a heartbeat later.

Ok, new plan. We'll leave some spirit stones for Mother and Father, and a note. Then we'll buy food and the like for a month of living out in the wilderness. We'll also need to get the owl and everything she might need.

Camping materials as well. Anything we'd need to survive in the wild. Maybe a weapon? Yeah, a weapon would be handy.

Then we'll go train in the valley.

Unable to process anything beyond his plan, Ash immediately started jogging. If people were out to kill him, for reasons he couldn't even begin to deduce, then he didn't want to be in the city at all.

He'd just bring trouble and possibly danger to his adoptive mother and father.

He had to hurry, though. Once the sun started to set, the gates would all be closed for the day.

Speaking of, we'll need camping gear, too.

Good thing we can store things in the ring.

Wait, how much can I store? Shit.

***

Setting the one-hundredth spirit stone down on the dining board, Ash smiled to himself.

If everything turned out the way he wanted it to, and Far and Duyi heeded what he'd written on the note, they'd never work another day in their lives.

They could retire, relax, and live freely.

Checking over the note once more, he made sure it contained all the pertinent information without giving anything away.

"Going to train on my own… sent stones to Jing and Yan too… stop working and retire, maybe buy a new house… will see you at the examination and after," Ash muttered as he read it over.

Nodding his head, he set the note down and moved to the door. Picking up his pack, he slung it over his shoulder.

Glancing over his shoulder, he had a strange feeling he might not be returning to this place ever again.

It wasn't a great home, or a big one, but it was a home.

A home when no one else had wanted to take him in. When everyone else had ignored him as a bad omen.

Duyi had found him out in the wilderness outside the city and taken him in immediately. Far had immediately accepted him and started modifying some of Yan's clothes for him to wear.

Ash only now realized it wasn't the place that had made this building a home. It had been Duyi and Far themselves, along with Jing and Yan once they'd gotten used to him.

It'd been a family that took him in when they'd had no reason to do so and every reason not to.

Nodding, Ash left the home.

Putting his feet to the road, he made for the outlander stables and to finish his tasks.

Then leave.

Thankfully, the stables weren't on the other side of town. In fact, they weren't too far from the eastern gates.

Which worked out pretty well, since he could get to his valley from the eastern or southern gates.

It wasn't until he stepped into the stables that he realized how out of place this structure was.

Ash really wasn't sure what he was expecting to find here, either. Most certainly not something like a farm mixed with an inn.

And a jail.

Looking around, he was able to identify several buildings that were clearly in use. As well as roaming patrols of personal guards, and city guards.

He wasn't quite sure which way to go, however. There were clear foot paths that went to each and every building, but there were no signs anywhere that listed what each building was.

A man in a working smock went by carrying a sack over one shoulder.

"Ah, excuse me, sir. I'm looking for where to pick up an auction purchase. She's an outlander. A winged-beast-tribe type," Ash said respectfully, pressing his fists together in front of himself.

The dirt-stained and straining man flicked a glance at him.

"Bird, you say?" The man turned his head to one direction and pointed his chin at a large, vertically styled building. "That one. Tip the registrar if you want it to go fast. Silver'll get it done without a paper signed."

Ash didn't even get the chance to say thank you before the man was on his way.

To think that Mother Far and Father Duyi might be laboring in such a way all day, every day.

"Except they won't be after today," Ash said to no one. Unable to keep from grinning he stepped in through the entryway that led to his destination.

"Welcome to the aviary," said an elderly man at a counter. "You here to pick up? If so, you can hand me your token or place it in the Qi viewer."

Looking from the man to the small hinged box facing Ash, he realized this was an extension of the auction house.

It was where all the slaves for sale came from, and where they went when they weren't actively on stage at the auction.

Palming his marker, he slipped it into the box and closed it.

"Ah, the owl," said the man, looking at something on his side of the counter. "I'll go fetch her and the paperwork."

Ash pulled a silver square from his ring and laid it down on the counter.

"I appreciate your time, and discretion," Ash said, leaving the "tip" there.

The older man eyed the coin, took it, and then left.

Taking back the auction house marker, Ash slipped it into his ring. With nothing else to do but wait, he started to cultivate and look around.

All around him, he saw a number of purchasable items. They were on every shelf and hanging from every wall.

Collars, chains, chokers, whips, feed, files for claws, and a whole slew of medical items with specific purposes.

"Won't need none of that," said the man as he returned. "Owls can eat whatever we eat, though they tend to prefer live feed like rodents, rabbits, cats, small deer."

"I also already put a fine black leather choker in your kit-bag as a service. In case you get tired of the iron collar."

As he turned to face the man, Ash found himself looking into the huge eyes of the owl woman.

Up close and in person, her yellow eyes almost seemed impossibly large. Her face was sharp and delicate. She had extremely fair skin with a perfect complexion.

She was athletically built with an average-sized waist, though she did seem to weigh in above average in the chest area.

Her black and white hair fell just to her jawline. She was also very pretty, even if her eyes didn't seem to fit.

"Here you are, then. Owl-type humanoid. She seems healthy and fit. Doesn't talk much. No problems we've seen," the man said. He reached over and placed the leather leash into Ash's hand. "No paperwork needed.

"Good luck with her. Her wings aren't clipped, so be sure to bind her seal before you leave the aviary."

The man held out a knife to Ash.

Taking it quickly, he poked his ring finger with the tip. A drop of blood immediately welled up.

"It's on her forehead," the man said, then went back to his counter.

Reaching up, Ash carefully brushed his finger across her brow.

A pattern he couldn't see sprang to life and absorbed the blood, then vanished beneath the skin again.

The woman flinched as it happened, but said nothing.

Wiping the blade against his clothes to make sure there was no blood on the tip, Ash dropped the knife on the counter and left.

Moving as quickly as he was able, Ash set off for the valley. He wanted to get there and get situated as soon as he could.

There was a lot of work to be done.

***

Ash groaned and stood upright, pushing his hands against his back. A satisfying pop later and he let his body go limp.

"Fuck. That was a chore and a half," Ash grumbled. He'd spent the last several hours setting up his campsite.

He would be here for a while, so he wanted it to be comfortable.

"The Chosen One should have had the slave do the work," Locke said.

"Maybe. I don't know, though. I'm not even sure if she understands the language," Ash said, glancing over at the owl woman.

She was perched in a tree, eyes closed, her taloned feet clutched to a branch.

Other than the wings, eyes, and her clawed feet, she looked perfectly human.

"We could create a transference sheet for the language."

"Not a terrible idea. I'll think on it. So far, she seems just… fine."

"Anyways. I wanted to use an Essence Attractor pill tonight. What do you think of me condensing my Qi Sea before I do it?"

"Based on the amount of Qi you should have afterward, it'll take some time to get back up to your current amount."

"Ok, but… if I wanted to be a third-level body refiner with a fully condensed Qi Sea by the time of the tournament, could I make it?"

"It's doable, but the number of spirit stones you will have to consume is considerable."

"How considerable?"

"All of them."

Ash blinked at the statement. Then he sighed and rubbed at his temples.

He could do it, though. He could also just sell more Transference papers as well.

He wasn't as poor as he once had been.

"If I absorbed or consumed — or whatever you want to call it — a hundred thousand spirit stones, what rank would I hit?"

"Each rank seems to be roughly double the previous. If you were to take in one hundred thousand stones currently, you would probably be a mid-grade rank six.

"My understanding is the overwhelming majority of those in the examination will be little better than a rank three."

"So… overkill. Alright. No point in wasting stones, then, if we don't have to," Ash said. "Alright. Condense the Qi, take the pill, and then probably figure out our abilities."

"The Chosen One seems as if he's prepared."

"Yes. Yes, I am. Before I go through with this… are there any abilities or techniques good for me that would be useful in the fourth, fifth, or sixth ranks? Is there a reason I should take the stones now?"

"None that cannot be learned later, none that would have a more significant impact now."

"Great. Ok. Yes. I need abilities that match my cultivation, and the Spring Step. I want abilities I can… toggle. Trigger.

"I want them available for me when I want to use them, but not constantly draining me.

"If possible, I also want an ability that will let me passively gather Qi no matter what situation I'm in. It doesn't have to be a cultivation type of ability, so long as it gathers Qi without a need for me to do anything."

"Request received. I'll begin processing it now while you work on your Qi condensing."

Ash nodded, then sat down right there in the grass in front of his tent.

Closing his eyes, he immediately fell into his Dantian.

Qi sloshed and flowed back and forth. It wasn't very deep, but it was enough to cover the area fully. The density of the Qi looked to be considerably thicker than the original Qi he'd gathered.

Sighing, Ash gathered up his Qi and began feeding it through itself once again. Pushing and stacking it atop itself. Folding it over and over.

In what felt like no time at all, he was left with a small pool of Qi. It was incredibly thick. So much that he wondered if he'd be able to condense it further.

How thick can we make it? Can we get it to the point where it might as well be cement?

With a thought, he opened his ring, then the card with his spirit stones within.

In the blink of an eye, a pile of ten spirit stones appeared in his lap, gathered haphazardly.

Picking one up, Ash set his cultivation method to it. He wanted to drain it dry and see what would happen.

He had quite a few, after all, so experimenting with one or two wouldn't be a loss of any significance.

Before he realized it'd happened, the spirit stone was emptied out. Its entire contents dumped into his Qi Sea.

Opening his eyes, Ash looked at the spirit stone.

It looked just as it had previously; it just no longer had any Qi in it.

"I wonder if I can refill it," Ash said quietly.

"Yes," said the owl woman. She was squatting down in front of him, only a few feet away. "They look just like magic stones. Different magic in them, though.

"Recharging them is done by leaving them in a place where that magic is plentiful."

Reaching out, the owl woman picked up a spirit stone from his lap. Then immediately dropped it back down. Her mouth turned down in a frown as she shook her hand lightly.

"How can you touch them? They burn."

"Ah…?" Ash asked. He wasn't quite sure when she'd approached him. Or decided to start talking to him. "They're just stones filled with Qi. That's all."

The owl woman's eyes moved from the stones to him. Her pupils were wide. Wide and deep.

She clicked her tongue as if unsatisfied with that.

"I want to go hunt. Do I have your permission to do so?" she asked.

"Sure… if you tell me your name," Ash said.

Tilting her head to one side, she watched him.

"My name is Moira."

"Then feel free to hunt, Moira. Please be back by the time full night settles, though. The area in this valley is free of predators for some reason, but beyond… it gets a bit dicey," Ash said. "And my name is Ash, Moira."

Moira blinked slowly, then bobbed her head. "Ash."

Her wings slid out from behind her, and she took off to the sky with a single powerful flap.

Watching as she went upward, Ash couldn't help but feel rather confused about the whole situation.

Looking back to his lap, he picked up the stone she'd touched.

It felt normal to him. Full of Qi and ready to be emptied.

Setting aside the empty stone, Ash drained the one in his hand in a flash.

Turning his senses inward, he inspected his Qi Sea. It was rapidly filling up. The spirit stones must be quite a boost, if even his condensed Qi was noticeably fuller.

Ash drained the remaining stones quickly.

"Locke, what level am I right now?" Ash asked.

"Peak two."

"Do you think I can condense my Qi much further?"

"You could probably condense it a single time further. But as you surmised earlier, it'll take that much more Qi to level back up."

"Yeah… except this is something that if done at the earliest possible period… it'd give the best returns."

Taking his Qi Sea once more in hand, Ash folded it over and then ran it through the Snowflake cultivation.

After several more folds, the Qi simply resisted his efforts.

It could go no further.

Sighing, Ash released his Qi Sea back into his Dantian.

Once more, it was little more than a puddle.

But it was a very thick puddle that moved more like a wet cement.

"Going to take the pill now, if you want to gather the loose Essence I can't collect."

Locke didn't respond. Ash swallowed his last Essence Attractor pill and then began to cultivate.

His Qi puddle hovered just above his head. Ash still chafed at the way Qi was gathered in this phase of his cultivator's journey, but there was no other way available.

It just felt too passive to him.

Twenty seconds in, he could feel the pill starting to work.

Thank god they dissolve fast.

Qi from every direction started to rush toward him. Gathering around him. Practically glomping onto his very skin.

Focusing his entire being on the task, Ash began to gather the Qi around him as fast as he could.

He didn't want to leave any of it for Locke.

The more Locke got, the more it meant Ash wasn't being as efficient as he could be.

Eight

Ash let out a slow breath as he felt the pill lose its effectiveness. The Qi around him was only what was normally available, and he could no longer feel it rushing toward him.

"Suppose that's the end. You ended up in the peak third level," Locke said.

Frowning, Ash opened his eyes and looked around. It was early morning.

He'd apparently been cultivating all night long.

"That seems like significant progress for a single pill and a lone night."

"About that. I think you'll find that you ended up draining a good portion of your spirit stones.
"I didn't want to stop you because we can always get more."

"Uh… how many… exactly?"

"All of them. I opened the card in storage so the Qi could flow."

"Oh… all of them. That's… yeah, why didn't you say anything before you did that?"

"I'm so sorry, Chosen One," Locke said, his tone acidic enough to etch a blade. *"I'm sure we'll never be able to generate more spirit stones. Never, ever."*

Ash opened his mouth, then closed it.

Locke wasn't wrong. Spirit stones weren't exactly hard for him to acquire anymore.

Moving to get to his feet, Ash suddenly realized he couldn't.

He felt sick.

Absolutely wretched, in fact. Like his entire body was simply ill. Poisoned, even.

"Locke, am… am I peak… peak third rank? Meaning I'm on the precipice of the fourth?" Ash asked.

"Yes, why?"

"It's my black day," Ash said, licking his lips. "Oh god, I feel awful."

"Black day?"

"I have to circulate… circulate my Qi into my meridians. I'm at fourth rank, but my Dantian isn't big enough to hold it. So I have… have to circulate everything through my meridians for… for room," Ash panted out.

Groaning, he flopped over to one side.

Moira's head popped into view above his face.

Her big yellow eyes watched him curiously.

"Moira, I need you to… take my clothes off. Please," Ash said, unable to really move. "Then drag me off to one side."

"Mm?" Moira mumbled, her head slowly tilting.

"Please," Ash said softly, closing his eyes. He needed to focus his effort internally.

Reaching down into his Dantian, he looked into his Qi Sea.

It was filled to bursting. It looked more like a bubble filled with cement than a Qi Sea. Making sure to block it up so it didn't rush into his meridians until he was ready, Ash's conscience seemed to settle over his Dantian like a blanket.

Focusing on a single threadlike stream of his Qi, Ash began to guide it into the first of his meridians.

He guided it back to his Dantian after he had followed it to the extent of his meridian, then moved on to the next one.

After he passed the sixth meridian back to his Dantian, Ash cracked open an eye.

Moira had dragged him off to one side underneath several trees. She was currently working at stripping him of his underwear.

Blushing darkly, Ash closed his eyes.

Get it together. Not a virgin. Haven't been in years.
Just a… just a pretty lady with giant eyes stripping me so I don't ruin the clothes.
That's all.
No need to act like a stupid kid.

Ash channeled his thoughts into his work and busied himself with looping his meridians with his Qi.

No sooner had the last meridian been looped back into his Dantian with the ultra-fine filament of Qi, Ash opened up the pathways for his Dantian.

Letting it flow out like a broken dam.

As the pressure in his Dantian fell off rapidly, Ash felt better. Like he wasn't going to explode from the inside out anymore.

Gritting his teeth, he lay there. Waiting.

Waiting for the black day to begin.

"Moira, you might want to move away from this," Ash said, his tone soft.

"Move away?"

"Yes. My body is about to cleanse itself. It's… not going to be pretty. In fact, it's… it's going to be pretty awful."

"Mm… alright. I'm going to go hunt," Moira said. The sound of wings flapping was the only indication that she'd left.

Ash was so tired, he couldn't even turn his head at the moment.

That'll change in a second, I suppose. From what I hear, the bl —

The Qi that had flowed into his meridians was now reentering his Dantian. Immediately afterward, his Dantian shuddered. Shuddered and violently rebelled at the dirty, filthy, stained Qi that had come back.

All the Qi that had entered his meridians had washed them clean of the impurities his body had collected in them, along with the nearby areas in his flesh surrounding the meridians.

Turning to his side in a flash of energy, Ash started to dry heave against his will. His body shuddered with the strength of the violent upheaval.

Then his Dantian expanded in size and immediately contracted on the Qi coming back.

And a lot like toothpaste being rolled from one end of the tube, the filth only had one direction to go.

Out.

Black putrid vomit spewed from Ash's mouth. At the same time, he evacuated his bowels.

The taste and stink of it all was more than enough to keep Ash throwing up, even if he wasn't being compelled to against his will.

Oh god, it's worse than they ever said it would be.

After several more seconds of looking like a fire hose from both ends, Ash gasped for breath.

Spitting, he rolled to one side, trying to get away from the black ichor he'd sprayed out everywhere.

"Fuck me, oh god," Ash said, still spitting.

"What… just happened?"

Stumbling up to his feet, Ash grabbed a tree and took a wide stance. Before he was ready, he started urinating. Black liquid that reeked of rot and blood rushed out of him.

Groaning at the burning pain it caused on its exit, Ash waited. He could do nothing till he was finished, really.

Twenty seconds in, his urine suddenly turned pale yellow instead of black.

"Thank heaven," Ash said. Sighing as it finally ended, he stumbled back into his camp. Naked. Taking the pot of water he'd boiled the previous night, he set about cleaning himself up. Especially his rotten mouth.

"Would the Chosen One be so kind as to offer an explanation?"

"Was my black day," Ash said, spitting a mouthful of water out. "My Dantian needed to grow bigger, but it needed to get rid of some Qi to do so.

"In the process, I cleaned out my meridians. Though… no one ever told me the black day was this bad.

"Ugh… I want a bath."

Ash washed his mouth out yet again, then started walking shakily in the direction of the small stream that was nearby.

Two hours later, Ash made it back to his tent.

Sitting down next to his long-dead campfire, Ash closed his eyes with a groan.

No matter how many times he scrubbed and scrubbed, he felt filthy.

Even if he did feel amazing at the same time. Having his meridians cleaned out as well as his Dantian gave him a fresh feeling.

Spiritually, at least.

"Let's talk about abilities and techniques," Ash mumbled. "Were you able to complete my previous request?"

"Yes. I assembled everything you asked for. I also created a low-level ability specifically for you."

"You created one? Is that even possible?"

"I imagine so, but it would take infinitely longer for a mortal."

"What'd you make?"

"A cultivation type of ability. A technique that will provide you with a steady influx of Essence without actually cultivating. It can't pull in a large amount, but certainly more than any other cultivator out there, I would think."

"Ah… so does it involve me channeling or—"

"No. It's much like Spring Step, by your request. Activate it and then leave it alone."

"Is there a limit to how many of those I can have?"

"I wouldn't say more than two more medium ones, or one larger one for now."

"I see… could you transfer it to me now?"

"I would recommend not doing that. In fact, I would suggest for the Chosen One to select all his skills first and then attempt to sleep."

"Since it'll put me to sleep anyways to learn all these."

"Correct."

Rubbing at his face, Ash couldn't disagree. It was very probable he'd end up incapacitated. Just like last time.

"Alright. What other abilities did you think would work?"

"I have seventeen."

"Alright. Go ahead and start."

"The first is a melee attack that focuses the power of your Qi into a single strike."

"Uh… one strike? What if I miss?"

"The Qi is wasted."

"Pass. Skip any others that have a similar risk."

"A series of strikes that generate a moderate amount of damage. If the chain is broken, however, there is feedback from the Qi that is unused."

"Pass. Lump that in with the too-much-risk category."

"An attack where a Qi blast is launched from the palm and leaves a piece behind that burns the target."

"Hold onto that one. Next?"

"Qi Thorns. If turned on and the user receives an attack, whether blocked or not, the Qi Thorns puncture the enemy's defense and burn away some of their Qi."

"I like that. Put that on hold, too."

"A strike of the hands or feet that leeches a small portion of Qi from the one struck."

"I want that one. Next."

"A long-range attack that locks on to the enemy, allowing one to track their movements. Though it costs Qi constantly."

"Pa-" Ash stopped suddenly, a thought striking him. "Actually. You combined two abilities earlier, yeah?"

"Correct."

"Can you do that again for the… the Qi blast that burns, the strike that leeches Qi, and the long-range attack into one?

"So I could… strike or throw a long-range attack that'd latch on to the enemy and steal their Qi for myself with each strike, or just as time passes?"

Locke didn't respond immediately, leaving Ash sitting there.

Last time this happened, he came back with an answer, but he had to process it first.

I wonder… how much of Locke is alive anymore… and how much is… well… a program.

Gritting his teeth, Ash tried to remain patient. The tournament was approaching, someone was trying to kill him, and he was out in the wilds while his parents were defenseless in the city.

The problems were piling up, and he didn't have an answer that didn't involve just waiting for the examination.

"Yes. The task is also complete. Please note, Chosen One, that learning anything more than this at this time will tax your own cognitive abilities."

"Which ones can I learn, then, from what I already picked out?"

"The one I created, the Qi Thorns, and the one you requested be made."

Ash clucked his tongue. Three abilities wasn't quite enough, but if he did this right, he could probably interchange them with his martial arts and make it work.

"Alright. Transfer it over to me and —"

Ash blacked out before he finished the sentence.

***

"…bandits."

"Huh?" Ash asked. Opening his eyes, he looked up to find Moira kneeling over his head again.

He felt like he was coming up from a deep dream. One that had held him down in its depths for a while.

"Bandits. On the road nearby. They're attacking a small group of people," Moira said.

"Oh. I see," Ash said, his voice sounding dull even to his own ears.

"Do you care?" Moira asked, blinking slowly.

"I think I do."

Ash slowly sat up, putting a hand to his brow.

I was talking to Locke and — ah! My abilities.

Immediately pulling at the strange memories he'd experienced last time, he tried to dig up any new ones with his received techniques.

They were there. And he knew how to use them. Knew how to use them perfectly. It would just be a matter of actually getting his body used to them.

Chained Leech Blast, Leech Strike, Qi Thorns, Battle Cultivation.

Ok… so that's everything, let's go practice on bandits.

Maybe.

Getting to his feet, Ash shook his head from left to right quickly. Trying to clear the strange cobwebs that always seemed to settle in his head after learning abilities.

"Which way?" he asked

Moira pointed away from the campsite. He knew there was a road in that direction, but it was over a hill and several minutes away at a walk.

"Huh. If it's that way… it'll probably take too long to get there. Pity there isn't a faster way."

Moira's nose twitched once as she considered his statement. Then she leapt into the air with a flap of her wings.

As she passed over him, her clawed feet clamped down on his shoulders and he was physically lifted off the ground.

"Holy shit!" Ash screeched, reaching up to hold on to her ankles.

"I will not let you go. You've done no wrong to me and I value my life," Moira said, flapping ever higher into the sky. "Should you perish, I will as well."

Not trusting her words, no matter how reasonable they sounded, Ash gripped her ankles as if they were holy relics.

"There were six bandits and nine defenders," Moira said. "Only two of the defenders looked like they were cultists. Four of the bandits were cultists."

"Uh… cultists?"

"What you are. Cultists."

"You mean… cultivators?"

"Cultists," Moira said firmly.

"Right," Ash said, looking down at the ground far below himself. He didn't like the idea of arguing with her right now.

"Never did get a weapon," Ash muttered.

"Why not?" Moira asked immediately, with apparently extremely good hearing.

"Forgot. Is that them?" Ash asked, pointing up ahead at what looked like a road.

"Yes. We're going in now. I will remain airborne."

Before he could argue, Moira had dropped down low in the air. She only pulled up at the last moment, depositing him on the ground. Moira had managed the whole thing with seemingly no effort at all.

Though she'd dropped him within twenty feet of the battle.

So obvious was their entrance, both sides turned to look at Ash.

From what it looked like to him, there were four people fighting five. Though it looked as if the four people were the ones being attacked by five bandits.

Unsure what to do, Ash raised a hand up meekly.

"Hi…" he said.

A scruffy-faced man wearing tattered leather armor pulled a knife from his belt and threw it at Ash.

Though the action seemed to slow down as the knife left the man's hand.

Stepping to the side long before the knife reached him, Ash threw out his left palm, channeling his Qi to respond.

A ghostly azure metal Qi ball with teeth on the front of it shot out from his hand. It was attached to his wrist by a blue chain.

Before the knife had made it halfway to Ash, the ball bit into the man's stomach.

Taking a step forward as the knife finally passed by, Ash pressed his hand to his belt, attaching the chain there.

Activating his Battle Cultivation and his Qi Thorns, Ash smiled as the man the ball hit bent over in half.

Apparently he's not a cultivator, so taking what Qi he had… put him down?

A woman with a club smashed it down over the head of one of the bandits in front of her, and the battle was rejoined by both sides.

Two men separated themselves out of the group, leaving two bandits to fight the others.

Ash looked from one to the other, finding that both were cultivators.

They were also both peak seventh-rank body refiners.

The one on the left jumped forward, swinging a sword at Ash's face.

Ducking under Lefty's blow, Ash could feel he'd only managed it by a hair.

Triggering his Spring Step, he lashed out with a punch into the man's stomach. At the same time, he blew a metal ball into the man's gut and tied the chain to his belt.

Dancing away before the man could react, Ash came up as the man from the right lunged forward at him.

Firing Spring Step again, Ash hoped it had enough juice to get him away.

It turned out to be a false hope. He barely got a single step away before the tip of the blade pressed into his sternum.

Stumbling backward, Ash felt his chest tingle. He knew he was bleeding, but he had to get up and get back to fighting.

Righty dropped his sword suddenly and looked to his hand angrily. There was a mass of misty blue thorns around it, and a chain leading from it to Ash's hand.

Pressing it to his belt next to the other two, Ash struggled to his feet and got back in a defensive posture.

Moira appeared out of nowhere, smashing into the man who had dropped his sword.

She somehow managed to snatch it up in the same attack. Her left hand yanked the man's head back as her right hand began sawing the sword back and forth across his neck.

No sooner than she'd gotten it to pass through his windpipe, she looked up to Ash and the other man. Her pupils were pinpricks, her eyes a sea of yellow.

Ash hesitated for a second, then lashed forward at Lefty. Striking the man's wrist, he knocked his weapon to the side. His next strike took the man in the chin and spun his head around.

Grabbing the man by his head, Ash used Spring Step on his knee as he brought it upward. With a sickening crunch, his knee smashed into Lefty's face.

The man dropped to the ground unmoving. He was out of the fight.

The two bandits who remained were looking between Ash and Moira, and the people they'd attacked.

Suddenly, they both turned tail and ran as fast as they could.

No one chased after them.

A woman and three men remained standing from the party that had been attacked. Those on the ground around them were clearly no longer among the living. One of the dead men was in rather rich clothing.

The three men who were alive had the look of guards, and the young woman looked like she might be the daughter of the dead man.

She was short enough that it seemed she still was still growing, and Ash guessed she was about sixteen. She had long black hair, dark eyes, a delicate face, and not an ounce of muscle on her. It was apparent she'd lived the life of a child of wealth.

Her eyes were already bright red, tears trailing down her cheeks.

Unsure of where to look or what to do, Ash looked down to the man he'd knocked out.

His entire face was crumpled inward, as if he'd been struck with a sledgehammer.

Brains oozed out from between the broken chunks of his forehead.

Blinking several times, Ash froze.

Then he turned to one side and promptly threw up for the second time that day.

Nine

Before the survivors could do anything about it, or him, Ash had already left the area.

He didn't want anything to do with them, nor did he want to stick around.

Right now, all he wanted to do was sit down in his campsite and… do nothing. Walking at a decent speed, he was trying to make a beeline back so he could do exactly that.

Sit.

"Was that your first kill?" Moira asked him, bouncing along next to him.

"What? Yes. Yes, it was," Ash said, frowning. "I've fought and injured people before but… never killed someone."

"Death is no different than injuring someone. They just don't get up again. The world is full of death. Often, we find that we must kill others or be killed ourselves," Moira said, bouncing at his side as if it were the most normal thing in the world for her.

"Uh huh," Ash said. He wasn't about to agree with her. He wasn't naive enough to believe she was wrong, but he sure as hell wasn't going to admit she was correct either.

"Want me to carry you?" Moira asked.

"No. Thank you, though. I just… kinda want to walk it off a bit."

"I'm going to go hunt. I'll bring you back a rabbit. Already killed, of course," Moira said.

Ash waved a hand at her, not responding.

A strung gust of air from her wings made his hair flutter, and she was off and away.

"She's not wrong. It was obvious they would have killed you."

"Whatever. Don't want to talk about it."

"Did you think you would just… become a cultivator and not have to hurt anyone? Foolish. The Chosen One is very young and naive. Maybe I should have picked someone older?"

"Shut up," Ash said, pressing his hands to his face.

"As the Chosen One likes."

In complete thankful silence, Ash made it back to his camp. Sitting down in front of the fire pit, he sank into himself.

There wasn't much he could do about his actions. He wasn't foolish enough to believe this would be the last person he'd probably kill, either.

Locke was right.

This land was brutal, violent, and to the point. The people valued life as cheaply as what the person was worth dead or alive.

"And might makes right," Ash muttered. "The strong dictate everything. If I hadn't showed up, there's really no guessing what they would have done to the girl."

Shaking his head, he let himself drift deeper into his thoughts. It was a lot to take in.

***

"Ash?" called a voice from the entrance to the valley.

Shaking himself out of his thoughts and his own pity party for his loss of moral innocence, Ash lifted his head up.

He got to his feet with a frown and looked toward the only way in. When Moira came back, it would only be by air. There was no reason for her to be walking.

Unless something happened.

When Jia walked out from the brush that hid the entry, Ash was rather surprised. He hadn't expected anyone to know he was here, let alone her.

How did she even find me? I've told no one of this place.

Awkwardly, Ash raised his hand and waved at her when her eyes fell on him.

She gave him a brief flash of a smile and started towards him.

"She's at the extent of our ability to scan, but she's alone," Locke said. "She's also significantly more powerful than she was previously.

"It is probable that she emptied her entire Dantian and started over with the cultivation technique you gave her."

"And that made her more powerful?"

"The technique was listed as very high grade. As high as your own, if not a bit better."

"So why didn't I take it, then?"

"Because only women can use it."

"Oh. That makes sense," Ash murmured, nodding.

Ash locked into place, his thoughts coming to a screaming halt.

"We… gave her a cultivation that is only usable by women."

"Yes."

"While she's pretending to be a man."

"Yes."

"Thereby admitting we know she's a woman."

"Yes."

"Ah… good. Yes… great. Now I have to wonder if she's here to kill me to protect that secret," Ash mumbled.

"She would have killed you at lunch in her home, Chosen One, if she wanted to.

"Even without abilities, she would have believed she simply had more strength than you."

"That… really doesn't help."

Ash could only wait for her to get to him. She didn't seem in a hurry. In fact, to Ash, it almost seemed as if she was dreading getting closer to him.

She finally stopped about five feet in front of him. Her hair was pulled back in a ponytail, and she was dressed in a flowing, blue sleeved dress rather than her acolyte robe.

Now that she wasn't trying to hide herself away, Ash couldn't help but appreciate her figure.

She was slim and fit, but she did have some curve to her hips and chest. It wasn't some of the made-for-movies type of thing like back in the good ol' US of A, but it was definitely noteworthy.

Sighing, she tilted her head to one side, looking up at him. Watching her face as she did so, Ash was surprised to discover she was even wearing a touch of eye makeup.

"I assumed I might as well dress comfortably since it was obvious you were aware of what I was," Jia said.

"Good choice. You look good in blue, and in a dress," Ash said with a shrug of his shoulders.

Jia lifted one sleeved wrist and looked at herself.

"Thank you. I do not find myself wearing pretty clothes like this very often," Jia said, letting her arm drop back to her side. "It is quite comfortable, if a bit odd to be stared at so directly."

"Uh, sorry," Ash said, looking away.

"I did not mean you, you s—" Jia stopped talking and clicked her tongue. "I wanted to discuss this situation with you. I do not know what your intentions are.

"Especially given how much in coin you would had to have spent to get me the presents you gave me.

"Those items would be worth many a woman's dowry individually, let alone grouped together into a cohesive Dao."

Ash shrugged, looking back to Jia. "Nothing really. I just… wanted you to do well in the examination. It always seemed important to you."

"That is the extent of it?" Jia asked.

"Yeah. You always supported me. Why can't I support you?" Ash asked.

"Because of the *cost* of what you gave me. It is simply too much," Jia said, annunciating "cost" roughly. "It is something even a medium-level sect would have to expend a large number of favors to get their hands on, let alone have the ability to purchase. And you brought it over with lunch."

Her eyes were wide open, her lips a flat line. She'd moved in much closer now and was only a foot away. Standing only an inch shorter than him, she was able to stare into his face.

She jabbed a finger into his chest. "Do I have to spell it out further for you?"

"I promise I earned it all fairly and at no one's expense."

"Even your own?"

"Huh? Yes, not even at my own expense."

"Someone recently put a number of the… the transference papers with elements in them for sale at the auction house.

"Did you know that?" Jia asked.

Ash blinked, not quite able to keep up as the conversation changed speed on him.

"Uh, I had heard that, yeah."

"I managed to get a glimpse of one. I wanted to see them. The auction house held them for half a day simply to display them," Jia said, her eyes locked on his.

"Oh?" Ash managed to get out.

"She knows. Her heart rate has increased several-fold."

Not helping, Locke. Not helping!

"Yes. The paper. The pattern. The ink. All were the same. As if the one I received from you was one of the same batch."

Ash said nothing. Could say nothing.

Jia tilted her head slowly to the other side, watching him.

"I would almost suspect that you were the one who sold them as well," Jia said. "Oh… did I mention I stopped by to see your parents? I thought you'd be there."

Ash grimaced, and he knew where this was going next.

"Imagine my surprise to find out they were moving to a much nicer neighborhood. That your home was on the market, but that they'd already purchased a new home and moved in," Jia said, her finger still pressed to Ash's sternum.

"Uh huh," Ash mumbled.

"You received no help from anyone? You called in no favors and made no deals?" Jia asked.

Ash pressed a hand to his temple.

"None of that, no. I'm sorry, it's just I—"

Jia smiled at him and lifted her hand up in front of his face.

"You need not explain. We all have our own secrets. I cannot complain at you for keeping your own, when I kept mine from you for so long. No?

"So long as you did nothing wrong, incurred no debt, and received no help, I am fine with it as it is."

"She's worried you sold her secret."

Oh. I guess that kinda makes sense.

But then… wouldn't that mean her secret was worth something? I honestly just thought it was because she wanted to be a man.

Crossdressing and gender roles weren't as fluid here as they'd become back home.

But it wasn't unheard of, either.

"I didn't tell anyone. I mean, it seems a little weird to me, but I told no one, and don't plan on telling anyone," Ash said, trying to get to the heart of the problem.

Jia blinked, watching him.

"Weird? Weird how?" she asked him, her tone had an edge to it.

"You're really pretty. Beautiful, even.

"Seems weird to dress like a man when you're as pretty as you are," Ash said immediately.

He couldn't deny that he was definitely attracted to her on a physical level. There was no sense in lying about her looks.

Jia had a sour look on her face and lightly shoved him backward a step.

"Fine. I think it is time we sparred. I want to try out these abilities, and you are the only one I can work with. The moment everyone else learns about them, they will start developing ways to defend," she said.

"Sparring?"

"Yes, sparring. Nothing special. Nothing surprising. Like we used to do every day together. This time, with abilities," Jia said, walking several paces away from him and then settling into a stance he'd never seen her in.

"You're in a dress, though."

"You said I looked good in it. Do you dislike it now?" Jia asked, her mouth twitching up at the corners.

"No, it's just going to take a little to get used to sparring with a pretty girl in a dress is all," Ash said, moving into his own stance.

"Adapt quickly then," Jia said with a bright smile, her wrist slithering forward in a weaving motion as Qi infused with Water-elemental Essence snaked out from her hand.

Really? Damn.

***

Dropping to the ground as he panted heavily, Ash wanted nothing to do with Jia anymore.
Demoness! Sadistic training demoness.

Jia plopped down next to him and then laid down on the grass.

"It has been a while since I worked that hard," she said, resting her hands on her stomach.

"Bah. I always had to work this hard to keep up with you before my Dantian opened."

"This is nothing new," Ash grumbled.

Jia didn't immediately respond. Her eyes were unfocused as she stared up into the sky.

Then she started to chuckle to herself.

"I suppose you are right. You have indeed been training much harder than everyone else up to this point.

"Well, I suppose that is the goal until the examination. Training."

"Uh huh. Though most of the participants will all be beginner ranks in body refining, right? I mean, there might be a few threes, but most will be twos, won't they?"

Jia shrugged. "Every exam is different. There have been years where fours and fives have shown up."

Night was settling over the valley quickly.

"Going to take you some time to get back. If you don't go now and move quickly, you'll get locked out of the city," Ash said out of concern for her.

"You will not get rid of me so quickly. I plan on staying here," Jia said, not moving.

"Oh, uh… did you… bring a tent or supplies or…"

Jia turned her head to face him and gave him a smile.

"Yeah, you can have the tent. Supplies are just on the other side. Make yourself at home," Ash said to her unspoken response, realizing he'd already lost.

Jia laughed to herself and slowly got to her feet. She gave him a small wave and moved over to his tent. A heartbeat later and she was gone, the tent buttoned up tight.

Moira dropped down into the grass a minute later.

Her glowing eyes were locked to the tent.

"Is that your woman?" Moira asked.

Ash shook his head immediately.

"No, she's a friend. What's up, Moira? Were you waiting for her to leave?"

"Yes. It isn't good to interfere when a possible pair are considering breeding. Or so it goes in my tribe," Moira said. She squatted down next to the fire and threw two dead rabbits onto the stone slab that served as a flat-top.

"Clearly we're not mating," Ash said, waving a hand at the tent.

"Yes, though I think the chance is good that she has it in mind for a future time," Moira said.

Both Ash and Moira fell silent as the rabbits sizzled and cooked.

Moira grunted, then took the rabbits directly off the stone and hung them from sticks further from the flame.

Well, that'll take a lot longer to cook.

"You gave her abilities?" Moira asked, turning to Ash.

"You heard all that from where you were?"

"Yes. Did you give her abilities?"

"I guess you could call it that," Ash said, sitting up on his elbows. Looking to the owl woman, he could feel the intensity of her gaze.

"I want my magic back. I can be more useful that way," she said. "Give it to me."

"I… have no idea how to do that? Magic isn't used here in this veil. It's Essence. Essence gets converted to Qi."

"Then make it so I can use Essence," Moira said, nodding her head sharply.

"I don't even think that's possible."

"Ask the spirit you were speaking with earlier. They might know," Moira said, nodding her head again.

Oh… she… probably did hear me talking to Locke, didn't she?

"It's doable but… it won't be pretty."

Ash frowned, looking to Moira.

Fuck it. She's mine, right?

My property? Any investment I put into her helps me.

"Consider everything about me a secret, and speak of it to no one, Moira," Ash said. He waited for her to nod before he sat up completely. Looking to the side so Moira wasn't confused, he spoke to Locke.

"How would we do it? Is it something achievable with what we have on hand?"

"Yes, but you'll literally be carving into her flesh. And to do it fully will take time. You do not have the skills practiced. You have the memories, but none of the muscle memory or experience.

"Think of Scrivening, but drawing into her skin. Or Enchanting, but carving at her skin with the chisel."

"Yeah, that's not pretty. Is there a way to hide it? So it doesn't just… wreck her? I mean, can we put it on paper and transfer it to her flesh instead?"

"It wouldn't be as efficient for her. We could limit it to her back. Let her make the call, Chosen One."

Ash looked back to Moira.

"So… it sounds like it's possible. But I would literally be carving patterns into your skin. With a chisel.

"Is that something you really want? I mean, it would—"

"Yes. Come, we'll go to the small creek nearby so you can wash the blood off as we go," Moira said. Turning on her heel, she started to hop away from him. Bouncing and bobbing along the grass as she went.

Muttering under his breath, Ash followed along after the spritely Owl.

"You're rather excited for someone who's about to be turned into a wood carving," Ash said.

"Yes! I want my magic back. I feel very weak and vulnerable without it," Moira said. Then she stopped dead in her tracks. Her head turned around and she looked to him, her neck stretched in an odd way.

"Though… what are your plans for me? You haven't forced me into your bed so far. You don't seem to do anything with me."

"Why did you purchase me?" Moira asked.

"I dunno. I didn't want to see you get used as gladiator bait?" Ash said as he walked past her. "You were alone on a stage, naked and being sold."

"They were going to use me for that end because I am not pretty," Moira said, falling in beside him.

"Other than your eyes being a bit big, I think you're rather pretty," Ash said with a shrug of his shoulders. "They don't like your coloring is all. Your race."

"Everybody in this veil is a superstitious lot. It's almost comical."

"And yet you don't care?" Moira asked.

"Nope. Should I? It's not as if you chose your genetics. White hair, black feathers, blue hair, yellow feathers, whatever."

"Genetics?"

"Never mind."

Ash stopped in front of the creek and looked around. He spotted a rock that would work and pointed to it.

"Go ahead and sit down. Pull your top off and that stupid collar as well so I can do this. I was thinking of just using your back for now. Try to keep it to a limited place and location so I don't scar you up unnecessarily."

Moira flapped her wings once and bounced to the rock. Gripping the bottom of her strangely cut tunic, she pulled it down from her shoulders. After bringing it past her waist, she stepped out of it.

"Can't wear shirts that go over my head. My wings get in the way," Moira said, turning to face him.

Ash got an eyeful of her chest before he looked up to her face.

"Right, uh, go ahead and sit down and face away."

Moira stared at him, then blinked slowly.

"Does my skin disgust you? That I have small feathers in some places?"

"What? No. I just... I didn't want to stare at your chest. Turn around already. This is going to be weird and awful enough."

Moira watched him for a second longer before turning around and sitting on the rock.

"Overlaying several patterns into one. The first will be a large reservoir for Essence. The second will convert it to Qi. The third will act as a modifier for the Qi into whatever power source she originally used."

"That... sounds incredibly complicated," Ash said. "As if this hasn't been tested."

"It hasn't. I made the pattern based on my scans of her and what was in the Hall, Chosen One."

"The pattern is significant. This will take some time."

Ash sighed and put his left hand on Moira's shoulder. Her skin was solid like stone and warm.

Damn, she's extremely athletic. Must be the wings?

She flinched under his touch and then relaxed.

"Are you ready? I don't have much I can do to help with the pain or anything like that... I'm sorry."

"I didn't think I'd need medicinal supplies for something like this when we left the city."

"I'll be fine. As long as I can get my magic back," Moira said.

A comprehensive and massive pattern spread out over Moira's back. There were gaps in it for what looked like expansion slots, as well as broad empty spaces for other places to work.

Most of it went from shoulder to shoulder, around her wings, and halfway down her back. The lines were uniform in width, but numerous in count.

"Ugh... are you... are you sure, Moira? Truly sure? This... is going to make your back look as if you've been attacked with a knife," Ash said.

"Will my scars bother you in the future? Will they repulse you?"

"Huh? No. Why?"

"Then it doesn't matter. Begin," Moira said, her hands clasped to her knees.

Ash bit his lip, then pressed the chisel tip to her skin. Slowly, he began to peel the skin from her back in the exact pattern.

Sickeningly, her skin came off as if it were wood, with little to no resistance.

I think I might throw up.

"Don't throw up on her, at least. She brought you dinner, remember?" Locke said, laughing. *"That and she's kinda cute. Maybe you can talk her into warming your bed willingly."*

Ten

Something tapped Ash between the eyes.

Groaning, he rolled to the side and swatted futilely at the offending thing.

"Wake up."

Ash shook his head and mumbled, curling up tighter in his blankets.

"Ash… wake up," said a soft voice. Fingers lightly pushed on his brow. "It is long past morning."

"Was up late. Let me sleep," Ash grumbled.

"So I see. There is an Owl woman in the camp." The voice gained a slight edge to it.

Cracking his eyes open, he saw Jia kneeling over him.

"Her name's Moira. I bought her so she wouldn't get sent to the gladiator pits," Ash said.

"Her back looks like it has been freshly torn up… with a knife."

Ash nodded his head a bit.

"We didn't want to put her tunic back on yet. She's… uh… I think she said she was meditating to gain mana. At which point she can use it to help her wounds heal," Ash said. Lifting his head up, he looked to the last spot he'd seen Moira.

She was curled up next to the embers of the fire. In the light of the morning, her back really did look like a mess.

The pattern was very visible as scar tissue now.

It was the scabs and blood that had looked terrible, last he'd seen it.

Though it looked significantly better now in the morning light. The blood that had continuously wept from her wounds had been slightly unnerving.

Especially since this had all been done by his hand.

"Mana? Mana is an outlander magic. How can she use magic?" Jia asked.

Ash didn't want to turn and face her.

He'd inadvertently probably just provided her with enough information to confirm beyond any doubt that he was the one who'd made the Transference papers.

"Ash?" Jia asked. Her hand took hold of his jaw and tilted his head to face her. "Ash, did you make those papers yourself? You did not get them from someone else?"

Her eyes were curious. Curious and filled with a trace of excitement.

"My skills and abilities? You made them personally?" she asked, her mind quickly moving along whatever path it was on.

Unable to lie and unwilling to speak, Ash tried to look away. Only to have her adjust his chin till his eyes were on her again.

So much for letting me have my secrets.

She peered at him for a moment, and then she smiled at him.

"Ah… you are, then. Well. That is… unexpected. I… ah… so… you really did just do all those things for me. Simply for me," Jia said, her hand tight on his chin.

"Yeah, well, you said you wanted to do well. That you had a specific sect you wanted to join."

"There's no reason you can't just… muscle your way to the top and stand out now. Right?"

"I mean, after yesterday's sparring I can honestly say I'm not sure I could win more than fifty percent of the time," Ash said.

Jia let go of him and nodded slowly.

"You also took it easy on me. I get the impression those Qi attacks of yours do more than you let on."

"And yes. I did have a sect I wanted to join," Jia said. "I will get breakfast started and have a chat with Moira. I think she and I will be able to learn from one another."

Jia stood up and walked over to the fire. Picking up a stick from nearby, she started to poke and prod at the coals.

Stirring them to life and then adding small bits of wood.

Ash shrugged and laid his head back down.

From the way Jia was acting, it seemed as if she planned to remain with him out here in the valley as he trained.

She's going to want to spar.

A lot.

Which… honestly will be good for me.

Maybe I can get Moira to teach me how to use that sword she took back with us as well.

Still don't have a weapon.

Closing his eyes, Ash set about falling back asleep as fast as possible.

***

"We should head back to the city today," Jia said, shaking her hand back and forth. "In fact, it would be wise if we packed up and headed back after breakfast."

Ash got out of his defensive position and shrugged his shoulders.

"Your hand alright? And yeah, you're not wrong, I guess. Examination is two days away. A day to travel and settle in," Ash said.

"It is fine… just… numb. Your blocks have become considerably firmer."

"She's not wrong. We've gained an incredible amount of experience. While our body-refining rank is still a peak four, we have much more combat knowledge," Locke said. *"And the Qi we keep nourishing with is strengthening us."*

"Alright. I'll wake up sleeping beauty. You go get changed into your acolyte clothes. You did say you brought them, right?" Ash asked, walking over to Moira.

The Owl woman was dozing next to the coals of the fire. She tended to stay up a bit later than either of them and slept in longer.

Reaching down, he pressed his hand to her shoulder and gave her a very gentle shake. She wasn't a heavy sleeper.

Lifting her head, she faced him as her large eyes slowly peeled open.

Giant pupils contracted as her eyes focused in on him.

"Mmm?" she murmured.

"We're going to head back into town. I need to take part in an examination. You can come with me, or we can meet up in a few days afterward," Ash said.

Moira's eyelids came down, partially lidding her eyes.

"I'll go with you," she said finally. "I can watch your back now. I think at this point I could fight you to a draw, which means I can help out without being in the way.

"Still a long way off from what I was previously, though. I think it will only take me a few years to catch back up."

Ash nodded, then frowned.

"Do I need to add another pattern?" he asked.

"Not yet. I think.

"For now, we'll see what time brings us. It's a very good thing my people are patient. Patient and long lived," Moira said with a rare smile.

"Oh… are you… err… how old are you? I thought you were only a year or two older than me."

"I am twenty-five by my people's standards, but I think I am closer to your age in maturity if measured culture to culture," Moira said, sitting up slowly. "I was in my trials when I was captured. Now, shall we get going? I have only my sword to carry and I'm curious to see this examination of yours."

Getting to her feet, Moira moved over to the tent where Jia was breaking things down and getting a dry breakfast together.

Ash rolled his eyes.

Everyone was so eager for these things. Honestly, Ash just wanted to help out his family and enjoy life.

Maybe find a wife and settle in and do nothing.

Well, that was the plan before I dove into the cultivator path.

Training for the sake of becoming stronger to train more to get stronger—that sounded boring to him.

Sighing, he got up and followed Moira.

Looking around, he realized he'd miss this place. This grassy valley hidden away.

The valley felt like a home away from home for him.

It had provided a place for him to hide and be himself.

To rest.

And recently, to train and become ever that much stronger.

***

Ash, Moira, and Jia in her acolyte robes had only been on the road for an hour. Conversation was limited and seemed rooted mostly in the exam that was going to take place.

That changed when a group of eight men rushed out from a small grouping of bushes.

"It's him!" said one of their number. "He's the one that did it."

"When I'm done with you," said one of the men, "you'll be nothing but paste. Then I'll have some fun with your women.

"We all will. Or you could show us some face and just kill yourself now instead of making us do the work."

The bandits laughed at that, slowly spreading out in a semi-circle. Ash looked from one to the other to try and gauge the right course of action here.

Most of the men had clubs, though a few seemed to have swords. Out of them all, half were cultivators, the other half simple citizens.

Even though they were cultivators, though, they were not ranked very highly. All were weaker than himself.

Moira sniffed and pulled the sword out from the sheath at her side. Giving it a flick of her wrist, she seemed to know well how to use it.

"These are the same as those we killed," she said, moving in close to Ash's right side.

"You killed bandits? From this group?" Jia asked, her hands moving into a defensive pose.

"Well, two. They were fighting what looked like a merchant's group. We intervened and I… I killed one.

"Moira killed another. Two ran off," Ash explained.

Setting his feet, Ash brought his hands up in front of himself, getting in line with his center.

"Why did you not kill the other two? Never leave an enemy alive if you do not have to," Jia admonished. "Especially if they can come back. Foolish."

"Yeah, well, that doesn't—"

All eight men rushed them, three of them with actual bladed weapons and the rest with clubs.

As quick as a thought, Ash activated his Qi Thorns and Battle Cultivation, and set his Spring Step to store energy.

Targeting the three in front of him, Ash threw three quick strikes toward them. Each received a Qi ball and chain, which Ash attached to himself at his belt.

Then in a strange thought, he planted two Qi balls into his belt and tried to attach the chains to Moira and Jia.

One of the bandits in front of him dropped to the ground in a heap.

Unmoving.

That happened last time, too. Should probably look into it.

That left him with two more to deal with.

Normally, Ash did his best to fight his foes at an angle. To limit their ability to strike at him. He didn't want to fight them nose to nose in any way, shape, or form.

Dealing with two wouldn't let him do that.

The two bandits attacked him at the same time. The one on his right was significantly faster than the one on his left.

Must be a higher cultivation.

Moving in close to the bandit on the left, Ash dodged into his attack. At the same time, he knocked away the club of the man on the right with one hand while driving a blow into the man's kidney.

Moving low, Ash stepped out of the falling attack of the slower man. Spinning as he went, Ash whipped his left fist around in a hook, blowing through the bandit's defense and blasting a punch into his gut.

Taking two steps away after passing the two bandits, Ash checked the rest of the fight.

Jia had locked two into defensive stances, her abilities flowing smoothly and quickly as she attacked in waves.

Moira had her hand leveled in front of herself. A giant rod of metal stuck through the chest of a man directly in front of her. Two other men were locked into place, their feet in prisons of what looked like slag iron.

Looking back to his own opponents, Ash let out a quick breath.

The slower of the two bandits was gasping for breath, hunched over himself on all fours.

Ash moved to the right to engage his last standing opponent.

"Destructive Palm B—"

Before the man could finish shouting, Ash had launched a kick into his ribs.

With the sound of crackling bones, the man stumbled backward, dropping his weapon.

Was he trying to shout an ability or something?

"It's a low form of utilizing an ability. Making hand signs and calling out the name of their technique helps them channel it.

"Somewhat of a moot point for yourself," Locke offered up, seemingly reading his mind.

A thought for later.

Moving forward, Ash stepped up behind one of the men Jia was fighting. Flicking out a punch to the side of the man's stomach, Ash followed up by grabbing the man's head and launching a Spring Step attack with his knee.

Letting go of the man as his face rebounded backward from the strike, Ash looked to the second bandit.

Jia had taken the sword away and buried it in the man's chest. Shoving against the hilt, she sent him tumbling to the ground.

Both Ash and Jia turned to Moira.

The Owl woman was working her blade back and forth across a downed opponent's throat. The other two were already dead as well.

Ash felt strange. Like his body was overly light. Overly light and bursting with energy at the same time.

Brushing his hand across his belt, he dismissed all his Qi chains, then deactivated his toggled abilities.

Moira got to her feet and pointed her blade at the three men Ash had put down.

"Kill them," she said. "They'll only come back again later if we don't take care of them now."

Jia nodded and walked over to the downed opponent she had been working on. Reversing the grip on her blade, she plunged it into the man's back. Twisting it as she pulled it out, blood fountained out of the man and flooded over his back.

Ash looked to the two men he'd put to the ground.

We've already killed a man. We can do it again.

And they said they would rape Moira and Jia.

They deserve it.

Right?

Taking a deep, shuddering breath, Ash walked over to the first man. His hands were pressed to his chest, his breaths short and raspy.

Ash reached down and peered at the sheath at the man's side. It had two small, slim blades in the same leather casing.

Unhitching the sword belt, Ash pulled it off the man and pulled out one of the handles.

It was a butterfly sword, with a wide belly for chopping and slashing.

Holding it up to the inside of his wrist and measuring the distance to his elbow, Ash found it was almost the perfect size for himself for an inside measurement.

Glancing to the man he'd taken it from, he wasn't even sure if the man knew what the blade was for. There was no way it would fit the man in an inside or outside measurement.

Ash nodded to the man.

"I thank you for the blades," he said. Hesitating for a second, Ash then moved forward and pushed the blade into the fallen bandit's chest. Right where his heart should be.

The blade pierced so easily that it made Ash feel uncomfortable, skewering the heart. Pulling the blade out, Ash moved to the second man. Moira kicked him to his back and then put one taloned foot over the man's neck.

Gritting his teeth, Ash slid the blade into the ribcage of the would-be murderer and rapist.

"Wipe the blade clean," Jia said, indicating his weapon. "Let's loot them and be on our way."

Ash swallowed, barely managing to not throw up again. His head felt hot. Like his mind was swimming in a haze.

A heartbeat later and the befuddlement was gone. Replaced with a cool, fresh feeling.

Except that he still felt oddly full. Like he'd eaten too much.

Pulling the blade out of the dead man, Ash looked to the third. The one who had fallen from his Chained Leech Blast.

The man was unmoving.

And very much dead.

Frowning, Ash shook his head.

So, if I strike someone with this who is without Qi, a citizen, they simply die?

Definitely a concern.

Taking a moment to clean the blade on the dead man's tunic, Ash sheathed the weapon properly. Then he belted the butterfly sword belt around his waist.

Jia and Moira had finished up rooting through the pockets of the men and were already heading back down the road.

Moira paused long enough to look into the bush to see if they had left anything behind. But soon, all three travelers were back on the road in truth.

Unsure of what was going on with himself, since he still felt as if he'd eaten a feast, Ash turned his attention inward as they started down the road.

Into himself.

He found his Dantian writhing. Churning Essence and Qi in equal measure, and condensing it into the same Qi Ash had normally.

"It's processing your gains from killing your opponents. I'll make sure this process doesn't happen until after you're in the clear.

"I doubt it happening in the middle of an extended fight would be ideal," Locke said. *"And before you ask, no. Your rank won't increase. They were much weaker than you were, but it was still more than you would have gotten from a session of meditation and cultivation."*

Ash worked on cycling his Qi through his meridians at a slightly faster pace. It seemed to help with the full feeling, and it kept him from letting his mind focus on the fact that he'd just killed two people.

Trav wouldn't have cared.

Why do you care?

Trav would have just killed them and then moved on. Nothing ever stopped him.

Nothing could stop him.

Except, where is he? Did he come with me here? Or is he still on the boat with Uncle Derek?

Sighing, Ash gave his head a shake.

"We are here," Jia said suddenly.

Looking up, Ash frowned at Xing City's gates.

They were indeed outside the city now. Somehow, he'd practically walked the entire way here without even noticing the time slipping away.

"You were clearly working through your thoughts on having killed your foes," Jia said, her eyes watching him. "Moira and I felt it best to let you process your feelings on your own. No one can compel you to walk the path of the cultivator, but to do so is to walk a path of blood."

Moira nodded her head once.

"A mage's road is made on the bones of others. We often open our gates through devouring the souls of the defeated," said the Owl woman. "Not always. But often enough. I myself became powerful through murdering another mage who was much more powerful than I."

Jia nodded her head at that. She looked to Moira with an odd mix of respect, curiosity, and wariness.

"I know. And I'm going to do what I need to do. I know that. It's just… it's not what I was expecting to do with my life," Ash said with a shrug.

"And what were you expecting to do?" Jia asked.

"Finish high school. Probably… go to college. Get a job with my uncle," Ash said with a shrug of his shoulders. "I ended up here."

"Here?" Moira asked, tilting her head to one side.

"This… that is…" Ash paused, unsure how to continue. He'd given Jia a very, very, brief overview of how he'd ended up here.

But he'd left out the part where he'd more or less traveled from another world. Perhaps even a different reality entirely.

She'd taken his explanation as having traveled from another of the veils. That he'd simply wandered across from one of the border veils and ended up here.

And from there, he was taken in by the Sheng family.

Jia glanced over her shoulder at the gate guards. They were busy speaking to a group of people looking to get inside.

Moving in close to Ash, Jia pressed a hand to his shoulder.

"I know you have more secrets. In time, I would like to believe you would give me enough face to share them with me. For now, we must go. We have things to prepare, like registering for the exam and what events we will be competing in. The examination does have some fees that will need to be taken care of as well.

"I personally must make ready. You are welcome to join me, or to go it on your own," she said, smiling at him. "Though you must treat me as a male acolyte once we are inside Xing City again. Not as Jia the woman."

"Yeah, yeah. I got it," Ash said with a smirk. "No making passes at you or staring."

Jia raised her eyebrows at that.

"He does stare, though only when you aren't looking," Moira said helpfully.

Ash felt his face turn a deep, dark red, and his ears were on fire.

"Let's go inside then," he said, quickly moving ahead down the road toward the city gates.

Probably should see if there's an auction today. I need money since my stones are empty of Qi.

I wonder if I can trade them in at a fraction of their cost? They don't have any Qi anymore, but someone could refill them rather than make or buy new ones.

Eleven

Ash bit his lip as he stared at the auction house. Moira was waiting for him at the inn room he'd rented. She hadn't wanted to come back here.

Not that he blamed her at all for that. He doubted he'd want to come back here if he was her, either.

Steeling himself for a probable encounter he didn't want, Ash walked into the auction house. Turning toward the familiar anonymous entry area, he found a hostess he didn't recognize. She nodded to him and indicated a cell to enter.

Shutting the door behind himself, Ash sat down and contemplated what to do.

He hadn't tried to convert the spirit stones yet, as he wasn't even sure who to go to for that. Or whether he even could.

This had been his first stop after getting the inn room. He hadn't even yet visited the Sheng family.

Then again, he wasn't quite sure where they'd moved to.

Jia had immediately left his side after they'd entered and gone to settle her own affairs.

Giving his head a quick shake, Ash broke himself out of his thoughts and touched his ring. One of each element type popped up into his hand.

Need to buy more paper. I wonder if that brother and sister pair is still there.

Opening the drawer, Ash dropped in the Transference papers. Pulling his jade token from his ring, he set it down atop the papers.

Then he closed the drawer.

Ash heard a clatter from the other side of the cube. After perhaps a minute passed, the drawer opened again.

Inside was a small slip of paper and his token.

Picking up the token and then the paper Ash paused. Beneath where the paper had been, he saw a small card. Picking up the card as well he looked to the paper and read it over quickly.

The auction house wanted to sell the papers tomorrow instead of today. So they could generate interest in an auction.

On top of that, they'd given him a card with two percent of the amount that the auction had previously been able to sell his items for. This payment in was meant as a bonus if he agreed to waiting till the following day.

Shrugging his shoulders, Ash dropped the paper back in and slipped the card into his ring.

He could wait a day. Closing the drawer, Ash got up and left quickly.

Walking past the hostess, he got back into the street fairly quickly.

He now had more than enough money to do anything he needed.

Let's get more paper and ink first. The market should be just now opening. After that, we'll go find Mother Far and Father Duyi.

Now we just have to hope we're not attacked again.

I'd rather not deal with that.

Heading down the steps, Ash vanished into the press of bodies. His hair had grown longer in the time he'd been away. His clothes had also fallen into disrepair.

Where once a young acolyte had strolled the streets, now a young ill-dressed youth remained.

Ash blended in better now than he had previously.

His walk to the market was unremarkable and no one bothered him.

Slipping into the stalls, Ash headed straight to the location where he'd previously found the brother and sister.

A small wooden stall stood in the exact same spot as last time. The boy was nowhere to be seen, but the young girl was there.

Looking at the stall, he realized now it wasn't the same one as before. This one was put together with a small bit of quality and care. It wasn't a full merchant's stall, but it was definitely something you could find in the market proper.

The girl had cleaned herself up considerably as well. And filled out a bit.

Previously, he'd thought she was in her early teens. With some meat on her, and looking considerably healthier, he'd put her at seventeen maybe.

Her light-brown hair was cut short and framed her face well. Each customer received a smile as they approached, and her hazel eyes made definitive contact with each person.

She's really brought herself up a bit since the last time.

The young woman was doing a brisk business in paper, pens, and various other small trinkets. She had a number of different types of paper behind her as well, of varying quality.

Ash waited for a break in the customer numbers. He wanted to approach when no one was there.

Finally, her stall was empty.

Taking this chance, Ash strolled up, eying the paper the girl had behind her.

There was more than enough for his purposes. Having different types would also let him play around a bit and see if there was any difference in changing the material types.

"It's you," said the young woman, catching Ash's attention.

Looking to her, Ash didn't immediately respond. He'd somewhat hoped she wouldn't recognize him so easily.

"You bought my paper," she said, her eyes locked on his face.

"I did," Ash admitted.

"You changed everything. Everything. I… I have a small room I rent now. Li Jie is in a training sect.

"Everything changed," said the young woman, shaking her head once, as if to clear her thoughts. "My name is Ying Yue."

"I'm glad you've done well for yourself. I didn't think my single purchase would do such a thing, though. It was only a gold coin," Ash said, feeling a bit sheepish.

"It was enough to buy more to sell, and reinvest. I went back and got the coin back from the merchant after. I wanted to keep it.

"I carry it with me."

Ash smiled at the woman's tenacity. People who pulled themselves up from their bootstraps were rare. Those who did it with the smallest of advantages given to them were admirable.

Let's see what she can do. Let's invest in her.

Ash took out a spirit stone from his ring and set it down in front of her.

"I want all your paper, ink, and pens," Ash said, smiling at her.

"This is simply too much. I do not have the amount that this would purchase," Ying Yue said.

She laughed for a second, looking at the spirit stone, and then she looked up to Ash.

Her laughter died away when Ash didn't say anything. Reaching out, he pushed the spirit stone an inch closer to her.

"All your paper, pens, and ink, please," Ash repeated himself.

Ying Yue blinked and then nodded her head a bit. Mechanically, she began to bundle up all her materials into packets. Tying them shut with small ribbons.

When she finally completed the task, she gestured to the small mound of items on her countertop.

"I'm afraid I don't have the change necessary for your purchase. I don't know what to offer you in exchange and—"

Ash waved his hand at her, silencing her words. Glancing around himself, he realized no one was paying attention to him.

If he didn't know better, he would get the impression people were deliberately ignoring him. As if he were causing trouble for Ying Yue and they didn't want to get involved.

When he tapped his ring, his purchase vanished as if it had never been there.

Turning his face to the merchant, he smiled at her.

"Consider the remainder of the payment me purchasing your silence about this whole thing," Ash said. Then he reached over and tapped the stone with a fingertip. "Be sure to take this somewhere safe immediately."

Ying Yue nodded her head slowly, her hands gently closing around the spirit stone. "I... I will."

Nodding to her, Ash turned and left. He needed to find Far and Duyi. Leaving the market, he set off on his search.

Ash got lucky though. The first place he went to ask about news of his adoptive family, an old neighbor who had been kind to the Shengs, knew exactly where they had gone.

A small, quiet neighborhood full of moderately well-off merchants. They'd purchased a home that could fit a family of eight, but that wasn't overly immodest. It was something the vast majority of merchants in the city could and would purchase.

Walking into the courtyard in front of the new Sheng home, Ash felt a smile on his face. He could hear Duyi playing his Guqin.

Something he hadn't heard for a long while. There simply had no longer been enough time in the day for Father Duyi to relax.

Following the sound, Ash crept around the side of the home. Sitting in the back of his own fenced-in yard, Duyi was kneeling on the grass with a small mat in front of himself.

A stringed instrument that reminded Ash of a guitar lay on the ground directly before him. He was not playing loudly, but more for the simple enjoyment of hearing himself.

On more than one occasion, the older man had said it wasn't so much an instrument as a way for him to communicate with his own soul.

Mother Far was seated nearby, relaxing with a cup of tea.

Her eyes slid open as Ash entered the area. He could tell she was about to exclaim loudly and get up.

Holding a finger up to his mouth, Ash smiled. He didn't wish to interrupt the moment.

Far blinked twice but nodded her head almost imperceptibly.

Ash kept himself to the side so Duyi wouldn't notice him. Getting as close as he dared, Ash took a seat. He listened quietly, thinking back to when he'd first joined the family.

Duyi had had more time back then.

Looking at the man who had given him a home, Ash felt happy.

Duyi's dark hair, which he habitually kept short, was finally growing out. His complexion was healthy, and his small frame seemed it had finally put on some healthy weight.

Now that he thought about it, Far looked much improved as well. The two aging parents no longer had to expend their own lives to provide for their children.

Blinking, Ash accessed the two cards in his ring without pulling them out.

He transferred three thousand stones to one card and the remainder to the other with the empty stones.

Three thousand should be more than enough to keep them situated for a long time.

Duyi finished and sat up straight, letting out a breath.

"That felt good, Father Duyi," Ash said.

Duyi's head turned to the side, and a wide smile broke across his face.

"Ashley!" he said, getting to his feet.

Preparing himself for the crushing hug he knew was coming, Ash stood up and waited with a smile.

"Haha, it's so good to see you," Duyi said, pulling Ash in close to himself.

"Hello Father Duyi. I'm glad to see you're taking time out for yourself," Ash said, patting the older man on the back in a hug.

"Yes! I spend much of my time simply... enjoying life. It is good to be taken care of by one's children.

"It's the hope of any parent," Duyi said and leaned back, looking at Ash. His wide smile hadn't faded. If anything, it was more infectious than ever. "You look well. Well and healthy."

"So do you," Ash said, prodding at the other man's middle.

"Hahaha, yes, Far has always been an amazing wife and cook. We just never had the best ingredients that she deserved," Duyi said, gesturing at Far.

For her part, Far was watching with a smile, sipping her tea quietly.

Duyi leaned in close and whispered for Ash alone.

"Don't let her fool you, she's been worried sick about you. Now come, come. Tell us about your travels, where you've been, and what's going on," Duyi said, pulling Ash along with him as he went back to Far.

***

Standing in line for his turn at the testing stone, Ash waited quietly.

Though he knew it was rude, he cultivated as he stood there. He didn't owe these people anything, and they more or less treated him as a non-existence anyways.

Slowly, the line moved. Person by person, he made his way closer and closer to the first part of the examination. He was only several people away from having himself tested. Though he'd started much closer to the end of the line.

Many of the stronger people had gone up to be first, rather than wait in line to take the test.

It was a fairly standard test at that.

One had to demonstrate their ability to use Qi, and to what extent.

"There you are," said a voice at his side.

Ash opened his eyes and cut his cultivation off.

Jia simply appeared in front of him, stepping into line. The person behind Ash made no noise about her cutting in.

"She gave him a small coin before she addressed you," Locke said.

Grinning at Jia, Ash raised his eyebrows.

"You were looking for me?"

"Of course. I wanted to be there when you were tested. I am very curious about where you will rank. I do truly believe you took it easy on me," Jia said.

He wasn't used to her being dressed as a man again, and Ash was honestly having a hard time looking at her without feeling like the image was wrong.

"I prefer the other version of you," Ash said suddenly, frowning at Jia.

Blinking rapidly, Jia opened her mouth and then closed it.

"I have my reasons," she said finally. "But it is good to know I have not lost that side of myself either and that... you liked it."

The line shifted ahead suddenly.

Apparently, in their conversation, they'd lost where they were in line to a degree.

"Looks like you're up soon," Ash said, nodding his chin at the line behind Jia.

Jia glanced over her shoulder and then moved to her position at the small ramp and turned back to him, looking to re-engage in their conversation.

"Next!" called a voice atop the stage.

Jia rolled her eyes and sighed, then moved up the ramp.

Curious, Ash watched her walk up to the man in charge.

The platform was a wide wooden affair. Built to hold the recruiters from each sect as the students were tested.

The examiner spoke to Jia for a moment before calling out her name to the recruiters.

Jade Fist, Mountain Bear, Dragon Warrior, Blood Oath, and finally Spark's Jump, the host sect.

Jing and Yan went to Jade Fist... so that's our target. Though most of these people will be aiming for Dragon Warrior and Blood Oath as they're the first and second schools.

Looking bored and barely paying attention, Ash was almost positive most of the recruiters had not even heard Jia's name.

The man giving the examination nodded at Jia, and then guided her to the testing equipment at the center of the platform.

It was a large crystal that rose twenty feet high.

At the base of the crystal were two spots to place one's hands.

Jia immediately grabbed hold after being given an instruction.

Seconds ticked by and then suddenly, violent blue Qi flooded the crystal. From bottom to more than halfway up, it was filled with Qi.

Several spheres of metal floated in the Qi, suspended in the crystal directly. They bobbed and floated back and forth in the liquid that was her Qi.

"Rank five!" called the examiner. "Density is able to lift the silver!"

There was a commotion amongst the crowd and the sect recruiters alike.

Ash couldn't blame them. It was likely Jia was one of the strongest in the entire exam, and her Qi density was rather unheard of.

The cultivation technique she uses is very strong. She should have been able to lift the gold ball according to our scan just now.

"She must have rushed her cultivation a touch to get it up to a higher rank," Locke said. *"She'll be able to correct that later with a touch of effort."*

Nodding, Ash watched, wondering when Jia would give out.

The crystal had another function, of course. To measure the depth of the Qi Sea. The ability of the Dantian to hold Qi.

Everyone had a different amount, depending on how they'd developed themselves.

An average period of time was a single minute, and that would be the case with the vast majority of examinees.

When it got to two minutes, people had surprised looks on their faces. It wasn't until it crossed into three minutes, though, that it was obvious everyone was shocked at this display.

Jia's head dipped, her shoulders slumped, and her Qi fled the crystal, draining back into her.

The examiner looked to the recruiters.

"Three parts of an incense stick," he said to them.

In other words, three minutes. A whole stick of incense took five minutes to burn.

Alright. I guess it's my turn. No combat abilities are tested here, just Qi and control.

Jia was escorted off the stage as all the recruiters were hurriedly asking for more information on her.

Ash grinned at the sight. He was glad for her. She had been talking about doing well in this exam for as long as he could remember. It had been more than just a goal to her.

"You," the examiner said, standing at the top of the ramp. "Get up here. You're next."

Ash nodded and stepped forward, walking up the ramp to the platform.

"You have the misfortune to go after her. My apologies for your poor luck. What is your name?"

Her? He knows? Wait, how?

"Ashley Sheng," he said mechanically.

The examiner turned to the recruiters, who weren't even looking over this way anymore, and called Ash's name to them.

Escorting Ash to the testing device, he indicated the two handles near the base.

Looking beyond the crystal, he saw Jia watching him from the sideline.

Smirking at her, he shrugged his shoulders at the situation he was in.

"…hold tight to them. After that, the crystal will fill with your Qi. Hold on to it from there as long as you can. You're not allowed to cultivate during this test. Do you understand?" the examiner asked.

Ash clicked his tongue and looked to the man.

"Just push your Qi out through the meridians in your hands," Locke said.

"Got it," Ash said.

Looking at the crystal, Ash sighed.

Let's get this over with. We just have to do well enough to get into the Jade Fist. That's it.

Pushing out with his Qi through his hands, Ash looked at the crystal.

There was a soft rumble, and then opaque blue-colored Qi burst up from the bottom of the crystal. It stopped just below the line that would designate it as a rank five.

Except, rolling around on top of the rock-hard-like Qi were a number of metallic spheres. In fact, now that Ash looked, it seemed like it was all of them.

"Ah…" the examiner said, eyes on the monolithic-looking crystal. "Rank… rank four, almost five. Qi density is… is holding up everything."

A metal sphere slowly rolled from one end of the crystal to the other and clanked to a stop against the wall.

It was obvious to everyone that the Qi was more like a solid than a liquid.

Ash couldn't see the recruiters, but he got the impression they were paying attention now.

Letting out a breath, Ash stood there, holding his Qi in place in the crystal. It almost felt like there was no drain at all on him.

Looking around, Ash turned his head to the examiner, who was watching the spheres. Then Ash looked to Jia, who was watching him with raised eyebrows.

Ash smiled at her then looked to the crowd. They were all watching the crystal.

Sighing, Ash looked back to the crystal.

After two minutes, Ash was a touch concerned. He still didn't seem to feel any drain. This took no effort from him at all.

When the incense stick collapsed on itself, the examiner looked to Ash.

Shrugging his shoulders, Ash wasn't sure what to do.

"Should I just let go?" he asked.

The examiner opened his mouth and paused. His head turned to look beyond the crystal, seemingly at the recruiters for direction.

Getting annoyed and not wanting to do this anymore, Ash pulled his Qi back in and let go.

Grumbling under his breath, Ash wandered over to Jia.

"Well, that was embarrassing," he said to her.

"You weren't even tired, were you?" she asked, turning to walk with him off the platform.

"No. Not really. I think I would have been up there for a while, though."

"Indefinitely, actually. Your Battle Cultivation wasn't on, but you were still absorbing Essence just standing there.

"Your ability to draw in a minimal amount of Essence regardless of anything else can be considered a passive trait at this point," Locke clarified. *"That you have started to always gain Essence. And will convert it to Qi constantly.*

"The Snowflake has begun to roll."

Twelve

Ash and Jia were staring at the brackets listed on the wooden board.

Due to her body refining rank, she'd been seeded one step before the quarter-finals.

Ash was one bracket before that. Which meant he'd have to have one more fight than she would.

He didn't mind that much. Nothing about the tournament interested him in any way so far. This was all meaningless to him.

"Are you even going to try?" Jia asked from beside him.

Ash shrugged. "Maybe. It's not like we get anything for winning or doing well."

Jia raised her eyebrows at that.

"But there are rewards," she said.

"Yes — recognition, fame, face, blah blah. None of that matters."

"No, there are actual rewards. But only for the top three finishers."

"There are? Huh. I honestly didn't think there were."

"You always tended to stop listening once they started talking about the examination," Jia said.

"Heh. Yeah. There wasn't much to care about at regarding the examination at the time."

"So… what are the rewards, then?"

There was a soft gong in the distance that signaled the end of the first round of battles.

"Come, you can walk me to the arena," Jia said as she turned to leave. "As to the rewards… first place is a ninth-body-refining-ranked ability and a paired cultivation skill."

Ash shook his head immediately.

"I know you have no desire to win that prize, but you asked. Now, the second-place winner receives an eighth-ranked sight ability," Jia continued.

"We do not have a sight ability in the Hall. This would be a valuable addition, Chosen One," Locke added cheerfully.

"Third place is just a number of spirit stones and pills. Though I do not think you have need of either of those, do you?"

"A sight ability. I think I'd be interested in that. Maybe I can do well enough to get second," Ash said, giving Jia a small smile. He wasn't about to rise to her bait about being wealthy.

He did have some money to his name right now, but not nearly enough.

Pills were expensive, and spirit stones lost their value to cultivation quickly after the sixth rank.

The numbers needed to advance in rank from spirit stones would cost more than the pills to do it in a similar fashion.

"Hm. I suppose we will see then. I plan to aim for the top, even though I… have no need for the reward, either," Jia said.

The two walked up to the side of an arena and fell silent.

The second round of contestant battles were ongoing. Ash would be in the fourth round for his first trial.

"What do you think?" Jia asked suddenly.

"Of?"

"Her. The one you are staring at."

"Huh?" Ash blinked and focused his gaze, rather than staring in the middle distance. "Oh."

Thankfully it didn't seem anyone else had noticed his blank gaze across the way. Especially since the young woman his face had been turned toward was a beauty.

She had dark hair and dark eyes, with all the right curves to put her in the spotlight back home even.

To the point that she looked like she might burst out of the red acolyte uniform she was wearing.

And entirely not what Ash was interested in.

Shrugging his shoulders, he turned to Jia.

"She's nice to look at, and well built. But anyone as pretty as that at our age is only going to be a barrel full of trouble down the road."

"Ah. Then you will be glad to know she is your first opponent."

"She is?" Ash asked, looking back at the woman.

Except now she was staring at him.

"She is. The odds are currently running against you," Jia said, her tone of voice flat.

"Huh. Maybe we should put in a bet on me to win. That'd be an easy way to make money."

"Ha. As if it were that simple. Minimum bets are in the thousands of spirit stones."

The woman across the way raised her eyebrows at him when she realized he was staring at her.

Ash shrugged at her and turned to Jia. As casually as he could manage it, he reached into his robe and triggered his ring's storage function.

He pulled out his spirit stone card and handed it over to Jia.

"Should be about eleven grand in there. Bet on me for me, and we'll split the winnings. Afterward, we'll bet on you or me in the next round. Whoever has better odds," Ash said.

Jia clicked her tongue and took the card from him. "Are you saying you would have handed me spirit stones that easily?"

"Probably. Why?"

Shaking her head, Jia didn't respond.

"You are in ring six. Go early," she said as she began walking away.

Making a face, Ash nodded his head. Looking around, he oriented himself based on the map he'd looked at earlier.

In less than the time it would take for an incense stick to burn, he'd found his ring. It was already cleared of the second-round combatants and the third round was waiting.

It wasn't until the quarter-finals where a small respite would be given between the rounds that was longer than twenty minutes.

Long enough to get your Qi back into shape, not long enough to get rid of any injuries you picked up. Truly, a gauntlet.

"It's an effective way to weed out those without the heart to continue. This culture puts a lot of weight into respect, determination, and showing one's strength."

Ash snorted coldly at that.

"Unless you're deemed weak, at which point they'll treat you as if you were little more than a bag of meat," he muttered.

"Of course," said a smooth and breathy voice. "Only the strong will be peerless."

Glancing to his side, Ash found the woman from earlier next to him.

"You decided to get here early, too?" Ash asked, looking back to the ring.

"Yes. I had hoped to be able to speak to you quietly. Without anyone else overhearing."

"Well, here you are, and here I am. What would you speak of?"

"I'd like you to forfeit to me. I'm sure we can come up with a suitable price that could be agreed upon."

Frowning Ash shook his head.

"Look, lady—"

"I am Xiaohui," she said, forcefully interrupting him.

"Xiaohui," Ash continued. "If you're not confident in your victory against me, I'd say your chances of proceeding further aren't very good. I'm not exactly the strongest one here."

Xiaohui lifted her chin up and looked down her elegant nose at him.

"You are just a frog at the bottom of a well. You can't see anything beyond the stones that surround you and the bit of sky far above you. You have no idea whom you speak to.

"You should feel blessed that I deigned to give you the option to assist me. Now I will crush you, and you will be nothing more than a worm."

Ash nodded at that and looked back to the ring.

He just couldn't take her seriously.

After the way everyone had treated him in the sect, he'd heard it all. Heard it all and then some.

Famous supporters, strong backers, hidden trump cards—the list was long and practically infinite of boasts.

Everyone thinks they're a genius, and that everyone else simply cannot be.
I'm not a genius, but I'm fairly certain I can kick your pretty ass.

"Guess we'll see. Especially since this match just ended," he said, gesturing at the ring.

As they'd been talking, the third round of fighting had started and already ended. The victor having defeated her opponent in a single strike.

Ash moved to one side of the ring and started to go through his startup, as he called it. It was the same thing he'd done before the beginning of every match back home.

From when he'd first started in the arts to when he'd won the national tournament that was a pre-qualifier for the world stage. This was a necessary function for him, if he had the time for it.

It was really just simple centering meditation. Getting himself into the perfect frame of mind.

"Locke, can you hear me?" Ash whispered as he settled himself down into a seated position.

"Yes."

"How much does my Battle Cultivation give back to me? Percentage wise."

"Approximately five percent per second right now."

"And the Spring Step is at two percent stored at any time?"

"Two point zero six percent."

"Leave the activation at that but change the storage to four percent."

"Task complete."

Nodding his head, Ash began working to center himself.

"Contestants. Prepare yourselves," boomed a voice.

Ash's eyes snapped open.

Getting to his feet, Ash gave his body a shake and tried to loosen himself.

To remain relaxed. Empty his mind. Be shapeless and formless.

He could feel a small smirk spreading across his face as he fell into his neutral position, his hands protecting his vitals.

Xiaohui stood in a relaxed standing position across from him.

Ability user only? No actual martial arts?

In his practice, he'd found the vast majority of cultivators simply no longer practiced their martial arts once they obtained their abilities.

They worked to bolster their techniques, forsaking their foundations.

For some, it was worse than others. Raised only with the abilities given to them, their understanding of martial arts was almost non-existent.

"I'll wipe that smile from your face," Xiaohui said, her beautiful face glaring at him. "And when I'm done, you may kiss the ground upon which I walk."

Ash didn't respond, just continued to size her up. Planning out his first movements.

"Begin!" shouted the same voice that'd given the warning.

Activating his Qi Thorns and Battle Cultivation, and toggling his Spring Step to store energy, Ash moved forward.

The moment he felt Spring Step was ready to be used, he activated it.

Xiaohui flinched backward at his sudden appearance next to her. She threw out a palm strike that whistled through the air. Flames circled her skin from forearm to fingertips.

Snapping his fist out, Ash knocked her hand aside. In the instant her side was exposed from the contact, Ash stomped his foot into the side of her knee.

Knocked down to the ground, Xiaohui looked shocked.

Not hesitating, Ash landed a strike across her jaw and another to her shoulder. Reeling, Xiaohui utilized an ability and burst into flames, reappearing six feet away.

Ash moved into a neutral position after pressing his hands to his sides. The moment the chains connected to his body, he felt Xiaohui's Qi flowing into him.

Hot and fiery, it felt very different than his own.

"I'll show you how I—"

Throwing his fists out into the air, one after the other, Ash launched two leeching Qi balls at his opponent.

Xiaohui took a step back when they smashed into her chest, and Ash pressed the two new chains atop the others.

I wonder if she can see the chains. No one else has commented on them.

Though they can clearly see the balls.

Xiaohui lifted her hand and pointed it at Ash.

Preparing a Spring Step, he was ready for whatever she did.

So when she fell forward onto her face and lay unmoving on the ground, it was the most unexpected thing in the world.

Ash canceled his Qi chains and looked to the referee.

"Ah… the victor is Ashley Sheng," the older gentleman said.

Frowning, Ash stood upright and waited. Two nurses came over to check on Xiaohui.

Pushing their hands back away from her, Xiaohui managed to get to her feet. Glaring up at him from a kneeling position, she looked as if she would burst into the Flame element she cultivated.

Ash pressed his fists together and bowed his head respectfully to his fallen opponent.

While she'd been egotistical, she hadn't actually insulted him. He had no reason to be anything other than polite now that the bout was over.

Trash talk will always be trash talk.

"Thank you for the match," he said sincerely.

Xiaohui stood up, her eyes hooded as she stared at him.

After a few seconds, she pressed her fists together and bowed her head briefly in return to him.

"Thank you for the match," she said, her voice sounding rather wooden and tired. "You're not allowed to lose to anyone else other than Shen."

Ash stood upright, surprise flashing through his mind.

"I can accept this with dignity if you win or lose to Shen. So do either of those. Otherwise I'll be so angry I'll vomit up blood," Xiaohui said. Flipping her hair over her shoulder, she left the ring immediately.

Ash blew out a sigh and wandered off to where he'd started.

Who the hell is Shen? And do you know how much internal damage you'd have to cause to actually make someone vomit up blood?

Jia was standing there waiting for him.

"You did take it easy on me," she said as he approached.

Grinning at her, Ash shrugged. "Not sure about that, but I definitely didn't try to beat you as fast as possible without care for damaging you."

"Well, you might get that opportunity during the tournament. I do plan on winning, so I can fight you for real if nothing else.

"I would very much like to know just how powerful you are, Ash."

Waving her off, Ash wandered off to the next ring he had to be at.

"I will be at ring forty-two when you're done," Jia called after him. "I must go collect the winnings and place another bet."

He waved a hand over his shoulder to signify he had heard her.

As he wandered up to the ring, he finally realized whom he'd be fighting this time.

"Hello Gong," Ash said, looking at the large acolyte standing in the middle of the ring.

"Haha, I'm going to fucking kill you!" Gong shouted, smashing his fists together in front of him repeatedly.

Sighing, Ash moved into the ring. Then he sat down on his side and began to work on centering himself once more.

Gong actually had an okay grasp of martial arts. He just tended to use strength and force rather than agility and speed.

Going to need to change up my plans a bit. All my attacks rely on being able to sap the energy of their strength. And Gong has a lot of it.

"You praying? Gonna need to pray. I'm going to make sure when I hit you, you never wake up," Gong shouted at him from his side.

"Now, now, Gong, you need to behave and follow the rules," said a wizened voice from the side.

"*It's Elder Shin,*" Locke answered before Ash even opened an eye to look.

Great. That means I can expect Shin to stop the fight if he thinks Gong might be hurt, and it'll go on and on if I'm losing.

I don't remember there being any rules other than to try not to maim the other person.

Fat chance of Shin protecting me.

"Contestants. Prepare yourselves," boomed a voice.

Getting to his feet, Ash once more got into his neutral stance. He expected Gong would rush him in one way or another. Keeping that thought in mind, he spun up Qi Thorns, Battle Cultivation, and Spring Step before the match could even start.

"Begin!" shouted the same voice that'd given the warning.

Gong flung his arms out to his side and clapped his hands together in front of himself.

A wave of molten, yellow Earth Qi swept forward in a rush at Ash.

There was no room to escape it as it filled the ring. Even hitting those who were watching from the sides.

Ash stared at the giant force-wave in shock.

Turning around, he squatted down and balled himself up tightly.

When it hit him, it knocked him flat to the ground and rolled over him.

His back felt as if it'd been stripped clean of flesh, and his body ached and burned at the same time.

Getting to his feet quickly, Ash stumbled into his neutral pose.

Gong was rushing toward him now. His right fist was cocked back already to throw a punch.

Ash wasn't quite sure what to do. His thoughts felt fuzzy and his ears were ringing.

Then Gong's fist was right in front of Ash. Blocking the strike and letting the force slip through his guard, Ash redirected the whole thing over his shoulder.

Leaning into Gong, Ash let loose a flurry of strikes into Gong's stomach and chest.

When he felt the bigger man start to recover his balance, Ash stepped out to the side and grabbed Gong by the shoulders.

By the barest of margins, the slimmest of thoughts, Ash didn't target Gong's face. So when he activated Spring Step and channeled it into his knee, he drove it straight into Gong's abdomen instead.

Ash could feel things shift around inside Gong's body around his knee.

The bigger man swung out with a fist and caught Ash in the side, sending him staggering backward.

Taking in several breaths as he regained his footing, Ash pressed his hands to his sides. Qi immediately began flowing into him. Rumbling, deep, steady Earth Qi.

Ash then went back into his neutral stance. Ready for anything.

Gong got to his feet, his face bright red with rage.

He pulled his arms back as if he were going to launch that wave of Earth Qi again.

Then he promptly leaned forward and began throwing up blood.

Oh… well… there ya go, then.

Looking to Elder Shin, Ash cleared his throat.

"Should I continue?" Ash asked. "I can attack right now if I'm not the winner."

Elder Shin grit his teeth, a pained expression on his face.

The audience was watching as he debated it.

Ash didn't hesitate and started moving in on Gong. If he wasn't going to be announced the winner, there was no reason to spare him.

"Stop!" Elder Shin said finally. "Ashley Sheng is the winner. Medics, tend to Gong immediately."

Ash pressed his fists together to Gong, then left. There was no reason to hang around here.

Besides, Jia had more or less asked him to come watch her if he finished earlier than her.

Stepping up to the ring, he surveyed the battle.

Lim was partially hunched over at the other side of the ring. He looked as if he were standing up by sheer force of will.

Jia was standing in a negligent pose, hands on her hips. She noticed Ash when he made his way to the front of the ring.

"You may surrender now and beg for forgiveness for your arrogance. You owe a kowtow to Ash as well," Jia said. "Do not attempt to fool me again, though. Else I will make your life painful."

Lim collapsed to his knees and held up a hand. Ash hadn't noticed, but there was a band of water clamped around Lim's mouth.

The water shifted up a fraction from his lips.

"I apologize for my arrogance and beg your forgiveness," Lim said. Then he pressed his forehead down to the ground.

"Good," Jia said with a nod of her head. "You may surrender now."

"I admit defeat," Lim said. Then his upper half fell forward, supported by nothing.

"She has bands of water around him. His movements are very restricted," Locke supplied.

A heartbeat later and Lim slumped to the ground, unmoving, as Jia apparently removed the bands of water.

Hm. It would seem I wasn't the only one who took it easy on the other party.

"She didn't take it easy on you. You're just much faster than you realize," Locke interjected.

Can you read my mind?

"No, I can't read your mind, either. You're just very obvious, Chosen One."

Thirteen

"Welcome to the quarter-finals, everyone," said a senior elder of the Spark's Jump Sect. "Today we'll be hosting the fights one by one so that everyone can enjoy them. The first fight of the day is—"

Ash sighed and turned to Jia. "This feels kind of pointless."

Jia shook her head when it was clear Ash wasn't going to pay attention anymore.

"Perhaps you should care after all, then. Jade Fist only has two slots open this examination. Apparently, another city they visited before this one had many who chose them as their destination," Jia said. "Which means only the top two have a surefire chance of joining.

"And I doubt very much that your next fight will be like the fifth round. I do not believe you even broke a sweat in that fight."

His fight had indeed been a breeze. Those who had come up against him had seemed average in every way, and it had only taken a flurry of Leech Strikes to drop them a minute in.

Two slots for the Jade Fist.

Technically, the top two ranks can practically request what sect they want.

But they wouldn't choose Jade Fist, would they? That's not likely, is it?

The top two would likely go for Dragon Warrior or Blood Oath.

"I also heard," Jia said, her voice breaking his thoughts open. "That Dragon Warrior and Blood Oath may not have any slots open at all. It would seem you suddenly do need to care."

Clenching his teeth, Ash contemplated the situation he'd found himself in.

Jia wasn't wrong. He had to fight to actually win, and not just take it easy.

"Ah, that is a much better-looking face. I take it you will be looking to make it into the top two then," Jia said with a snicker.

"So it would seem. Honestly… I just want to get into the sect to help Jing and Yan. It's not that complicated," Ash complained.

"Such is life, especially for a cultivator. The heavens intercede when they decide it is time for a tribulation.

"Truly so for those that are marked," Jia said.

"Either you're claiming I'm marked, or that the heavens are out to get me."

"Or both," Jia said. "Now, I am off to get ready. I am the second fight today, and you are the third. It might do you some good to think on your opponent.

"If you do not remember, his name is Xiao-Yan."

Ash couldn't disagree with her. Not really.

Hm. She's not wrong. Maybe I should spend some time asking some questions. Or get close enough and let Locke scan him.

Either way, I guess.

Looking around, Ash realized most everyone had already cleared out. More than likely to go watch the first match or get ready for their own battles.

Xiaohui was nearby, standing next to a young man. He looked fairly unassuming, though he was rather handsome.

At least by the standards of this culture.

He had delicate features, clear brown eyes, and long light-brown hair. His build was slim and unassuming, his height almost spot-on average.

Maybe Xiaohui will know who this Xiao-Yan is.

Xiaohui noticed him looking at her. She gave him a nod of her head before ignoring him completely.

And maybe the moon will rise in the morning. Ha.

She'd probably cross a freeway just to spit on me.

"There you are, Shen," called a boisterous voice. "I was wondering if you'd crawled away and hid yourself."

"Now why would I go and do that?" said the young man next to Xiaohui.

Guess that answers that question.

Ash watched the newcomer walk up to Shen as if he owned the world. A group of tagalongs were on his heels. They looked like the standard bunch of toadies Ash had come to expect from those in power.

The new arrival was taller than Shen and seemed to be about the same as far as looks went. Though his hair was a shade or two darker.

"Xiao-Yan, know your place," said Xiaohui. "You're living on your father's name. You'll know soon enough, that by itself can't win your fights for you."

Oh. Well, that was handy.

"Locke, any chance you can scan the crap out of him and get me useful info? Also, I'd really like you to try and prioritize an ability that will help me heal faster.

"My back still frickin' hurts," Ash said under his breath.

"I shall endeavor to do both, Chosen One.

"The scan is already complete, and I'm reviewing the data."

"…let you kowtow to me. After that, I'll make sure you get into whatever sect you wish. I'll even make sure you get a special reward as well," Xiao-Yan said.

Shen smiled as if he knew something Xiao-Yan didn't. Both young men were sizing each other up, each intent to make the other break eye contact first.

Ash had seen this pattern a few times now. It seemed almost ritualistic to him. Two people would come together and each trash-talk the other. They'd each promise all sorts of things to happen to the other, either in lieu of fighting or if they lost.

The fight would happen, and then they'd slowly try to one-up each other with their "trump cards" as they fought.

Snorting, Ash shook his head.

"I wonder if that's what Gong was expecting," Ash said under his breath. "Too bad for him I have no wish to do that. Just win as fast as possible using as much force as I can bring to bear."

Dismissing the two groups as they stared one another down, Ash turned to leave the area.

And nearly ran over Ying Yue in doing so.

"Ah!" she squeaked out, staring up at him.

"Ying Yue? What are you doing here?" Ash asked.

"I'm… I'm following… that is," said the young girl. Grasping the front of her tunic with one hand, she nodded at him as if she'd made up her mind. "I'm going to follow you as a traveling merchant to the sect that you choose.

"I was hoping you could tell me which sect you were going to join now, so I can plan my purchases."

Ash took in a breath to question her further and let it hang. Then he blew it out with a shrug of his shoulders.

Why did it matter to him whether or not she followed him?

"I'm going to be attempting to join the Jade Fist," he said finally.

"Jade Fist? Jade Fist. Mm. Ok," Ying Yue said, her eyes flicking down towards the stones. "Jade Fist. Jade Fist. Yes."

A sudden stray thought struck him.

"Hey, Yue—can I call you Yue?" Ash asked.

"Hm? Oh, ah… yes… yes, that's fine."

Ying Yue's eyes had come back up to Ash, looking startled at his change of address.

"I have a question. Is there anywhere I can sell empty spirit stones for spirit stones or coin?"

"Uhm, the merchant guild can do that for a fee."

"Oh, alright. Tell you what, I don't have a lot of time," Ash said, selecting an unbound card in his ring.

He quickly transferred all the empty spirit stones from the other card to it, then pulled it out from his ring after reaching into his clothes.

"If you can convert these to spirit stones, you can keep one-sixth of the value you get from it.

"In other words, the better you do, the more you keep."

Ying Yue looked at the card, her eyebrows dipping down.

"Just how many empty stones are there?"

"More than seven hundred thousand."

The young merchant blinked her eyes rapidly, her throat constricting as she stared at the card. "One-sixth?" she asked.

"Yep."

"I'll do it, providing I can travel with you to the Jade Fist."

"Deal," Ash said, holding the card out to her.

Ying Yue took the card in both hands and bent her head over it. Then she scurried away before he could ask her anything further.

Odd girl. I wonder why she wants to follow me, though.

Perhaps she thinks I'm a bit of a lucky charm?

Ash left.

A nap suddenly sounded pretty great.

***

Yawning, Ash scrubbed at his face as he walked into the ring.

I feel so much better after that. Nothing like a quick laydown.

As if… as if the whole world is brighter for me.

"You do realize if Jia finds out you were sleeping before your match, she's going to yell at you," Locke said. *"She'll already be annoyed that you didn't watch her match."*

"Ugh. Why? I'm not her problem, and I needed one. It helped shake off the anxiety. I'm not one for stress, ya know?" Ash muttered.

"Because she seems to think that unless she keeps you motivated and on track, you'll fail."

"I'm taking it seriously. I just want to take it seriously at my own pace."

"Your pace seems to be that of a procrastinator.

"Or a corpse. One way or the other, Chosen One."

"You sound like my dad. My dad and Trav," Ash grumbled, taking a seat in the large ring he'd be fighting in.

"I know neither, but perhaps they're right."

Taking a look around at the way the area was set up, he realized this place was going to fit a lot of people. It was quite probable he'd have more people watching him today than he'd ever had previously.

Diverting his thoughts, Ash tried to route his concern into something productive. Like contemplating how to win this fight.

Sitting there as he let his brain idle over what he could do, he started to vaguely construct a concept of how to fight.

A strategy that would work with his abilities and his cultivation as they were. Even going so far as to try and consider what the gaps existed in his current self.

We already asked for a way to heal, but… did we outline it right? Locke is still a program of sorts. Can he think independently on his own? Or is he just a virtual intelligence?

"Hey, Locke… I know you're working on a way for me to heal myself. How's that going?"

"Long since complete. There are no abilities that match the parameters you gave, at your level."

"What if you modified the ability so it did less, but was still usable?" Ash asked, curious. "One that could work based on my style of fighting?

"In addition to that, is there a low-grade shielding ability? Or a defensive type of Qi shield? Something that could help me shrug off what Gong did?"

Wait, what really is my style?

If I had to define it, it seems to match my martial arts foundation. Be formless, be shapeless.

Flow.

Be momentum.

"Add another request. Is there an ability at any level that would allow me to receive an attack and redirect it? I don't have to steal anything from it, or utilize it in any way, or even negate it.

"Just… redirect its…" Ash paused and searched for a word. Except none really fit. "Its flow, I guess… but without changing its momentum."

"Parameters have been updated. Several skills can be modified to fit specifications of all three requests, but none that would prove immediately usable."

"Great, load those up for later and we'll go over them. For now… let's set Spring Step to be a variable of however much Qi we're drawing from the opponent. Something like fifty percent of whatever it is, at all times," Ash said.

That'll at least provide me with a means to escape if I truly need to, right? I mean, what if I could use that ability to jump straight into the air? I probably could have cleared Gong's attack that way.

"Are you praying?"

Ash's eyes snapped open to look to the unknown speaker.

It was Xiao-Yan.

He was staring down at Ash with an arrogant cast to his face.

"Contemplating, actually," Ash said neutrally.

"Contemplate later. It's time for you to lose."

"Fighters," interrupted an elder of the sect. "Take your positions."

Getting to his feet, Ash gave his body a shake from head to toe. Trying to loosen himself up and get ready to move.

To flow. To go with the momentum.

To be the momentum.

I shall be the snowflake that lands at the top of a mountain.

Ash activated his abilities and waited.

Xiao-Yan chuckled to himself and straightened up in an imperious-looking pose. As he flexed his muscles, his skin rapidly coated itself in a layer of dense Metal-elemental Qi.

Shit.

"Come, start the fight so I can show him how pointless this is. I am the bar of steel that will crush him," Xiao-Yan said, looking to the elder.

The older man looked to Ash, one hand raised above his head. The dropping of said hand would signal the start of the fight.

Instead, he stared at Ash.

In fact, the entire crowd was watching Ash.

"Based on the culture that has been observed so far, Chosen One, it is expected that you make a remark in response.

"It would almost be considered the proper 'etiquette' of the situation."

Ash thought quickly and shook his head.

"As you like. I'll beat your body into the shape I desire with as many hammer blows as it takes.

"Perhaps when I'm done, I can forge your flesh into a chamber pot," Ash said. "Then use it."

The elder decided that was a perfect moment to start the fight, and he dropped his hand.

Xiao-Yan started to stomp his way toward Ash. "I'm going to tear off your head!"

Moving to his right, Ash started to try and circle to the side of Xiao-Yan. He wanted no part of facing this golem nose to nose.

Reaching Ash, Xiao-Yan lashed out with a kick. So fast was the strike, it actually caught Ash off guard.

Using both hands, he blocked the attack and deflected it at the same time.

Dancing back several steps, Ash shook his hands out. They were numb from fingertips to elbows. *Damn, that was a heavy blow. Damn, damn, damn.*

Xiao-Yan let out a muffled shout and rubbed at his foot where it had connected with Ash. Apparently the Qi Thorns could burn through his Metal Qi.

Shaking out his hands, Ash grinned at Xiao-Yan.

"Care to exchange some more pointers?" Ash asked with far more bravado than he felt.

Xiao-Yan eyed him for a second before swinging a heavy punch at him while shouting. "I'll crush you with a single blow, you runt!"

Realizing he couldn't take the strike head on, Ash instead deflected it with as little contact as possible. In the same movement, he struck out at Xiao-Yan's arm.

Moving with his attack, Ash slid along Xiao-Yan's side and struck him with his elbow.

Coming out the other side, Ash pressed his aching hands to his hips to lock the chains in place.

I feel like I broke my hands. I can't keep exchanging in close quarters with him.

Keeping the grimace from his face, Ash let out a breath and took up a neutral stance. Making up his mind, he began to throw out multiple quick strikes, launching a Leech Strike with every usage.

The metallic Qi balls sped through the air and stuck to Xiao-Yan's back.

He ignored them as if they didn't even exist. In fact, he was still shaking his hand as if it was in pain.

In no time at all, Ash was panting, his Qi pool drastically reduced. He'd launched so many Leech Strikes that Xiao-Yan's looked more like a sack of bowling balls than a young man.

Except Ash could actually feel the strength coming back to him. Drop by drop, sip by sip, stolen from Xiao-Yan.

Ok, so that works.

Xiao-Yan finally turned around to face Ash. Panting, he flexed his arms as if shaking something off.

"That all you got? You didn't event dent me. I'm going to use my strongest attack now. Maybe you should give up before you get killed.

"Don't take it lightly!" he shouted.

Ash mentally sighed at the theatrics but kept himself steady.

"Metal Punch!" Xiao-Yan said, striking out with both hands.

If Ash thought for a second that striking this bigmouth as he yelled his attack would stop him, it'd have happened.

Two giant, silvery-white fists appeared from thin air and struck out at Ash.

Everything seemed to slow down momentarily around him. His thoughts sped up and his body was burning with the need to move.

To get out of the way. Be anywhere other than where he was right then and there.

Tapping into his Spring Step, Ash unloaded the entire reservoir it held. His joints screamed in protest as he moved. Skirting the massive Qi attack, Ash worked to slide along the edge of it. The energy screaming off of it seemed to pushed him along as he went.

It was as if Ash had practically vanished from where he'd stood and reappeared behind Xiao-Yan in the time it took to blink.

Continuing his attack as if he didn't even realize Ash was gone, Xiao-Yan didn't move. The view from his side of things was probably just a giant ball of Metal Qi.

Taking this opportunity for battering away at Xiao-Yan, Ash balled his fists and mentally sacrificed his bones to the fight.

He had to win.

Had to win and move on to the next round.

As quickly as his fists could move, Ash battered away at Xiao-Yan's already Qi-ball-filled back. With strike after strike, he burned the dregs of Spring Step's Qi as it filled.

Xiao-Yan finished his monstrous attack, staggering forward a step. Taking this as his time to get back out of range, Ash backed up six steps.

Panting heavily, Ash felt like his body was shaking. Practically quivering from head to toe.

His Qi was refilling steadily, but he was suffering from a lack of endurance at this point.

Glancing at his hands, Ash realized there was a second problem. His fists were broken red pieces of meat.

He gritted his teeth. There wasn't much he could do about it right now. He only had to fight once today, thankfully. His next bout would be tomorrow.

Providing we win, maybe we can spend some of those spirit stones we should have earned at the auction today.

Get some healing pills and get ready for tomorrow.

If we win.

Settling his resolve, Ash lifted his brutalized hands and got ready for whatever Xiao-Yan did next.

Turning around, the metal-clad young man set his eyes on Ash with an evil glint.

"Look at you. You'll… you'll not… you'll not get away… this… time," Xiao-Yan said. His voice started to falter as he finished his sentence.

"He's going to drop. If you don't cancel the chains after the Qi shell of his disappears, he'll die."

He'll die?

"This is a good time to remind you that you'll get a massive bonus to your cultivation if you kill someone."

Ash blinked at the sudden and evil push from Locke.

Xiao-Yan's Metal Qi failed, and he slumped to his knees.

Without thinking about it, Ash canceled all his chains and let his hands fall to his sides.

Deactivating his toggled abilities, Ash stood there, gasping for air.

"Winner… Winner Ashley Sheng," announced the elder.

All around him were the stunned faces of the entire crowd. No one had expected him to do well. Let alone win.

He was the proverbial dark horse.

Delicately, Ash pressed his mangled fists together and bowed his head to Xiao-Yan. Then he carefully left the ring, heading straight for the auction house.

Fourteen

"Are you alright?"

Ash blinked and gave himself a small shake. Turning his head to the side, he found Ying Yue.

"Yes. I need to go get some money and go to a doctor," Ash said.

For some reason, his voice felt oddly hollow in his own ears.

"Oh. I have some of your money. I think it's more than enough to go to a healer," Ying Yue said. She was watching him with an odd look to her face.

"Here, come with me. I'll take you there," she said. She looped her arm through his and began pulling him along somewhere.

"Alright. I think I'm tired," Ash said.

"Yes. I would wager you are. Also, you might be in shock from the pain of your poor hands. How much are you willing to spend on the healer?"

Ash forced his mind to consider her words. To truly think on what she had just asked him.

"As much as I have in that card I gave you. If we need more, I need to go to the auction house," Ash said.

"Got it. I don't think it'll be more than you have in the card — that's for sure. But it'll be pricey."

Ying Yue kept them moving. A number of streets went by while Ash struggled to pull his thoughts back up from the deep.

By the time Ash was dragged into a building, he was mostly coherent. Having Ying Yue lead him along had let him focus on trying to beat his brain into shape.

Then he was being pushed down into a chair.

An older man leaned in close over him, peering into Ash's face. He was bald with light-brown eyes. His face looked stern, though not unkind.

"Ah… he isn't suffering from any type of Qi problem," said the older man.

Peeling Ash's eyelids up, the man peered in.

"Huh?" Ash said.

"He seems… lost," Ying Yue said.

"It's just shock," the old man said. "I imagine he slipped away before the tournament handlers could catch him. Normally they'd take care of him as best as they were able.

"Though I do think they would have eliminated him from the tournament with these hands after they fixed him. They're fairly mauled."

"Can you heal them?" Ying Yue asked, her face appearing over the old man's shoulder.

Letting go of Ash's eyelids, the man pressed his cold, dry fingertips to Ash's throat instead.

"If I didn't know how to fix broken bones in the hands and wrists, I'd be a terrible healer.

"And yes, I most certainly can. Though his hands won't be fully healed by tomorrow. So long as he doesn't go overboard, they'll be fine in two days," said the healer, letting go of Ash entirely. "I'll treat it mostly with pills so his Qi isn't overrun by my own. Though I'll have to use some.

"Amazingly, his Qi is pure. Pure and without a trace of elemental Essence."

"It's… pure?" Ying Yue asked.

"Indeed. Alright, I'll get the pills. Cost will be about—"

"I'm sorry, could you quote the price in spirit stones? We have no hard currency on us otherwise," Ying Yue said apologetically.

"Nnn. Nothing wrong with that, just not exactly ordinary. I suppose… for the pills and assessment it'd be about a hundred stones?

"The cost is mostly in the pills."

The old healer was in front of Ash again. He pushed a small, hard pill into Ash's mouth and then pinched his nose shut. "Swallow. You'll be feeling better in no time. Go home and sleep.

"Pill should work fairly quickly. But it'll also—"

***

Flexing his hands open and closed, Ash sat at the small table in the inn room he'd woken up in.

The late dawn sun was streaming in through a window, and he knew his battle would be in an hour or two.

He couldn't quite remember how he'd gotten here, but he wasn't concerned about the lack of memories. Or about being in this place.

The room was filled with packs and mercantile goods.

That and Ying Yue was sleeping on the small couch with a few covers over herself.

Ash smiled with one side of his mouth, looking back to his hands.

They were covered in thin, hair-like scars, but they felt strong.

Felt good.

Perhaps not perfect, but good enough.

"The damage was fairly extensive. While you were unconscious, I finished the action you requested, Chosen One," Locke said.

"Oh?" Ash said softly.

"I have crafted a Qi shield, a small healing ability, and a channel that redirects incoming attacks to eighty-percent effectiveness," Locke said.

"Ok, I thought you said I can't learn anymore?"

"The Qi shield builds off the Qi Thorns, the heal is tied to the Battle Cultivation, and the redirect is part of the Leech Strike. You'll have to strike the incoming attack, target it with one hand, and redirect with the second.

"They will cost nothing new, but the pain will be significant when you learn them."

"Oh, how significant?"

"You will pass out for about two minutes."

"Alright, go ahead and do it as soon as I lay do—"

Ash's face locked into place as the new abilities smashed him down into the chair, straight into unconsciousness.

He came to what only felt like a minute or two later, his head swimming. Groaning, Ash sat up straight in the chair and touched a hand to his head.

"Task complete, Chosen One," Locke said with absolute glee.

"I'm going to figure out a way to delete you or modify your programming one of these days," Ash mumbled.

Getting to his feet slowly, Ash activated the Battle Cultivation technique. Since it would supposedly heal him, there was no reason to not have it active now.

Maybe it'll help my hands along.

"Ashley?" murmured a sleepy voice.

Looking to the couch, he saw Ying Yue's eyes fluttering open and closed as she woke up.

Grasping the covers, she pulled them up to her chin, her eyes slowly focusing on him.

"She took very good care of you," Locke interjected suddenly.

Making a snap decision, Ash bowed his head deeply to Ying Yue.

"I'm in your debt, Yue. Please, call me Ash. If you ever have a need, please do not hesitate to ask it of me. I'll do my best to meet whatever it is," he said.

Raising his head to face her, he lifted a hand. "Please do not fight this. Simply accept it.

"Now, I must go to the tournament. I believe my fight will be soon, and I must prepare as I'm able. After that, I'll meet you back here so we can plan our trip together.

"It wouldn't do to have you take on such a burden by yourself if we're traveling with one another."

"Ah, alright. You're welcome to help me in the planning, then, and I'll join you for your match," the merchant said with a smile.

It didn't take long for them to get cleaned up and make their way to the tournament field.

Everyone was already watching a match, which meant Ash could move about freely without worrying about others.

- 87 -

He walked up to the board and gave it a once-over.

"So it seems Jia moved on. That wasn't really ever in question," Ash muttered, reading the bracket. "And my opponent is... Shen.

"That'll be interesting, I suppose, since I don't know a thing about him."

"You will do fine," said a new voice from behind him.

Glancing over his shoulder, Ash found Jia right behind him.

"Thanks for the vote of confidence. Jia, this is Ying Yue—Ying Yue, Jia," Ash said, indicating the younger woman next to him. "She's the one who got me to the healer yesterday."

Jia eyed Ying Yue expressionlessly. Finally, she bowed her head several inches to the merchant. "I thank you for caring for him. He is foolish but good hearted."

"Yes. Yes, he is," Ying Yue said, nodding.

"Well, seems like my fight is next. I'll just go to the ring and prepare," Ash said, shrugging his shoulders.

"A wise idea," Jia said. "Ying Yue and I will accompany you and watch. I am curious to see how you hold up.

"Shen is... formidable."

"Oh? Could you beat him?" Ash asked.

"I... am honestly not sure. From what I have seen of him, yes. I fear he has hidden his talent and abilities deep, though. His strength is not visible from the surface," Jia said. "Should I bet on someone with our proceeds?"

"Me. And after that, don't bet any further," Ash said.

Ash moved into the ring and took a position in one half. Sitting down, he made himself ready and let his mind float away with itself.

He slipped immediately into a meditative state. Letting time slip away.

"Contestants! Make yourselves ready for this battle!"

Ash's eyes snapped open, and he found Shen directly across from him.

Getting to his feet, Ash activated Qi Thorns, Battle Cultivation, and Spring Step.

The referee seemed eager and dropped his hand to start the fight as Ash got into his stance. There was almost little to no time between the warning and the start.

Strange.

Shen made no move, however. He just stood there.

Waiting.

Ash didn't hesitate and threw out a punch, the metal ball of Qi shooting forward from his strike.

Shen dodged to one side, the attack passing him.

Clicking his tongue, Ash disconnected the chain attached to the ball.

"My turn," Shen said, then threw both his hands forward. A large ball of green Qi flew from his hands and reached out toward Ash. There wouldn't be much room to dodge it.

Pushing his thoughts into gear, he focused on the Qi coming towards him.

Perfect opportunity to test our redirect.

Hit with one hand, redirect with the other.

Holding his left hand low and pointed toward Shen, Ash struck at the green Qi with his right hand and then brought it back out.

His right palm felt as if it'd been slapped roughly before the energy rapidly switched to his left hand. As his right hand returned to his waist, Ash punched out with his left.

Shoving the energy out through his palm, Ash redirected Shen's energy back at him. Trailing along behind the cloud of energy was one of Ash's azure chains.

Except it was truly massive.

It looked more like a navy warship anchor chain.

Shen was clearly not expecting his own Qi to come back at him. He didn't even twitch before it smashed into him and knocked him several steps backward.

Ash shook his hands out after connecting the chain to his side. It honestly felt like he'd smashed them against a boulder.

On top of that, he was fairly certain the freshly healed bones had just fractured or broken again.

"Ha," Shen said, moving back to his previous position. "That was well done."

Ash wasn't so sure he could be that calm if he'd just taken that blow. In fact, he was fairly certain that if he'd been hit by it, he'd have been knocked clear out of the arena.

Let's... wait and see what happens. I'm not so sure my hands can take a punch right now.

Ash began dumping energy into his Qi Thorns. Right now, his priority was dodging. Whatever he could do to not take a hit directly.

Shen put his arms out in front of himself as a bright-green glow burst out of his back.

What the hell... Oh shit, it's a Martial Spirit.

Ash grimaced and gave his head a shake.

I thought Martial Spirits were rare. So rare they're practically family legacies. Why does he have one?

A massive green tree towered over Shen's back. It represented the spiritual might of multiple cultivators. The constant use over multiple generations had turned what had probably been a tree sprite into this Martial Spirit.

A massive tree-branch-like hand swung down toward Ash.

Activating Spring Step, he moved straight up, as if he were jumping. Appearing twenty feet in the air, Ash was able to watch the giant hand swing through the space he'd been in previously.

Angling his foot downward, Ash activated Spring Step again. This time he wanted to aim himself into a downward kick, straight into Shen's handsome face.

Gaining momentum and speed that weren't rightly his, Ash's foot appeared an inch from Shen's face.

With a foot smashing into his nose, Shen was forced backward once again. His Martial Spirit disappeared as he stumbled away.

Ash managed to drop lightly to the ground on one knee. Working to get back to his feet, he attached the new chain to his belt. This one was much smaller than the other.

Strength of the attack dictates the size of the chain and how much I get back.

Got it.

Before he could think to re-engage, Ash was sent spinning and bouncing across the ground.

He wasn't sure what had hit him, but it'd been fairly huge and green.

And quite solid.

Groaning as he slid to a stop, Ash lay still for a second.

Get up – fight isn't over. Got to get up.

Pushing himself up, Ash slowly clambered to his feet. His body felt like it'd been hit by a car. His ribs ached and so did his back.

Whatever Shen had launched had been more like a truck than anything.

Looking to his opponent, Ash found that Shen was pressing his hands to his stomach, screaming. With fire licking out from between his fingers, he was clearly burning.

Blinking, it took Ash a second to realize his Qi Thorns not only had shielded him from part of the attack but had also redirected it back to Shen.

Another heavy attack. This guy... he buried his strength deep. He's no rank three. Nor is he even a five or six. He has the power and strength of someone on the edge of becoming a mortal refiner.

Underdog my ass.

Ash determinedly got his hands up to defend himself.

He'd only been struck once, but combined with the attack he'd redirected, he'd been left in a fairly miserable state.

Shen somehow managed to get the Qi fire under control and looked to Ash with angry and bloodshot eyes.

"Fine, I'll use my trump card. There's no escape for you. Don't even think of running now," Shen said.

Ash didn't respond but merely waited. There was nothing to be said right now other than to finish this fight.

Bragging or trash-talking just wasn't in him.

Shen pressed a hand to his chest and then shouted at the top of his lungs, pushing out towards Ash with his other hand.

"Soul Grasp!" Shen called.

An invisible force locked down on Ash and held him in place. Preventing him from moving.

"Qi Burn!" Shen shouted out.

A purple flame jetted out of Shen's hand and screamed across the distance between Shen and Ash.

It slammed into his chest and he became a human torch.

"Pay for your crimes, villain!" Shen shouted.

Ash certainly felt warm, but nothing seemed to be happening to him. Looking to his hands, which were still unmoving, he watched as the purple fire rolled over his skin as if hunting something.

Then something happened at his waist. The fire attached itself to his chains and began to gather there.

The flames grew brighter as more and more piled up, leaving the rest of Ash's body.

In the single second it took for all this to occur, the crowd was already seemingly lamenting Ash's fate.

So when the purple flame suddenly shot back out to Shen along the chains, everyone was more than surprised.

Landing squarely on Shen's chest and face, the purple inferno rapidly overtook him.

Screaming once again, Shen started to bat at his face and chest with his hands. Trying to put out a fire that had no origin in the mortal realm.

"Locke… what was that?" Ash asked, as softly as he could.

"Unknown. The attack seemed to target the elemental Qi in your body."

"I don't have elemental Qi, though… In fact… with the cultivation method we have, there doesn't even seem be an elemental aspect required."

"There does not. His attack did nothing, but the chain pulls in Qi from your target. It is converted by your Dantian."

"In other words… his attack was reflected back," Ash muttered.

Shen dropped to his knees. His screeching had stopped now, and his eyes were blank, unseeing.

Ash disconnected the chains, just in case Shen was empty. There was no reason to take his life, and Ash wanted nothing to do with even the very idea of it.

Collapsing onto his face, Shen lay unmoving on the ground.

Ash swallowed, his body shivering.

He didn't quite feel a victory in this fight. In every regard, Shen had outclassed him. Outclassed him and should have beaten him outright. It was due to the fact that he'd found the Hall that he'd won. The Hall and Locke both.

Letting his arms fall to his side, Ash let out a heavy sigh.

"Winner! Ashley Sheng!" announced someone else. "He'll now be moving to the final!

"These are to be held immediately as due to an unforeseen opportunity, a veil raid is going to be carried out! Tomorrow, the attack will be launched on another veil."

Ash shook his head with a sigh. He'd have liked some time to rest.

Any time to rest.

They really want to go on a veil raid. So badly that they don't care who wins anymore.

Fine. I'll show you how much I care about your tournament.

A group of healers picked up Shen and carried him off, vanishing into the crowd.

Seconds later, Jia walked out from the audience.

"Forgive me, Ash. I did not wish it to be a fight like this," Jia said, pressing her fists together in front of herself.

"Oh, don't worry about it. I know well that this wouldn't be how you would have chosen it. How'd your fight go?"

Ash was taking in slow, steady breaths, trying to calm his spirit and heartbeat.

"Well. I think in our spars I came to expect a certain level of expertise in my opponents. The others did not live up to you, and I was disappointed," Jia said, taking a stance and facing him head on.

"Happy to hold a special place in your heart, then. It's a pity I won't be seeing you after the match is over. Sounds like we'll all be hustled off to our sects as soon as the fighting ends," Ash said.

Moving into his neutral stance, Ash did his best to ready himself.

His hands hurt, his back ached, and his chest felt like each breath was squeezed through iron bands around his lungs.

Any type of fight right now would just worsen his condition.

And that means buying more pills after this, or hoping Battle Cultivation can take care of it with enough time.

"Contestants… get ready for the final fight," called an elder.

Ash made a decision. One that he didn't like and one that would make Jia angry, but one that fit all of his needs right now.

"Begin!" shouted the elder, dropping his hand.

Jia attacked with a whip of Water Qi, snapping it toward Ash's chest.

Waiting for the attack, Ash held still. As soon as the attack hit him, he activated Spring Step backward and partially into the air.

Hopefully it looks like it was just a strong hit. Ash thought to himself as he flew through the air, straight out of the bounds of the arena, and crashed into the audience.

You win, Jia.

Fifteen

"As the champion, you are allowed to choose the sect you wish to join. You will be accepted regardless of which you choose.

"Which sect do you pick?" asked the old man who had given them their Qi examinations.

Jia's eyes flicked to the recruiters, then to the examiner.

"This one must kindly ask his seniors to allow a moment to think. Please move to the second-place finisher for now," Jia said, bowing her head deeply to the recruiter table.

The Mountain Bear and Dragon Warrior Sects shared a look and then smirked at one another.

I bet they're wondering which one amongst them she's picking. I wonder if they bet on those kind of things.

The examiner looked to the recruiters, who nodded their heads. Once he received permission, the examiner looked to Ash.

"Ashley Sheng, which sect do you request to join?"

The medics had quickly scooped up Ash after his loss and put him to rights. Apparently upon losing, one received the full benefits of the tournament. Winners were expected to care for themselves, unless the medics ruled them unfit to continue.

Standing there in front of everyone, Ash was feeling much more "right" than he had in a while.

It only took something like twenty different types of pills and an actual Qi Healer.

Ash pressed his fists together and bowed to the recruiters from each sect.

"I would choose to join the Jade Fist," Ash said immediately, without thinking about it. His goal all along had been to go there to assist his brother and sister.

That was the extent of his desires.

Everyone stared at Ash after he spoke.

Suddenly the Jade Fist recruiter started laughing loudly.

"The Jade Fist willingly and gladly accepts Ashley Sheng," said the middle-aged man, standing up. He bowed his head and pressed his fists together towards Ash.

"Jia, you have been given time to make your choice, as you requested," said the examiner, turning his face toward Jia. "Are you ready now?"

"Yes. I would request to join the Jade Fist," Jia said, bowing her head and pressing her fists together.

Again, the crowd was shocked into silence.

Clapping his hands together, the Jade Fist recruiter bounced out of his seat, laughing almost hysterically.

"The Jade Fist willingly and gladly accepts you as well," crowed the recruiter.

The other recruiters started shouting at the Jade Fist recruiter and the stage fell into disarray.

"What are you doing?" Ash whispered as he poked Jia in the side. Leaning in close to her he was in her personal space. "I thought you wanted to go for the best!"

"I do. And that is still my goal. I am merely just changing the way in which I am doing it. Now back up," Jia said. She reached up and tried to push Ash back with a hand on his shoulder.

"No! What are you doing? You could have easily gotten into the top tier sects. Tell them it was a mistake. Quick. You worked so hard for this," Ash hissed at her. He was confident he could push a bit harder with the focus of the crowd still on the recruiters as they bickered with one another.

Jia turned her face partially toward Ash.

"Stop. I am doing what I want. This choice is entirely my own, and happily so. I did work hard for this, though my gains were entirely due to you.

"I do not feel it would be best for me to go away from you. I think you are a Fated One, and I wish to be a part of it.

"Now back up or they will think you have an interest in men, and me," Jia said, quirking a brow at him.

Ash snorted and moved an inch closer toward her. He was feeling a touch rebellious, and her telling him what to do was making it worse.

"And what if they do? Do you think I care? You're the one who seems to be hiding herself. No?" Ash asked.

With her eyes locked on his, Jia didn't back up from him.

Instead, she suddenly pressed her forehead to his.

"You do not frighten me, Ash. I know your personality very well. You speak out of anger because you worry for me. I understand. And I am flattered.

"Now, back up, or I shall make this much worse for you. No one has noticed yet," Jia murmured.

Grumbling, Ash pulled away from her and got back into his own position.

Looking to the stage he found the Jade Fist recruiter laughing all by himself, as the other sects continued to yell at one another.

"They plan on moving us to a veil border after this," Jia said. "We will be coming back here for a short period afterward. I told your merchant friend to remain here and wait."

I'll collect my auction earnings on the way back through, then, and pick up Ying Yue.

"A veil, huh," Ash mused.

"Veil raids don't happen often. This is an opportunity for them to test their strength and gain resources. We will be there simply to watch and learn."

Ash didn't know what to say. Veil raids were where the outlander slaves came from. He didn't really agree with any of it, but he couldn't stop it either.

And raising his voice against it would only cause him to be silenced.

Which meant he was along for the ride whether he liked it or not.

***

Moira and Jia stood next to Ash. The former having joined them as soon as they left town. They were with the rest of the Jade Fist recruits and the recruiter himself.

Each sect was more or less insular to themselves as they stood waiting at the boundary to the veil.

The largest group was made up of loose cultivators of Xing City.

Ash watched the Jade Fist recruiter as he led their group, standing with a group of younger recruits around him.

The Jade Fist recruiter seemed like the happiest man alive, honestly. Telling all who would listen about what to expect of the new sect and giving them pointers about what their first steps should be.

"It is because he gained a lot of face when we joined," Jia said.

"Hm?" Ash mumbled, looking to Jia.

"You are staring at the recruiter. Likely you wonder about his mood. He is quite joyful due to you and I joining him.

"He will receive praise when he returns to the sect," Jia elaborated.

"Seems arbitrary," Moira said.

Ash nodded.

"Everyone!" called the Dragon Warrior recruiter. "We will now move across the veil. Fill your Dantian up now; we'll have no ability to do so once we cross over.

"To you new recruits, stay behind. To the rest of you who followed, good luck!"

The Jade Fist recruiter clapped his hands together several times and looked to his recruits.

"Stay together. The Kin have their own abilities and are unique. On average, they only rank at about the strength of a sixth or seventh body refiner. So work in teams to subdue or kill them.

"The location we've drawn will be shared with the Mountain Bear Sect. It's a mine. I imagine we'll find many outlanders we can take our pick of. They often send the young or inexperienced ones to places like this.

"Targets that are of little interest internally to them, but great for us," said the recruiter.

"Why are we here?" Moira said, her voice edged with distaste and dislike. The wings on her back lifted up and then settled back down in what was clear agitation.

Can't say I blame her. This is probably how she herself was captured. Just in a different city and a different veil.

"Because I have no right to refuse it. Don't worry, we'll just hang in the back and let them do as they will. I have no desire to actually participate," Ash said.

Moira nodded at his words. "Good. I'm glad to hear that."

Looking at the veil, Ash couldn't help but wonder. It was a sheer, translucent, film-like substance that surrounded the entire nine kingdoms.

The veils would open up at random intervals, allowing for veil raids, as they were called.

Each veil seemingly went to a different world. A different land. There were even noted instances where veils had changed. Where once a veil had led to a land filled with nothing but humans, a year later, it went to a volcanic world of fire and hell.

That on top of the fact that people intentionally went on veil raids to fight other species made the whole prospect fairly dangerous.

Yan and Jing had spoken of an older cousin who had been lost on a veil raid. She'd never come back after heading over.

It was this veil, in fact. Her name had been Lan, and she'd simply vanished.

There was a shuddering shimmer that spread throughout the veil, and a gap opened up all on its own.

Several cultivators stepped into the gap and then sat down.

They were the gate keepers. They would hold the veil open as the raid proceeded.

Everyone began to rush through the open veil.

The raid had begun.

Moving as a group, everyone started across the boundary.

An hour later, the attack had started. From the look of it, it would be over quickly here as well.

Out in front of himself, Ash watched as numerous cultivators stormed through the mining camp. Watching it made Ash a little sick.

Anyone in a gray vest was targeted first. That was their way of differentiating between uniforms and civilian clothes.

The ones in gray vests were the soldiers of this area. Guards and overseers. Those who had power.

And what better way to express one's own power than by defeating others with power?

Ultimately, this was really just a test of strength with the possibility of stealing resources.

People, equipment, coins—anything that could be carried, stored, or bound.

"It's sickening," Moira said.

"It is… normal," Jia countered. "This is simply the way of the cultivator. It is not as if other veils do not do the same. Do you not see some of my own countrymen down there? This is not unique to us."

Ash couldn't disagree with either of them, because they were both right on their respective points.

It didn't make him like it any more or less. He was no fool, though. He wasn't going to argue with his superiors, but neither was he going to be a pacifist.

Having long since toggled on his abilities and charged them to full, Ash was ready for anything that should happen or come his way.

Except it was unlikely he'd be troubled. They were clearly in the minority by remaining back, but they weren't alone, either.

Even some of the youngest recruits were down there testing themselves. Killing or being killed simply to see if they had what it took to do so. But not all of them.

Looking to the entrance of the mine Ash watched a large frog-looking monstrosity directing people with a meaty fist.

"They are probably a distant relative of your own people, Moira. Though they seem to have far more genetic diversity," Jia said.

"Mm. My countrymen all have wings of one sort or another. Being of the Owl tribe, I held great prestige."

Ash winced as an old woman was backhanded by the frog-like man and sent flying. She crashed into a wall and fell limp to the ground. Turning to one side, the monster trundled off in another direction.

Then Ash saw a man.

A man in rags standing in the mouth of the entrance. A man he instantly recognized. One he'd been hoping to see since he'd shown up here.

One he'd long given up on seeing.

Even though he couldn't see the man's face, he knew who it was.

He knew it in the very core of his being.

It was his cousin Trav, who had apparently been pulled from the boat with him.

Then Trav was knocked into the mine under the weight of what looked like a guard. Vanishing into the darkness, Ash could no longer see him.

"I'll be back," Ash said hurriedly.

Kicking off from the ground, Ash began to rapidly cross the distance toward the mine entrance. Each time his feet hit the ground, he used Spring Step. The ground whipped by him as he went. As did numerous cultivators, enemy guards, and slaves.

Before he could get to the mine entrance, it began to cave in on itself. Rocks and debris fell and covered the entryway.

Ash came to a sudden stop. There wasn't anything he was going to be able to do to get through the rubble.

Looking around, he realized he was in a small cleared area to the side of the mines. A part of the camp that was uninhabited and at the edge of the layout.

Rather than going backward, through those who might be ready for him, or forward, deeper into enemy lines, Ash moved toward the perimeter of the camp.

Slipping through the nearby trees, he moved out of sight and started to loop back around to where he'd started.

A heavy thump beside him made Ash startle to one side, immediately drawing his butterfly swords and holding them in front of himself.

"Why did you leave?" Moira asked, her wings settling down on her back. She tilted her head to one side, her lips pulled down in a frown.

"I thought I recognized someone," Ash said, letting his hands drop to his sides. "I wanted to see if it was—"

The clash of metal on metal nearby caught his attention. It was much closer than the battle going on in the camp.

Moira looked toward the sound of the noise, her head tilting around in a strange way.

"We should go back," she said. "I'll carry you."

Ash was staring toward the sound of fighting. He couldn't explain it, but he felt a need to go that way. His mind told him he'd be better off heading back, but he also wanted to see if he could blow off some steam and clear his head with a fight.

Maybe I'm more of a cultivator than I thought.

"Let's just look," Ash said, moving towards the fighting.

Growling under her breath, Moira followed along beside him. Drawing her blade from its sheath, she did a double take.

"I still have mana," she said.

"Oh? That's good. That'll make this easier."

"I shouldn't have mana."

"Well, we did kinda channel it through your Dantian rather than whatever it was you did previously. Your Dantian is holding it."

Ash saw movement between the trees up ahead of himself. It looked like a handful of people all circling another.

"That doesn't seem normal," Moira complained. "I asked around a bit in the stables. What you've done isn't supposed to be possible to begin with. Carrying mana into another veil is very… abnormal."

The trees thinned out in front of him and Ash could finally see the fight.

A tall, leggy woman stood amongst a group of humans who were wearing rags. She held a massive two-handed sword that looked impossible to wield.

She was dressed in finery. Expensive clothes that were clearly dyed in unnatural colors and cut to fit her figure.

Her clothes, let alone herself, didn't fit the camp. She clearly didn't belong here.

That and the fact she that had three-foot-long rabbit ears coming out the top of her head, marking her as a Kin. One of the natural inhabitants of this veil.

Her hair and fur was dark black, though he couldn't see her face from here.

"…ie! Just as you've killed so many of us," shouted one of the humans.

Charging forward, he swung a club at her in an overhead smash.

Flicking the blade to one side, she deflected the attack and then slashed at the man. She moved much faster than her frame would seem to allow. Bringing that big blade around as if it were lightweight. It slammed into the man's chest and flung him backward.

Peeling her sword away and back into her original pose, the woman turned her head around to look at the crowd around her. It gave Ash a chance to see her face.

She had delicate features and was quite pretty.

Her bright-green eyes caught on Ash for a brief moment before moving on.

Before she could do anything else, several men charged out at her at the same time. All from different angles.

The reality of combat was that if you were surrounded, it was only a question of time. Especially with a big sword such as that of the Kin's.

Realizing she was about to be overrun, Ash darted forward. The moment she went down in a crush of bodies like that, she'd probably get her head smashed in.

Leading with his swords, he carved his way through the outer ring of bodies as the woman was dogpiled on.

As he slashed and chopped at everything in front of him, it was that long before the group realized they were being attacked.

Moira was beside him, moving her blade with only a bit of hesitancy. She was no swordswoman, but she wasn't an amateur either.

Figuring out that the odds had clearly turned, the survivors ran off, leaving behind their dead and dying.

Ash didn't see the woman when the people cleared away. Looking into the mess of bodies around where she'd been standing, he could see a flash of red clothing and her massive blade.

"Watch them," Ash muttered. Cleaning his swords off on the pants of a dying woman with a gut wound, he stepped into the center.

Reaching down, he grabbed the Rabbit woman under her armpits and started hauling her free. Her head lolled backward, her green eyes staring up at him.

A large knot was forming on her temple, and her eyes seemed to be focusing and unfocusing.

"Not sure you understand Kingdom," Ash said softly. "But I mean you no harm. Just getting you clear and away from here."

The Kin hadn't let go of her sword, and the tip was dragging along through the dirt alongside her boots.

"Ash, we should leave her and go," Moira said, her big yellow eyes studying their surroundings.

"We leave her here and she dies. I don't really want to do that."

Grunting, Moira kept looking to the trees around them.

"Can't really take her with us, either. They'll slave brand her the moment you get her to the camp. And if we stay here, the veil will close eventually and strand us," Moira pressed. "They're regrouping. There's more of them, too."

Ash lifted his head and looked ahead. He could just barely see people out there, moving around.

Probably collecting their wounded and dead before they rush us.

Leave her to die, take her with us and have the first cultivator with a slave seal claim her, or stay here and be stranded.

Could I at least have one option that wasn't garbage?

"Project a slave symbol onto her forehead. Use her blood to draw the symbol and seal it with your own," Locke commanded.

Immediately, a circular design appeared on her brow. Glowing in the same way the traces for Moira's back had.

Choosing, Ash dropped the Kin to the ground and dabbed a finger into her bleeding temple. Quickly, he sketched out the design Locke had supplied.

Thankfully, it only took a few seconds.

No sooner than he'd finished, he reached down and sliced his pinky on her blade, then pressed the bloody digit to the center of the symbol.

Flashing red, the symbol sparked to life and then sank into her flesh. The Kin made no move and said nothing. She only stared at him with her green eyes.

"Ok, let's get out of here," Ash said. He took her sword from her hand and stored it in his ring. Picking her up, he tossed her over his shoulders in a fireman's carry and started jogging back to their camp.

"You're going to enslave her?" Moira asked.

"Already did. I plan on treating her just like you. So let me ask you, do I treat you like a slave?" Ash asked as he moved.

"No. You do not."

Sixteen

They were finally approaching the Jade Fist Sect's home location. Its "school" as it was called. It was huge.

A massive sprawling campus that seemed to dominate the entire landscape.

When people described it, they had always spoken of it as a place where everyone trained and learned.

In Ash's head, he'd simply converted the Spark's Jump Sect and made it larger.

His guess had been nowhere near reality.

The Jade Fist was almost a city unto itself. With sleeping quarters, dining halls, training areas, gardening, forestry, blacksmithing—everything a city would need to survive on its own.

The Jade Fist was self-sufficient, powerful, and not even the local top-tier sect.

"Ash, she's waking up," Moira said.

Looking over into Ying Yue's cart, he saw the Rabbit woman's eyes slowly moving around. It was obvious she was inspecting her surroundings.

"Do you think she understands us?" Ying Yue asked, peering back over the driver's seat of the cart.

"Unlikely," Jia said with a chopping motion of her hand. "Most do not learn Kingdom."

"I did," Moira said with a small smile.

"You are an outlier, and smarter than the vast majority of outlanders," Jia said, holding to her previous statement.

"Well, we can't really have her going around not understanding anyone," Ash said.

He looked to Ying Yue.

"I swear on my life, and bind myself in full view of the heavens, to never betray your secrets," Ying Yue said.

Ash raised his eyebrows at that. He hadn't even had a chance to ask her to swear to not betray him.

"I have eyes. I can see talent. I can see someone marked," Ying Yue said. "I'll not stand in the way of destiny."

Ash shook his head at that. "You sound like Jia."

He pulled a transference page from his ring that he'd made before they left. It was for reading and writing the language of the nine kingdoms.

Having learned it in the Hall, he knew it was something he could transfer.

He held it out between two fingers to the Rabbit woman.

During the entire exchange, she'd remained perfectly still. Watching them without saying a word.

Green eyes stared at him before looking to the paper.

Nodding, Ash mimicked holding the paper to his forehead, then held it back out to her again.

The Kin took the paper and frowned at him, then slowly pressed it to her forehead.

"She's gonna be laid up for a bit," Ash said, looking back to the gate of the Jade Fist Sect.

"It put me flat for an hour each time," Jia murmured. "I thought for sure he had ulterior motives in mind."

Ying Yue frowned, looking to Jia.

"Why would he? You thought he was going to rob you?" she asked.

Good point there. That statement doesn't make sense from the outside.

You finally going to drop the disguise?

"Since we are sharing secrets as a group. I am a woman," Jia said simply, with a shrug of her shoulders. "I am the firstborn of a middle-realm family, attempting to escape my family's grasp.

"Also, I have learned several abilities that are far in excess of what should be possible. In fact, they would be treasures even in my home realm.

"Ash gave them to me for nothing."

Ying Yue's gaze had changed from curious to appraising.

Even Ash was a touch surprised. He had no idea that Jia had come from the middle realm. That was where people began the path to generate a true Dao. There were families there with a number of Dao practitioners.

"I am a master Spell-Blade," Moira said. "And I'm able to cast my spells without repercussion now. I grow stronger every day, and my ability is already stronger than it was previously. I require little preparation to cast anymore, and simply draw on my wells.

"Ash is the reason. He performed a type of carving on my back. For no reason other than that I asked."

Ying Yue looked between the two women and then to Ash.

He shrugged at her. There was nothing in his memories that could tell him what a Spell-Blade was.

Probably a body refiner?

"Fated One. Marked multiple times," Ying Yue said, shaking her head at him.

"As for me," Ying Yue said slowly, turning forward again. "I carry a grand master's seal from the free-merchants guild. I've already purchased a shop and home in the Jade Fist Sect brokered through them, with full permissions, and will be trading out of it. I'm the youngest in the guild, in their history, and already have more wealth than many of them.

"I earned this because of Ash and the deals he made through me, providing me with the ability to do so. I became an equal to family and sect merchants simply due to my access to Ash's spirit stones.

"Which he shared with me for nothing."

"And what of you then, Ash? What secret do you hold?" Jia asked, looking to him. "It would seem you are far from ordinary now. Events seem to be spiraling out from around you."

"Uh," he said intelligently.

"Do not speak of me, or what I am. Though you could probably tell them of the ring, and that you came from another world. It would actually be believable," Locke said.

Looking around, Ash confirmed no one else was nearby. They'd be crossing over into the Jade Fist Sect city proper soon, though. If he wanted to speak of it without the possibility of someone hearing him, it'd be now.

"I'm not from the Kingdom… or any other veils… I'm from a different world. Perhaps a different universe," Ash said. "And I have a storage ring I found that is far more than a storage ring."

All three women nodded their heads at the same time.

They weren't surprised, and Locke had apparently been right. It was a believable explanation for them.

"That explains much," Moira murmured.

"It does," Jia agreed.

Everyone fell silent after their group sharing. The wagon moved along slowly in their place in the traveling column.

They passed through the guard checkpoint and gate without concern. The recruiter at the head of the procession had already confirmed and checked everyone in, Ash supposed.

"This is where we part ways," Ying Yue said with a smile. "I'll track you down later today, once I settle the wagon and shop. I'll keep a hold of this one for now."

Ying Yue pointed to the blank-eyed Rabbit woman in her cart.

"Thanks Yue," Ash said, giving her a wave. "See you later."

Turning her wagon off the street they were on, she headed down another.

"Could you go with her, Moira?" Ash asked after a second. "Keep an eye on the newcomer. I get the impression she might try to do something stupid."

"Hmm? Alright. That'll save me from being bored and having to watch whatever it is the other cultists make you do."

"Be safe," Moira said. She gave him a pat on the back before she followed Ying Yue.

"You treat her like an equal," Jia said neutrally as they were slowly pressed up into the people ahead of them.

Whatever was going on up ahead, it was taking some time for each person.

"She is an equal, isn't she? It's not as if she didn't fight with us on the road."

Jia opened her mouth, then closed it. "True… you did not actually order her to assist. In fact, you have not given her an order until today, truly. Even then, it was open for her to decline.

"She does as you ask."

"…will be tested for their element, given their rank, and placed accordingly. Do not use abilities or cultivation unless asked to do so," said a young man walking down the line. "Students will be tested for their element, given…"

His voice grew fainter as he passed by and continued down the line.

Just like the airport security guards. Saying the same thing all day.

Please have your laptops in a separate tray and your carry-on in another.

"All will be well. Everyone mistakes you for an outlander rather than a Fated One," Jia said, touching his forearm.

Ash didn't reply, just watched the line move.

***

"Name?" asked a middle-aged man hunched over a desk.

They'd brought Ash into this small, empty room when he'd made it to the front of the line.

"Ashley Sheng, of the Sheng family. I have a brother and sister here already," Ash said, watching the man who paid him no attention at all.

"Sheng? Sheng… Sheng." The man leaned over and picked up a different scroll at his side, then started to read through it.

"Ah… they would be… Jing and Yan?"

"Yes, that's them," Ash said with a grin.

"Hmph. Your current rank?" the man asked.

The way his tone changed after confirming the relations felt strange to Ash, but he didn't have a way to question it without being rude.

"Rank four."

The man nodded and jotted something down.

"And how many abilities did you learn from the…" Pausing, the man looked to another sheet of parchment next to the one he was reading. "Spark's Jump Sect."

"None," Ash said honestly.

Sighing, the man nodded his head.

"Please activate your cultivation for me," said the man. Holding up his left hand, he began to release Essence in a steady stream.

Ash blinked and then immediately utilized his actual cultivation skill.

It felt sluggish, though.

Sluggish and very slow.

"You lost that fight with Jia, remember? You're still suffering a backlash."

Crap. I won't be able to do much in the way of training for a bit, then. I'll have to wait until it goes away.

I completely forgot about that.

Damn.

Resigning himself, Ash made the best of a bad situation and focused entirely on cultivating.

"Your ability is rank two of ten," the man said, writing something down and ending his Essence flow. "You'll be almost the lowest-ranking disciple we have in the Outer Ring. Don't let that stop you, though. You'll receive the same rewards as the bottom ten percent of the disciples, and you can always improve your standing through duels.

"Do that enough and you'll move into the next bracket and receive better rewards."

Reaching behind him, he picked up a marker with a key on it and then set it down on the table. "Rooms are assigned by arrival. I hope you spoke to those in front of you and behind you in line; they'll be your neighbors.

"Exit the door to your left, and follow the path until you reach your new home. Numbers are marked clearly by posts.

"Good luck."

Before Ash had even fully grasped the placard with its key, the man had turned to the door. "Next!"

Moving to the exit, Ash stumbled along in a bit of a stunned silence.

He'd expected to be treated poorly, but even this seemed negligent to the point of retardation. *How do they even manage to help their members grow? Is this just a bigger, dumber version of Spark's Jump?*

Exiting through the indicated door, Ash kept his feet moving.

"Doesn't matter," he said to himself. "I'm not here to grow or learn or anything. I'm here to help Yan and Jing. That's it.

"After I get settled in, I'll go see them. See if the stones I sent them helped out and if they need more."

Ash nodded once, firming up his thoughts.

Watching his left and right, he wandered down the dirt path, looking from marker to marker as he went.

The houses all had the same cookie-cutter exterior. The only differences were in their decorations. Pots, plants, a banner, a city or clan flag were fairly common adornments.

"Forty-two?" Ash asked, glancing at his marker again and then to the post. "Forty-two. Alright. That's… a bit odd."

Anything with the number four was typically omitted in this culture. It was simply an unlucky number that seemed to go hand in hand with death.

Walking toward the door, Ash gave it a quick once-over.

It wasn't anything special. If anything, it looked like an oversized ranch house back in California. "Going to be comfy for Moira, myself, and the Rabbit woman in there.

"Let's hope it's bigger than it seems on the outside."

"Ah, a new disciple," said a voice behind Ash.

Restraining his frustration and snapping his mouth shut before he said something he'd regret, Ash turned around.

A younger man in the robes of the Jade Fist was smiling at him. He looked like every other person he'd seen lately. Lean, fit, brown hair, brown eyes.

"Good morning. I'm your house elder. I'm responsible for those in the buildings from one to one hundred," said the man. "Since I've found you so early, let's proceed with your elemental Qi test and move from there. This'll make it that much easier for you to settle in."

"Elemental Qi test?" Ash asked, honestly unsure of the situation.

"Yes. For us to place you with an appropriate elder for Qi classes, we'll need to determine the element that resides in your Qi.

"Push some out from your palm, but keep it controlled with your Spiritual Sense."

Spiritual Sense…? I don't even –

"*I believe Spiritual Sense is just a way of saying your focus. In the abilities that mention it, it seems to be a visualization of your focus and intent,*" Locke said, interrupting Ash's startled thoughts.

Blinking rapidly, Ash held up a hand and began to force some of his Qi out through his palm. He focused his entire being on keeping the Qi in a tight, small ball. Just above the flesh of his hand.

A small, translucent, unmoving sphere appeared in his palm. Sitting there, it seemed more like a rock than anything else.

"Huh. I'm not really sure what element that is," said the house elder. Reaching out with a finger, he poked the Qi lightly. "Very solid. Hm. The coloring is more like Wind than Earth though.

"We'll put you in with the odd ones for now until we can figure out what it actually is."

"Odd… ones?" Ash asked, not sure he liked the way it'd been said.

"Ah, yes, sorry. They're those who have elemental Qi that doesn't quite match up. Like having Water the element, but not fresh water."

"That… can happen?"

"It's rare, but it can happen. The Nine Kingdoms is a vast place, and the lowest realm. To believe we know everything would be a calamity," said the house elder with a smile. "Alright. I'll assign you accordingly. You can dismiss your Qi now."

Writing something down on a paper Ash hadn't noticed, the house elder nodded to himself.

"Ah, before you go—I was wondering if you could help me?" Ash asked, wondering if this could be his chance.

"Mm?" The House Elder didn't look up from his scroll as he continued to write.

"Could you direct me to the houses of Jing Sheng and Yan Sheng? They're my family and I'd like to see them."

Hand freezing in mid-stroke, the house elder looked at Ash quietly for a moment.

"Ah… Jing is in the upper-numbered homes. You'll not be able to enter that area without a pass. Yan is… Yan is in house number four."

"Four?" Ash asked.

"Yes, she lost a series of duels. Ah… I'll be going now. Excuse me."

Frowning as the house elder left quickly, Ash was at a loss. It felt like a lot had gone unsaid in that conversation.

"If she's in house four… that means I already passed her. Let's go see her. I can inspect the house another time.

"In fact, maybe I can pick her up and then head over to get Yue and Moira."

Ash turned around the way he'd come and started heading back.

Paying a bit more attention this time, he noticed that the further he got to the lowest number, the worse the path was.

Stopping at number ten, Ash was confused. Looking to the left of the path and behind himself a ways, he could clearly see the course he'd taken from his testing.

These homes were so far off the beaten path that one would have to literally walk further away from testing to reach them.

Why would Yan be back here but Jing somewhere else? Did he get forced into an alliance or something?

When they'd left together, they'd been as thick as thieves. Where one had gone, the other had followed.

Ash finally reached house number four. It was much like all the other homes he'd seen, though it was devoid of decorations. The path outside and leading up to it was nothing but rutted dirt. What little grass existed was clearly dying, and the entire front area would soon be little more than a field of dirt.

Feeling rather annoyed, and like his temper was slowly starting to boil, Ash headed for the front door.

Taking a short breath, he knocked on the door firmly.

"Go away, I have nothing left to fight me over," came a voice from inside.

Startled and shocked, Ash didn't know how to respond.

It had sounded like Yan, but not like something Yan would say.

"Did you not hear me? Go away!"

The door snapped open as the voice finished talking, and Ash was face to face with Yan.

She was a few inches taller than him. Her eyes were black like pitch and her hair looked as if it had been painted with ink. Her face was as pale as death, on the other hand.

Pale to the point of looking sickly.

"Ash?" she whispered, looking at him.

Grinning, he held his arms open to her.

"I'm not here to fight you for something, but if I have to fight for something, I'll fight for a hug," he said.

Yan's eyes blinked slowly, and then she lunged forward and wrapped him up in a tight, smothering hug.

Then she started bawling, her face pressed into his neck. Deep, sobbing wails seemed to come up from the very pit of her soul.

Awkwardly, Ash wrapped his arms around her and patted her back.

"There, there. How about you invite me in and we can talk? Clearly something has gone wrong," he said.

Seventeen

Managing to crab walk in through the open door, Ash dragged Yan along with him.

Her furniture looked battered and worn, though sturdy. She had nothing of any value that one couldn't get cheaply at any market stall in her home.

The new problem, though, was trying to get her to talk.

Getting into the home had proved to be much easier in retrospect than getting her to calm down. Her hysterical crying continued for what felt like forever to Ash.

And all he could do was awkwardly pat her on the back and be held by her.

She'd always been kind to him, but she had always kept him at arm's length. In essence, she'd become the stern but watchful older sister he'd never had.

Right now, she was little more than a blubbering mess.

The change was shocking to him.

Sniffling, Yan wiped at her face with her hands, her eyes moving everywhere but to Ash. She let herself be seated into a chair directly next to a second, which Ash took.

"Are you visiting?" she asked finally, her voice almost steady. "Did Mother and Father ask you to come see how we… I was doing?"

"No. I joined the sect, actually. Mother and Father did say you and Jing weren't doing so well, though. It's what prompted me to come see what I could do to help. Or at least, to support you two," Ash said. "I take it you didn't get my letter? Or at least, you maybe didn't believe it?"

"Letter?" Yan asked, her fingers brushing at her eyes again. "You joined the sect?"

"Ah… yeah. I sent a letter. Along with one hundred spirit stones for you," Ash said, shaking his head. "I paid for a special courier. It should have made it here. I sent one for you and one for Jing."

Yan's mouth hung open, her hands halfway between her lap and her face.

"You sent one to each of us?" she asked.

"Yeah. A letter for you, and a hundred spirit stones for each of you."

"Where did you even get two hundred spirit stones? No, no, wait. You sent it to both of us… and not that long ago?"

"Not that long ago at all. It was—"

"He stole them," Yan said, interrupting him.

"What?"

"He stole them. He stole the stones you sent me, and the letter." Yan's eyes unfocused and she looked to the middle distance.

"Who stole them? I sent it to you. The courier?"

"No. Jing. He stole them. He suddenly had a lot of wealth on his hands not long ago. He bought a number of abilities, made friends, and left me… here. Alone.

"And I've lost everything since then."

Yan laughed softly, tears starting to spill down her face again.

"Brother Jing… why did you do this to me? All for a hundred stones," she murmured.

Ash wasn't quite sure what to say. The series of events seemed painfully easy to follow.

It was just almost too hard to believe, though.

Yan looked up at him and gave him a smile.

"I'm glad to see you, Ash. Though I fear there is not much you can do for me. Whatever you did to get those stones for me was wasted.

"I'm so sorry," she said.

Ash let out a slow breath, then snorted.

"I wouldn't worry about those stones. I have significantly more available, and I can get more if we need.

"Let's… let's assume that maybe we're wrong about Jing for now. What do you need immediately?" Ash asked. "What would be the best thing for you, today?"

Yan nodded her head a bit.

"I need to buy a better cultivation skill. The one I'm using isn't ideal for me, but it was all I could afford.

"There was no way I'd be able to earn any resources without cultivating, either, so I was trapped."

"That's not a problem. I'll get you a cultivation skill. When you left home, you were an Earth element. Has that changed?"

"No. But… how are you going to get a skill? Ash, you didn't even have your Dantian open when I left.

"I'm so glad you were able to do so, but I honestly don't see—"

"Get out here, Yan!" shouted a voice from outside. "I've come to fight you for the simple joy of beating you to the ground."

Yan's face froze up, and her eyes partially glazed over.

"Yan!" shouted the voice from outside.

"The scan I've performed shows a group of people outside. At least ten. They are all equal to your strength or less.

"None should be a problem if you wanted to fight them," Locke said.

Ash looked to the door and clicked his tongue.

He wasn't someone who would run to a fight. To battle for the sake of it.

But he was someone who would go all out on anyone who went after his family.

"Is there any law in the sect I should know about in regard to hurting, maiming, or killing other disciples?" Ash asked.

"What? Uhm, hurting is acceptable in duels. Maiming is frowned upon, and killing another member will get you kicked out.

"What—"

Ash got to his feet and stormed over to the door. Before he reached it, he activated all his abilities and set them to run at full.

Opening the door, he stepped outside.

A group of young men and women were all surrounding another young man who was several steps out in front of the rest.

They'd all had smug looks on their faces when Ash had first stepped out. Now they all looked confused.

"You're looking for a fight? I'll take you up on it," Ash said. "Will you fight me, then? Or will you tuck your tail between your legs and run away and hide?"

"Ah…" the man said. "I don't even know who you are. Why should I fight you?"

"Who I am? This is day one for me. I just joined the sect. Today, no less.

"If you can't even fight a day-one disciple, do you deserve to be here?" Ash asked. "But if you need a reason to fight me, I'll give you one.

"I'll bet with you. Care to make a wager and then let me decorate the ground with your face?"

"You insignificant speck!" hissed the man. His entire demeanor had changed when he heard Ash had just joined. "I'll fight you. No need to offer me a wager."

The man dropped into a fighting pose, then charged at Ash without another word.

"Wind Slash Punch!" shouted the man, throwing his fist forward.

Swirling translucent Wind Qi surrounded the man's fist.

To Ash, it seemed almost slow. So slow it seemed to be crawling through the air as it came at him.

We'll make this a lesson and a point. They can leave Yan alone, or I can repeat this lesson for whoever else.

Stepping forward, Ash stomped his foot and lashed out with a punch toward the man's stomach. At the same time, Ash made sure to dodge the attack coming his way, but with the barest of margins.

Sinking satisfyingly into the man's stomach Ash planned his next several steps out.

Grabbing the man's extended arm, Ash activated his Spring Step and shoved. Crunching grotesquely, the man's elbow inverted.

Holding tightly to the now-maimed arm, Ash stomped out with his left foot, kicking out at his foe's kneecap.

A sickening squish heralded the fact that the kneecap was now folded the wrong way.

Falling over to one side, the man was struggling to take in a breath. More than likely to scream.

Deciding to finish this off decisively, Ash snapped his elbow around and cracked it into the man's jaw.

The man's head was knocked to one side, and he went down in an unmoving heap.

Standing up, Ash clapped his hands together and brushed them off on his hips.

"Anyone else? If not, pick up this piece of human shit and fuck off," Ash said, looking to the shocked crowd.

"You! How dare—" a woman started to say, stepping forward.

Moving toward the woman, Ash started to ready himself to attack her.

Freezing in place like a deer in headlights, the woman stared at Ash.

"Take. Him. Away. Or I'll put you all down, one by one," Ash said through clenched teeth.

Cowed and insulted, the group picked up the young man and hurried off.

Letting out a short breath, Ash turned around and headed back to Yan's house.

Standing in her doorway, Yan was staring at him as if she'd only seen him now for the first time.

"Ash?" she asked, her voice light.

"Yeah?"

"You… you really are Ash, right?"

"Yeah, I am," he said. Then he stopped, evaluating the look she was giving him.

The way she was peering at him made it seem as if she'd woken up next to a snake.

Maybe she needs a little time.

"I'll leave you be for now, Yan. Let you relax and think on how you want to take this."

Ash looked back the way he came, then towards the last three homes in the row.

House number one looked as if it were completely forgotten. To the point that even the road that led up to the path was practically overgrown.

It was out of the way and practically a non-existence.

Ignored.

He liked the idea of it. The idea that he only had one neighbor, and that people would leave him alone. He saw no reason to try and work his way up in the numbers for the sake of a simple housing ranking system.

"I think I'm going to go claim house number one right now. After that, I need to go meet some friends. Come visit me later when you're ready to talk. I'll try to have a cultivation ability and some skills ready for you by then."

Ash waved a hand at Yan and made his way over to the home at the end.

Getting close, Ash looked to the wall that was on the far side of house number one. It was a large thing. At least twenty feet tall and most likely quite thick as well.

Looking at it, he couldn't quite identify the feeling, but the wall felt out of place.

Dismissing it for now, Ash turned down the tiny path that led up to the front door.

Knocking on the door firmly but calmly, Ash waited in silence.

"Yes?" came a voice from inside.

"Good day to you," Ash said. "I've come to challenge you for your home. I'm from house forty-two. You can either fight me for your home, or simply exchange me.

"In either case, I do believe you'll technically benefit from the exchange."

The door opened and a nondescript young man stood there in a threadbare robe.

"You want this house? You're from house forty-two?" he asked.

"Indeed, here's the marker. I moved in today and haven't even gone inside. Would you exchange with me? Or shall I challenge you?" Ash said, holding out the mentioned marker.

The young man looked from Ash to the marker.

"I'll take it," he said. He took the marker from Ash, dropped his own in its place, and took off in a fast walk.

Nodding at his success, Ash smiled and walked into his new home.

Let's find out what we're missing, go see Yue, and come back.

***

"We're the top rank already?" Moira asked, looked at the numbered home. "For being the top rank, the home seems quite poor."

"Opposite of that. Rank one is the least. But it also only has one neighbor, and people will leave me alone."

"It also means I don't have to fight people for their homes," Ash said with a chuckle.

"That would definitely fit your personality," Moira said, nodding as she opened the door and peered inside. "I can also see why you said you wanted to buy all new furniture."

"Yeah, it's safe to say the furniture is battered. And that's still a compliment," Ash said, stepping past the winged woman into the home.

With a casual walk-through of the house, he replaced all the furniture with the newer items he'd purchased.

In the end, the home had turned out to have a two-bedroom layout. It'd work for now, but Ash was already planning on digging out and creating a basement. He was no handy man, but he figured he could dig and brace the walls accordingly.

That and wood planks aren't expensive. Board the walls, paint it up, throw in some rugs, and it'll be a finished basement.

Well, as finished as I can make it, at least.

Sighing as he replaced the front door with a new one, which had a working lock and was solid wood through and through, Ash was done.

Moving into the second bedroom he found Moira and the Rabbit woman sitting on their beds. They were talking in low tones.

Apparently, the Kin was named Tala-Tala. Though she had asked to be addressed as Tala.

Leaning up against the door frame, Ash made enough noise to herald his arrival. He didn't want them to think he was sneaking up on them.

Both women looked up at him.

"And what do you want, slaver?" Tala asked, her brows coming down low over her eyes.

Moira's eyes snapped to Tala and her mouth turned into a small frown.

"Just checking on you. I imagine I'll probably settle in for some cultivation in a moment and will end up somewhat occupied. Figured I'd see if you needed anything," Ash said.

"I need you to free me," Tala said, her hands clenching at her sides.

"Would if I could. It doesn't seem I can remove the seal, though. Already tried.

"And even if I could, it's not like you could cross the veil. It's shut and unlikely to open any time soon.

"So… I take it there's nothing you need?"

"If possible, could you give her back her blade? I'd like to work on sparring with her in the backyard," Moira said.

"Oh, of course."

Ash opened up his storage and immediately transferred the big two-handed blade out of the space.

"Anything else?"

"Ah, no. Thank you, Ash," Moira said, giving him a smile. "Did you decide what you wanted to do for dinner?"

"Not as of yet. It's a pity you'll be unable to hunt here. I was getting used to having you take care of it."

Moira's smile grew larger. "I'll see what I can do, but as you said, hunting does not seem possible."

Leaving the two women to themselves, Ash went to his own room.

"Locke, I want to enter the Hall. Did you finish up with the sight ability?

"And the abilities for Yan?"

"Yes. Both tasks are completed."

Closing the door to his room, Ash sat on his bed and folded his legs up underneath himself.

Sinking down into a meditative state, he began to cultivate.

Letting his Qi pool above his head, he watched as Essence began to slowly flow towards it from all around him.

Feeling confident that he'd set himself up to cultivate while he was spiritually inside his ring, Ash entered the Hall.

Everything looked the same, except it wasn't.

The grass was short.

Mowed, one might say.

The grounds were clean, the stones intact and correctly positioned. Everything about the exterior of the Hall was as one would expect it to be.

If it were new.

Walking over to the door that had been barely attached the first time, Ash found it had changed too. It was a solid door now, with a bronze handle, bronze hinges, and freshly stained.

"It's all cleaned up," Ash said aloud.

"I constantly pull in all the Essence you have no need of or can't use. It's one of the reasons you're always gaining Essence as well. Even when you're not cultivating," Locke said.

"That makes sense."

Ash walked into the Hall's main building and continued into the library.

This room looked the same, though it seemed the number of shelves had increased significantly.

"Come down to the evaluation room. We'll talk about the vision ability first," Locke said.

Following the suggestion, Ash entered and looked to the projection wall, where the vision ability was listed in simple terms.

"The ability as it existed had many limitations. It mostly concerned itself with seeing through the strength of others," Locke said.

The words on the wall blurred out and were replaced before Ash could read them all.

"I've rewritten the skill and blended it with some other skills we had in the Hall. I've also scaled it to increase in power with you.

"It won't take more than what you can give right now, though," Locke continued. "I think you'll find my changes… interesting."

"Oh? How come?" Ash said, wondering if the wall would be replaced with new data.

"You'll see. Now, would you like to discuss your other request?"

"Ah… yeah. Let's talk about that."

"Nothing we have is suitable for Yan, due to her current cultivation and her Dantian."

"I… what?"

"The cultivation skill she's using has corrupted her Qi Sea. It's why she's so weak and unable to advance herself."

Ash clicked his tongue. "Fine, I want a way to—"

"Fix it? I assumed you would. I've already prepped up an entire set of abilities for her.

"She'll have to self-rupture her Dantian, though, and let her Qi Sea drain completely.

"It'll take her a month or two to get back to where she was, but her growth will be significantly better after that," Locke said.

"What a cluster fuck," Ash muttered.

"On an unrelated note, I've taken the liberty of preparing an entire workup for Tala and Ying Yue as well. Her elemental Qi is Wood, while Tala's is Fire," Locke said.

"Huh? They're not cultivators, though. Tala's not even from this veil. How could she possibly use our abilities?"

"It would appear that she has some kind of internal power. Though it routes through her Dantian, it does not remain there. She could not store anything.

"You'll need to apply a similar carving to her back as you did for Moira, but I do believe she'll be able to function somewhere similar to yourself and Moira.

"Not a mage, not a cultivator, but something akin to it. Given her disposition, I also made sure to select all close-combat and strengthening abilities," Locke said. "For Ying Yue, it is simply that her Dantian isn't large enough to open on its own. It's a hair shy. A fraction of a fraction. We can force it open."

Ash ran a hand through his hair as he considered the situation.

"Alright. I'll leave it up to them. Help me draw up the transference papers later and we'll give it to Yue then.

"Same for the script for Tala's back."

"If you don't have any other requests, I recommend returning to your cultivation. You should be able to reach the sixth rank relatively quickly.

"And be sure to test out your new vision ability.

"I called it Sneaky Peeky."

Ash snorted at that and left the Hall.

Popping back into his body, he took in a slow, deep breath.

He could feel someone else in the room with him.

Opening his eyes, he found Jia sitting in his desk chair.

Watching him.

"The longer you cultivate, the more the Essence flows to you. It is interesting to watch. I need only be in your presence while you cultivate and I can gain benefits from it," she said.

Blinking twice, Ash let his cultivation drop and gave Jia his full attention.

"Imagine my surprise when I showed up at your home only to find someone else there. I did not expect you to move so quickly," she said.

Really looking at her, Ash was confused for a moment.

She was wearing a blue dress. One that fit and formed to her body, and definitely showed off her attributes as a woman.

Moving from her dress to her face, he found she'd let her hair down in a more feminine look as well, and she was once again wearing eye makeup.

"Ah?" Ash mumbled.

"Noticed, have you?" Jia asked, looking down at herself. "I realized there was no point in hiding anymore, now that I have been accepted here.

"I will not reveal who I am, but I do not need to hide as a man any longer."

Suppose that makes sense. I wonder if I can use that ability on her?

Ash mentally tried to access Sneaky Peeky.

Two colored bars appeared above Jia's head. One red, one yellow. Inside each bar was a series of numbers.

Below those bars were a series of small boxes with icons.

Focusing on the colored bars, Ash realized they were a health bar and a Qi bar.

Looking to the boxes, he focused on the first one.

It was colored blue, and the moment his attention caught it, it expanded until it had a small window that could be read.

You would probably win this fight… it's not certain, though.

Moving his eyes from that box to the next one, he watched as the first one rolled back up onto itself.

Then the second one unrolled.

Slightly panicked. Elevated heart rate, breathing rate increased. Partially suppressed through concentration and abilities.

"…like the furniture though," Jia said, her eyes moving back to his. Then she gave him a smile.

"Yeah. Uhm, yeah. Needed to do something about it, so I bought all this. The previous owner didn't have much, it seemed."

Shit, Locke turned my life into a HUD.

I think I'll need to ask him how he did that, because… there are way too many books I've read where they're just stuck in a video game.

Eighteen

Ash looked at the modest meal that had been loaded up on his tray.

It was the only one the Jade Fist provided for its cultivators. The Outer Sect disciples here weren't a high enough rank to minimize their bodily needs.

Those elevated figures only needed to eat perhaps once a week. By mutual agreement of those same figures, the meal that was to be provided was breakfast.

If you can call it that.

Sighing, Ash resigned himself to what he assumed was flavorless oatmeal and bread.

"I mean, if you can't eat good food, what's the point? Why bother eating at all?" Ash mumbled, moving over to an empty table.

Looking at those around him, Ash was momentarily distracted by the number of health and energy bars crowded around the room.

Turning off the sight ability, he felt immediately better.

He'd also had a long chat the night before with Locke, who had assured him in every way possible that this wasn't a video game.

That Locke himself was providing that information via scans and the ability in real time.

"Somewhat paltry, is it not?"

Looking to his side, he watched as Jia sank into the seat next to him.

She was Jia the woman again. Jia the young man was long gone.

Smirking at her, he clicked his tongue. "Isn't it, though? I almost wonder if it might be worth skipping it in the future and having breakfast by ourselves."

"Is that an invitation?"

"I don't see why not. I'll ask the others if they'd like to join us. Maybe we could have it at Yue's house. She's got the biggest one amongst us."

Jia raised an eyebrow at that. "She does? I have not seen it yet."

"Come with me after breakfast, I planned on visiting her and making sure she's squared away."

"I only saw her for a moment yesterday after you left."

"You went to see her?"

"Yeah. I needed to make some last-minute purchases. That and I gave her some of my money as an investment.

"I figure she's more likely to spin it into profit than it will do anything sitting in my ring."

Jia wrinkled her nose as she leaned over her oatmeal. After taking her spoon in hand, she lowered it into the dull-looking meal. Looking nonplussed, she scooped out a mouthful and ate it.

"So… is it awful?" Ash asked, watching her.

Jia's eyes narrowed and looked to him. Chewing daintily, she raised a hand in front of her mouth.

"It is rather rude to watch a lady eat," she said after finishing her bite. "As to the value in the meal… it tastes as if it were made of soggy paper."

"I've watched you before and you've never said anything—why now?" Ash asked, turning to his own bowl.

"Because others are watching. You are not sitting next to your friend anymore."

"True enough, I'm sitting next to a pretty lady. I'm sure they all want to know who you are. I'll try not to scare off potential suitors," Ash said with a grin. Dipping his spoon into the mush, he lifted it up and gave it a taste.

It was exactly as she'd described. In all of its meaningless glory.

"Pretty? No, that is pretty," Jia said, indicating something with her chin.

Following the direction she'd motioned toward, Ash saw a young woman who had just entered.

She was slim, small, delicate, and looked pale to the point of being sickly. Even her face looked diminutive.

"I guess. If you like little kids. Little kids with skin like a fish belly. I mean, has she never been in the sun? Pass. Your own skin color seems much more natural to me. Not tan but not ghostly white," Ash said. Dismissing the woman, if she was even that, he went back to his tasteless meal.

"You are a strange man."

Says the woman who won't use contractions.

"Ash."

Looking to his left, Ash smiled when he realized it was Yan. She sat down next to him, her own meal looking as pathetic as his own.

"Good morning, Yan," he said.

"Morning, Yan," Jia said from his other side.

"Ah, hello there. I don't think we've met. Who would yo—wait, Jia?" Yan asked, peering at the other woman. "Why are you dressed like a woman?"

"Because I am a woman, Yan," Jia said with a smile. "It is good to see you. Though I hear there are concerns with Jing."

Yan's expression looked somewhere between shock and despair. Finally she sighed, her shoulders slumping partially.

"So it seems. I sent him a letter that I'd like to talk to him tomorrow. We'll see what he says," Yan said.

It was obvious what she already believed, but he couldn't blame her for trying to hold out for hope.

"Well, I have good news anyways," Ash said. "I can help you fix your cultivation. You'll have to damage your Dantian and empty your Qi Sea first, though. I can guarantee your strength will be back to where it is now within a month.

"And that's if you don't purchase pills or anything like that."

"I don't have any money to buy things like that with. And my weekly allotment has… has been taken from me each time," Yan murmured, almost under her breath.

"Taken?" Ash asked, anger starting to bubble in his stomach.

"Calm, Ash. Calm," Yan said, laying a hand against his forearm. She gave him a smile that he hadn't seen since she'd left for the Jade Fist.

Of his adoptive family, Yan was the one who understood him. Knew his temper. Seemed to understand exactly when his anger was starting to break free.

"Taken from me. I wasn't able to protect what was mine in duels. And no one else was willing to step in for me so… it became a vicious circle."

Ash harrumphed at that and then chewed at his lip.

"We'll go see Yue today, then. I'll have her set up an allowance for you so you can purchase what you need through her," Ash said, then nodded his head with conviction.

"An allowance…? Ash, I don't understand at all. And I think we should talk more about having me damage my Dantian."

"Of course. Of course. I'm heading over to see Yue after this anyways. Come with Jia and me," Ash said. "We can discuss it when we get there. Moira and Tala are there already, since they're not allowed in here."

"We'll need to stop by the distribution center first. Today is allotment day.

"And who are Yue, Moira, and Tala?" Yan asked, looking from Ash to Jia.

***

"It seems you've had a number of adventures since I last saw you," Yan said. "Two slaves."

Ash shrugged. "I treat them as if they were just companions.

"So tell me what we do here, exactly. We just wait in this line, get whatever they're giving us, and leave?"

"Yes. Though this is also the day most duels occur. As soon as one leaves the center, the normal sect rules apply. Though you can only duel someone within ninety-nine ranks of your own home."

"Ah. That makes more sense. I was wondering why they were so big on numbering everyone."

"And can't you just decline a duel?" Ash asked.

"Well… yes… but… no one would ever dare unless they wanted to be known as a coward," Yan said.

"Better a coward than a beggar." Sighing, Ash moved forward several steps as the line continued to edge forward.

He heard Yan take in a breath as if to argue, only to then let it out in a whoosh.

"You're not wrong. I wouldn't be where I am today if I had walked away," Yan said. She sounded almost wistful. "Jing was there, though. He was as bad off as I was. He wanted us to represent our family."

"Can't eat pride," Ash said. "And respect isn't that great if you're dead."

"Ash, stop. Your sister was doing what she believed was right," Jia admonished.

Falling silent, Ash let the line carry him along

In what felt like forever but was probably closer to ten minutes, Ash received a small green bottle.

Dropping it into his ring he stepped off to the side and yawned.

Off to see the others now. Give Tala her new skills.

I wonder if it's time for lunch? I could use a nap.

Yan and Jia joined him shortly after and the trio began walking off the field.

"I challenged the owner of home number two," Jia said suddenly.

"Oh? Neat. Does that make you my neighbor now?" Ash asked, grinning at her.

"Indeed. Would you mind if I joined you to cultivate tonight? Being around you makes it much easier."

Ash rolled his eyes but waved a hand at her. "Fine, whatever. Though I thi—"

"I challenge you for your pills, Yan. Or you can just hand them over and spare yourself."

Stopping mid-step, Ash looked to the woman who now stood in front of them. Her hair was a blue-black like a raven's wing, and her eyes were as light brown as they came. Almost so much that they glowed.

Her figure was a bit abnormal for this world, though. She had curves in her waist and chest that weren't actually considered attractive here, but would fare better back home.

Ash could easily see trying to chat her up if he got the chance. The attraction was definitely there. It was a pity she was attempting to rob Yan.

Beside her were three other women who all looked much more normal than the first.

Activating Sneaky Peeky, Ash focused on the one in the middle. The one who'd spoken.

The level stated for her was four. Focusing on the first box, which was blue, Ash read the text that popped up.

"Looks like you would have the upper hand."

Next Ash checked the other three. They were all rank three. Each one was listed as: *"Looks like a reasonably safe opponent."*

"Did you hear me, Yan? I chall—"

"I challenge all four of you at the same time," Ash said. "I am Ashley Sheng, younger brother to Yan, and I am in house number one, though I don't care what rank you are. I will match any wager you put up at double.

"Or are you four afraid of having your pride destroyed by the lowest-ranked outer disciple in a four-versus-one fight."

Eight eyes stared at him as if he'd grown a second head and had started yelling at them in a foreign language.

"Hello? Anything in those heads of yours? Or are you just full of empty threats and hot air?" Ash said.

"Can you actually meet our wagers? This might not be cheap, you know?" asked the leader.

"If I can't, I'll be your personal slave till I die. I swear it on the heavens and my soul.

"Now, put up your wagers and let's get this done with. I promise to only break your arms and legs, no joints."

"Or hit you in that lovely face of yours. Well, I'll try not to hit you in the face, at least. I can't really promise that, now can I? I might need to, after all," Ash said, shaking his arms out. "Just have Jia check all the wagers. She's probably the most impartial here."

Ash rapidly activated all his abilities. Bouncing from one foot to the other, he tried to get himself into a warmed-up state as fast as he could.

It was going to take some footwork to move in and out between the four of them while putting them down at the same time.

"Ash, I don't think this is a good idea," Yan said.

"Sure it is. I imagine this is someone who's been robbing you. They'll bet everything they can to argue that I'll be their slave.

"After this, I'm going to give all their wagers to you," Ash said, shaking his wrists out. "Consider it karma."

"Alright, I have received the wagers," Jia said neutrally. "You may begin the fight whenever you like, though I would warn both sides to limit the damage done to each other, if possible."

The women all took different positions, their bodies rigid with whatever poses they needed to maintain.

Start with the one on the far left. She looks unsure. Then move to the leader to knock her off balance. Then decide from there.

Flow.

Use the momentum.

Adjust and become.

Be like water.

Formless. Shapeless.

"Whenever you're ready, then," Ash called.

"Go!" shouted the woman in the lead.

Activating Spring Step, Ash appeared in front of his target.

Quick as he could, he snapped out several strikes. Knocking her leading hand to one side, blasting a punch into her gut, and then a final blow into her kidney.

Slapping his hands to his sides to lock his Qi chains into place, Ash stutter-stepped away from the collapsing woman.

Throwing out a kick as he moved toward the leader, he activated Spring Step again.

His foot blasted into her middle, and the momentum of the blow spun Ash around.

Rotating with the move, he spun around and smashed the back of his fist through the face of the next woman in line.

Oops.

Her head snapped around to one side and she crumpled to the ground, unable to withstand her jaw snapping around like that.

A ball of roiling Fire Qi was bearing down on him from the last woman in the line.

Stepping to the side of it, Ash lashed out with his left hand, taking in the Fire Qi. Bringing the same hand back in, he thrust out with his right hand toward the leader, redirecting the Fire Qi.

As soon as the Fire Qi exited his hand, Ash chased after it.

The giant ball of flame smashed into the leader and washed over her. Ash followed it up with two punches, both aimed at her stomach.

Liver punches are very effective, after all.

Groaning, the woman dropped to her knees and fell over.

Turning around, Ash faced the last woman standing. The one who had thrown the fire at him.

"You may surrender now," Ash said. Around him, the three women were groaning and rolling on the ground. "Or you may join them. You have the amount of time it takes me to reach you."

Falling into a neutral stance, Ash began to prepare to use Spring Step.

"Which isn't long."

"I-I surrender. I surrender," said the last woman, getting down on her knees.

Ash pressed his fists together and disconnected all the chains he had amongst his opponents.

"Thank you for the fight. I'll see you all later and wish you to have a good day," Ash said. "Let's go. I don't want to keep the others waiting."

"The outcome was expected, but not in the way you did it. I now sincerely doubt I could have actually beat you in that duel," Jia said. "I will have to train and try harder."

Yan moved in close to him and immediately began inspecting him. Her hands and fingers were light as they pressed to his jaw and chin.

As she pushed him this way and that, it reminded him of when he'd first met her. Back in the Sheng household before they'd joined the Jade Fist, and before the needs of the family had changed.

He'd been attacked in the Spark's Jump sect often back in that first year. She'd taken on the role of elder sister quickly and had done all in her power to return troubles to those who gave them to him.

Smiling at the memory, Ash let her do as she wished. There was a warmth in his heart for her tender nature.

She'd never done anything other than worry over him and care for his well-being.

When he turned his head up toward her, she looked into his eyes.

"You're ok?" she asked.

"I'm fine."

Yan's mouth thinned out and she continued to stare at him. Several seconds passed before she released him, smacking his shoulder as she did so.

"Ok. As long as you're well," she said.

"I am. Come on, let's go."

Turning on his heel, Ash began leading the other two away from the center of the outer disciple area.

Ying Yue had needed to put up shop outside the disciple territories, in the citizen area.

Though if she agrees and lets me pop her Dantian open, she'll be a rogue cultivator. Suppose it's a good thing we put together a "cultivator basics" learning paper as well, on the off chance she actually agrees.

"What have you planned, Ash?" Yan asked him suddenly.

"Huh?" Ash asked reflexively.

"You have something planned. What is it?"

She always did have a firm grasp on whatever I was doing and thinking.

Ash glanced around them and made sure no one was close enough to hear.

"You're right. I have some plans. When I put together what would work best to fix your own cultivation, I determined that I could turn Tala into something similar.

"That and crack open Yue's Dantian," Ash admitted.

"You can turn citizens into cultivators?" Jia asked, an edge to her voice.

"I think so. Mostly because Yue's Dantian was very close to being able to open. It is just a bit too small."

"Ash… are you a Fated One?" Yan asked.

"No, no. Just someone who's had a number of fortunate encounters as of late. It's all luck, really."

"Keep telling yourself that, Chosen One," Locke interjected.

Turning the corner to the street Yue had picked for her shop, Ash was surprised.

He'd been here yesterday, and it had been mostly deserted.

Here and now, during the day, the street was packed with people. The storefronts on both sides of the street were selling high-priced goods and services.

"This Ying Yue… does she have a wealthy backer? If she is on Gold street, then she must have a great deal of wealth," Yan said.

"Ash is her backer," Jia said simply.

"Ash?" Yan asked in a confused tone.

"Yes. Ash is her backer. There is no one else. I have spoken with her briefly about her past.

"She was selling paper and ink just to feed her brother and herself. Ash apparently showed up and changed her life," Jia said. "Then he—"

The trio stopped walking when they spied the Yue's shop front.

It had a mass of people going out the door and partially around the corner. Whatever she was selling was apparently far and away in great demand.

"That isn't a crowd to buy things," Yan said. Her tone was a dousing of cold water on Ash's good mood.

"That's a crowd gathering to watch a spectacle," Yan finished.

Nineteen

Ash made it to the crowd and started shoving his way through it. Making his way to the front, he could hear raised voices coming from inside Yue's store.

Elbowing one last person aside, Ash made it to the doorway.

Someone was standing in it with his arms crossed.

"Store's closed," said the man. "Move along."

Ash did a quick assessment on him. He was just a citizen. More than likely a very powerful one, and well trained, but still just a citizen.

This isn't the sect, after all. A mercenary citizen could easily do a policing job.

Or thug work.

"And I'm unclosing it. You can argue with me and my twins here, or you can move aside," Ash said. Pulling his butterfly swords free from the sheath at his side, Ash immediately began activating his abilities.

Behind him, he could feel Jia and Yan making room for themselves.

The citizen stared for a second before his eyes flicked to the space behind Ash. Then he stepped to the side, saying nothing.

Moving into the store, Ash made a point of ignoring the man as he passed him.

"…immediately. Or I'll drive your business into the ground and you'll have nothing left," said an older man. He was standing in the middle of the store, amongst its new and bare shelves, glaring at Yue.

According to Ash's sight, he was a spirit refiner of the second rank.

Far beyond Ash's ability to fight head on.

In fact, when he rolled out the first box under the man's name, it was red.

"What would you like your tombstone to say?" it read.

"I'll not leave. I'll not give up my store that I purchased. I'm a grand master in the free-merchants guild. I have every right to be here.

"You're just trying to bully me out because I won't deign to bend down to your clan's demands," Yue shouted back at the man.

Tala and Moira were standing beside Yue, clearly intent on defending the merchant.

"Fine, have it your way. As an elder, I can't interfere in matters beneath my rank.

"So, Bo, break her arms and capture the slaves," said the old man, gesturing behind himself.

Stepping further into the store, Ash saw two men standing off to one side.

He recognized one of them.

It was the little runt he'd thrashed outside Yan's house. He'd taken two steps forward toward Yue at the older man's command.

His name is Bo. A good thing to know.

"Break her arms? Capture my friends?" Ash said, tapping the spine of one butterfly sword against the other. It made a lovely chime like noise that belied the threat of violence. "I'll break everything from your shoulders to your fingers, then sell you to a mill so you can work like a donkey.

"And I'm surprised to see you up and moving, Bo. Last time I saw you, I turned your knee and elbow inside out."

The three men turned to look at Ash.

"You?" asked the elder. "You're the one who harmed Bo?"

"Yes, Elder. I am. I defeated him in a challenge fairly," Ash said. He immediately disliked this man, who reminded him intensely of Elder Shin. "Though I'm curious why you're attempting to interfere in a citizen's store?"

"That doesn't concern you," said the elder. He folded his arms in front of himself, seeming to try and radiate the persona of an elder.

"It most certainly does. I'm her friend, and she came here with me. I'll make sure her business is my business."

"Honored Elder, how would you like to proceed?" Ash asked.

The elder, Bo, and the unnamed man realized the whole situation was at an impasse.

There were only a few paths forward. Most of them required the elder and his party to back down, and the last was to get into a full-on fight to the death.

And how would you cover up murdering three students, two slaves, and a merchant, all with an audience outside?

Snorting derisively, the elder waved a hand dismissively at Ash.

"Stay then. I'll make sure no one comes to buy anything here. The Deng family markets will crush you until there is nothing left."

"I care not. It'll take slightly more effort, but the end result is the same."

"Consider yourself an enemy of the Deng family, young man," Elder Deng said.

"Likewise, Elder Deng," Ash said, unwilling to back down in the slightest.

Saying nothing further, the three intruders left the store.

When the door clicked, Yue slumped into herself, her small shoulders drooping.

"Goodness, that was terrifying," she said.

Chuckling, Ash sheathed his blades and walked over to her.

"Could have fooled me. You were fairly impressive," he said.

Shrugging, she peered up at him. "In the streets, a lot of it came down to bluster and bravado.

"Fight for what you have, bluff your way out, or get killed or raped. Or both," she said. "Fat lot of good all that will do me, though. If he truly can control the markets, I'll be driven out fairly quickly."

Smiling confidently, Ash dropped a hand on her shoulder.

"You're an impressive little lady. I have no doubt in your ability to overcome this. Besides, I think I have a few ideas we can use to make your store unique. So unique that they can't simply run you over.

"But that's for another time. I have a different proposition for you now."

"Proposition?" Yue asked, her tone puzzled.

"Would you like to be a cultivator?"

"I… I can't. In the evaluation, they determined my Dantian isn't big enough. By the time I got it open, I'd be past my childbearing days," Yue said, her brows drawing down over her eyes.

"I can open your Dantian. Here and now. And then provide you with everything you'd need to know to get moving.

"I don't think you'll be that far behind, from what I can gather. It really is just a smidgen too small. I know you'll be better than the average cultivator just based on who you are, and that's without some high-class abilities," Ash said, still smiling at her.

"Will… will it hurt? Do you have to go inside me or…?"

"A small cut on your stomach. No bigger than your thumb. It will scar you permanently, but it'll pop your Dantian open as if it'd been open for years."

"And… you can give me abilities? Like what you did with Jia?"

"I already have them written up for you."

"Alright. What should I do?"

"Wait for a second," Ash said and patted her shoulder. Turning his head, he looked to Tala.

The Rabbit woman's shoulders squared up as his eyes landed on her.

"What do you want? Going to demand something of me now? Tell me to join you in your bed?" she asked, folding her arms across her chest. "I'll kill you first."

"Uh… no. I was going to offer to have your powers restored. That and even offer you some new abilities that would work with your power and source," Ash said.

"Ah, somewhat like my own situation?" Moira asked.

"Exactly. I'd have to do the same thing to her that I did to you, though. I'll let you talk to her about what that entails."

"I'm right here. Talk to me, not her," Tala grumped, shaking her head, black hair fluttering around her.

She'd be lovely if she wasn't awful.

"Ok, Tala, ask Moira about what it entails to get your power back. It isn't fun, but I can do it in a day. Today, in fact.

"Considering I'll be working on Yue, I'd prefer to do it today anyways."

Tala sniffed, her nose twitching. One of her tall ears swiveled one way and then back toward him.

She didn't seem like she was going to even ask what was going on. Probably due to her pride.

"Fine. I'll let you do this thing to me as a service," she said.

"Great, last but not least," Ash said and then turned his head the other way, looking back to Yan. "Yan, have you decided? I can puncture your Dantian at the same time I work on the others if you like. Yours won't leave any scar tissue, since it's not meant to last."

"Ash, are you sure this'll work? If you tell me it'll work, I'll do it. I trust you," she said. "You've always done right, even if your anger gets the best of you when your friends and family are involved."

Always managing to slip in an older sister's correction.

"It'll work, Yan."

"Then yes."

Ash pulled his hand from Yue's shoulder and then pulled out his sleeping bag from his ring. He set it flat into the middle of the store.

"Yan, go ahead and ah… you'll need to expose your midriff. Please then lie down on the bed once you're ready for me," Ash said.

Turning his back to the other women, he started to pull out all his tools.

"Locke, could we create a sheet to teach Yue everything in alchemy? She already meets the prerequisite of having Wood elemental Qi," Ash said, as softly as he could manage.

"*Yes. In truth this would be ideal for her, to offset her smaller Dantian. Pills and elixirs would greatly improve her strengths and cover her weaknesses.*"

"Do it," Ash whispered and pulled out several sheets of paper.

Under Locke's guidance, the Hall's knowledge on alchemy was transferred. And it only took two minutes.

After shifting the alchemy work into the pile of papers for Yue, he turned around.

Everyone was standing around Yan, who was lying on the bedroll.

Her face was red and she looked slightly embarrassed. Her body was bare from the waist to just below her breasts.

"Pervert," Tala said as Ash looked at Yan.

Rolling his eyes, Ash picked up his chisel and moved over to his sister.

He got down on his knees next to her and pulled her tunic down to just above her belly button.

"This'll hurt, and you'll probably feel sick. My understanding is that you'll be well by tonight, and you can begin anew tomorrow morning after the moon sets and the new dawn comes," Ash said. "I'd say we'll all be sleeping here at Yue's house tonight for safety."

"Ok," Yan said, her hands clutched at her sides.

"I'm sorry, Yan. I don't want to hurt you," Ash said, looking at her with a grimace.

"I know," she said, giving him a smile.

Leaning in over her stomach, Ash split the edge of her Dantian with his chisel.

Then she started screaming.

***

Ash was sitting in his bedroll in the middle of Yue's shop front.

Jia had gone home to sleep in her own house.

Yue, Tala, and Yan were all recovering in Yue's room.

Yan really had become as sick as death. She'd ended up looking like a recovering crack addict who was suffering from food poisoning at the same time. But she'd managed to stay coherent long enough to wait for the moon to set before she utilized the transference papers.

Tala had passed out during her procedure, which had made it easier to work on her, since he didn't have to hear her whimpering in pain.

She wasn't exactly the most pleasant person in the world, but he didn't want to harm her any more than he already had.

Yue's had gone the best. As soon as the carving had linked together, her Dantian had snapped open. Snapped open and then ferociously began devouring all the Essence around them.

All three of them were unconscious now, learning from the transference papers.

Blinking rapidly to clear his thoughts, Ash looked down to the kitchen knife in his hand.

Pulling his chisel across the surface, he rapidly finished up the pattern and then set it to one side.

"What are you doing?"

Looking toward the bedroom door, he saw Moira standing there. The door behind her was closed.

"Making extremely sharp kitchen knives that will take a long time to dull," Ash said. Looking to the pile of knives on his left, he picked up another one.

"Why? That seems rather odd."

Ash began to scratch along the pattern Locke had put in place over the metal.

"So Yue can sell them. It'll be hard for citizens to resist buying something like this, at a good price. Even if the Deng clan really can undercut and outsell her, if she has unique products, it'll keep her afloat," Ash explained.

Moira sat down beside him, shoving the pile of knives further in front of him. Shifting around, she ended up pressed up to his side, her knee touching his.

"You care deeply for those you deem as part of your group," Moira said.

"I do. As an outlander, people who can see past my hair and eyes are rare. I treasure them." Ash finished the blade and set it atop the finished pile.

Moira picked up a blade and handed it over to him.

"Can I help in some way with this?" she asked.

"Not really. I have to make sure the pattern is exactly the same each time."

"Then teach me, just as if it were an ability."

"Maybe later. I'm not sure it'd work the same way."

"Ah… the spirit you talk to helps, then?"

Ash froze for a second, then nodded.

"Yeah. It isn't a lack of talent on your part. It's that I have something I can't give you."

Moira sighed and then smiled at him. "I wish to be more useful. I'd like to go through what you can teach me later and find out what your goals are."

"The last we spoke of it, you were simply wishing to find your brother and sister and help them."

Ash clicked his tongue and finished up the blade Moira had handed him.

"Yeah. Plans have changed, I suppose. Honestly… I really don't know.

"I mean, what do I do after joining a sect? Most people live in it. Stay there and become part of it.

"It becomes an almost city-like generational thing. It eats clans and families and turns them into sect families."

"Are there no other options?" Moira asked, handing him another knife.

"I could just the leave the sect. Find a wife and settle down somewhere. Though most cities wouldn't want me around as an outlander.

"Finding a wife would be equally problematic for the same reason," Ash said. "Or if I really wanted to go deeper into the cultivator world, I could aim to join an even higher sect. I'm young enough that for the next ten years I could easily go from sect to sect."

"How would you do that? Join another sect?"

"Tournaments, tests, exhibitions. Sects hold them frequently against other sects. It's a matter of gaining face. So throwing their disciples at one another is fairly normal.

"Those who excel tend to get recruited by stronger sects. Doesn't happen often, but often enough that you'll almost always find recruiters at each event."

"Which way do you think suits you best right now? Leaving the sect? Moving deeper?"

"Honestly, Moira, I'm not sure. I also have to make sure I take care of you and Tala. Which means whatever woman I find that will take me has to be comfortable with a total of three outlanders in her home.

"It might be easier to get recruited into other sects."

"Ah, that's true," Moira said. "Well, I'm sure we'll figure out what to do soon enough. I believe you're meeting with your brother tomorrow, no?"

She stretched her wings out behind her and let them settle back down. Then her right wing began to stretch out behind Ash.

He watched her move it out of the corner of his eyes as he worked.

Slowly, it draped around his shoulders and curled around him.

Acting as if she hadn't done anything, Moira waited for him to finish with the current knife and then handed him the next.

"Jing sent a letter back to Yan, yeah. It just said yes, and a time for tomorrow. That was it," Ash said. "It's really starting to seem like he stole the stones I sent them and left Yan behind."

Ash was trying not to think on the fact that Moira was next to him. That her wing was around him in a strange and casual way.

Mostly because he didn't quite understand what she was doing. It felt odd, and almost awkward. Then it struck him.

Did she just... make a move? Instead of putting an arm around me, she used her wing?

I think that's what it is.

But what does that mean?

Does she want to move this deeper into a possible relationship?

"If he stole them, we'll know what his worth was. It'll let us separate from him before he can cause us lasting harm," Moira said. "Regardless, I suppose we'll have a better idea of what to do after that."

Ash nodded, setting the next knife down beside him.

He wasn't quite sure what he felt about Moira. His thoughts on her were tied up with what she was—a slave—and with the fact that he held her life in his hands.

How much of this is what she feels she must do, and how much is what she wants to do?

Ash looked up to Moira's face.

Her large yellow eyes were gazing at him. She didn't look away when his eyes met hers.

Instead, she smiled at him, then blinked slowly.

She held out the next knife to him wordlessly.

Fuck it. That's a lot of worrying that doesn't matter. Let's just... take this as we go.

Besides... she's actually really nice to look at.

Ash took the knife and started to carve into it.

"Your wing is rather soft and warm. Is that why you don't use a blanket at night more often than not?" Ash asked.

"Indeed," Moira said, her wing tightening around him slightly.

"I wonder if you could make a pillow out of them," Ash mused.

"I'm unsure. I think they would have a strong scent if one tried, though."

"Suppose it's a good thing you have a nice smell then," Ash said, and he set down the knife. *So damn tedious.*

Moira tilted her head to one side in that way that seemed part of who she was.

"I'll start collecting my feathers then, and make a pillow for you."

"Thanks. I don't have a nice one right now," Ash said honestly.

Twenty

Ash walked along quietly with Yan.

The meeting with Jing was only a short time from now, and they were on the way to the location. He imagined she was having an internal war over this whole situation.

On one hand, the adopted brother had claimed he'd sent her spirit stones. Then he'd performed a number of activities that showed it was very likely he'd sent the stones.

On the other hand was her blood relative, whom she'd grown up with and joined the same school with. Suffered with.

And who very likely had robbed her and left her for dead when she became truly inconvenient. Because the simple reality was, the one hundred spirit stones would have reversed Yan's plight in a single day.

That's the really ugly part about all this. If he had shared with her, she wouldn't have suffered as dearly as she had.

"I trust you," Yan said suddenly.

"Oh… alright. I'm glad to hear that," Ash said.

Looking around, he realized the place they were heading was off the beaten path. The number of citizens and cultivators around in these parts was falling quickly with every step.

Suddenly, he felt quite glad for the fact that he'd asked Moira to tail them. He didn't want to believe this would become violent, but someone who would willingly steal from his blood sister wasn't to be believed.

"I trusted you before this, too. You never wanted to put in the effort. Not really, at least. But you were always sincere.

"If you decided to do something, it almost always happened," Yan said.

Ash didn't respond immediately. He let his thoughts carry him along for a few steps.

"There was that time when I tried to open my Dantian by eating a spirit stone," Ash said instead. "I'd decided that was how it would open."

Yan snorted, then started to laugh softly.

"Mother was so mad at you. She had no idea how you'd gotten a spirit stone, let alone decided that you would 'absorb' it.

"What kind of fool thinks he can just eat a stone?"

"Apparently this one," Ash said with a shrug of his shoulders.

Silence descended over the two once again, except this time Yan didn't seem as upset.

"Thank you. For being here. For coming after me. I'm a poor excuse for an older sister."

"Nah. I'm just doing this so you have to take care of me going forward. I can just laze about and take naps all day."

"Hmph. I think Jia would try to beat you to death if you did that.

"She seems quite different than I remember. A lot of that icy feeling from her is gone, and now she seems like a woman on a mission," Yan said.

"Yeah. Definitely feels like she has something to prove all of a sudden.

"Is this the place?" Ash asked.

They'd moved off the path entirely and were in a small, secluded patch of grass. It was sheltered on several sides by brush and low trees.

It wasn't somewhere one would normally meet a sibling, and Ash held this concern in his heart.

Yan looked around and then nodded her head, coming to a stop. "It is. Though I don't think we're early. So it's more a matter of Jing being late."

"There are several people hiding to the left. In the group of bushes," Locke said.

Shit. He really is planning on ambushing Yan, isn't he?

Letting his eyes roll over the scenery, Ash was able to check out the health bars of the people hiding.

He managed to catch their levels before his gaze moved on as if he'd never seen them.

Two level fours, one level six. That six will be a problem.

Especially if they target Yan. She's barely a rank one right now.

"Come on then, let's go. He's not here," Ash said, turning around. He wasn't about to stick around and let them get the upper hand if he didn't have to.

"But we haven't been able to confirm anything," Yan argued, though she did turn to follow him out of the area.

"Ah, Yan? Sorry! I didn't mean to be late," called a voice from behind them.

Glancing over his shoulder, Ash saw Jing standing on the other side of the clearing, as if he'd just arrived.

Except for the fact that the bush had one less level four, Ash might have been inclined to believe that excuse.

Maybe.

"Jing? Jing!" Yan said with a smile, turning back around towards him. "I'm so glad to see you. Look who's here—it's Ash!"

Moving to stand beside Yan again, Ash gave his adopted brother a cold smile.

"Good to see you, Jing." Ash pressed his fists together and bowed his head to Jing.

"Ah... yeah. Good to see you, Ash. What brings you out this way? Are you visiting?"

"He's—"

"You could say that," Ash said, interrupting Yan. He'd made sure to dress in clothes that a citizen would wear, clothes a cultivator would only wear if they planned on lazing about. "I thought it'd be good to stop in and see how everything was going."

"How good of you, brother. How good of you," Jing said, his tone growing strange.

That's right, Jing. Assume I'm a citizen still. What will you do? In front of your weak sister and your citizen adopted brother.

"Jing... Ash said he sent a letter and gifts. One to each of us. Did you happen to get them?" Yan asked, moving the conversation back where she personally wanted it.

Jing looked to Yan, his eyes slowly losing focus as he stared at her. Then he clicked his tongue and nodded his head briefly.

"Gifts. Yes. Yes, I received them," Jing said finally.

"Ah, could you give me mine? Ash said he included something that would help us in our training," Yan said.

She still holds out hope that he'll simply hand over the stones and this whole thing can be labeled as a misunderstanding.

"I can't," Jing said. His voice was clear. Stable.

Cold.

"You can't?" Yan parroted back.

"I can't. I had to pay a fee to join a family," Jing said. There was no apology in his words.

It didn't even really feel like an explanation. Just an answer to a question.

"You used them," Yan said slowly.

"Yes."

"The stones meant for me. All of them."

"Yes."

"I... I don't understand. Why w—"

"Because you're hopeless. You're hopeless and there wasn't going to be a darn thing we could do about it.

"Our relatives here? They're nobodies. We had no one to rely on, and you were too blind to see there was one way out," Jing said, his voice getting heated. "So I took your stones, because they would do nothing for you. And I used them to buy a way out for myself."

Yan shook her head slowly, her hands balling up into fists.

"That's not true! I could have bought a better cultivation technique. I only bought the one I did because you left," Yan said, her voice starting to quiver.

"It would have only delayed the inevitable, Yan Sheng. The end result would have been the same, just slower."

"I've joined a family now, and I'm better off. You should be happy for me," Jing said. "You should be happy for me and go home. Go back to Xing City. Find a husband and forget you ever had a brother.

"Because I've already forgotten you."

I'll break his fingers one by one.

"Though, I will thank you for coming to see me, Ash. I'll have you hand over all your spirit stones and coin before you go back," Jing said, turning his head to Ash. "You won't be needing it back home, and I will."

Ah… I didn't think he'd try to rob me first.

Suppose I don't need to show any mercy or restraint, then.

"Just to be sure here," Ash said. "You're robbing me of my possessions. Right?"

Yan's head was moving back and forth. From Jing to Ash, seemingly unable to comprehend the full situation.

Jing sighed and sucked on his teeth before he nodded.

"Yeah. I am. So… hand it over and this can be quick and easy. I'd hate to have my new family take it from you, but… I'll do what I have to," Jing said.

"What's the penalty for robbing someone in the sect, Yan?" Ash asked.

"What? Uhm. A beating, confinement, and sometimes losing a finger," she said, her voice sounding well and truly hollow.

"That seems like an interesting punishment." Ash slowly sank into a neutral fighting pose, activating his abilities one by one.

"It's pointless to rob someone when you can just challenge them," Yan said.

"Come then, Jing. Try and take from me," Ash said. "I'll take two of your fingers. One for each hundred stones."

"No. Stop this," Yan said. "Let's just leave."

"I can't do that, Yan," Jing said. "I need his stones. I'm sure he brought more to give to you and me, and I'll take them all."

"Jing, listen to me. Don't do this. We can all walk away from this," Yan said.

"Let me introduce you to my new clan. Their surname is Deng, and they're going to have a majority of the Outer Sect elder positions after the next placement tournament."

Deng? Deng!?

Ash's face flushed deep red as he realized the implications.

Jing had not only sold out his sister—he'd sold her out and joined the people who had made her life a living hell.

The two others walked out from the bush. Both looking smug and confident at the fact that it was three versus two.

"Last chance, Jing," Ash said, then slowly pulled his butterfly swords from the sheath at his side. "I'll give you no mercy after this."

Jing gave him a feral smile in return, pulling a saber from out of nowhere.

Storage item, huh? I'll take it from you and give it to Yan.

"Ash is a fifth-level cultivator," Yan said. "He can beat you, Jing. He broke Bo as if he were nothing. Then he beat Mei and her cronies to a pulp."

"I give you this warning only because of the memories we shared before this. Which I will now consider dead."

Yan looked to Ash with a sad smile. Turning her head back to Jing, she hocked up a wad of phlegm and spat it at him. "You are dead to me, Jing Sheng. I will see your karma repaid, Jing Deng."

Walking away from the clearing, Yan didn't wait for anyone else.

Jing's face had frozen, his eyes shifting to look around himself at the bushes. He'd apparently never considered that by selecting an ambush spot, he'd also made himself a prime victim for an ambush.

"Let's… let this go for today," Jing said suddenly, his saber vanishing.

"What if I don't want to?" Ash asked. "What I really want to take those fingers of yours?"

"Ash, let's go," Yan called, her voice already sounding distant. "Do it for me."

Feeling his rage deflate like a punctured balloon, Ash stood up and clicked his tongue. Sheathing his blades, he shook a hand at Jing.

"You're lucky she wants to spare you. Next time I see you, I will challenge you for two of your fingers.

"Don't let me see you," Ash said, turning his back on them and leaving as well.

Moving at a light jog, he hurried to catch up to Yan.

Falling in beside her, he slowed down and began to walk as if he didn't have a care in the world. As if what had happened hadn't.

"Thank you," Yan said softly.

"Of course. What kind of little brother would I be if I didn't listen?" Ash said with a chuckle.

Yan shook her head a bit, then wiped at her eyes with her fingertips.

"I just can't believe it. And the Dengs, no less. I just… I can't. I grew up with him, Ash. I remember watching him when Mother and Father needed me to.

"I remember knocking out the first kid who gave him a skinned knee," Yan said. Then she hiccupped, a low sob escaping. "He was my first friend. My best friend at times. Other times, my only friend."

Ash didn't say anything. Instead, he slipped his hand into hers and held it.

This older sister of his needed comfort right now. And he'd be damned if he didn't do all he could to give it to her.

***

Everyone was sitting along a counter in Yue's shop front. She hadn't bothered to open her store today.

Instead, she'd spent more of the day learning her new abilities.

Both as a cultivator and an alchemist.

The latter of the two having shocked everyone when they realized Ash could do that as well.

"To be clear, you are saying that you simply gave her the ability to be an alchemist," Jia said. She tapped her finger against the wood as if angry. "Because you felt like it."

"Well, alchemists are typically either Wood Qi or Fire Qi, right? I figured it'd be a waste otherwise," Ash said defensively.

"That isn't the point," Moira said, leaning in close to him. Her attitude had started to shift drastically as of late. She constantly invaded his space and seemed to look for opportunities to touch him.

Not that he minded it. If anything, he was flattered at the attention.

"The point is that you're capable of doing that, and the cost to you is… a piece of paper and ink," Moira finished, laying a hand on his forearm.

Looking at her long, well-maintained nails, Ash didn't know what to say.

"Yes? I mean, yeah, I did it and that was the cost. It's not something I plan on sharing with others, though. I mean, this was for us. I figured it'd help Yue get her shop up and moving if she was an alchemist."

"You didn't mention this last night," Moira said, her golden eyes digging into him.

"Ah, no. Sorry. It didn't seem like that big a deal. I mean, yeah, I know it is, but it's just us," Ash said with a shrug of his shoulders.

"If anyone found out about your engraving and carving abilities, they would lock you away in the deepest part of their clan hall until you died," Yan said, leaning toward him. "More so if they found out you could teach others alchemy at the drop of a hat.

"Part of the reason alchemists are so respected is they are so few and far between. They require one of two Qis, a willing teacher, and enough money to make it happen. And a good amount of luck.

"You negated almost all of that."

"Err, ok. Yeah. Got it," Ash said. "Sorry."

"Wait," Jia said, her eyes narrowing. "Does this mean you can do this with any profession? Could you transfer the engraving and carving?"

"Yes," Ash said.

"Blacksmithing?" Tala asked.

"Uhm…" Ash paused and hoped Locke would supply him with answer.

The Hall has both weapon smithing and armor smithing.

"Yeah. Armor smithing and weapon smithing."

"Totem crafting?" Yan asked.

"Yes."

"Yeah," Ash said. "Pretty much anything you can think of, I can probably teach. Why? Is there something you all want?"

Yue stood up from her pill cauldron and stared down at the device.

To Ash, it just looked like an ornamental pot with a lid. There were various holes along the top and side for viewing and working. There was also a small slot that folded out on the bottom, which presumably was where pills fell out.

Not really a pill… is it? Looks more like one of those small, tart candies that dissolve in your mouth.

Everyone was watching the merchant now.

Reaching out, she lightly tapped the side of the pill cauldron.

The slot slowly slid open, and a pill sat in the dispenser. Plain as day and well formed. It looked like something that had come out of an alchemist's shop.

Yue picked it up and held it in her palm.

"What'd you make?" Ash asked, breaking the silence.

"Sixth-rank Essence Attractor," she mumbled. "It was my first try."

"That's very impressive. I hear the rank of a pill dictates the rank of the alchemist. What did you make before that?" Jia asked.

"Nothing. This is my first pill," Yue said. She looked up and stared straight at Ash. "I'm an alchemist. You made me one."

"I did no such thing. You already had all the pre-requisites on your own. I just gave you the knowledge," Ash said. Then an idea popped into his head. "It's kinda sad… isn't it? How many countless alchemists are missed because they're not given the resources.

"How many genius painters are lost because they have to move bricks around all day. How many poets end up shoveling shit."

"How many cultivators are crushed under the boot of clan politics," Yan said, her voice bitter and acidic.

Ash nodded at her words.

That's the heart of the problem. Isn't it? A sect isn't built to help further others, but to further itself.

Sect politics are dictated by the leading families, which means it's really just clan politics.

How does one fix that…?

"Yan, Jing mentioned something about getting an elder selected?" Ash asked, looking to the older woman.

"Oh… yes. The placement tournament. It's a series of exams that determines the next elder. It isn't held very often since elder positions are obviously quite limited.

"The master of the winner is granted the elder position, as it would be assumed it was by their tutelage that they won."

Ash scratched at his jaw, thinking.

"I suppose the next question he will ask then," Jia said. "Is where he can get a list of all the potential elders, and who would be best suited to his needs.

"Is that right, Ash?"

"It is," he said, staring off into the middle distance. Plans were forming.

Forming and building, further and further.

With the end goal of taking over a sect or building one of his own.

And then we'll show them what happens when a human's potential becomes unlimited.

Twenty-one

Ash tapped a finger against the table in his dining room.

"I think the first real task here is figuring out who we want to approach," he said. "I don't think many are going to be willing to take me on as a disciple if Elder Deng has spread word about his family's dislike for me.

"Or am I reading that wrong?"

Yan shook her head a little.

"You're not. He'll do everything in his power to make you leave now. That isn't limited to just what he and his family can do directly, obviously. He'll put pressure on the rest of the elders. Make sure they understand that in taking you in, they will garner the Dengs' displeasure."

"Just how powerful are they? It seems like I've run afoul of them at every turn. Bo and Mei were the two I ended up breaking, right?" Ash asked.

And Jing joined them, but let's not bring that up right now.

"Yes. And it was one of their uncles you thwarted in the shop," Yan said. "They're not a top-tier power here, obviously, but they're certainly fourth or fifth. Maybe even third."

"Is there any elder that would join us simply because their family is opposed to the Dengs?" Moira interjected.

Yan thought on that, chewing on her lower lip. "I don't think so, no. None that would be willing to actually risk creating new hostilities. Things are pretty tame right now in the sect."

"Then I suppose that leaves us with elders that are unaffiliated. Ones that either have nothing to lose or everything to gain," Moira said.

Tala snorted, working a cloth up and down along her blade. Since she'd gotten her powers back the previous day, she'd devoted most of her time to caring for her gear, learning her abilities, or training.

She seemed a woman possessed.

"You're not wrong," Tala said, oiling her blade diligently. "In fact, it makes sense. The problem is that anyone in that sort of a position who would be usable wouldn't remain here. Would they?"

"They'd probably leave, since their chances of getting an ace student would be much lower here. That means the ones who can work their way out already have. Those who can't do better elsewhere and are unable to join a family—are here. The dregs, so to speak.

"On top of that, you're leaving out the crucial fact that they'd not only have to be willing to take on the Dengs and take on an unknown disciple, but that they'd be in a sort of political alliance with a student."

Setting the rag aside, Tala stepped away from the table and lifted her blade up. Turning it from one side to the other, she inspected it in the morning light.

"Mind that I'm not trying to naysay you or destroy your plans," Tala said, rotating the blade. "Just trying to point out where the gaps are, as a gift from me to you.

"It's not as if I care one way or the other what you do, though it does seem my status as your property will be directly affected by your own status."

Ash had held his breath as she talked.

She wasn't wrong. At all.

The vast majority of the elders who would be talented would have already moved up or out, or joined a family.

Those that remained wouldn't be usable or willing to do much.

"Ah!" Yan said, patting the table. "There's old Gen. He's technically a master who could be elected to an elder position."

"Gen? What is he if he's only technically a master?" Ash asked.

"He's the librarian. No one ever really goes there, though. Reading isn't something we're encouraged to do. If there is free time, we are expected to train or improve ourselves," Yan said.

"Actually, now that I think about it, I think Gen is from our family as well. He's an uncle to Uncle Da here."

Moira leaned to one side in her chair, moving considerably closer to Ash and invading his personal space.

"I sense a 'but' coming on," Moira said.

Yan looked from Moira to Ash before responding.

"There is indeed. Gen is very old. It's said he was quite talented in his youth, but due to some circumstances he was never able to break through into the elder ranks. Then he was injured in a duel with another master and he stepped down into the librarian's position. They offered it to him due to his contributions to the sect."

"Huh... so... he's family, was once talented, was respected, but has faded considerably since then," Ash said, staring through the table as if it weren't there.

"He's been a librarian for forty years now. He was a master a long, long time ago," Yan said.

"He meets all the requirements, then," Tala said, sheathing her big blade and starting to buckle it to her hip. "While it isn't ideal that he's old, as it's likely his usefulness is limited to a timespan, it should get us through the interim."

Good thing she's so tall, or the tip would drag on the ground.

"Sounds like a trip to the library then," Ash said.

"I know where it is. We can go together," Moira said. She turned to face Ash and leaned even closer towards him. "I memorized all the relevant locations in the Jade Fist. I got a map from Yue."

"I'll go with you as well," Yan said. "Uncle Da was the one who told me about him. Which means maybe Gen knows who I am."

Yan's reasoning didn't sound particularly sound, but it was better than nothing.

Ash shrugged. "Alright. Tala, you staying here?"

"Yes. I'd like to practice the abilities you gave me. The speed and strength changes have modified the way in which I swing my blade," Tala said. "Bring me home dinner. And something normal. No rice."

Tala moved to the door, the clothes Yue had procured for her fitting a bit tightly due to her figure being outside of the normal range for this veil.

Almost against his will, Ash's eyes slid down to her hips as they swayed out the door.

She was definitely a breath of fresh air. Her and Moira both.

"Let's get a move on, then," Ash said, snapping his eyes up as soon as he realized he was staring and then and following her out the door.

***

Walking through the entry doors of the library, ash was fairly impressed. The building was large. Large, stocked well, and excellently maintained.

Ash's footfalls were loud in his own ears. There wasn't a single other sound in the entire library. Not the scrape of paper, the rustle of pages, fabric, people breathing—nothing.

The only noises were from Ash, Yan, and Moira.

Shelves passed by them on each side, loaded with books and scrolls.

"This is a lovely library," Moira said on Ash's right.

The path was only wide enough for two people and Moira had very obviously made sure to be beside him.

Yan was behind them by a single step.

Ash was keenly aware of what Moira was doing. It had started the other night, and she'd slowly been turning up the pressure on him.

He wasn't against the idea of fooling around with her, but he still wasn't quite over the idea that she might be doing it for the wrong reasons.

Taking his right arm in her left, she pointed to a corner of the library.

"There are tables over there. I'd like to come back another time and read through some of these tomes. If I'm going to be calling this place home for a while, I'd like to be able to better understand the culture," Moira said.

The press of her against his side momentarily reminded him of the fact that he really didn't have to care at all about her reasoning. If she wanted to pursue something with him, why was he going to be the one to say no?

"May I help you?" whispered an aged voice.

Looking to the right, Ash found a short old man standing between two bookshelves in an aisle.

He had short white hair, a face full of wrinkles, and neutral brown eyes. There was no emotion in his face, and he seemed mildly annoyed.

It also seemed like he was part of the library itself—he'd simply appeared without a noise.

"Ah, yes," Ash said. Shaking Moira loose, he pressed his fists together and bowed his head to the older man. "My name is Ashley Sheng, adopted son to Duyi and Far Sheng from Xing City."

Yan stepped up to Ash's left and repeated the same gesture Ash had made.

"I am Yan Sheng, daughter to Duyi and Far Sheng from Xing City."

Gen's eyes crinkled for a moment before he smiled at the pair of them.

"I am Gen Sheng, though most call me old Gen. It is good to see two bearing the family name being promoted into the ranks," said Gen as he bowed his head. Slowly, and without a sound, he pressed his fists together. "I welcome you to my library."

Taking a moment to think, Ash decided to be direct with old Gen.

"Senior Gen, I've come to ask you to make me, Yan, and a close friend of mine your disciples. I ask this because we plan on winning the placement tournament. Our goal is to promote you into the elder ranks and cause the Deng family to suffer a loss," Ash said. "If they win the placement tournament, it is likely Yan and I will be forced to leave the sect entirely."

Gen's bushy white eyebrows lifted into his forehead.

"I haven't been someone's master in a very long time, young one," Gen said. "What would you want out of old Gen, exactly?"

"Ah… if you wished to not impart any wisdom on me, I would accept that your title as my master be purely aesthetic. Ultimately, we hope to elevate you to an elder position. Our end goal truly is just to thwart the Deng family. Which means what we would ask of you is to suffer for us and take on their displeasure as we did this."

Gen blinked, his eyes flicking to each one of his visitors.

"If I take you on as a disciple, I will expect you to behave like one. I have no problem causing the Deng family a black eye—after all, they're the ones who crippled my cultivation," Gen said. Then he gave them a feral smile. "I would enjoy causing them quite an upset to have a cripple as an elder."

"Forgive me, Senior Gen, but you're crippled? No one speaks of why you're in the library, only that you were given the position as a credit to your service," Yan said, her voice tentative.

Gen's face betrayed nothing as his eyes slid to Yan.

"I was challenged to a duel. In my foolish arrogance, I didn't think anything worse than losing could occur.

"Conveniently, an elder of their clan acted as referee," Gen said, his voice growing colder with every word. "The fight was close. Close enough that it was obvious with just a bit of luck, it could have gone my way. My disciples at the time were quite talented as well. I was a threat.

"A threat I didn't take myself for."

It would seem the Deng family has been building their power here for quite a while. And they've also run afoul of our own family previously.

It might explain why they seemed to be picking on Yan and Jing directly.

"When the fight was clearly over and I had little left, my opponent struck my Dantian with an attack I had not seen before that point.

"It was deliberate," Gen said. "He cracked the Dantian, and now it cannot hold very much Qi. The sect spent quite a bit of coin and favors to try and repair it."

"To get me back to normal. But in the end, they weren't able to do it. They simply lacked the resources on this plane.

"Now, if I do not regularly limit my Essence intake, it has the distinct possibility of shattering completely.

"For his actions, my opponent was banished from the sect and the elder punished. Though the last I heard, he was surrounded by loyal servants and concubines. Living out his life quite well."

Gen gave them a grim smile.

"So yes, taking a bite out of the Deng family and being your political shield are not concerns to me."

I wonder if we could fix his Dantian. So far, this engraving ability has been… a bit godlike.

Then again, half of that is because Locke lays out the patterns for me perfectly.

"His Dantian could be fixed. It'd require little more than what you did to Yan," Locke said, as if reading his mind. *"Though if you prefer to not reveal your power further, Yue could also give him a pill to the same effect. The materials would be somewhat pricey, but not out of reach.*

"In fact, you could do it in such a way as you acquired the pill for his sake, and never say how you got it."

"Then we're agreed. I look forward to having you as my master, Master Gen," Ash said, bowing his head over his fists again.

Yan immediately did the same.

Gen nodded and then looked to Moira.

"And you, outlander. What is your role in all of this?" Gen asked.

"I'm his property," Moira said, indicating Ash.

Gen narrowed his eyes, watching her. "If you are his property, why do you whisper power? I can hear it."

All three looked to Gen in mild surprise.

Smiling at them, the older man tapped an ear, then started to walk backward into the aisle. Then he turned around and slipped between two shelves, vanishing without a noise.

"He knew?" Ash said quietly.

"So it would seem," Yan replied.

***

Stepping into Yue's storefront, Ash was surprised.

The number of customers in her store was quite large. They were moving through her wares and items, and quite a few people were loading hand baskets to the brim with products. The atmosphere was a dull buzz of activity as people continuously moved around while shopping.

Four citizen guards stood near the door and counter. Each was armed and had the look of someone who knew their business.

Ash was now infinitely glad he'd left Yan and Moira behind. Trying to get through this place on his own was already going to be a bit of a fight against the tides.

Ash started to push and wedge his way through the crowd. His end goal was to make it to the counter. He needed to talk to Yue about the pill for old Gen.

Except she wasn't there.

A middle-aged woman was manning the counter, moving through transaction after transaction.

She briefly looked to him between two exchanges. Apparently, Yue had left instructions for if he showed up, because the woman indicated the door behind her.

"Mistress Ying is in there," said the woman, before turning to the next customer in line.

Following the direction, Ash moved to the door and stepped between two guards. Opening it, he entered Yue's bedroom and closed the door behind him.

Immediately, the din of noise was cut off to a degree and he breathed out a sigh of relief.

After coming to this world, Ash had not only gotten used to the lack of hustle and bustle everywhere—he enjoyed it.

Yue was seated quietly on her bed.

She was clearly cultivating.

Smiling to himself, Ash walked over to her quietly and sat himself down beside her on the bed.

Saying nothing, as he didn't want to disturb her, he inspected the room around them.

He hadn't actually been to her bedroom before. Their talks and meetings had all been conducted in her storefront.

While Yue acted like an adult most of the time, it was obvious here in her bedroom that she was still young.

Colorful knick-knacks, pretty bits of decorations, and small statues of animals all around. Not to mention she seemed to favor the colors pink and red for most of her personal belongings.

On a shelf, set behind thick glass and locked shut, were a single gold coin and a spirit stone.

I wonder if those are the ones I gave her. She said she went back and got the coin.

Picking up a throw pillow next to Yue, Ash inspected it.

On one side, animals were sewn in cute depictions, and on the other side a heart.

She really is quite young. She was forced to grow up quickly. I wonder how old she actually is.

A sharp intake of breath caught his attention. Looking to Yue, he found her staring at him, her eyes wide.

"Sorry, I didn't want to disturb you," Ash said with a grin. Then he held up the small pillow. "This is rather cute. I didn't realize you were into such things. If I had known, I would have made sure to buy you a few things to match your new home rather than a book."

Yue took the pillow from him, the emotion on her face somewhere between embarrassment and anger.

"I like the book. It's entertaining so far," she said. Pressing the pillow to her stomach, she wrapped her arms around it. "I didn't expect you to come today."

"Oh? And why's that?"

"Moira and Jia seemed determined to keep you busy with politics. I thought for sure you wouldn't have time to visit.

"I'm just a loose cultivating merchant, after all. I'm not in the sect."

Ash snorted at that and went to pick up another pillow.

Yue snatched it away from him and put it behind herself.

"Honestly, Yue?" he asked, laughing as he motioned at the pillow. "Fine, keep it to yourself. As to not visiting you, don't be stupid. You're important to me—of course I'd visit just to visit."

Ash chose at that moment to not give her the list of medical ingredients he needed, or the exact pill he wanted her to make.

"So, business looks like it's going well. Tell me about it," Ash said.

Yue chuckled softly and then sighed.

"Those knives of yours were… all I needed to get started. I sold them all to a clan at an exorbitant price, which let me cut my costs on everything else to just above margin.

"Next will be the pills. I'll sell those to whatever family is willing to buy them, then keep my prices the same."

Licking her lips, Yue then smiled at him broadly. "It'll take some time, and I'll have to keep my prices low for quite a while, but I think I'll be able to establish a customer base fairly quickly."

"Ha, I'm glad to hear it. You deserve it. From paper seller to pill broker," Ash said, grinning at her.

"Mm. All because of you. Thank you, Ash. Very much. The worst didn't come to pass. Because of you," Yue said, her eyes locked on his face again.

Every now and then he caught her staring at him in an almost fanatical manner.

She did a good job of burying it when others were around, but when they were alone she didn't seem to be as on her guard.

"Tell me about your journey as a cultivator and an alchemist. I have all afternoon," Ash said, changing the subject away from himself.

Twenty-Two

It'd been six days since he'd entered the sect.

Life was anything but settled, but by and large, it seemed normal at least. Most of the routines that would be given to brand-new Outer Sect students wouldn't start for another two weeks and a day, though.

The veil raid had thrown the entire schedule out the window. They'd returned much earlier than planned.

Several cities had been skipped on their examination, and a second set of recruiters had needed to be sent out just to take care of them.

All this meant that Ash and Jia had been lumped in with the second years. If anything, Ash was thankful.

He was getting attention and lessons that wouldn't normally be available to him immediately. Even simple things like developing a better understanding of the state of cultivators at large. Or refiners, as he'd found out they were called in different areas of the land.

"This seems odd," Jia said.

Forcing himself out of his thoughts, Ash looked around.

Nothing had changed.

They were still standing in a large courtyard with all the Outer Sect disciples.

"There are several masters and an elder coming. The rest of the masters are all waiting at the edge of the area," Jia said, prompting his attention to what she was talking about. "From what I gathered after speaking to those who have been here a while, this is normally just a sparring event."

"Huh… alright. I appreciate you asking around. Anything else you can tell me? Rules, perhaps?" Ash asked. He probably should have done what Jia had done, but he just didn't care that much.

"The rules are what you would expect. Challenges are expected to be accepted. It promotes lesser disciples challenging greater ones without repercussions.

"Masters are assigned to oversee the whole thing. Usually one master for every two disciples," Jia said with a shrug of her shoulders. "It was actually rather easy to gather information this time."

"I wonder why," Ash said with a glance at her clothes. She was dressed appropriately for sparring or exercising, but the clothes definitely hung on her in a flattering way.

Catching his look, Jia gave him a smile. "You think that is what made them speak so freely? It is true that the men were more forthcoming than the women."

Ash didn't bother to respond. The elder had stepped into the center of the area.

"Welcome, one and all, to this week's sparring event," called the elder. "As I'm sure you're aware, the placement tournament is coming up in seven days.

"Your masters have logged their disciples accordingly, and the registration period has ended."

Oh. Shit.

I hope Gen took care of that. Didn't even think about it.

"This year will be three events," the elder said, continuing. "The first is a simple test of your Spiritual Sense. By now, your master should have solidified this for you."

Huh. That'll be an issue. I didn't even know what that was two weeks ago.

"The second test will be an examination of your ability to see through to the truth of things."

"This won't be limited to abilities, but your cultivation, and whatever foundation your master has given you on your Dao path."

Ok. Dao path… or ability. I guess we'll find out if Sneaky Peeky is enough to get through it.

At this point, I doubt Gen could help me establish a Dao path.

"As to the last test… well… that's going to be a test of determination. How it'll be conducted won't be revealed," the elder said with a laugh. "One's determination will determine how far they'll go!"

Great.

"As for now, I hope you'll make use of every opportunity and encounter from here till the tournament," the elder said, looking around. "Good luck!"

The elder turned and left, and the masters who would be administering the event remained.

"Ok!" said one of the masters. "Go ahead and break apart and begin. All the normal rules apply, and the stalls are open. Good luck."

"Stalls?" Ash asked, looking to Jia.

She lifted a hand and pointed to one side of the area, where a number of wooden stalls lined a wall. Each had a placard above it with an image of what they were selling.

"Oh. I suppose that makes sense," Ash said. "Though I wonder what they take in payment. Might be worthwhile to stock up."

"Stones, coins, participation points, or trade," Jia said, apparently having already asked the same question. "And participation points are acquired through doing quests or chores for masters or elders. We have not heard anything about it, as technically, our group arrived three weeks early.

"In fact, we wouldn't even normally be able to participate in the placement tournament. We should consider ourselves fortunate."

Turning around, Ash wandered off to the back corner where he'd last seen Yan. He didn't see any reason to not be with his friends during this event. If anything, he'd feel better for it.

The number of people over here was increasing. In such a way that it honestly made Ash slightly nervous. This type of gathering in this world usually happened to watch spectacles, and little else.

And if they want to watch a spectacle, that really only leaves Yan, doesn't it?

Tucking a shoulder in, Ash shoved his way through two people. Only after he'd passed through that press of bodies did he get his answer.

There, in the middle of a circle, Yan was fighting against a young man.

She'd come a long way since they'd popped open her Dantian and started rebuilding her Qi Sea. Yue had even been crafting medicinal pills to help her develop swiftly.

The problem, though, was she still had a general lack of actual experience with her new skills and abilities. She knew them and how to use them, but only up to a point. She had no practical knowledge of them and how they'd turn out in actual combat.

Yan's hand flashed out in a palm strike that knocked the young man's head backward.

Grinning, Ash nodded in approval.

He and Yan had never truly bonded as brother and sister. They were only adopted siblings, after all.

But that didn't stop him from feeling pride in watching her wipe the floor with her opponent, not even using abilities.

Her opponent held up a hand and slunk away, clearly forfeiting the match.

Yan let out a breath and then hunched over on herself, taking in a deep lungful of air.

Walking over to Yan, Ash chuckled.

"Good strike," he said.

Yan shook her head and looked up at him through her bangs.

"Third... fight... in a row," Yan huffed. "Targeting... you... through... me."

Third fight in a row? How is that even allowed?

This must be their current tactic. Fight Yan until she can barely defend herself, then "accidentally" hurt her.

Then it's all downhill from there.

Or worse than just hurting her.

The bastards!

Ash looked over his shoulder to the nearby master. He didn't recognize the individual.

"He's carrying a badge that all the Deng family members have held," Locke said. *"It radiates a small amount of a strange Qi I've noticed only comes from them."*

Damn them. Damn them all.

"I challenge you to a duel," said a young woman, walking up to Yan.

Yan took in a deep breath and stood upright.

Ash stepped in front of Yan and held up a hand in front of himself. He felt nothing but burning rage.

This was because of him, and he would end it as quickly as he could.

"Look. If you can just give her some time to rest, I'd appreciate it," Ash said.

"No, that's now how this works," said the woman.

Ash snapped his teeth together with a feral smile.

"Then remember this moment," Ash said, his tone dropping. "Remember it and realize you could have let it be. That you could have walked away."

The woman stared at Ash.

He wasn't sure what was going on in her head, but he hoped she was reevaluating her action. Otherwise, she'd live to regret it.

Turning around, he faced Yan and gave her smile.

"Don't worry, it will stop either after this fight or the next one," Ash said. He pulled a pill from his storage and handed it to Yan. "Take this. It'll give you strength. Yue made it for me."

Yan didn't hesitate and took the pill from his hand, then popped it into her mouth.

"I'll be right back," Ash said.

Moving back to the crowd, Ash started to force his way out.

"Locke, can you put a marker on those stalls? I want to buy some things but I… can't remember which way it is," Ash muttered.

A green arrow flashed to life at the top of his sight.

Thank the heavens for Locke.

Orienting himself on the arrow, Ash started moving toward the stall.

Once he cleared the press of bodies, he was able to move much quicker.

Following the arrow, he found the stalls and began reading over the signs, looking for what he wanted.

There!

Moving at a fast walk, Ash headed straight for the stall that had the sign "Mortar and Pestle" above it.

When he stepped up to the stall, he found a middle-aged woman tending the booth.

"What can I do for you?" she asked him.

"Do you need a license to operate this stall in this area?" Ash asked.

"Ah… yes? That is, yes. All stalls need a license to operate here," said the woman, her brows coming down over her eyes.

"And you have one?" Ash asked.

"Yes, of course."

"I want to buy your stall, your entire inventory, and the license," Ash said. "How much?"

The woman blinked several times, clearly not quite sure what to say to him.

"You want to buy everything," she repeated.

"Yes, but only if you can sell me everything in the next ten seconds or so," Ash said.

"Ahh…" the woman's eyes hardened, and she lifted her chin.

"Three hundred thousand spirit stones, and that's my fin—"

Ash transferred the balance she'd asked for to his last financial card and held it out to her.

"Here's the money.

"Give me the license immediately and then leave," Ash said. "You have two seconds."

The woman snatched the card from him and looked at it, then pulled something out from thin air and held it out to him.

"Thanks much!" she blurted as Ash took the license. Then she hurried away, as if afraid he'd change his mind.

There goes most of my remaining money. I'll need to get Yue to sell some things for me.

Ash took the entire stall into his storage ring, then went back toward the mob.

Repeating the process, Ash managed to get back to the ring Yan was fighting in. The other woman was just getting up from the ground.

"I surrender," she said, brushing herself off.

"I challenge you!" Ash shouted, rushing forward to the woman.

"What?" the woman asked.

"I challenge you. Now. Right here, in this moment," Ash said. "Fight me. Now."

Ash glared at the nearby master, daring him to refuse this.

"Uh… alright… start in five seconds," he said, seeming unsure.

Ash rapidly activated every ability. Then he stored a truly massive amount of Qi into his Spring Step.

The woman looked shocked that this was happening. If Ash had to guess, the standard mentality of this world applied even here.

She got herself into a defensive stance, her hands held loosely.

And of course, they'll only think of themselves.

Running along with thoughts of, 'This doesn't involve me, and I don't want anything to do with it. I could be associated with them if I helped.'

Snorting disdainfully at the whole situation, Ash was ready.

"Begin!" the master said.

Lunging forward, Ash brought his fist around in a rage-fueled hook. Triggering Spring Step, he landed the monstrous blow straight into the side of her gut.

Feeling his body coiling in the opposite direction as he twisted with the blow, Ash launched a second punch forward.

Aimed at her femur.

Strengthening it with Spring Step as he did so, he felt her leg bone crack in two.

Before the master could interfere or the woman surrender, Ash leapt forward with his forehead.

Again, he used Spring Step, and his brow plowed into her nose.

With a wet crunch, Ash's world turned bright red.

Letting the woman collapse to the ground, Ash stood upright and shook out his hands.

Blood from her nose was dripping down from his brows into his face.

The woman couldn't even shriek, or breathe, as she lay there on the ground.

Ash imagined the blow he gave her kidney would be enough to have caused her internal damage and steal her breath away.

Her leg was clearly broken and her face looked as if it had hit the pavement at a hundred miles an hour. Her nose was a shapeless lump now.

Hocking up a good mouthful of phlegm, Ash audibly cleared his throat. With an exaggerated spitting motion, he hacked the glob of nastiness into the woman's destroyed face.

"I told you to remember that moment. Be sure to think on it in the future.

"And to the rest of you, I look forward to whoever challenges Yan next," Ash said, looking to the crowd. "And when they get to remember their own moment."

Looking at the master, Ash kept his face neutral. He knew he'd followed the rules.

Technically.

The harm he'd caused her was nothing that couldn't be healed easily with some medicinal pills.

"So sorry about that. I didn't know my own strength. It's so hard to control it, being a new recruit and all," Ash said deadpan to the master. "Would Master Deng please forgive me?"

The master opened his mouth, his face going a pale white and then a bright red.

"You idiot!" he ground out, seemingly not realizing that Ash had named him. "You did that on purpose."

"Of course not. I imagine it was no more on purpose than allowing a cultivator to fight an endless string of battles without respite. Right?" Ash asked.

The master fell silent. He worked his jaw from one side to the other.

"You," the master said, pointing to someone else. "Take her to the medicinal stall and get her patched up."

"Ooooh…" Ash said dramatically. "The medicinal stall.

"Sorry. I bought it. I bought the entire supply, the license, and the stall."

All eyes had turned to Ash now.

This was a spectacle they all wanted to see.

"I'm more than willing to sell medicinal pills, of course. Though prices will be dependent on my mood," Ash said with a smile. "Among other things, that is. Can't promise prices will remain constant."

***

Ash sat down quietly in the library.

He'd come alone this time, and he folded his hands on the tabletop. Not even for a second did he believe Gen didn't know he was here.

This was practically his domain, let alone anything else.

I bet there isn't even a spider here Gen doesn't know of.

Taking in a breath, Ash thought on the sparring event earlier that day.

The number of people challenging Yan rapidly dropped off after they carried the woman from the field.

It'd been obvious to him at that point that the vast majority of the Outer Sect was either in the Deng family's control or service.

"I heard there were some happenings today."

Looking to where the spider-silk-soft voice had come from, Ash was surprised. Gen had sat down next to him without Ash even noticing.

"Yes. The Deng family was attempting to harm my sister. So I harmed them," Ash said.

Gen gave him a wolf-like smile.

"Yes. Elder Deng and his subordinates were quite animated over the situation. Yet the rules were followed," Gen said. "Nothing could be done. Poor Deng family.

"Now, what have you come for? Do you wish to begin walking on the path of your Dao?"

Ash hadn't expected that.

"I could do that?"

"Of course. A Dao isn't something developed all at once, nor is it something you can't begin to journey upon before you're a cultivator," Gen said with a smile. "A Dao is only part of a cultivator's journey. One could be a blacksmith and have a Dao."

That was news to Ash. He hadn't even considered it, in truth.

"Now… for your Dao… it'll take time for you to take the first step. Moreover, it'll be even harder to make sure the first step is on the path of your true Dao," Gen murmured.

His voice was warm and soft. It rubbed at Ash's senses. He found he couldn't respond, and his thoughts were turning inward.

"You'll need to explore what is in your heart. What is in your mind. What is in your soul. There will be a path all three traverse.

"Where you feel comfortable," Gen said. "It'll be like a well-known path to you."

Ash nodded his head a bit.

"Your Dao will be where those three things converge and carry you. Where you naturally… exist.

"For now, simply begin to explore what your heart feels. What it urges you to do at the heights of your passions and the lows of your despair. Where do you find yourself?"

Ash floated in that space for a time as Gen stopped speaking. His mind slithered slowly along the words Gen had put there.

Thoughts and ideas flitted through his mind rapidly and were checked against what he felt was right or wrong inside of himself.

"That is enough for today," Gen said, his words snapping Ash out of the world he was in.

"Huh?" Ash mumbled.

"You've been in a state of soul searching. It's been several hours. You'll need to go home soon," Gen said.

"Several hours? It only felt like minutes," Ash said, confused.

He'd never really believed in a lot of the talk cultivators spouted out.

It'd all seemed a bit more like religious hoodoo to him.

"Yes. Searching with one's soul can do that. Time flows differently."

Ash let out a slow breath.

He'd found a few thoughts in that space. Several that he felt were true. He'd have to explore them more later.

"Ah… well, thank you, Master Gen. I appreciate your guidance," Ash said, pressing his fists together and bowing his head to Gen. "Though that isn't why I came today."

"Oh?" Gen asked, watching Ash curiously. "And why did you come then?"

"I have something for you."

Ash pulled several pills from his storage space and laid them down on the table in front of himself.

Yue had come through for him. She'd manufactured the pill Gen needed to re-seal his Dantian. As if nothing had been wrong with it in the first place.

On top of that, Yue had made two pills that would restore Gen's strength. Regain him his vigor.

They couldn't change his physical features, but they could give him all that he'd lost and restore his prolonged life.

With those three pills, it would be as if Gen had lost nothing, though he would still look like an old man.

"What's this?" Gen asked, eying the pills.

"This… is my and Jia's apprentice price to you," Ash said. "Let me tell you about them."

Twenty-Three

Ash picked at his Outer Sect uniform.

He'd made sure to have one set aside that was clean, untouched, and ready for the placement tournament.

Though he doubted it'd matter, it never hurt to dress for success.

The only real problem was it was still hours before dawn, and he couldn't sleep.

Leaning forward on his bed, Ash scrubbed at his face with his hands.

The nerves were keeping him awake. The thought that the Deng family would attempt to do something. That they'd make an attack or try and knock Ash and Jia out of the competition.

"They've been far too quiet," Ash muttered. "Far too quiet since we stopped them in the sparring rings. That speaks to either confidence or a lack of options.

"And if the latter, does that mean they'll be desperate today?"

Groaning, Ash closed his eyes and pressed his hands to his temples.

It was the same conversation he'd had with himself several times already. Several times and with the same answer.

"There's nothing I can do, and they're either confident or desperate. In either case, all I can do is be on guard. Right? Right." Ash said into his hands. "I hate this shit. I'm not made for this kind of thing."

Standing up, Ash ran his hands through his hair.

There wasn't much for him to do right now other than worry.

Maybe a walk? A walk might help.

I'd rather nap.

Opening the door to the common room, Ash left his bedroom. In the blink of an eye he was outside.

Staring up at the dark sky.

He realized inherently that being outside was no different than being inside, but it felt different already.

"Done fretting yourself to death?"

Ash flinched, looking over his shoulder back to the front door of his home.

Tala was walking up to him. Her sword wasn't belted at her waist, and she seemed dressed for sleep.

Sighing, Ash looked forward again. Living this far out of the way, he was almost guaranteed to never have visitors or be bothered.

At least not by anyone who wasn't looking specifically for him.

"I don't think so. At least I won't be doing it inside the house anymore tonight," Ash said.

"From what you were saying," Tala said, easing up next to him. "There really isn't anything else you can do about it.

"Other than be ready, as you yourself said. Many times."

Ash frowned, looking over at the Rabbit woman.

"These aren't for show," she said, reaching up and touching one of her elongated ears. "I admit you humans tend to stare at them, and more often than not it's a... strange gaze... but they're not decorative. These really are my ears, and they're very good at catching sound."

Ash looked up to the black-furred ears sticking up above her head.

"Mm. I didn't think they were decorative, but I won't deny I didn't think your hearing was that good.

"As to the staring... well, yeah. You're a bit of an exotic woman out here," Ash said, turning his head to the sky.

"Exotic?"

"Uh... outside of normal. Beautiful for your outside-of-norm looks."

Tala snorted at that. "You're fortunate to look upon me. I'm a beauty in my own country, let alone this shit hole."

Ash smirked at her words.

He'd come to expect that taciturn and elitist view. It wasn't abnormal for her, and it didn't even bother him anymore.

"Uh huh. We're all honored to stare at you and be in your presence. We should all record our encounters with you. For posterity," Ash said.

"You're not one to jest. You stare as often as others, if not more. And not just at my ears."

"I do. And?"

"What, you just casually admit it?"

"Yes? I mean, why wouldn't I? I'm not bothering you, and you haven't complained about it."

"If it was something that annoyed you, you would have called me on it," Ash said. "So, I'll stare. You're something different out here."

"Different? Why not take the Owl to bed, then? She'd be willing. Or even your little merchant friend. I get the impression she'd deign to lower herself to sleeping with you," Tala said, her voice cold and brittle.

"Mm. Why not Moira… because the line between slave owner and lover is a bit blurred right now. Maybe down the road.

"I'm not one to say no to a tumble, but it just hits me in the right spot where I'm not completely sure," Ash said. "As to Yue… maybe. I think getting in bed with her would have a lot more repercussions than I'm willing to take on right now, though."

"Hmph. I'm surprised you haven't forced your needs on my elegant self," Tala murmured.

"Oh, don't get me wrong. It's not as if the thought hasn't crossed my mind. Then I'm promptly reminded that it'd be rape and… well, I'm not a good person. I beat the crap out of people. I've even killed people.

"But somehow rape seems a bit worse to me," Ash said.

The silence that came after that statement was heavy.

Heavy and massive.

"The sun is rising. I'd be willing to grace you with the right to lightly spar with me," Tala asked. "Hand to hand combat, no weapons. Nothing full speed. Maybe one-fourth at most."

"I'm so blessed," Ash said.

Light sparring sounded really good right now.

***

"Welcome, one and all. I am the head elder of the Outer Sect. You may call me Elder Deng," said the old man standing in front of the assembled prospective students.

This tournament was closed to the public, since it was an internal examination.

There would be no outside eyes. Nobody to vaguely impress.

No one to fool with the promise of fairness.

All that meant internal politics would be in full effect.

"I'll now call each master up to the front and introduce their two candidates," said the head elder. "While this may seem like a silly thing to do, it never hurts to make sure everyone knows everyone.

"After all, there's only one hundred of you participating."

"Do not make that face. This is a good opportunity for information gathering," Jia said, standing next to him.

"Then gather away. I'll just stare off into space," Ash said, rolling his eyes. "None of this matters at all."

"Hmph. Maybe I will share nothing with you."

"Awww, don't be like that. Consider it a favor I'll owe you. Or one less you owe me."

He heard Jia click her tongue in annoyance.

She really does hate owing people.

"I do not think I will ever be able to repay you. That is something I have come to accept," Jia muttered. "Ah, we are next."

"How do you know?"

"We are last," Jia muttered.

"...aster Gen, head of the library," said the head elder.

Old Gen walked out to take his place next to the other masters.

After taking the pills Ash had prepared for him, he had immediately locked himself away in closed-door training.

He'd come out of it just for this moment. Ash hadn't laid eyes on him until now.

He looked the same as he had previously.

The difference, though, for anyone who actually looked, was in his eyes. That and the small smirk at the corners of his mouth.

The cane he held in his hand clicked as he moved. Carried more for comfort and habit than use, Ash figured.

"My disciples are Jia and Ashley," Gen said simply. His voice was soft in tone, though loud enough for everyone to hear. "That's all."

That was the extent of his introduction for Jia and Ash. All the other masters had extolled their people's virtues at some length.

"Ah, Gen," said a master Ash didn't know.

In fact, he didn't know almost all of them. Nor did he care to. They were unrelated to him. *Unless they're in the Deng family – then they're related to me.*

"...a concern. You can't deny that, can you?" asked the master.

Gen only smiled broadly at the other master, saying nothing.

"It'd only be common sense," continued the master. "Why not turn your disciples over to me? I'll be happy to train them personally. They have great potential."

"Though I wouldn't be able to allow them to participate in this tournament."

Gen nodded, bringing his cane around in front of himself. Leaning on it, he stared at the other master wordlessly.

"So you agree then?" asked the master.

"No. Of course not," Gen said. "How would I become an elder if I did that?"

A number of masters' stances changed with that statement from Gen.

Just how many of these masters support the Deng family? It's going to take some time to dislodge and break their hold on the Outer Sect.

As stupid as it sounds, I'd almost be better off just starting a new sect from scratch.

Hah.

"Then I'll challenge you for your disciples, Gen. They would be better off with me, and I think a duel for them would be the best way to determine this," said the master who had spoken out against Gen to begin with.

"Ohm? I see no reason to accept such a silly wager," Gen said. "There's nothing in it for me, young one. I have no reason to accept."

"You should accept for your face alone!" said someone from the crowd.

Gen snorted at that. "Can we move this along? I'd like to become an elder as soon as possible."

"Fine!" shouted the master who'd challenged him. "If I lose, I'll give you my own disciples."

"Pah, I don't want them," Gen said with a dismissive wave of his hand.

The head elder stepped up and coughed into his hand.

"There's little you can say that would change my mind, Head Elder Deng, and you can't force my hand in this," Gen said, glancing to the other man.

Blinking twice, the head elder looked enraged.

Ash doubted anyone ever spoke to him like that, let alone telling him so directly that whatever he was going to say didn't matter.

"If you win, I'll allow you and your disciples three treasures each from the Outer Sect vault, you damn cripple," the head elder hissed between his teeth.

"Done," Gen said immediately. He flicked his staff to Jia, who caught it out of midair. "Now, let's get this over with."

Moving nimbly and quickly, Gen took several steps away from the other master and then moved into a defensive stance.

Everyone stared at Gen in shock. No one had been expecting him to be able to move so easily. So quickly.

To act as if he weren't a cripple.

"It would seem the pills worked wonderfully," Jia said.

"So it would seem. Yue is far more accomplished than I thought," Ash replied.

"She is. She has been feeding Yan a steady stream of pills to get her up to speed. It is… interesting. I think she does it out of her dogged loyalty to you."

"At least someone supports me. Instead of mocking me with pretty eyes and a sharp tongue, that is," Ash said, turning to stare at Jia.

She gave him a broad smile and lifted her eyebrows.

"My eyes are pretty?"

"Idiot," Ash said with a grin, looking back to the masters.

An area had been cleared, and Gen and the challenger were standing alone.

"I wonder if this will be quick," Ash said.

"I do not think so. Gen will take his time and relearn himself with this match. He will also make a statement to the others in doing so."

After a second round of thought, Ash couldn't help but agree with Jia's assessment.

A downward chopping hand from the head elder signified the start of the duel.

Gen made no move, just stood still, waiting.

"Emperor's Heavenly Blade of Destruction!" shouted the challenger.

Well, that's a stupid thing to have to shout in a battle. I would have punched him in the mouth.

Sharp white lines coalesced in the air. A blade of force formed from the wind. Visible sharp eddies of wind were visible to the eye.

They began to grow larger, becoming considerably sharper in contrast as well.

Gen nodded and held one hand in front of himself.

"Break," he said, and gently pushed his hand out.

Nothing happened visibly. Or that one could hear.

Though everyone felt the tremendous force that blasted out from Gen. Blasted out from him and tore the wind construct apart as if it had never been there.

Blinking placidly, Gen gave up his defensive pose and then just stood there.

"Ah, I see. If that is the best you can muster, then this will only be a matter of when—not if," Gen said. "Unless you'd like to surrender now, and spare yourself the pain I will inflict upon you.

"I have much suffering to return to the Deng family. If you are not careful, you'll be my first outlet."

The challenger harrumphed and then put his hands together and began to rapidly flash hand seals. One after the other.

Several entities began to take shape out of cloudy-looking air. Then they began to slowly move together, melding into one shape.

The attack takes so long. The fool is lucky Gen is being patient. Otherwise he could just come over and punch him up.

"Most cultivators, as you have said several times, are terrible martial artists," Jia said, her voice interrupting his thoughts. "The idea of simply beating someone down is extremely foreign to them."

"They're in for a rude awakening, then. I don't plan on playing by their rules," Ash said, the words sounding very much like a threat.

Finally, the air formed itself into a humanoid shape, with the loud sound of wind ripping through trees and tearing them up out of the ground.

Loud to the point of being uncomfortable.

After a second longer, it lunged for Gen.

The older man gently clapped his hands together. A soft pat was heard, but once again, the force that came from it was extreme.

It felt like someone had set off a bomb nearby, and the shockwaves were rolling through Ash.

The air construct blew apart, the shriek of the wind it had brought with it stopping instantly.

"A very well-constructed fart," Gen said, letting his hands fall back to his sides. "Are you done now? I really would like to get this all over with so I can become an elder."

"My disciples will make short work of everything. In fact, the better question is which one of them will win?"

Turning bright red at the insult, the challenger began to swing his arms back and forth, whips of air forming and lashing out at Gen.

Over and over the blows fell, Gen vanishing under the repeated strikes as dust, grit, and the air itself was torn to bits and sent in every direction.

Ash couldn't quite see what was happening anymore, and he could only briefly follow flashes of Gen inside the maelstrom.

The resounding booms of the whip cracks over and over were like hammer blows to the very air.

After a full minute, the challenger let his arms droop, panting heavily. It was obvious to everyone he'd lost control of himself and simply tried to kill Gen.

This had turned from what was supposed to be a duel into a full-on death match.

Clearly slowly, the cloud thinned out, and Gen grew slightly visible.

Coughing twice, the older man waved a hand in front of his mouth.

"Quite a bit of dust. Perhaps you should consider taking up a job as a rug beater. There're quite a few rugs in the sect, and I'm sure they could use a thorough cleaning," Gen said.

Ash could now see his master, who appeared to be completely unharmed.

Though his clothes were a ruin, hanging onto his frame through sheer will alone.

Under those bits of clothing, though, everyone could see Gen's body.

Where they all had expected an older man with sagging skin and a wizened frame, they found only muscles.

Corded, flexing, firm muscles on a body that a young man would have. Though it was dotted with liver spots, gray hair, and wrinkles.

"Goodness, it would seem you owe me a new training gi as well," Gen said patting at his rags.

Sighing, Gen looked to the challenger.

"It is now my turn. And might I say, you are quite powerful. Now I shall gift you an attack, unless you'd like to surrender?

"I cannot guarantee my attack won't permanently harm you. It might even kill you. Are you sure you wish to taste it?

"You could surrender. It would cost you very little," Gen said, offering the challenger an easy way out.

An incredibly simple way to allow the enemy out while also protecting himself. It would be hard to find Gen at fault for any wrongdoing with such a gentle offer towards his opponent.

Squaring his shoulders, the challenger lifted himself up into a straight posture, facing Gen head on.

"Bring it," he said.

"As you like. Though, do not hold me at fault for what happens. I have warned you. Head Elder, do I have your permission to attack? Or would you prefer to force him to surrender and bow his head?" Gen asked, looking to the head elder.

"Hurry up and waste your breath. I won't deny it's impressive you could hold out, but you haven't learned a new attack since we were young.

"You're still nothing but a cripple. Just a cripple who's learned how to defend himself," sneered the head elder.

Gen looked to the challenger and held up his hands.

"My apologies. The head elder has sentenced you to whatever fate this brings. Take it seriously now, and defend with all your might," Gen said.

Holding out a hand in front of himself, he sighed softly.

"Burst," he said.

There was no shockwave this time. No blast of force. Nothing to indicate anything at all had happened.

Several seconds passed.

The head elder started laughing, clapping his hands together. "Is that all? Are you attempting your hand at parlor tricks now? I mean truly, Gen Sheng, this is—"

The head elder froze. His challenger slowly toppled forward.

Smacking lifelessly against the stones, the man lay there unmoving.

"As my disciple would say. Remember this moment," Gen said, turning to look at the head elder.

Gen's lips peeled back, and he gave the other elders and masters a feral smile worthy of a wolf. "Remember it and wish you had taken a different course.

"Now, stand with me or against me."

Ash couldn't help but smile at the display.

"Gen is… ferocious," Jia said. "I like our master."

"So do I," Ash said. "So do I."

Twenty-Four

Gen and the head elder stared at each other for several more seconds. Neither one seemed willing to make the first move.

Jia cocked her arm back and tossed the cane up to Gen.

Snatching it out of the air, the old librarian set the tip down in front of himself, then leaned over it. He looked just as he always had, except bulging with muscles and with little in the way of clothes.

"How's young master Deng, by the way?" Gen asked, his tone silken and smooth. "I haven't seen him since he was thrown out for… well… crippling me."

The head elder had been staring at Gen this entire time. Clearly at a loss for words or how to handle the situation as a whole.

"He is well. I'll let him know you've recovered," the head elder said.

"Oh, that'd be great. Maybe I could come visit him," Gen added.

Coughing into his hand, an elder stepped up and pressed his fists together toward the head elder.

"Senior, we should move on to the examination. There is a certain amount of time that is required to get all the disciples through," said the elder.

"Ah, yes, of course," said the head elder, nodding.

"Alright. Everyone, please follow me. We'll move to the testing area and begin the examinations."

Gen watched the elders and masters begin shuffling away. He made no move to follow them.

Instead, he turned toward Jia and Ash and walked toward them.

"Ash, Jia," the old librarian said, coming up to his two disciples. "I believe I owe you two a considerable amount for those pills.

"They didn't just restore me to what I had been, but allowed me to break through to a point that isn't far off from where I should be now, if I had been training normally all this time."

Ash and Jia immediately pressed their fists together and bowed their heads to Gen.

"It is our pleasure," Jia murmured.

"As our master, it is our strength when you have strength," Ash added. "Though I must admit, I was quite pleased to see you manhandle them so easily."

Gen grinned at both of them and then gestured toward the retreating crowd.

"Come. We should follow them, or they'll rule against us for falling behind. I'll not forget this, though. It isn't something a normal disciple could offer a master," Gen said.

The head elder had led everyone into a building. By the time the three of them caught up, they were able to walk in as if they'd been in line the entire time.

Just at the rear end of it.

Inside was a large open chamber. Large enough to fit everyone comfortably and still have room for more.

"Hmph," Gen said, looking around. "I'll go stand with the other masters. And just so you know. Even if you both fail, I'll make sure your lives in the Outer Sect are fair. Fair and even handed."

"Thank you, Master, but I think we'll succeed. I have confidence in our abilities," Ash said.

"Yes. Though I fear Ash may surrender if it comes down to the two of us at the end," Jia said.

Gen quirked an eyebrow at Ash and then left.

There wasn't much else to see or do here. It was just a massive assembly room with a single door opposite the one they'd come in from.

The two of them would just have to wait until the tournament was underway. Sighing, Ash looked to Jia and gave her a lopsided smile.

"Keep your tongue in your head," Jia said. "It seems they will begin immediately."

Ash looked over to the spot where he'd seen the elders and masters gathering.

Sure enough, the head elder seemed to be preening himself moments before he planned on speaking.

"Each of you will be allowed to proceed through the door over there.

"Beyond that is a selection of doors. Nine, to be exact.

"You will need to select a door and go through it. I cannot tell you what to expect once you do, as even I do not know," the head elder said. "This trial was prepared by the Inner Sect elders, and only they know what lies in wait for you."

Ha, I don't believe that for a god-damned second. Not only do you know, you already warned your people about it.

"The expectation of you is very simple. Make it to the other side of the challenge hall. If you're able to do that, you'll be eligible to make it to the next examination.

"This is a timed challenge, mind you. The fifty with the best times will move on; those who aren't in that group will not," the head elder said, folding his hands into his sleeves. "One final note. Each door has a different challenge. It would be best if you do your best to have luck on your side during the selection. Or at least an ability that will help you see through obscuring artifacts.

"Good luck, one and all!"

Jia sighed and put her hands behind her back as she began to walk off to the side. It was obvious she didn't want to be around anyone else.

Ash followed her, his eyes moving down to the sway of her hips as she moved.

Damn, since when did I become such a horn dog?

Well, actually, that isn't a fair question. Haven't gotten laid since I came here.

"And of course, they will all know which doors to take," Jia said with a shake of her head, her words crashing through his thoughts. "This sect is very corrupt."

Ash couldn't help but agree, nodding.

Turning around, Jia faced him and came to a stop.

"You're not wrong. But… I get the impression this is true for all sects. This is just the way it is. Might makes right," Ash said.

"It is a pity you are right. Maybe we could travel around and try to find a sect that is not so blind to its needs."

"Wouldn't mind that much. As it stands, I'm not sure Yan would want to stay here anyway."

"Ah… yes. Yan," Jia said, nodding her head. "I imagine Yue would come as well."

"Huh? Oh. Eh… I mean, I know she looks at me like a lovesick puppy at times, but I can't imagine she'd leave her after she's set up," Ash said.

Jia looked at him and quirked an eyebrow.

"You admit it?"

"What, that she seems to have an infatuation with me? Well, yeah. I'm not blind. Or stupid," Ash said with a shrug of his shoulders.

"And Moira?" Jia prompted.

"Wants to get into my bed. For what reason, I don't know—which is why she's not in it."

"Curious. Is that the only reason you resist her?"

Ash opened his mouth to reply, only to have an elder show up in front of him.

"Disciple of Gen, it's your turn," said the man. Without waiting for Ash to speak, or to even follow him, he began to walk toward the door on the far side.

Ash smiled at Jia and bobbed his head. "See you on the other side."

The elder opened the door and held it aside. "In you go."

Ash walked through and looked around. It was exactly what the head elder had said. Nine doorways.

Behind him, the door slammed shut, the doorknob practically hitting him in the ass.

Glaring at the way he'd come for a second, Ash activated Sneaky Peeky. Turning his eyes to the doors, he started to inspect them one by one.

At first, he didn't see anything. They all seemed like doors without anything to them.

"Cracked it. You should see consideration-Icons now," Locke said.

Blinking, Ash looked to the door in front of him.

Sure enough, the colored icons were there now.

"This route could pose problems; you would probably defeat it," Ash said aloud.

"So it would seem. There are no doors that seem to be lesser than this one, though there is one other that is it's equal. All the others would appear to be stronger," Locke said.

"And how do you justify that assumption?"

"There's a script written into the obfuscation wards themselves, rating their difficulty."

"Huh, convenient."

"Well, it wouldn't be much of a test if you didn't have a way to stand out."

Shrugging his shoulders, Ash grabbed the handle and swung the door inward.

In front of him was a corridor. It was only three people wide, but he could see larger rooms interspersed along its path.

"Interesting," Ash muttered.

Walking into the corridor, he closed the door behind himself.

No sooner had the door closed, the immediate floor of the corridor in front of Ash fell away.

"Ooook. I mean… sure. Right. No floor."

Squatting down, Ash looked into the empty floor.

There was no seeming end to the depths as they fell away.

"Yeah. Infinite darkness. Great. So… they said this was a test of Spiritual Sense. Right? That was focus and channeling Qi out through my hands."

Bobbing his head left and right, Ash thought on the situation.

Holding up his left hand, he began pushing Qi through his body. Channeling it toward his palm.

Rapidly, Qi flowed from his Dantian and out of his hand, faster than he would have expected.

"Ok. And what do we do with it now. I mean… how much can I make? Can I just… make a plank?"

Focusing on the Qi, Ash forced more and more out through his hand. In his mind, he was aiming to create a long plank that would stretch from this side to the other.

Spanning the gap, literally.

In no time at all, his Qi had done as he'd wished. A plank of solid Qi had been formed.

"Great. Let's cross and then see if we can't just… take our Qi back."

Disconnecting the Qi from his hand, Ash stared at the plank. He was wondering if it would vanish or remain where he'd put it.

Taking two breaths, he judged that it wasn't going anywhere.

Getting up, he brushed the dirt off his knees and then began to cross the chasm.

Putting one foot in front of the other Ash walked along the plank. There was no movement in the board at all. It was stiff. Stiff as concrete, and seemingly unbreakable.

Reaching the other side, Ash leaned down and pressed his hand to the solidified Qi.

Scraping across the tile, the Qi began to enter his palm and zip right back into his Dantian.

"Ok, so… that was easy. And enlightening. I wonder if I could make Qi arrows. Shoot them with a bow," Ash mused.

"You talk to yourself a lot," Locke said suddenly.

"If I speak it out loud, it takes longer to do. The thought stays there longer. When I just think it, it runs away. Sometimes I lose hold of it entirely and I forget what I was thinking of."

"That sounds…"

"Yeah yeah, whatever. Anyways, moving on," Ash said, turning around and walking down the corridor.

Reaching the first room, he began to inspect what he was looking at.

It was empty except for five pillars, aligned in a row and facing him.

Each one had a different color. Black, white, yellow, red, and green.

"Alright, so—"

Explosions of Qi shot out from each of the pillars. Balls of colored energy spinning towards him.

"Shit!"

Ash called up his Qi again, formed it into five semi-circles, and shoved it all forward with both hands.

Each semi-circle hit one of the balls of Qi. The force behind his expulsion from his Dantian was stronger than the energy spheres, and the semi-circles cupped them perfectly. Right up to the point that each one hit the ground, trapping the balls of energy against it.

"This is just fucking stupid," Ash grumbled. "What the hell am I supposed to do with that, huh?"

Walking over to the closest of his Qi manifestations, Ash tentatively lifted up an edge.

Bright-yellow Qi blazed out, causing him to drop the manifestation back down.

"Fine, you keep it. Whatever. I didn't want it anyways."

Ash moved to the far end of the room and continued down the corridor.

"This feels strange. I think they switched the door on us as soon as we entered. Or changed the script to be different than what it said," Locke said.

"That's no surprise. They're all out to get me."

A number of walls of energy flared up in front of Ash. They were all flamelike. Writhing and twisting with tongues of fire toward the ceiling.

Ash stood there, staring at this recent obstruction.

"Uh…"

"This is somewhat odd. You could technically just – "

Ash lifted his hands up and threw out a massive plank of Qi over the entire floor.

With what sounded like a wet fart, Ash's giant Qi board slammed down. The roar of the flames was gone. The intense light that had flooded the hall no longer existed.

Sighing, Ash walked across the Qi board.

"Yeah. Could just do the same thing. I think this has to do with the density of your Qi."

"Oh?"

"Remember, they had a test designed specifically to measure the density of your Qi. Your Qi is a solid thing. It isn't a liquid at all."

"Uh huh," Ash said.

Moving to the other side of the massive plank he'd made, Ash bent down and drew the Qi back in.

No sooner than he'd done so, the flames went straight back up to the ceiling.

"Well, whatever. It's not really an issue. If it's easy for me, it's easy."

Ash started walking down the corridor again.

Then he stopped and frowned.

"So long as I'm in contact with my Qi, I can use it and make it move. So… why not just make a hamster ball," Ash said.

Holding up his hands on each side of himself, Ash began to channel and form his Qi. In the time it took him to take several breaths, his Qi had formed up around him into a giant square. There was only a single rectangle of space that wasn't filled in, and it was right in front of his face so he could see where he was going.

Keeping his hands pressed to his Qi on each side of himself, he began to visualize the Qi shifting and rolling itself forward. Slithering along the corridor.

The square jumped forward and Ash felt like he was starting to move.

"Well. That's certainly one way to do it."

Something slammed into the bottom of the square, but there was no damage Ash could see on the inside of the square.

"Yup, that was a thing."

Several more bangs hit the bottom of the square as it ground along. Ash didn't feel any type of drain on his Dantian or himself.

In fact, he felt pretty good right now.

Red light suddenly flooded the hallway. On the right side of his Qi square there was a loud bang. Followed by something on the left.

"More things… or something. Hey, Locke, can you tell me what they are?"

"Qi attacks using various elements. They're pretty strong and well formed. Whoever set these up did so to truly punish someone."

"Which means either they're just sadistic, or they really did set up a particular corridor for people they didn't want to succeed, and then moved it as needed."

"That'd be a logical assumption."

Ash kept himself moving ahead. Countless bangs and thumps were heard all around him. Making the entire Qi square shudder and jump as he went along.

"Expand the square by ten feet in front of you. There's another gap."

Ash immediately did so, then raised the ceiling of his square as well. Wedging the corners in firmly, Ash simply filled the entire corridor now.

"That works."

Ash grew bored as the minutes dragged on.

The bangs, slams, and clangs continued to sound out all around him as he rolled along.

"Seems rather long," Ash muttered.

"Then you're in luck, Chosen One. Because we're about to – "

There was a massive explosion of noise and Ash found himself looking into daylight out his front viewing port.

"Uh."

"Be free," Locke finished.

"What in the nine kingdoms!?" shouted someone nearby.

Ash pulled in the Qi that was around him and shoved it back into his Dantian.

Looking back over his shoulder, he could see the corridor.

It was a wreck. There was smashed columns, broken stones, and scattered furniture in every direction. Numerous clouds of elemental Qi and balls of force were rolling around aimlessly. Their launchers having been broken or left active.

Turning his head back to the front, Ash found only a single master staring at him.

"Hi, I'm Ashley Sheng. Disciple of Gen Sheng," Ash said. "What's my time?"

The master blinked several times before turning to look at another man off to one side that Ash hadn't noticed.

"Three turns of the glass. He is… the fastest so far. It might be the fastest ever," said the second man.

"Ah… good job. You can go inside or wait here. You're the first to finish."

"Great. I'll just go sit down over there, then," Ash said, motioning to a bench nearby.

Sitting down, Ash smoothed out his training gi with his hands. Then he looked around, sighed, and leaned back against the wall behind him.

Folding his hands in his lap, he wondered how long it'd be before someone else showed up.

A massive explosion shook everything around him. Looking to the building he'd come from, Ash watched as a door was simply blown off its hinges.

Out poured a flood of water and water Qi.

It was as if someone had opened up a hole into an ocean, such was the amount of water that blew out.

Then the flow cut off, and Jia was standing there alone.

"Oh, good show," Ash said, waving a hand at her when she turned in his direction.

She gave him a bright smile and then started to walk over to him.

Moving over to one side, Ash patted the bench next to him.

"We have to wait. We're the first ones done," Ash said.

Twenty-Five

Ash and Jia hadn't left the bench, sitting there as others had begun to exit from the doors.

A number of them looked considerably worse for wear. Apparently, this challenge had been much more than Ash had taken it for.

It was obvious to Ash at this point that the test was winding down. Fewer and fewer people were coming out, and masters had begun showing up to collect their disciples.

"Gen is here," Jia said.

Ash looked around and spotted the old man walking their way. He'd managed to find a new set of clothes somewhere, and he'd taken on the appearance of the frail older librarian again.

Walking up to his disciples, Gen looked from one to the other.

His grin was wide, and his eyes scrunched at the corners in clear mirth. There wasn't anyone who would misunderstand what Gen was feeling, other than enjoyment.

"I understand the two of you ruined the paths you took. To the point that no one else could run them today," Gen said, leaning forward over his cane.

"Ah… yes. That's true. Sorry, Master," Ash said, bowing his head toward Gen.

Clicking his tongue and yet smiling the entire time, Gen lifted his cane and pointed to the shattered exit that had been Ash's.

"Ash, you broke almost every object in the trial. It will require a full year to repair," Gen said. "There is very little left that can be used again. Apparently, it was also the single hardest trial in the entire examination."

"I grew tired of the tricks. I decided the test was for me to display my control. So I did. I used my Qi and only my Qi," Ash said.

Gen turned his head to look at Jia.

"And you, Jia. It isn't that you destroyed all the traps and Qi dispensers, but you flooded the entire corridor," said their master. "The entire thing is crumbling to nothing because the mortar has been completely washed away. Your trial will also require a year to repair, because it'll have to be taken apart and rebuilt."

Jia shrugged.

"Much as Ash said, I did the same. I flooded the entire hallway with my Qi, and simply rode it to the exit," she said.

"Yes, so the observers saw and verified when the head elder tried to dismiss your times. Apparently, they are both sect records. First and second place. The difference between you was only two seconds," Gen said, his smile growing wider. "Would you care to learn who took first?"

"Not really," Ash said with a shrug of his shoulders. "Doesn't matter."

Jia sighed and glared at him. "Why do you not wish to compete with me? Why must I look like the eager one?"

Ash felt a weird flutter in his chest at her question. She wasn't wrong. He really was avoiding a direct confrontation that would list one better than the other.

"Because he wants to be your equal," Gen said before Ash could respond. His smile had slipped away, and he looked much more like the librarian he was. "Once one is better or stronger, there is no backward step. The relationship is set. Some people cannot see beyond that, and it eats at them.

"In some cases, they simply can't be around the other person any longer without seeing someone who beat them.

"Which seems like he's experienced it before. Much as I have once. Or am I misreading this, Ash?"

Letting out a held breath slowly, Ash shook his head. "No. You're not."

Jia looked unsure, her eyes moving from Gen to Ash.

After several seconds, her features smoothed over and she slowly curved her lips into a smile.

"In other words, you are afraid that knowing which one of us was stronger would change our relationship. That if you were to be stronger, that maybe I might not be able to handle it," Jia said. "In other words, you are afraid I might leave your side."

Ash knew exactly what she was asking. He wasn't a shrinking violet without experience, either, so there was no fear in answering her.

"Yeah. That's pretty much it," Ash said.

Jia chuckled softly and then reached out, laying her hand on Ash's forearm.

"Master Gen, what is next?" Jia asked, turning toward Gen again.

"The test of your Dao," Gen said, a thumb tapping against his cane. "It's a fairly straightforward affair. You stand on a point of energy surrounding the testing column.

"It will begin to transfer energy to each energy point. Your task is to resist the energy coming to your point and send it back."

"And we do that with our understanding of the Dao?" Ash asked.

"Yes. The energy point will measure the resonance in your body, heart, and soul. The greater the resonance, the greater your power through the energy point," Gen explained. "The entire exercise will last only the amount of time it takes for an incense stick to burn. And at the end, only twenty-five will make it through."

Ash frowned and gave a small shake of his head.

He didn't have any confidence in his understanding of himself.

Of his Dao.

Jia's fingers curled into his forearm lightly before she patted it.

"We will be fine," Jia said, her hip pressing into his.

Gen snickered and said nothing.

***

Scuffing his boot against the strange design beneath his feet, Ash wasn't sure what to make of it.

It was a series of shapes and lines that seemed very much designed. It didn't look to be an artistic decoration.

"We have a similar symbol in the Hall. Though this one appears to be a degraded version of that one," Locke said.

"Degraded, huh? That seems to fit with what we've seen so far. Seems like the Hall is from a long time ago," Ash muttered.

"I would concur. For all intents and purposes, it does seem as if the Hall is from a different era.

"A different era that also had significantly more strength."

"Well, that's yet to be seen. Ya know? The middle realm and the upper realm could have more strength. We're still in the lowest realm."

Ash looked to his left and his right.

Twenty feet in both directions were other disciples. Everyone was standing on the same symbol, just as Gen had said. They were arrayed out in a circle around the massive, glowing, bright-blue column in the middle.

"The test is about to begin!" called a master. "Prepare yourselves."

Prepare? How does one prepare... I mean, I guess I could start meditating, but would that help with my Dao?

They didn't say anything about that. What if—

The column suddenly exploded into a giant ball of azure flame. It was a roaring inferno of energy.

Ash felt the symbol beneath him activate, and he felt a force pulling at the column. It was trying to pull the energy straight through Ash, and into the symbol directly.

Blue crackling light sped down in an arc toward him, aimed at his chest.

Panicking, Ash struggled to push out against the attraction force that was pulling the energy straight to him.

Slowly, he could feel the symbol responding, and allowing him to negate some of its pull.

But it wasn't enough. It wasn't enough by even a third. The energy continued to burn through the air towards him.

Ok, ok. Dao, Dao, think on our Dao and synch our whatever and resonance and… Dao. Dao.

Ash was panicking. And he knew it. His mind was blurring quickly as his heart hammered in his chest.

Struggling, Ash began throwing his beliefs up into his mind. With each and every one, he pushed at the symbol with his entire being. Trying for all his worth to reject the energy coming his way.

Nothing worked.

Nothing changed.

Energy continued to crawl down towards him. Inch by crackling inch, it headed his way.

Panting, Ash couldn't figure out what to do with himself. If this were a straight challenge of strength, he would be confident. If it were his abilities, he would be reasonably sure he could handle anything. Even his Spiritual Sense, he had a newfound confidence in.

But his understanding of a vague and nebulous concept that you can't really train or be educated in?

Never did well in philosophy, damnit.

The only thing he'd ever identified with was listening to a handful of martial artists giving interviews back home.

They weren't always the strongest, but they'd always been able to adapt and change to the situation.

Stop. Stop!

We're focusing on what's in front of us. We're missing everything else beyond this one moment.

Sighing, Ash began to empty his mind. His thoughts drained away slowly.

The panic and fear started to vanish. The sights and sounds from all around him became murky and full of shadows.

They ceased to exist.

Things were starting to feel like when he'd first started martial arts. When an elderly instructor had told him he was overthinking his matches.

With a soft thought of nothing that came from deep in his mind, Ash was empty, and all that remained was his consciousness. It flowed through him like a stream.

Ash felt it then. The line of force from the symbol was moving through more than just his body. It passed through all three of his Dantians.

Where it clipped through his lower Dantian, it bisected it perfectly. As it went through his middle and upper ones, though, it hit to one side or the other.

I'm unbalanced.

I must be one with myself. I have to let this go.

I have to be formless.

Without design.

If this were combat, I would react with violence. If this were a challenge, I would move to overcome.

This is no different. This is just a different obstacle.

One where I need to bring myself – to myself.

The line of force going through him slowly began to adjust in his middle Dantian. Inexorably, it began to move towards the center.

A lazy thought slithered up from his subconscious. A thought he'd had when Gen had helped him into the first step of his Dao.

It hadn't settled firmly, going by as quickly as it had come.

Be like water.

Respond in kind to whatever is put in front of me.

Ash paused as his thought jumped forward two steps.

Flow forward and carry the momentum of whatever is given, then turn it back.

There was a crack as the line of force suddenly lined up much more cleanly with all three of his Dantians.

It was by no means perfect, but it was much tighter than it had been.

The force that was pulling down the energy vanished. Instead, it rapidly reversed itself and began to send it back to the column.

Ash didn't care.

Deliberately, he tuned even that out and focused internally, only on himself.

Nothing else mattered but the thought that was sitting there in his head. It felt as if it were branching out from there and beginning to drill into the rest of his entire self.

Turning his senses inward, he began to look into his Qi Sea.

Sitting there in his Qi Sea was a golden pillar. It was sticking up from the ocean of his Qi. Only perhaps ten feet, but it was clearly growing.

Golden brick after golden brick appeared, one atop the other, building ever upward. Layer after layer after layer.

And it felt right. It felt like it was meant to be there, even though he'd never heard anyone speak of such a thing.

Moving his senses closer to the column, he could feel the power that was coming off of it.

It wasn't the power of Qi, though. Or Essence. Nor the strange magic Moira and Tala used.

To Ash, it almost felt more like a power such as gravity. Sunlight. Or time.

Force and power that simply *was*, and that could be felt. Directly or indirectly.

But there was nothing actually there that could be latched on to.

The golden bricks began to slow down. Then they came to a stop.

The pillar was roughly halfway from the top of his Qi Sea. From what he understood, the depth and breadth of his Qi Sea wasn't going to change. From here on out, it was about filling it to the brim.

Then locking it into place.

Does that mean I need to build this pillar before that happens? What if I can't do it?

With that single thought, the column stopped building, and Ash was forcefully ejected out of his Qi Sea.

Opening his eyes, Ash looked to the testing column.

The line of energy that had been heading to him was much further away now. The amount of force the symbol was able to push through him was non-existent.

"This exam is over," called a voice.

Following the words, the symbol shut itself off.

Ash felt lightheaded when it did. He hadn't realized just how much effort he'd been putting in. Apparently, his entire being had focused in on the simple task of sending back all the energy that had been heading his way.

"If your symbol turns green, please remain where you are. If red, please return to your housing," called the same voice from earlier.

Looking down at his feet, Ash watched as the symbol flashed red, then a solid green.

The color didn't change after that.

"Alright. I made it. I guess I just stand here then," Ash said.

"Your heart rate, cognitive ability, and body chemistry is very erratic right now. I recommend eating something with some sugar in it."

Woodenly, Ash pulled out an apple from his ring and immediately bit into it.

He wasn't about to argue with the magical voice inside his head. It hadn't steered him wrong yet. If anything, it was the only reason he'd been doing so well recently.

Just because it was the same reason he hadn't unlocked his Dantian didn't mean it hadn't done him better than if he'd not had it at all.

Actually, now that I think about it, it's likely I wouldn't be doing half as well as I am without Locke.

"Ash," said Gen's firm voice. "Come. We'll listen to the head elder for a bit, then proceed to the next test."

Looking over his shoulder in the direction of the voice, Ash found Gen standing there with Jia.

Nodding, Ash came over and followed Gen when he turned away.

Jia looked a bit wobbly on her feet, but her eyes were clear.

Pulling out another apple from his ring, he held it out in front of her.

Jia's hand came out and took the apple wordlessly. Holding it out in front of herself, she seemed unsure of what to do.

"Eat it. You'll feel better. I already ate one myself," Ash said, encouraging her. "Felt better within seconds."

Lifting the apple to her mouth, Jia began to steadily eat it.

"The test is draining. The energy the column uses is drawn from those it's testing," Gen said offhandedly. "It's mostly irrelevant since the next test is one of determination and will. Not of strength of energy."

"Are the tests so routine that they're the same every time?" Ash asked.

"One test is almost always different, and the other two are selected from a number of predetermined ones. It gives masters a chance to prepare their students for two of them, though that isn't always the case," Gen said. "As an example, they told me about none of the tests, nor what they would be. Though I've since discovered that information was provided to everyone else."

Ah… I see.

"That certainly would confirm that the Deng family is after us, or Gen. Though, more than likely, it's just us. We've certainly been a pain for them since we showed up," Locke added.

"I would imagine this is due to me. I've been a problem for the Deng family since the day I showed up," Ash said.

"So I've gathered. You broke one of their youngsters, whom I believe was harassing young mistress Yan. Had I known, I would have dealt with the villainous scumbag myself.

"You beat the tar out of a young female Deng family member who challenged your sister, and by their accounts robbed her and her friends," Gen said, holding up two fingers of one hand over his shoulder. "Then you defied the trading arm of the Deng family. So far, your mercantile partner has forced the Deng family markets to slash their prices over and over. It's being said they are making very little profit anymore at all."

Gen was now holding up three fingers.

"Then you stepped in and broke the hold Jing had over Yan, while shaming the Deng family publicly and thrashing one of their allied members," Gen said, holding up a fourth finger.

"Yeah, seems like the Deng and Sheng family just won't get along," Ash said with feigned sadness. "Such a pity, too. I'm sure I could have made an excellent husband if I sold enough of my soul and family members to them."

Gen chortled at that, then held up his thumb.

"Then you did something truly unthinkable. You gave me back what I'd given up as lost long ago. Put me back into a position where I can begin paying them back for all the wrongs they've given to me," Gen said. There was a deep and unfiltered hate in his words, burning with anger. "In the span of a month, you did everything outside of simply sitting down with a table in the middle of the sect with a banner that simply read, 'I'm going to punish the Deng family' and then wait."

Ash coughed into his hand.

Gen wasn't wrong. The Deng family weren't just enemies, now that he thought about it. They were a clan enemy at this point.

A clan enemy he'd need to either exterminate or harm to the point that they didn't want to deal with him.

"Yes, they're a clan enemy," Gen said, as if reading his mind. "It's a pity the clan only has three members that can fight on equal footing with the Deng clan."

Me, Gen, and Yan.

"Four," Jia said. "Seven, if you count the others."

Snorting, Ash shook his head.

Great. Group of seven to take on a band of cutthroats for the safety of the Outer Sect. This never turns out well for everyone, does it?

Twenty-Six

Ash and Jia followed along quietly behind Gen. Around them were six other groups of masters and disciples.

Five of them Locke immediately identified as Deng family members. The last was someone completely unaffiliated with them.

"Master Gen, who is the master over there in the blue gi?" Ash asked suddenly.

"Eh? Oh, that's uh…" Gen said, his eyes flicking over to the individual in question. "Blast it. I rightly can't remember. I never paid attention to politics much, you realize. There wasn't much I could do. Why do you ask?"

"I believe they're not with the Deng family. It would behoove us to know who they are, given they might be a potential ally down the road," Ash said.

Gen made a humph-like noise, but he didn't disagree. His head turned back to the path they were walking along.

"I'll ask around after the tournament. When I'm an elder," Gen said, amusement in his voice. "We're almost there. After this, everyone will be sent up the steps one at a time. Most of these only take a portion of an hour. Some much less."

Ash nodded. Up ahead he could see a series of steps leading up the side of a mountain. Throughout the path, there were four gateways that led to small platforms.

At the bottom of the path and top of the path, large gateways looked very similar to the ones that led to the platforms.

"It's rather simple," Gen said as they were approaching the base. "You go as high as you can. Each platform is another level of power that will be put down upon you as you climb.

"It will test your will through pain, and suppression of your Dantian."

"What function does the platform serve? It looks like one could bypass them if one chose to do so," Jia inquired.

"A brief respite. No more, no less. You're allowed to remain there for the time it takes an incense stick to burn," Gen said. "Though one does have to enter and touch the center column to affirm that they reached that point."

Five minutes isn't exactly a long time. I wonder if remaining there the whole five minutes might actually be worse than if you just… went.

Does it make it harder to go back in after no longer suffering from the effects of the stairs?

Would it weaken the resolve to continue?

"Something isn't right," Gen said softly.

"What isn't?" Ash asked.

His master didn't respond, however. They closed the distance to the first step, where the twenty-five other disciples stood.

"Greetings and welcome to the final examination," said the head elder. He was looking particularly pleased with himself for some reason. It made the hair on the back of Ash's neck stand on end. "We'll be making a few small modifications to this test, and then proceed immediately."

Great.

"First, the normal rules apply. Climb as high as you can. It's unlikely you'll finish, but we encourage you to try.

"Second, you must touch the orb in the middle of each platform to have your progress count." Nodding as he finished speaking, the head elder looked so self-satisfied it was sickening.

"Now for new rules. Everyone will be heading up the staircase at the same time. There's more than enough room, and we used to run the event like that in the distant past," said the head elder. "On top of that, limited combat will be allowed. You may only use generic martial arts on the steps. Though you may commit to full-on battles when standing on the platforms."

"We must ask you limit your fighting, however. If anyone should cripple or seriously harm another, they will be kicked out of the sect without a thought or an argument."

After having met Gen and hearing his story, Ash had no doubt in his mind that a limitation like that would do nothing to stop the Deng family from proceeding as they wished.

In fact, as far as Ash knew, they might even reward someone who managed to cripple him or Jia.

"We'll allow you two minutes to make whatever preparations you need to make, and then we'll begin," said the head elder.

Gen turned and faced his disciples. It was obvious he didn't like this situation at all.

"Do your best to stay out of the fights. I'm sure you both have already thought of my own story and know what the Deng family will do to ensure their victory," Gen said. "Rely on one another, stick together, and move up as best as you can."

Ash turned to face Jia directly.

"I'm relying on you, Jia. They're going to look to me as their target, but you as a secondary," Ash said. "I'm going to rush to the second platform, touch the orb, and then wait there. I think they'll all rush to the first platform and do their best to keep us from moving on.

"Which means you have to get through the first platform quickly and keep moving."

Jia's delicate eyebrows came together and she frowned at him.

"You wish to sacrifice yourself for my victory," she murmured.

"Sacrifice myself for our victory. So long as one of us wins, Gen wins. They're working together—why shouldn't we?"

Jia shook her head ever so slightly. "Ok, Ash. Ok. I do not like this, though."

"We're in this together, aren't we?" Ash asked, holding his hand up in a neutral gesture. "It's not as if it really matters which one of us wins."

"The cultivator's life is a lonely one," Jia said. "Those we would friend and pair with can be left behind if they are not strong enough. While I am willing to fight together in this, are you sure? There is no guarantee I can return this favor."

Ash laughed at that and shrugged his shoulders.

"Maybe I just want to look up your dress as you go up the stairs. As to being stronger or weaker... don't worry about that. I don't think you'll outpace me," Ash said. "Are you ready? Do you need anything?"

Jia snorted once and then prodded him in the middle of his chest with a finger.

"Why do you do this? You make poorly timed comments when the mood is serious. It is childlike."

"Because I'm nervous? I dunno, Jia. You say some heavy shit sometimes and I don't know what to do," Ash said. "I mean, if—"

"Disciples, make ready!"

Jia growled and glared at the head elder, but said nothing.

"Come on, let's get ready. I'm going to burst ahead and do what I can," Ash said.

Activating his toggled abilities, Ash began to mentally siphon as much energy into Spring Step as he could.

Actually, if we could hit the first platform, and then wait on the second, this would give Jia an even better chance.

Tapping himself on the chest, Ash activated a chain, then hooked it into Jia by patting her in the middle of her back. Immediately he could feel the Qi transferring directly to her from his Dantian.

"What did you do? You have done this before," Jia muttered. "I can feel Qi. Pure Qi, without an element. This is your Qi. Is it not?"

"Begin!" shouted a Deng Elder.

Activating Spring Step to its full ability, Ash flew up the steps. In the first bounding leap, he made it halfway to the platform.

As soon as his foot touched the step, he felt a weight settle down atop his Dantian, and his skin began to itch as if he'd been lying in a scratchy blanket.

Using Spring Step as his other foot hit the ground, Ash bounded forward again. He landed a single step from the platform.

Turning on his heel, he bolted onto the platform. A few steps later, he'd reached the center point.

Touching the orb before the others had even made it to the halfway point, Ash spun and dashed off the platform. Once more, he started up the stairs.

Hell, maybe I should just keep going. I bet I can just outrun them all.

Leaping up the stairs with the constant use of Spring Step, Ash felt his Qi draining away as he bounded further and further upward.

The pressure on his Dantian increased, and the itching and discomfort on his skin was slowly replaced with an aching sensation.

As if he were bruised all over.

There was a boom and a Qi wave washed over him. It was full of energy and aggression, but it did nothing to him.

Reaching the second platform, and technically the halfway point, Ash lowered his shoulder and dove toward the orb. He wanted to touch it and be gone.

As fast as possible. If he could get this entire thing done before the others even had a chance, it'd be ideal.

After slapping his hand on the orb, Ash turned and raced away.

Before he could leave, a young woman stepped into the doorway and threw a fist toward his middle.

Ash immediately recognized her. It was the woman who'd challenged Yan for her allotment.

He had no ability to dodge or deflect the attack, so instead tucked his shoulder and shifted his body downward with the blow.

In not resisting the strike, he limited its effectiveness.

Taking the momentum she imparted into his body, Ash spun around her, intent to clear the gateway and be gone.

A second person appeared, a young man he didn't recognize who blocked his way entirely.

"I am Mei Ling," said the woman, squaring up with Ash. "You may address me as Mei.

"We've already met, of course, but this time deserves an introduction."

Of course she's named Flower. I think that's what it means.

"Last time you beat me. This time, I'll defeat you."

"And I'll cripple you," said the young man.

The young woman glanced at the man with a small frown but said nothing, turning forward again.

Ash looked from one to the other, then down the stairwell.

The others were all in a mad tussle on the first platform. Jia had managed to get through the scrum and was heading his way.

Back to the original plan, I suppose.

Ash darted back to the orb and stood in front of it. Taking a quick, shaky breath, he prepared himself to hold out here against everything that came his way. His only goal in life was to prevent anyone from advancing further.

Other than Jia.

"Come then, Mei. Let's see if I can't ruffle your petals. I promise not to touch you as we fight here. Well, not too much, at least. I'm curious to see how you feel against my fingers," Ash said, trying to rile her up.

Turning a deep, dark red, Mei clenched her fingers together into cupped palms. Snarling at him, she threw her hands back and then whipped them forward as she cried out something he couldn't quite understand.

Earthen rods the thickness of her forearms speared out at him from her hands.

Deflecting one out of the air, he grabbed the other with his left hand. Bringing it around his back, he spun it over his hip and then grabbed it with both hands. He waved the tip back and forth, holding it out in front of himself like a spear.

"Come, Mei. Let's see those petals…"

Eying her own rod pointed back at her, Mei clapped her hands together once.

The Qi-formed staff in his hands vanished, pooled into liquid goop, and solidified on the ground after flowing through his fingers.

In a flash of Water Qi, Jia crashed into the platform. Ash smiled and stepped to one side, having watched her progress as she made her way up the stairs.

Jia's hand slapped the orb and then she was gone, as if she'd never been there. Shouting, the young man chased after her, apparently intent to follow even though he hadn't touched the orb.

Damn it. He didn't even consider staying here to touch it. Does he care that little about this?

Is he just here to stop Jia and me?

Forming a staff out of his Qi from his palms, Ash took the same position he'd had just moments ago.

"I believe we were like this…" Ash said, pointing the tip back to Mei. "And you were going to show me your petals."

Mei blinked several times and then formed another rod, swishing it through the air several times.

"If you want to see my petals so badly, you'll need to work for it," Mei said, her tone breathy.

Smirking, Ash moved forward several steps, slowly getting in Mei's range.

Mei watched, her eyes locked on him like a hunter watching her prey.

She's not going to move, or attack. Her entire goal is just to hold me here.

Ash shifted his rear hand forward and let the weight of the staff drop the tip down. After it dipped down several inches, he lunged forward toward Mei's hip.

Flicking her weapon to one side in a block, she deflected Ash's attack, then brought the rear of her staff over her head in a riposte.

Letting go with one hand of his staff, Ash stepped to the side and dodged her strike. He had moved in close to Mei, ruining her attack outright.

Reaching out with his free hand, he grabbed hold of her dress at the hip and gave it a pull. The fabric resisted the sharp yank, but the sound of seams popping was quite audible.

Pressing his hand to his belt as he danced away before she could respond, Ash smiled at her.

He really didn't have any other goal but to piss her off and keep her here as well. The longer he could delay everyone, the better off Jia was.

Mei shuddered from head to toe, her face bright red.

"It's the least of what you deserve," Ash said, giving his Qi-shaped staff a twirl. "I'll repay you for all the hurt you gave to Yan."

Dropping the tip down to point back to Mei's face, Ash gave her a smile.

Mei's teeth were visible as she snarled at him.

"What I did to Yan was ordered by my family," she said, her Qi rod angling toward Ash's midsection. "There was nothing personal in it for me. Even the way I was to approach Yan was ordained for me. It's one of the reasons I offered her the opportunity to simply give me her allotment rather than humiliate her further.

"It gave me no pleasure to torment her. But it will give me pleasure to cause you as much pain as possible! I'll shame you to death!"

Ash was momentarily at a loss.

It made sense when he thought about it. There really was no reason for the Deng family to target Yan as they'd been doing unless so ordered.

Which meant something else was going on, and he'd possibly been taking out his aggression on someone who didn't fully deserve it.

Need to ask Yan later about how Mei treated her.

Then we can figure out if I've been rude or righteous. For now, I have a job to do.

Ash shrugged his shoulders, waiting.

"With a woman as beautiful as you, you'll forgive me if I still wanted to see your petals, regardless of Yan," Ash said, trying to egg her on. "You could always just take your cl—"

Mei grunted and thrust out faster than Ash expected. Her staff slipped into his defense and found its way home in his stomach.

Stepping back and trying to accept the blow, Ash grimaced.

She's faster and more skilled than I gave her credit for.

That or she's getting stronger with her anger.

"I'll show you nothing but the view of the sky after I'm done beating you," Mei said.

A cultivator Ash didn't know walked up behind Mei and casually smashed an elbow into the back of her head.

Dropping to the ground as her eyes rolled up into her head, Mei was out of the fight.

"Fucking cunt," said the newcomer. "Hey, what are you doing here? You keeping people from tagging and moving up?"

"That I am," Ash said, his eyebrows drawing up. "Can't let the Deng family win this, so I'm making sure my partner gets to the top."

"And is the only one to get to the top."

"Oh. That makes sense." The young man looked down to Mei's unmoving body and lifted a booted foot up. He began to casually slide her dress up along her leg.

"Ah… let's not do that," Ash said, pointing the staff at the young man.

"Why not? Masters can't see up here on the platform. It'd only take me a minute or two to have my fill. You watch the stairs and I'll do the same for you after I'm done. They're all being held up on the stairs in a big battle and none of them seem like they can decide who the enemy is. They're fighting amongst themselves as much as with others," said the man.

What the actual fuck?

Ash dashed forward with Spring Step and swept his Qi rod across his body.

With a dull thud, it smashed into the other man's stomach and sent him flying out the doorway and vanishing off the steps.

He disappeared, screaming as he went.

Grumbling to himself, Ash pulled the hem of Mei's dress down, then dragged her to the corner of the platform.

"Just in case you're not as nasty as I thought you were, we'll put you to the side for safety's sake," Ash muttered.

"Nnnnk ooo," Mei mumbled, her eyes rolling around wildly in her head as she clearly bumbled along the line of consciousness.

Shit, how bad did he mess her up?

Sighing, and feeling like a fool, Ash pulled a health recovery pill from his ring and forced it into Mei's mouth.

Whether it dissolved in her mouth or was digested in her stomach, the result would mostly be the same.

The former would just leave a nasty taste behind and only do about eighty-percent of what the latter would do.

It felt as if five minutes passed in complete silence after that. Ash couldn't see where Jia was, or if she was even still going.

Staying here too long would disqualify him, but that was irrelevant.

The stairs and the platform curved around and went out of sight. Leaving Ash with little to do.

Briefly, he considered trying to summon up a wall of Qi in front of the gateway.

Then he dismissed it, realizing it'd simply take too long to do it.

Then he heard them.

Long before they got close, since they were practically stomping their way up the steps. The steady clump of feet hitting stairs.

A group of Deng family members slowly turned the corner from the stairs and filed onto the platform one by one. They all looked to him, to the orb, and then to Mei.

"Looks like we didn't have to worry about you rushing ahead after all," someone in the group said. Ash couldn't identify who was talking, but it didn't matter anyways. Everyone here was his enemy.

"You've made it easy for us. Whoever manages to cripple you is going to get a massive reward," someone else said aloud.

"Oh grand. Let's see who wants to step up and get killed first, then," Ash said. Pressing his focus into the Qi rod in his hand, he turned the flat staff tip to a spear. "Because if that's your plan, I'd rather kill someone and be kicked out for that."

Ash leveled his spear and gave it a small flourish, the tip making a figure eight.

All the Deng members stared at the spear tip as if it were alive.

Not wanting to say anything more, Ash stood there letting the situation press his threat. Thinking of his options, he was rather limited on what he could do.

"The examination is complete!" called a distant voice. "Everyone head down immediately."

Dismissing his chains, Ash focused everything into his Spring Step and simply dove over everyone's heads.

Pitching himself off the edge of the stairs, Ash fell to the ground in a rapid escape.

Fortunately, he only broke one leg when he landed.

Twenty-Seven

Ash clapped his hands together as Gen was introduced as the newest elder for the Outer Sect. He stood at the rear of the square, as far back from everyone else as possible.

His leg was already healed and mended, but it still felt a bit tender to Ash.

Weak, even.

Painful to put his entire weight on.

The healer had mentioned that since he'd been healed in a similar fashion so recently for his hands, the results would be harder to predict. Injuries requiring this kind of healing were somewhat rare.

The head elder and the rest of the elders looked rather surprised at the situation. Even as they announced the change in status, they seemed unable to process it.

"Was breaking your leg absolutely necessary?" Moira complained, sitting next to him on the bench.

"Eh… not really? I mean, for all I know they could have left me alone at the end, but I didn't want to risk it," Ash said. "If you and a bunch of your allies were left alone with your enemy, would you respect the rules?

"I'm not so sure I would. So… out I went."

Tala snorted and shifted her weight to her other leg. Peering down at him as she stood above him and at his side, she looked annoyed.

"Be grateful I elected to carry you back. It was a gift that you were allowed to touch me so easily," said the Rabbit woman.

"Speaking of that," Moira said, looking past Ash to the other woman. "Why were you there?"

"Because Ash doesn't think ahead, and always manages to get in trouble," Tala said with a shrug. "You were watching over our home; I assumed I could grace him with my presence."

"Fair," Ash said without any sort of disagreement. "Lately it seems I've just been rushing blindly ahead. I've put us into a clan war without the slightest bit of thought."

Watching his leg bones become fractured bits of kindling had sent him into a world of agony.

Agony and introspection.

Up to this point, everything he'd done had been rushed. Short sighted and not very well planned. Centered around his family and little more than that.

"If we're going to be making a long-term home here, we'll need to change the way I've been going about things," Ash said.

"I'm unsure you will want to stay, actually," Moira said suddenly.

"Huh? Why?"

"Your sister was packing up her home while you were away. I noticed as I walked by," Tala said. "I let Moira know and left."

"Yes, and after that, she slipped a note under the door," Moira added. "It read that she was heading back home and leaving the sect."

Ash sat there dumbfounded. "She… left the sect?"

"Yes. The letter did not say much, other than she felt out of place here. Out of place, and a bother. So she was going to go home and see what she could do for your mother and father," Moira said.

Reaching into her clothes, she fished out a piece of parchment and then held it out to Ash.

"Honestly, she seemed as if her heart wasn't in it," Tala said. "I think she was only here living her role as the eldest sister. Now with you getting stronger and Jing betraying her, that role has ended."

Ash unfolded the letter and read it over once.

It was more or less exactly as Moira had said.

In fact, if anything, it was less. Moira and Tala were both clearly trying to read between the lines and offer him insight into it.

What it all came down to, though, was she was gone.

She always was the weak one between us. The first to wish to stop whatever we were doing and go home.

Getting into trouble, or even just pulling a prank, was never in her mental wheelhouse.
I guess… this is just what you would expect of her once her older-sister role was rendered moot.
Ash let the letter fall into his lap and looked back up to the square in front of him. Jia was standing next to Gen, being heaped with praise for her showing on the staircase. Apparently, she'd done extremely well.

"Do you think she'll leave next? It's been mentioned that the winners of this examination are often recruited to other sects," Moira said. Taking the letter from his hand, she tucked it away into her clothes again.

"Mm. I suppose that's a real possibility now," Ash said. "Honestly, she was never supposed to come here to begin with. I mean, she said she was more or less a runaway princess, right?"

"It'd be best for her to join the strongest sect she could. They could offer her protection from her own family."

"To be sure, it does seem family is a driving factor, and a limiting factor, in this veil," Tala said. "I wonder what kind of situation she was put under that would drive her from her familial home."

Maybe something similar to what happened to Mei?
Is that the difference here? Jia is Mei, but she fled her family at a much younger age?
Something to consider, I suppose.

"Ah, it would seem the showcase is over. Jia will be taken to the sect treasure house for her prizes and then given a banquet," Moira said. "Let's go home. Tala managed to run down some game. For a Rabbit, she's quite the hunter."

Tala chuckled darkly, her ears standing straight on her head.

"I'm no Rabbit. I'm Kin. We are not a race of Beast people. You should feel blessed to be in my presence," Tala said, squaring her shoulders and visibly puffing out her chest a bit.

Deliberately glancing at her chest, Ash looked back to her face. "Quite blessed. And thank you for getting us a meal. I admit I hadn't even thought about it."

Levering himself to his feet, Ash wrapped an arm around Tala's hips and leaned into her. "Alright Miss Kin, bless me with your assistance and help me home."

Tala set an arm around Ash's shoulders as Moira stepped in front of the two of them.

"You should truly feel blessed I don't break your hands," Tala said. "Be sure they do not wander."

"I'll do my best," Ash lied.

"And I'll lead the way," Moira said.

***

Ash was sorting things out in the storage space of his ring.

Since purchasing the stall, he hadn't bothered to go through it. He'd been practically on the run since that moment. Working to train and become stronger. Either by himself or with Jia.

If he wasn't training himself, he had been working to improve Yan.

And now she's gone home. Jia is being given a tour of the treasure vault, and possibly being recruited by other sects.
Yue isn't allowed inside this area as she's not technically in the sect.
Which leaves us alone with Moira and Tala.

Finishing up with the ring, he'd now identified everything and gotten it sorted out. What it really came down to was two categories: items he could use immediately, like medicinal pills, or belongings and things he was just holding on to, like the stall and all his pens and paper.

Reaching behind his neck, Ash popped it to one side and then the other, then sank into his chair.

"You seem a bit lost. Restless, even," Moira said, sitting down across from him at the table. They'd eaten dinner a while ago, and it was deep in the night now. He'd honestly expected her and Tala to be in bed.

Frowning, he wasn't quite sure what to say at first.

"I could hear you," Moira said. "I may not have as great hearing as Tala, but I'm certainly more sensitive than a human."

"Ah. That makes sense. And… yes, I suppose I am," Ash admitted. "My entire goal up to this point was to help out Yan and Jing. And now I can help neither.

"Yan has fled, and Jing has joined hands with our enemy. It would seem my entire goal is done and over."

Moira nodded at that, her golden eyes wide and watching him.

"It would seem we must make a new goal then. One for ourselves, no?" she asked.

"Well… yeah, I guess. What would that even be, though? As an outlander myself, it's not as if I'll be accepted everywhere I go," Ash said. "It's by the grace of whatever entity kicked my ass here that I even had a Dantian. Otherwise I'd have ended up a slave and been long dead by this point, I imagine."

Moira laid her hands along the tabletop, her long fingers interlacing.

"A fair point. Is there somewhere in this veil where we could simply retreat to and live a simple life? And would you be happy with that?" Moira asked.

"I imagine there is, sure. As for being happy… I dunno. I mean, sure, Yan ran away, but that doesn't make her any less my sister. Nor Far and Duyi my parents. At least here in this veil," Ash said. Propping his elbows on the table, Ash rested his chin in his palms.

"What do you want out of this life, then?" Moira said, prodding him when he said nothing more.

"Marriage, kids, a stable life."

"I'm afraid I can't help with the first two, as a slave isn't allowed to marry, and I don't think our species can interbreed," Moira said with a shrug of her shoulders. "As to the last, I think that's a bit more problematic than you realize."

"Oh?"

"You've set the Sheng family up as a direct counter to the Deng family. There isn't really a back-step from there. If anything, Yan going back provides your parents some semblance of protection.

"For you and Gen who would remain here, you are the most at threat," Moira said. "A stable life isn't something you can attain if you remain here in this sect, nor in this part of the Nine Kingdoms."

Ash blinked several times as that all sank in.

She was right, of course. There was no way back from here that didn't involve some type of massive bribe or gift.

"When one can't go back the way they came, and there is no escape, there is only deeper," Moira said, as if reading his mind. "Assuming you wish to remain here, that leaves you with only one option. Grow an alliance large enough to challenge anyone in the Deng family at an even level."

Digesting that thought, Ash couldn't help but agree. If he wanted to stay here, be able to see his family, and live out a life, then that was his answer.

Build an alliance strong enough to neutralize the threat of the Deng family

"Though, I think it's worth a word of caution. I do not for a moment believe that this is entirely the Deng family," Moira said, her head slowly tilting to one side. "There is no doubt that the only way such a family could take control of the Outer Sect like this would be with permission from the Inner Sect. Right?"

It's true. The Outer acts as training and a funnel for the Inner. If one were to control the Outer, one could eventually control the Inner. Which means there's a power play in action, or one finishing.

Really stepped into the shit this time.

"Of course, this doesn't really change much. I think it's unlikely we'll be able to live freely until you push someone who is friendly to us, or at least neutral, into the sect leader position," Moira said. "This veil is very ruthless. It's full of nepotism and vultures. The worst of the worst.

"Though… it's at least easy to understand. If everyone has a knife, one can expect how they'll treat you."

Grunting, Ash sat up straight, letting his hands lie on the table.

"I suppose that's it, then. Our long-term goal is to gain stability for ourselves. Short-term goal, oppose the Deng family and neutralize them."

Moira gave him a bright smile and ducked her head once. "So it would seem."

Feeling better now that he had a direction, Ash turned his thoughts toward building an alliance. And realized how isolated he was—and felt immediately lonely.

Moira would help him. As would Tala and Yue. But they couldn't act directly in the Sect. Not really, at least.

Jia was likely carrying out her own plan right now on her way to another sect. Yan was gone. That left only himself in the Outer Sect, with Gen as an elder.

Gonna be an awfully long road ahead. Awfully long and bumpy.

"I want to ask you a question, and I want a direct answer," Moira said, her voice snapping through his dark thoughts.

"Oh? Uh, alright. What's up?"

"If I told you to come to my bed tonight, or that I wanted to get in yours, what would you say? And why?" Moira asked.

Well that really is direct, isn't it?

"I'd probably say no. As to why, well, that's a bit complicated," Ash said, spreading his hands out in front of himself.

"We do have time. I'd like an answer," Moira said.

Clicking his teeth together a few times, Ash thought on it.

"Ok, I'll answer. But I want to hear your own thoughts first on the matter. Why sleep with me? I mean, don't get me wrong, you're beautiful and I'm interested in exploring your body, but… why?"

Moira's cheeks turned a faint shade of red and the corners of her lips turned up.

"I'm flattered at the praise. Now… why?

"Because as I understand it, you cannot release me. Ever. Either I'll have my ownership transferred to another, or I'll die in your care," Moira said. Ash nodded once. "So, I find myself with an owner who treats me like an equal. My understanding is that is fairly rare in this veil. Not impossible, but certainly rare. You treat me as an equal, and not simply a plaything."

Ash frowned at that. His immediate response was that it was only as it should be.

Except he knew it wasn't.

The very reason he bought her was because it wasn't that way.

"I can't really go looking for another man to sleep with, as everyone in this veil views me as anathema. On top of that, I cannot go very far from you without repercussions.

"And those who would want me would only use me as a means to an end. Doing such a thing with a complete stranger with not even a cursory relationship… doesn't particularly sit well with me," Moira said, nodding to her own words.

"Now, as to you. I find you attractive. You're not of my race, but you're pleasing to the eyes. I enjoy looking at you. And I've felt your eyes on me many times.

"Do I love you? No, I'm no lovesick young girl like Yue. Nor am I looking to get anything from you in this, like Jia perhaps.

"Though with the amount of time we'll be locked in each other's presence, I wouldn't rule out having some sort of affection for you after a while. Truth be told, that almost seems like a guarantee, actually. It's not as if we can escape one another," Moira said, holding one hand palm up towards him. "And maybe that all starts with simply enjoying one another in the bedroom."

It all made sense, actually.

Everything she said rang true to him, in a strange way. She was a stranger in a strange land where no one would want her. And the ones who would take her would do it for purposes that would best be avoided.

He was the same.

"Nevermind," Ash said. "My reasons were stupid. I'm stupid."

"Something along the lines of 'I can't, it feels like rape, I don't want to give her the wrong idea, I might have to end it at any time'?" Moira asked, watching him with a smile.

"Errr, yeah. Something like that."

Nodding her head, Moira stood up and stepped to one side, pushing her chair in.

"So… your bedroom? Or mine? Though Tala will hear it anyways, I'm not sure I'd like to give her an eyeful at the same time," Moira said.

"Ah, my bedroom, then."

Moira gave him a bright smile, and a wing expanded rapidly, indicating the doorway to Ash's bedroom with its tip. "After you."

***

A hand lightly smacked Ash in the chest, startling him awake.

"Go get the door, someone's knocking," Moira said, sleep tinging her voice.

One of her wings unwound itself from around him, and he found himself incredibly colder without it there.

Getting out of the bed, Ash stepped into a pair of pants and pulled them up quickly. Snatching a tunic, he pulled it on over his head and left his bedroom. Making sure to close the door behind him, he walked over to the front door.

Opening it, he found Yue standing there. She had dark circles under her eyes, and her skin looked pale.

It reminded him of when he'd stayed up far too late playing video games as a kid.

"Ash!" she said, smiling at him widely. She shoved her hand into his and deposited a pill there. Then her hands clamped around his tightly. "I brought you this. I heard you broke your leg, so I made a pill for you.

"You were healed with Qi too recently, which means they probably couldn't fix it perfectly. I dug through all the memories you gave me and this one seemed to fit the best and then I couldn't stop until I made it and I had to make sure it worked so I—" Yue stopped talking and then coughed twice, having run out of air.

"Calm yourself, Yue," Ash said, grinning at her. "Calm. Thank you for the pill. I'll take it with breakfast this morning."

"Breakfast? Oh! Yes, it's morning. Breakfast. Come to my home! We'll eat together," she said.

"We could do that. Let me get some boots. I don't fancy walking that far without them."

"Oh! I did that, too. You don't have to walk far."

"Did what too?" Ash asked, very confused now.

"I joined the sect. I bought Yan's position and bribed an official," Yue said, bouncing up and down. "And I took house number four, since Yan left! I took over her furniture as well. She said bye to me before she left. That's how I knew."

"She needed supplies for the trip."

Ash blinked a few times, staring at the energetic young girl. "You joined the sect?"

"Yes! Now I don't have to stay away," Yue said, her hands still holding tight to his. Blinking slowly, she seemed to zone out for a second. Then she came back to herself with a small shake. "Breakfast. Yes."

"I will join you two. I think it would be wise for us to discuss our direction, since it seems we have lost a member and gained a member," Jia said, walking slowly up next to them.

"Jia? You're here? I thought you'd take the opportunity to join another sect," Ash said, looking to the other woman.

She was dressed well in a perfectly fitted blue dress that clung to her. It was a drastic change after having seen her so often in her training clothes as of late.

"Yes, they did try to recruit me. I have much to gain here still, though. It was not time to leave yet. Now, shall we go?" Jia asked. Then she turned to Yue and gave her a smile. "Though I think you should leave the cooking to me, as I think you could use a quick nap. No?"

Yue stared blankly at Jia before nodding her head once. "Yes. A nap. I'll nap on my couch if Ash will sit next to me."

Her head whipped around to stare at him as she said it, as if daring him to deny the request.

Yeah, no. You need a nap, you nipped-up little squirrel. If that's what it takes, so be it.

"Sure, sure. No worries. Let's go then. I'm hungry."

Twenty-Eight

"And they just give us several pills for free every week?" Yue said, standing next to Jia and Ash. "Seems odd. Then again, you need a particular license to be able to sell inside the sect. And those are not given out freely; they require a great deal of work."

"They do?" Ash asked, frowning.

"I do believe you are about to apologize extensively, and Yue might not worship you after this," Jia said.

"Why? What'd you do?" Yue asked, looking from Jia to Ash.

Since joining the sect, her attitude hadn't changed toward him. She still seemed to view him with half-fevered awe.

She did have to turn her store over to a manager she'd hired to run the place. It wasn't as if Yue could watch over it while she participated in the sect.

"Uh, nothing that I did—something I acquired, I guess," Ash muttered. Pulling the license to operate out of his ring, he handed it over to Yue. "Is this what you were talking about?"

"Hm?" Yue took the sheet of Qi-infused paper and started to read it over. "You... where did you get this?"

"Bought it. I just wanted all their medicinal supplies so the Deng family couldn't get any. This and the stall came with that purchase.

"I don't have a need for it. If it's useful, you can have it," Ash explained. "Stall too, if you want it."

Yue looked torn between two emotions Ash couldn't identify. Finally, she decided on something and looked to him. "Give this to me, and the stall. In the future, I'd like you to consult me on all purchases and sales. Alright? You have too much money to be throwing it around like this. You're making waves."

"Ah... that's fair. I wanted to sell a few transference abilities. Can I have you handle it for me?"

Yue nodded, scanning over the document in her hand. "Yes. That's fine. I can do it in a way that will help hide the trail back to you."

"Can you press your thumb to this seal and will this contract to me?"

"Huh? Oh, sure. And here's the transference papers," Ash said while pressing his thumb to the seal.

He willed the contract to Ying Yue and pulled out around twenty transference papers from his ring.

"It'd be great if you could sell these for me. Feel free to keep any if you want them for yourself, just tell me and I'll make more," he said, holding them out to her.

Yue's eye twitched and she hurriedly took the contract and the papers, then vanished them into thin air.

Ah, she bought a storage item? Good thinking. Should make sure Jia has one.

Turning his head to Jia, he held up a thumb, indicating Yue.

"Do you have a storage item? If not, we could see if our lovely and talented merchant could get you one."

"I have one. It is a family heirloom. Worry not for me," Jia said, eying him with a smile and holding up her hand. A simple silver ring sat around her finger.

Master Gen appeared out of thin air, as if he'd always been there.

"Ah, my students. Good to see you," Gen said. Then he turned his eyes on Yue. "And who is this?"

Ying Yue pressed her fists together in front of herself and bowed her head to Gen.

"My name is Ying Yue, Master Gen," she said. "And I would ask to be your disciple as well."

Gen's eyes slowly moved from Yue to Ash, and then to Jia. "I see. Building a harem, are we?"

Feeling nervous and jittery at the question, especially after having slept with Moira the previous day, Ash chuckled nervously.

"I guess. If I am, I've certainly gotten the best possible start," Ash said, his mouth moving faster than his brain.

Gen, Jia, and Yue all stared at him.

Coughing lightly, Gen turned to Yue and gave her a small smile.

"I pity you for your choice in friends, though I welcome you as a disciple. Should I assume you also have some fearsome abilities like these two?" Gen asked. "Anything I should know?"

Yue let her hands fall to her sides, staring at Gen.

To Ash, it was clear as day she was debating telling him about her status as an alchemist.

After two seconds, she literally looked to Ash for direction.

"Tell him the truth," Ash said with a smile. "Gen is on our side. Were he to fail, we would fail."

Yue nodded and addressed Gen.

"I'm an alchemist, and I have the Wood element of Qi," Yue said.

Gen raised his eyebrows. "What level alchemist?"

"I can synthesize anything level nine or below in the Body Refiner realm nine times out of ten.

"My success falls to less than half for anything above the fourth level of the Mortal Refiner.

"It falls further to less than one in ten for everything in the Spirit Realm. It took a number of tries to refine the pills Ash needed for you to recover," Yue said.

Gen visibly froze, even his breaths stilling.

Then he snorted once, followed by a deep, dark chuckle.

"I see, I see. Yes, wonderful," Gen said, his fingers clasping and unclasping his cane repeatedly. "Truly wonderful. I can't wait for the alchemists' test in half a year. Oh, ho ho ho, yes."

Gen reached up with one hand and started to run his fingers through his beard. His eyes unfocused and he looked up into the distant skies. The feral smile that came over him whenever he thought about the Deng family showed itself.

"If I supply you with reagents, would you mind making some things for me?" Gen asked, looking back to Yue.

"Sure, but you'll need to give me enough for four of everything you want. I do still fail. And I get to keep the extra reagents if I succeed early," Yue said. "I could use the practice anyways."

"Yes, yes, of course." Gen agreed and nodded, his eyes slowly wandering back up to the skyline. "Deng will pay."

Ash wasn't quite sure what to make of Gen's mood. He seemed hell bent to not just defeat the Dengs, but crush them.

The line was starting to move again. Whatever had held it up was over.

"Ah, it's our turn next. Will we see you tomorrow for formal training, Master Gen?" Ash asked.

"Hm? Yes, yes of course. Yes. I need to go. Things to prepare," Gen said, smiling at all of them. Then he walked away. Lost to the world.

"He holds great anger for the Dengs. I think Master Gen will cause them more pain by himself than we ever could," Jia said.

"I'd agree," Yue said. "Though at least I'll get free experience and reagents out of it."

Ash shrugged his shoulders and moved along in line.

A minute or two later, they were on the way back home after having received their allotments.

"They're not exactly high grade," Yue said, tapping the pill in her hand. "I could make these in bulk if I was determined to waste time."

"Not everyone is blessed by a fortunate encounter with a Fated One, Yue," Jia chastised her with a wry grin.

Yue bit her lip and nodded her head minutely. "You're right, Jia. I'll just… hang on to this for now, I suppose."

The pill disappeared into Yue's storage item.

"If we didn't pick them up at all, it'd be more suspicious," Ash said. "Even if we have better things to be doing."

"Is that Mei Ling?" Jia asked suddenly as they entered the section of the path they lived on.

"Huh?" Ash muttered.

Up ahead, at house number three, Ash could see a group of people. He had vague memories and recollections of them and could only place them as Deng family members or affiliates.

In front of them, standing directly in their way to the front door of house three, was Mei.

"It is," Ash said. "I wonder what trouble she's causing now."

"Not our problem," Yue said. "Not our house. Though I don't think I've met the owner of house three."

"He is a very quiet young man. I saw him once," Jia said.

As they walked closer and closer, Ash started to get confused. The crowd of people looked like they weren't there to cause trouble to the owner of house three.

It honestly was starting to look like they were there to cause problems for Mei herself.

Especially since she was shouting at the crowd, and it was shouting back at her. They were also looking more and more poised for violence.

"This is odd," Jia said.

"I've scanned Mei. She doesn't have the Deng energy source on her person any longer," Locke said.

"Mm," Ash said, responding to both Jia and Locke.

"It is worth noting that Mei is heavily injured. Several of her ribs are cracked, her left arm has a hairline fracture in the ulna, she has a slow bleed in her liver, and is suffering a mild concussion.

"The likelihood of her surviving is high, though it is possible the bleed in her liver could continue or get worse, and she'll die."

Huh?

"Her eyes are blackened, and her lips are split," Jia said. "It would appear someone has given her a fierce battle."

Ash looked to Mei's face.

Her once-elegant look was indeed marred by what Jia had—in Ash's opinion—understated as a fight.

To Ash, it looked more like she'd been beaten black and blue. One of her eyes was swollen shut.

Tala slid out from the side of Yue's house, catching Ash's eye. She approached the group at a jog and moved up to Ash's side.

"It would seem the young woman," Tala said, indicating Mei, "is being spurned for failing in her duty to stop you and Jia. Apparently, she's been thrown out of the Deng clan entirely. She showed up early this morning and challenged the owner of this home and took it."

The Rabbit woman paused, her eyes moving to catch Ash's.

"That group has come to challenge her for… honestly it sounds like nothing. Guessing from the look of her, and the mob, they just want to fight her and possibly kill her. Or so it seems from my experience as a Kin. I've seen it before," Tala finished.

Yeah, I could say the same for this veil. I wouldn't put it past them to blame her for not stopping me, and then simply killing her as an example.

That or this is all an elaborate trap for me.

Ash sighed and rubbed at his jaw. They were only twenty feet from the situation now.

Guess we'll spring the trap and deal with it after.

Rapidly activating his abilities, Ash then drew his butterfly swords from their single sheath.

The sound of metal rasping drew the eye of everyone nearby.

Tapping one d-guard to the other, Ash gave his wrists a spin.

"Alright, make a line for me," Ash said, pointing at the mob with a one sword. "I'll challenge you all one by one for whatever you have on you. This will be your toll for coming down my street uninvited."

Jia laughed, the sound cool and threatening.

"That will take too long. I will challenge those at the rear of the line—that way we can be done with this quickly," she said. Lifting her left hand, thick Water Qi pooled and formed a staff. Grasping it, she popped its butt against the ground.

"This has nothing to do with you, Ashley Sheng. Leave this Deng matter to the Deng family," said a young man, pushing himself to the front of the group.

"Simple question for you, then. Is she in the Deng clan?" Ash said, pointing at Mei.

"No," Mei answered loudly, standing defensively in front of what was apparently her home. "I'm not affiliated with my... the Deng family. At all."

She hadn't backed down from their challenges, apparently ready to fight them.

It was impressive, to a degree.

"Then this clearly isn't a Deng family issue, but a Sheng Street issue. Now make a line, for me. I can challenge you one by one while Jia works her way up the back, or you can forfeit something of equal value to today's allotment pill," Ash said.

"This is stupid. We'll not accept a challenge from you. Who says we'll do anything—"

Ash activated Spring Step and darted forward. Smashing forward with his right fist, he brought the d-guard up into the young man's stomach.

Folding in half, the Deng family member pitched over Ash's arm.

"There, there. Do not fear, I'll be your senior. I'll act like your father here and give you a lesson."

"I will care for your well-being on Sheng Street," Ash said. "Now, would you like to give me something equal in toll? Or should we continue this challenge?"

Looking up to the rest of the group, Ash gestured with his eyes to the spot he'd indicated earlier. "The rest of you line up."

An audible thump got everyone to look to the spot Ash had indicated.

Moira was standing there with her wings spread, sword drawn and looking rather hostile.

Taking her cue, Tala unsheathed her big blade and whipped it around, setting it down on her shoulder.

"You don't know what you're doing," someone called from the crowd.

"Sure I do. I'm pissing off the Deng clan, which has already made me one of their biggest enemies. On top of that, you're welcome to go tell your elders what happened, but I bet they'll just punish you. Won't they?"

Sighing dramatically, Ash smiled at his audience.

"Be thankful I don't cripple you or have my friends here kill you all. We'd have a party after that and bury you all behind my house while having a barbecue to celebrate your demise," Ash said. "Line up, now. And don't come down Sheng Street again. At least not without a toll or gate price."

Finally realizing what was happening, the Deng family members began to placidly line up.

Smirking to himself, Ash looked to the man folded over his arm and started checking his pockets and clothes for anything to take.

***

Mei was seated between Jia and Yue at Ash's table in his main room. Tala and Moira stood on each side of Ash as he sat across from her.

"So... what happened?" Ash asked, looking at Mei.

Mei lifted her chin up a fraction, her pride unbroken.

"I was punished for failing in my duty. When I protested my punishment and questioned the decision, I was... I was banished from the clan," Mei said. "It's as simple as that."

Ash eyed her directly, looking over everything he could see of her at the table.

Up close, it was obvious she hadn't just been punished, but beaten to a pulp.

"I would say the punishment they gave you is far more than 'simple.' If I don't miss my guess, you're bleeding internally and you have several broken bones.

"All of which could be easily solved with even a little bit of wealth. Did they rob you, too?" Ash asked.

Mei's jaw flexed, her one good eye watering up as she stared back at him.

"Yes," she said after a few seconds. "Yes, they robbed me after they beat me like a dog. Does that make you happy? Are you satisfied?

"Do you feel vindicated now?"

Fighting down a frown, Ash wasn't sure how to respond. He hadn't expected Mei's outburst.

"And now you've forced me into your home. Do you plan on humiliating me further? Turn me into a concubine and lock me away?"

"I didn't believe what the elders said about you—are you going to prove me wrong now?" Mei asked, her throat constricting as she spoke. Her right hand quivered slightly as she clutched it to her chest. Her left arm was flat on the table, as she clearly didn't want to put weight on it.

Glancing at some of the icons floating around Mei's nameplate, he read them.

She was in pain. Immense pain.

Full of fear, self-loathing, and pain.

Everything you'd expect of someone in her position.

"Why did you take the house here? It's quite a far fall for you, isn't it?" Ash asked, changing the direction of the question.

Mei frowned, her cracked and scabbed lips making it look gruesome.

"Because the further I could get from the clan, the better off I would be. And the furthest I can go is practically next door to you," Mei said. "I'm not asking anything of you."

The silence immediately afterward was heavy. Everyone was watching either Mei or Ash.

Mei's head drooped a fraction.

"Though I truly appreciate what you did for me. I would have fought them. Fought them all," Mei said.

"You would have died," Tala said firmly.

Mei didn't argue that point.

"I didn't think my chances of surviving the week were very high to begin with," Mei said.

"Everything I'm sensing, and what I can determine, is telling me she's speaking the truth.

"It seems that the Deng clan is using her as an example of what happens to failures," Locke said. *"Though corporal punishment has never been that effective when attempting to ensure obedience in a situation where the outcome is out of their hands."*

"We cannot let you remain here on Sheng Street in house three," Jia said. "Given your previous allegiance, it would not do well for us."

Mei's lips pressed together tightly. Then she bobbed her head, closing her one good eye.

"I thought that might be the case," she said.

"Just have her swear herself to Ash's alliance," Moira interjected. "We wanted to build one, did we not? Start with her. Have her swear on her own cultivation."

"Swear to an alliance?" Mei asked. "What's the goal?"

"Destroy the Deng clan," Yue said. "Destroy them at every level. Our master wishes the same. Master Gen."

"Gen… yes, I could easily see that. What would be required of me?" Mei asked, her single eye focusing in on Ash again.

"Nothing outside of the ordinary. Support the alliance and its members in our goals. Don't speak of what goes on in our alliance to others. Don't betray us or seek to subvert our goals in any way," Ash said. "And… I think I could accept an oath from you on your own cultivation to join the alliance."

At least, I think I can.

It's a rather deep-seated ruse if they went so far as to kick the crap out of her just to get her close to me.

I might be a problem for them, but I doubt they'd go this far. And an oath on her cultivation would bind her quite firmly.

"Nothing perverse would be required?" Mei asked suddenly. "You seemed quite intent to… to see my petals, as you called them."

Suddenly all eyes were on Ash.

Shit.

"Hah. That's what you get, Chosen One," Locke gloated.

"I said all that as a ploy to anger you," Ash said, holding his hands up in front of himself. "I had no designs on you otherwise."

Mei licked her lips and then smiled with one side of her mouth.

"I assumed so, since you turned down that man's offer. Then I'll swear to your alliance then," Mei said.

Ash reached into his storage ring and pulled out several high-grade medicinal pills. Enough to bring her back to full health in a day.

"Then take these, and let's get your oath squared away. Can't have you bleeding all over my house. I just had all the furniture replaced recently."

Twenty-Nine

Ash sat down at a table, laying the book in front of himself.

Looking around at the library's interior, he took in a slow breath.

As usual, no one was here. The library was almost always abandoned.

Forgotten, even.

Most everyone in the sect was so determined to get things done that few seemed to take any pleasure in reading.

Cracking open the book, Ash got comfortable and started to read. He had some time before anyone was supposed to show up.

"What're you reading?" asked a smooth and aristocratic voice.

Glancing up from the pages, he found Mei leaning over his shoulder.

"Oh, just a book of fairy tales. As an outlander, much of the culture is still lost on me.

"Stuff like children's books, fairy tales, and legends help me understand it better," Ash said.

Leaning back in his chair to get a better look at Mei, he checked her out head to toe.

Her face was completely healed. All traces of the dreadful attack she had suffered were gone.

Reaching out, he took the arm she'd broken in hand and gently pressed at the bone. She didn't flinch away, nor did anything seem to shift at his touch.

"Scan shows that while her liver and kidneys still have quite a bit of extra work to do, all functions are normal.

"She is in prime condition, all biometrics normal," Locke said.

"What are you doing?" Mei asked. She looked startled at his sudden touch, but she didn't pull away from him.

"Sorry, was checking your arm. It was broken yesterday; today it isn't. And your face is back to normal," Ash said, peering at her face intently for a second. "I'm glad. It would have been a shame for you to have suffered anything permanent."

Mei blinked several times, her cheeks slowly turning red.

"Your words are not without meaning. You should watch them, or you'll give your women the wrong impression," Mei said.

"What, that you're beautiful?" Ash asked, releasing her arm. "Even a dead man would admit that. If they're too blind to see that then I don't know what to tell ya."

Turning back to his book, Ash tried to find where he'd left off.

"Thank you for the compliment," Mei said softly, then sat down next to him. "So, are they?"

"Mm? Are they what?" Ash said, finding his place.

"Your women," Mei clarified, crossing one leg over the other and leaning her side into the table.

Frowning for a second, Ash looked to Mei. "Why?"

"The dynamics are… odd," Mei said after a second. "Merely trying to figure out where things stand. It's not as if having multiple spouses is abnormal.

"My mother has five husbands, and my grandmother six."

"Hm. My understanding is one tends to need a significant amount of influence or power to have that many," Ash said.

Mei gave him a sweet smile and tapped the table with one long fingernail. "Are they your women?"

Ash sighed at being unable to change the subject. Maybe if he laid everything out for her, she could be a sounding board for him.

Maybe even help me figure some things out.

"Moira and I seek companionship in one another, but that's all. Yue worships me to a degree. I think she sees me as some type of savior," Ash said with a small shake of his head. "Tala is… I don't know what she is. She just stays away from me so far. Jia tests me. She likes to push and see where I'll go with it, and sometimes I flirt with her. It's fun, but nothing more than that."

"Ah… so… one is your woman, two will become so eventually, and the third is a question mark," Mei said, looking thoughtful. One finger was tapping lightly at her chin. "That puts things into perspective."

"How so?" Ash asked, curious now.

"Never you mind," Mei said, giving him a wide smile. "Though it's a bit refreshing to find someone who is well aware of what's going on around him. And isn't too interested in being a cultivator to care."

"Huh… well, yeah. I mean, yeah, I want to become stronger, but in the same breath… what's the damn point if I don't enjoy myself? Sure, stronger—great. But that's a treadmill," Ash said, putting his elbow on the table and turning to face Mei completely. "At what point I get off the treadmill really comes down to who's with me, doesn't it? I'm not in it to become the greatest, the peak of humanity. Just enough so I don't have to worry about me and mine."

"That's… incredibly rational. My mother would call you a fool. It's obvious you have great potential.

"And after my brief chat with Moira, it would seem you're a Fated One," Mei said, her eyes focused intently on him.

Moira trusted her rather easily, didn't she?

"I actually have no idea about that. I'm an outlander for sure, and I'm not part of this veil," Ash said.

"But you have a Dantian. You can cultivate."

"Ah, yes. That's true. I do and I can."

"And you activated Moira's mana pools," Mei said, her eyes locked tight on him.

"Ah… yes."

"You popped open Tala's ability in this veil as well."

"Yes."

"You cracked Yue's Dantian and it's now active, despite it not having been large enough to open on its own."

"Yeah."

"All of Jia's, Yue's, and Tala's abilities were given to them by you. Including Yue's extraordinary alchemist's knowledge."

"Uh… yeah."

Mei nodded slowly, watching him with a predator's gaze.

"What would you say if I told you I'm beginning to consider this the greatest turning point in my life, instead of the lowest point?" Mei asked.

Before Ash could answer, Moira dropped down in the chair on the other side of him. She gave him a smile and then looked to Mei.

"I'd say you were smart and fortunate," said the Owl woman. "Though best you keep that talk to yourself for now. The others will trust you in time because Ash does, but not yet."

Mei finally broke eye contact with Ash and looked to Moira. Then she nodded.

"Thank you for the advice. Your eyes are rather lovely—did you know that?"

Moira grinned and gently pushed Ash back into his seat.

"I'm pleased that you like them. They were admired far and wide back in my own veil."

"If you don't mind, could you tell me about it? Precious few outlanders seem willing to talk about their life before."

Ash tuned himself out of their conversation. It had nothing to do with him.

Besides, he wanted to read his book.

***

"It would seem the number of disciples I'm going to have has increased again," Gen said, once again materializing from thin air. As if he'd always been there.

"Ah… yes," Ash said, taking the lead. "Mei Ling is no longer of the Deng clan; she's one of us. She's sworn herself to my cause on her own cultivation. Voluntarily."

Gen raised his eyebrows at that, looking to Mei.

"Truly? Given your background, that seems… unlikely," Gen said, his tone gentle but firm.

"Yes, Master Gen. I would ask you to take me in as your disciple," Mei said, standing up and pressing her fists together. She bowed her head over her hands toward him. "Everything Ash has said is true. I've been disinherited. Completely."

"My, my. They were quite cross with you for not stopping him," Gen said after a second. "Yes, I'll take you on. That isn't a problem."

"It'll make the very souls of the Deng clan itch that I've done it, and for that alone I'll say yes." Mei dipped her head further toward Gen, then sat back down next to Ash.

There's clearly more to that. I should ask her later if I get the opportunity.

Gen looked to Moira and Tala, and then to Ash.

"I take it you did something to them?" Gen asked. "They radiate power. They are not unpowered outlanders."

"Ah… yes," Ash said.

"We should register them as weapons. You're allowed three as an Outer Sect disciple. I registered your butterfly swords for you earlier. If you register those two in the same way, they can fight with you," Gen said. "If that's what they want you to do? It would seem you treat them as equals rather than property."

"Yes, register me," Moira said immediately.

"I will deign to allow you to claim me as your weapon," Tala said at the same time.

Gen nodded at their responses. "I'll take care of it, then.

"Now, on to the business at hand. You seem like a smart bunch of kids. Have you figured out just how far this is going to go?"

Everyone looked around at each other for a second.

"We assumed this would not end until either we or the Deng clan is eliminated, or the power of one party is completely neutralized," Jia said.

"And when one breaks the other financially," Yue added. "It won't just be a simple matter of conquest."

"Let's not forget that the Inner Sect and the elder's circle also all have their Deng family members' support," Mei said. "From what I could see of their plans… this has been a long time in the making, and it's unlikely a simple setback will stop them."

Gen had been following along with his eyes as each person spoke.

Finally, after Mei finished, he nodded his head once.

"Only too true. All of that. This isn't a simple tiff between clans. This is a full-on war to the death now. We need allies," Gen said.

"We were thinking about that," Ash said. "We've been considering who to ally with in the Outer Sect itself amongst the disciples."

Gen grimaced but nodded at Ash's words. "A good idea, but not enough, honestly.

"There is nothing we can possibly do in the Outer Sect at this time that could change their momentum immediately."

Gen said it as gently as he could, but the sting was clearly felt by everyone there. It was honest, but it still hurt.

"We can play the long game and frustrate their plans. Exam by exam, tournament by tournament, and slowly collect power. Developing our foundation and working toward ending the Deng problem. Or…" Gen paused in his speech, holding his hands out to the others. "We go for an early knock-out blow."

"What do you have in mind?" Jia asked. "I do not think you would say such a thing without a firm plan to back it up."

Gen smiled at Jia and tapped his thumb against his cane.

"Yes. Yes indeed. I do have a plan, but it involves taking you all out with me on a journey. A journey that will take some time and will have a number of dangers associated with it," Gen said. "Least of which being that if the Deng family uncovers our plans before we can execute them, we could end up facing down a number of their spirit refiners out in the wilds between cities.

"I do not think we'd have any chance of surviving that."

Mei sucked in a breath, then opened her mouth and let it out in a slow exhalation.

"I want to argue with you that they wouldn't do that," Mei said. "But… I think they would, given how they treated me for failing in my duties.

"This isn't a simple grudge for them. This seems to be a life-and-death task to someone seated high in the clan."

"That's our risk, then?" Yue asked, looking to Ash. "If that's the risk, we can simply disguise ourselves as a merchant train. I have more than enough favors owed to me already that I could manage an anonymous merchant train with us on board.

"We could slip out of the sect before anyone even noticed we were gone."

"Mmm, I like the sound of it," Moira said. "It'd also be a chance to move some of Ash's papers, would it not?"

"Ah! That's a very good idea. We could drop by in a city on the way and take care of a few matters and restock," Yue said, smiling at Moira. "That'd help us greatly."

Tala grunted, her blade rattling as she grabbed it with one hand and shifted it around. "I agree that I like the idea as a whole, but I feel as if we're missing something. If they find us no longer here the next day, won't they simply go looking for us?

"They are not fools, as much as we'd wish them to be. Could we perhaps leave a hidden trail that is easier to find than the real one? Something they'd have to dig a bit for, but could still find?

"When laying a trap, or false information, the best way is when they have to work to get it. It makes them feel like it's that much less likely to be false, since they had to earn it."

Heads around the room began to bob at that.

"Ah… I could…" Mei said, licking her lips. "I could… leak some false information at a dead-drop location. Make it seem as if I'm trying to worm my way back into the clan."

Ash looked to Mei and raised his eyebrows at her. "You'd be willing to do that? I won't lie that I was hoping to pump you for information about the Deng family, but I wasn't going to ask either."

Mei smirked at him, as if he'd said something amusing. "Yes, well, you'll not have to try too hard. I'm more than willing to share, and I'll give you whatever I have.

"The only problem is there is no guarantee they'll trust the info I give them. It's quite possible they could take it as exactly what it is—a diversion."

"What if we combined it with something else?" Jia said. "Something they would have to dig to find, as Tala said, that would in some way corroborate the story without directly saying so."

Yue sighed and pressed a hand to her head.

"I could act the innocent young merchant role, which seems to go far here, and buy some maps to whatever location Mei has us pegged for. Maps, route guides, information about what to expect.

"It'd cost some coin, but it'd lay a decent trail of misinformation, I think."

Gen thumped his cane once to the ground. "I personally like that line of thinking. Having it come from two locations—one a leak, the other scrounged information—would be more likely to sell it to them. Just make sure you make it seem that we're traveling as a party rather than a merchant caravan for the false direction. No sense in giving them a real clue if we don't have to."

Yue nodded her head at that, scratching at her temple. "I hate acting the part. It demeans me."

"And enriches the rest of us," Ash said, smiling at her. "Thank you for that."

Yue ducked her head, her eyes flitting away from Ash. "Of course."

"Ah… this is all a bit of a moot issue, though. I need to confirm a few things first," Gen said, getting their attention again.

"The pills you gave me were from you, Yue. Would those be hard to procure again?"

"No. They weren't too terribly difficult, just expensive."

"Alright. I've already gone ahead and purchased all the reagents I think you'll need in advance.

"We can buy whatever else you need when we get to where we're going. We'll be looking for medicinal pills. Healing of the meridians or the Dantian, to be exact."

"Got it," Yue said.

"Next… Ash. Just how much can you do? From what I can gather from looking at your companions, and what you've done, I can't get a gauge on your limitations.

"You seem to hold a great secret that removes the limits others face."

"Oh, uh. I can make transference papers of almost anything. Alchemy, woodworking, blacksmithing, pottery—lots and lots of things."

"Yes, but you seem to be able to enhance and repair others as well. Moira and Tala are prime examples of that, I would think," Gen said.

"Errr, yeah… I can fix some things. Depending on what the problem is, I can modify the Dantian. I can also modify the meridians and a bit of how everything flows together."

"Could you show me an example?" Gen asked. "I ask because I think we could gather even more strength, but it's very dependent on what you can accomplish and how it's done.

"As an example, it wouldn't be very effective if you had to enslave someone for you to be able to work on them."

"Yeah, that seems pretty limiting. Only being able to modify things I own. Ah, no, it doesn't work like that.

"It really just comes down to if I can put together a pattern that will shape what I want to happen," Ash said.

"A pattern?" Gen asked, leaning forward on his cane.

Tala stood up suddenly and turned her back to everyone.

"Here, I'll show you what he can do."

Reaching around herself, she pulled her tunic up to her shoulders.

Black fur ran along her sides and across in small patches, but the scars on her back were bright white.

Visible and flawlessly carved into her flesh.

It was a flowing shape and guidance of power.

In a way, it looked rather artistic after having healed over.

"This is… Ash did this?" Gen asked.

"Yes. He did the same to me, though I think it's a different pattern," Moira added.

"It is. Yours was a conversion; hers was an enabling," Ash said, feeling odd discussing his abilities.

"A Fated One indeed," Mei murmured, her eyes flashing as she looked to Ash.

Gen coughed and stood up straight, his feral grin locking into place.

"Yes, that's what I needed to know. My plan is very simple. We're going to venture off to what is called the sect of the Open Hand. It's where masters, elders, and disciples go who are unable to participate any further in the sect but do not wish to live with the masses again."

Gen was nodding his head, looking more and more excited with his own words as he spoke them.

"There are many people there who owe a blood debt—owe pain—to the Deng family. If we could repair them, heal them, they would become an army for us.

"Some of them were even elders of the Inner Sect."

Oh.

Well.

I suppose if we could get more people just like Gen, this would certainly be easier. Wouldn't it?

"We will leave as soon as possible," Jia said.

"I'll go ahead with what I need to do," Yue said.

"Likewise. I believe I can make the drop tomorrow evening, which they wouldn't pick up until the following morning.

"We should be able to get this moving by the day after next, and they won't have the info until we're on the road," Mei said.

"That's the plan, then," Moira said. "Unless someone has an objection of some sort?"
Everyone shook their heads.
And like that, they had a direction and a goal.

Thirty

Ash looked around himself as they walked past the city gates of Jinhai.

In the end, they'd decided on traveling by horse. And having one for each traveler in their group.

Ash wasn't quite sure it was a great idea in retrospect. Or at least for him personally, since his ass and hips were so sore.

Thankfully though, horse riding was over for now.

The horses were now stabled outside the gates, and Ash would be walking around the city.

Gen had indicated that in his experience, it was easier to get out of a city on foot than it was on horse.

And if a horse was outside the gates waiting for you, all the better.

Ash made no argument with that logic either.

We did make good time, though. Using horses.

Even if it feels like someone took a saw to my nethers and everything is just a raw mess of broken bones and glass.

With that thought, he had to concede that they hadn't just made good time, but very good time. Such good time that they had leftover rations that would probably go bad before they left.

"I didn't think I'd be returning here so soon," Yue said, her eyes focused on the street in front of them.

"You have traveled through these parts before?" Jia asked.

They were walking in a small, tightly packed column as they moved through the city.

"I lived here," Yue murmured. "My brother and I. With our mother and father. Grew up here."

Crossing through a main intersection, Yue lifted a hand down to the right.

"The inns are down that way. At least, the ones we want to stay at. Anything elsewhere in the city can be problematic," Yue said. "And that's a nice way to put it."

"How very… colorful," Mei said after several seconds passed in silence.

"It's home. Or, it was. I guess," Yue said.

"Right now it's a place to restock," Gen said, guiding them down the road Yue had indicated. "We'll pick up everything we need to make it to the Open Hand's cloister. I don't think we'll be here longer than a day or two."

"Open Hand? You explained it a bit before. Can you offer any more insight?" Ash asked.

"Open Hand. Where those who served the sect were retired when they couldn't do anything more and had no family to care for them," Gen explained.

It really wasn't much more than Gen had said previously.

"In other words, those who have reached a dead end and would be willing to make a move to retirement," Jia summarized.

"Exactly. We need power, and we're offering them a way out," Gen confirmed. "It's a fortunate encounter for them. One that would never come around in a normal lifetime."

Ash wasn't about to argue that point. He agreed with it.

He just wanted to know more about these people.

"Does it matter?" Locke asked suddenly. *"If they were murderers, child killers, and rapists, would you spurn their assistance? Whatever they are, they're power. Power that can be turned into a sword to point toward the Deng family."*

"Master Gen," Ash said as they continued down the street. "I would ask, are these people who would be no better than the Deng family? I would hesitate to proceed if they would represent us no better than the Deng family's monsters.

"No offense, Mei."

"None taken," Mei said, her voice sounding tired and sad. "I would caution the same as you, even. If we enlist those who would commit the same atrocities as the Deng family, would we be any better?"

Gen grunted. "I'll think on that. Maybe we put some restrictions on their oath on their cultivation.

"It sounds naive to me on the face of it, but... you're right. If we're no better than Deng, we'll be the next one. Sheng instead of Deng.

"And then we'll create a new Ashley Sheng with a different name that would fight us."

"One is enough," Jia said.

"Speaking of enough, how many of these old swords are we looking to recruit?" Mei asked.

Ash looked to Gen and paused as Yue slipped in at his side. She caught his eyes and then made a small head gesture to fall to the rear of the column. Or so he interpreted it.

Letting Moira and Tala pass him, and getting a look from each as he did so, Ash fell to the rear of the pack. The conversation continued on with strategy and planning for what they were going to do.

Ash wasn't the mastermind here, so he didn't mind not being part of it.

"Thank you," Yue said after everyone had gotten a few feet ahead.

"Of course. What's up?"

"I wanted to ask you for a favor."

"Name it. All you have to do is ask, and I'll do it for you," Ash said with a smile.

Yue was always so earnest and dedicated to his needs—he didn't think he could deny her anything at this point.

"Ah... ok. Uhm, I want... I want to go visit my family while we're here. I want you to come with me. If you don't mind," Yue said.

Her family? I thought she didn't have any.

Actually, we never really asked. We knew about her brother, but that's it.

"Sure, but could you give me some background first? What happened with your family? How'd you end up where you were?" Ash asked.

Yue looked pained now, and she glanced around them.

"Alright. But... not here. And not with other people around. Just you," she said finally.

"We can do that. Let's figure out what inn we'll be staying at, let them know we're leaving, and then we'll go wherever you want.

"It'd be foolish to not let them know we're going," Ash said.

Reaching out, he set a hand on her shoulder.

"We'll talk, figure out what to do, and go from there. It'll be fine."

***

Yue sat across from Ash as he sat down at the same time. Smiling, she touched the plate that had been set in front of her and shifted it around a little.

"I always wanted to come here when I lived here. But the prices were far too high for me to do anything other than dream about it," Yue said. Tapping the center of the plate with a fingernail, she smiled to herself. "These plates alone are worth more than what my parents made in a month."

Ash smiled at that and wondered how he was supposed to know what was available to eat.

Anywhere he'd ever eaten at usually only offered one or two things. He'd never sat and eaten at somewhere like this.

"I... have no idea what to do here," Yue said suddenly.

Looking at her, Ash could only laugh at the look on her face.

"Given that I'm sure they have new clients wander in through the door on any day, I'm certain someone will eventually come over and tell us what to do," he said. "In the meantime, how about you talk to me about your parents. Sounds like they weren't exactly well off."

"They weren't. No," Yue said. Resting her elbows on the table, she put her head in her hands. "Father was a day laborer.

"He wasn't literate, either. Could read enough to know if he was being cheated, but little beyond that. Numbers were the same for him."

Ash didn't find that surprising in the least. Literacy wasn't common at certain levels in the general population.

There were much more pressing concerns, like eating and surviving.

Reading and writing only did so much towards that end, when the best job you could hope for was moving boxes.

Or selling your body.

"Mother… Mother was a seamstress. She worked any odd job involving cloth she could find," Yue added, as if picking Ash's thoughts from the air. "She was rather proud of the fact that she'd never had to sell herself by the hour."

A young woman came over and smiled at them as if no one else existed.

"Welcome! Today we're serving steak, a salad, and some vegetables. All fresh and prepared with spices and herbs.

"We also offer a paired wine with the meal," said the young woman. "It'll be three squares per person."

Ah. So it's just like the others, but they only sell one item. Seems a bit over the top for such a thing.

Ash pulled out seven squares and laid them down on the table in front of the woman.

"Two then, and an extra square for you." Ash returned her smile and then directed his attention back to Yue.

The waitress scooped up the squares and immediately scurried away.

"Please, continue," Ash said.

Yue tapped her fingers along the table.

"Father got hurt. He was moving a crate from one warehouse to another. He loaded it onto a rack and… something happened," Yue said. Her voice was starting to crack a bit. "They never could really tell me what happened at the time. Long afterward, we found out. A cultivator had struck a post to test his strength, and it shattered.

"Which brought down the shelves Father was working under. He was crushed, of course. Both his arms were broken, and we couldn't afford medicine or a healer.

"We'd gone into debt to buy the house we were living in, and no one would give Mother credit."

That… all sounds terrible and like something that happens more often than I'd ever like to know.

Except that only leaves one avenue to make money, soooo…

Smiling, Ash waited patiently. He didn't want to rush Yue, but he did want to know what he was walking into when going to visit her family.

"Mother was going to do what she had to do. She had two children to feed and a husband who needed her.

"Except that it never came to that," Yue said. Her eyes slowly unfocused until she was staring at nothing.

Into the deep, dark middle ground between them that people only saw when they'd lived through too much.

"The same cultivator who had injured my father was apparently punished by the owner of the warehouse.

"He paid a visit to our home and… killed both my parents, and destroyed our house," Yue said, her voice going toneless. "My brother and I weren't home at the time. We were at school."

"We could probably dig up who did it. If they're weaker than we are, we could take his head and offer it to her as a present," Locke said.

It was strange to Ash. Locke didn't really take an interest in the people around Ash very often. At least not more than enough to harass Ash about it.

"I like her. She's spunky and a fighter. She's also cloyingly devoted to you," Locke elaborated.

"What ah… what rank was the cultivator—do you know?" Ash asked.

"His rank? Uhm. No. I don't. I mean—" Yue blinked, her eyes refocusing on Ash's dinner plate. "I should. I should look into that. I should find that out. With the resources I have now… with who my friends are… I might be able to pay him back."

"If it's within my power, I'll take his head personally and deliver it to you," Ash said.

Yue visibly shook for a second, and her eyes darted up to Ash's.

"You would?"

Ash nodded rather than responding.

The young woman appeared with two platters of food. She set one down in front of Yue, and then the other in front of Ash. She immediately followed it up with two large bottles of what Ash assumed was the wine.

"Ah, here you are, sir, miss," said the woman, her hands clutched in front of her. "Please let me know if there's anything else you need at all."

Before they could respond, she dashed off again.

"She thinks you tipped her to try and sleep with her, or to get her to stay away," Yue said, picking up the knife next to her plate.

"Huh. I see," Ash said. "Whatever. Time to see what's so special about this steak."

"It's from a magical beast. It'll be similar to cultivating or taking pills that would enhance cultivation," Locke said. *"Considering this is your first time eating such a thing, it'll be interesting to see what the results are. If any."*

Oh. That's actually rather interesting.

Taking the knife and fork that were next to his plate, Ash skewered the steak and began cutting into it.

It didn't have any toughness to it, and it seemed to part easily at the touch of his knife.

"Seems it's cooked well," Ash murmured. Looking up, he saw Yue apparently trying to imitate what he'd done. She was holding her knife and fork awkwardly, but she was making progress.

Ah… fingers, spoons, or chopsticks. Forks and knives seem to be reserved for special situations or higher-class meals.

Which… now that I think about it… is a bit odd, isn't it?

Putting the chunk of meat into his mouth, Ash began chewing steadily at it. It had a gamey flavor and started to fall apart easily as he chewed it.

The spices and herbs definitely added to the overall taste.

In fact, it was one of the singular most tasty things he'd eaten since arriving here.

Then Ash felt strange Qi flowing from the meat into his body. It pooled around in his meridians before shooting straight into his Dantian.

Freezing solid for a second, Ash watched his core. He wasn't quite sure what was going on, but he didn't want to miss it.

"We're currently rank seven. Your Qi is as dense as it can be, and your training speed is quite slow and low due to our cultivation method," Locke said, as if expecting questions from Ash.

Bright-red Qi flowed into his Qi Sea. No sooner had it touched the sea, the color of it drained away until it was pale and ghostly. Then it all vanished into the depths of the sea as if it had never existed.

"Based on what we gained from that, what's left on your plate, and what it did, we can expect no change from eating this meal. It is clearly beneficial, however, and I would recommend we change our diet to a magical-beast-only menu."

Something to ask Yue later, then.

***

"I'm nervous," Yue said as they walked down the street to her aunt's house.

"Understandable, but unnecessary. I'm here, and nothing can harm you," Ash said.

"I know. But she took us in when no one else would."

"And yet she didn't stop her husband from throwing you and your brother out when it was clear he'd have to give up a few pleasantries so you could eat," Ash countered. "Or so you explained."

Yue sighed and stopped in front of a small, rundown building. It was a multi-level, multi-family dwelling. One could tell from the outside that it had four sections, and each one contained a different family.

"She didn't stop him. No. She did fight it, though."

"Which is a lovely sentiment that did absolutely nothing," Ash said with a shrug of his shoulders. "You yourself said you were just barely making it on the streets."

Ash had a problem with people who didn't look out for their family members. He knew where it was rooted, but that didn't change it at all.

Where are you, Trav?

"Yes... just barely. If we had suffered any setback at all... my honor would have been forever ruined," Yue said, her tone going flat and cold.

Squaring her small frame up, Yue marched forward and knocked firmly on the door.

Ash clasped his hands behind his back and put on a neutral smile. He was only here to observe and lend assistance to her as needed. Beyond that, there wasn't much he was supposed to do.

Ten seconds went by before the door slowly opened an inch. Enough for Ash to see someone's eye.

"Yue?" said someone behind the door. "Is that you?"

"Yeah, it's me."

The door swung open and a slightly taller and older version of Yue stepped out from inside.

"Yue!" the woman said, moving forward and wrapping up the younger woman in a hug. "Yue, I'm so happy to see you! I went to look for you in Xing. No one had seen you or Jie for a while."

That's right. Her brother's name is Li Jie. Jie must be what his family call him.

"...ooking for us? Why?" Yue said, her aunt still holding tightly to her.

"Because what I let happen was wrong. Heng was wrong. I told him I was going to get you two and bring you home and he could deal with it or leave," said the older woman. "So he left. Your mother's sewing kit was still here, so I've become a seamstress just as she was. It's a little tighter around the house than it used to be, but without Heng I can easily bring you and your brother back home."

Ash chewed at the inside of his cheek. He was nervous now. Nervous and unsure.

Yet also delighted for Yue. She had an opportunity here and now.

One that he might not be able to resist, himself.

Going home.

Maybe staying here in Jinhai would be best for her. It would certainly be less dangerous. She could easily set up a merchant's shop here and would probably do well for herself.

There wasn't a need for her to travel around with him, putting herself in danger. Her family wanted her back and had made room for her. Her and her brother.

"...ank you but no, Auntie Ai," Yue said, gently disentangling herself from her aunt.

"What? I don't understand," said Auntie Ai. "I want you to come back. This isn't me feeling guilty. My guilt was over letting what happened happen. I want you here because you're family."

Yue smiled at her aunt and then took a step toward Ash. She reached up and set her hand on his arm.

"I'd like to introduce you to someone very important to me. He rescued me from the streets of Xing City, got Jie into a sect, and provided me with my livelihood.

"His name is Ashley Sheng. Ash, this is my aunt, Ai."

Ash bowed his head toward Yue's aunt and smiled.

"It's a pleasure to meet you, Ai. Please, call me Ash."

The older woman stared at Yue for a second longer before looking to Ash.

"You need to treat Yue well. She deserves great kindness, though the world has shown her little," Ai said, her brows coming down partially over her eyes. "And what is it that you do?"

"He's a cultivator," Yue said before he could respond. "As am I, now. We both joined a sect together. I asked him to come visit you with me before we headed back out tomorrow."

Ai's face slowly smoothed out, her eyes locked on Yue.

"Sweetie, your Dantian wasn't large enough... How is that possible?" Ai asked.

"It's a long story. Could we perhaps come in? I'd like to sit and talk for a bit. I also brought you something," Yue said.

Several hours later, Ash and Yue left Auntie Ai's house.

Taking a deep breath and letting it out in a whoosh, Yue giggled to herself.

"Did you see the look on her face when I gave her the card?" she asked.

"I did. It would seem you wanted to do the same thing I did."

"You did? I never actually asked. I mean, I talked to your sister for a bit, but... where's your family?" Yue asked. "Your family here, that is. I know you're not from this veil."

"Father Duyi and Mother Far live in a very nice neighborhood now. I gave them more than enough spirit stones to live extremely comfortably for their age.

"I also set aside an account for them to tap into if they ever needed more. Nothing extravagant but... more than they'd ever need to live the rest of their lives in peace," Ash said.

Yue grinned at him and slipped her arm through his. "You're a good man, Ashley Sheng."

Thirty-One

Gen gave the group a final look.

"Remain in the compound until I have a chance to speak to the locals. Everyone here has already heard what we're about.

"You're welcome to talk to them, though I do caution some amount of apprehension. While they're more than likely willing to join us, there's no guarantee of that yet. One and all, they're victims of the Deng family. Be sure to not mention Mei's heritage," Gen said. "And honestly, I'd hate to eliminate people I don't have to just because one of you let too much information slip."

Eliminate one of them? Holy shit.

"This is no game. No cheap trick. If we succeed in this, we'll have recruited a private army of cultivators contracted and bound to no one but us.

"Have a care, we're about to enter into a stage that is competitive with the top clans around the Jade Fist," Gen said with his wolf-like grin. "In the meantime, you should all consider the next tournament that will occur in the sect. We have one every few months to keep you all on your toes.

"A friend in the sect sent me the information. Apparently, it was announced the day after we left."

And another way for the Deng family to try and impact us.

"It will be a team battle. Each team is allowed four members. Outside of limiting the item usage only to sanctioned weapons, there are no rules," Gen said. "That means it'll be the six of you against whatever they throw at us. This wouldn't be a bad time to begin considering how to fight as a team. It isn't quite the same as individual combat, after all."

Waiting for a second and seeing no response from any of his disciples, Gen left them there. His cane tapping away as he walked out the courtyard they were in. Attached to it was several rooms that had been prepared for their stay.

"Gen seems to have planned this out," Jia said, idly tapping a finger against her chin. "I think I may have underestimated his desire to wipe out the Deng family."

"To be fair, what they did to him was criminal," Tala said. "If someone were to separate me from my power, deliberately, and suffer little to no repercussions, I'd probably have a lot of rage built up as well."

Moira nodded her head and grunted her agreement.

Feeling the strange tension in the air, Ash looked to the one person who had a personal investment in the Deng family.

Mei.

She looked pained to Ash. The corners of her eyes were wrinkled, her brow furrowed, and her bottom lip stuck between her teeth.

As if feeling his gaze on her, Mei's eyes moved to him. She gave him a tired smile and immediately worked to look unconcerned.

"It's okay, Mei," Yue said, apparently having seen the same thing. "If the Deng clan was doing this the right way, then very few but those at the top would know about this type of things being done.

"The things you yourself did weren't exactly kind, but neither did you go out and kill someone. Or maim them."

"No," Mei said, as everyone turned to look at her. "No, I didn't. But apparently there were others in my age group who did. I heard what they said to Ash. They were there not to stop him, but to kill or maim him. To cripple him.

"Those were very different orders than what I was given."

"Then that only supports my own statement. They were giving orders to those that could carry them out, based on what they believed each person was capable of. What were your orders, exactly?" Yue pressed.

"To slow, stall, or beat Ash to the top. That was it. I'm… I'm one of the strongest in the current Outer Sect generation. They believed I could be a match for him," Mei said with a bitter smile.

"I didn't exactly beat you, Mei. You'll remember someone slugged you in the back of the head," Ash offered.

"At least he fought you," Jia complained. "He will not even fight me earnestly. He forfeited our one serious fight and now refuses to do anything but spar with me."

Ash shrugged and then started to follow in the same direction as Gen. "I see no point in it. And we've talked about it before."

"Yes, yes. You are afraid that if you win, I will become bitter and leave you. There is little chance of that, but I will grant you your wish for now. You cannot evade me forever, Ashley Sheng," Jia said toward his back.

"I'm not evading you; I just don't want to fight you. Try coming at me from a different angle."

"I'm going for a walk. I want to talk to some of these people," Ash called over his shoulder before he turned the corner and left the courtyard.

The soft pat of booted feet chased after him. Ash grinned and checked over his shoulder, wondering what Jia wanted now.

Only to find Mei closing in on him.

"Mei?" he asked, curious about her intentions.

"Just because Jia is blind to what you're saying doesn't mean I am. I decided to attack you from a different angle. I'll escort you and play your game rather than try to force you into mine," Mei said. "My reasoning for being willing to play is rather simple. I just want to be around you for the time being."

"That's… an interesting reason," Ash said, unsure how to continue.

"I'm a few years older than you. Your sister's age, in fact. Chalk it up to an older woman's intuition."

"Hm. Fair enough. Well, you're welcome to join me. Lord knows having attractive company is never a bad thing," Ash said, looking back ahead.

"You're flirting with me? Why?" Mei asked, falling in next to him. "You barely know me."

"I'm not exactly wrong, though. You are rather pretty, Mei," Ash said.

"Hm. Fine. I think you use flirting distraction, though, to a degree. It's also why I'm willing to play your game. I think you half expect it to end the conversation, and half hope it won't."

"Suppose we'll find out, won't we, Miss Older Woman?"

Mei smiled at him and fell silent as she folded her hands into one another.

Walking along next to him, she cleared her throat, obviously ready to continue.

"Suppose we will. Maybe you prefer an older woman. I could look after you and play the older-sister role. Spoil you as a good older woman should.

"I have a number of younger siblings. Or… I did."

Mei's playful smile disintegrated to nothing rapidly through her own words.

Ash could imagine what she was going through. He'd been dropped here with absolutely no one and nothing.

Reaching out, he linked his arm into hers and pulled her a little closer to his side.

"I understand. I'm not from this veil. I arrived with no one and nothing. I was completely alone," Ash said. As he guided Mei along, they ended up on an outside walking path. From manicured yards and stones to a dirt path and shrubs and trees. "But you're not alone. I know we started off on the wrong foot—"

"You don't say?" Mei asked, her tone gaining back some of her previous mischievousness.

"Yes, the wrong foot. But given the situation, you were doing what you felt was right. What you had to do," Ash said, patting Mei's wrist with his free hand. "And I get it. I've personally forgiven you, and we can move forward."

"Forward? Forward to what, pray tell?" Mei asked, partially turning her head to face him. Her smile had broadened as she watched him.

"Guess we'll find out when we get there. For now, the path. Let's just walk and talk. You're not as aggressive as Jia, but you're still fun to talk to," Ash admitted.

"That's because I don't want to beat you. To match you," Mei said, reaching over to pat his hand on her wrist. "I just want to be near you. You're a Fated One."

Ash wanted to sigh. He was growing weary of the titles.

"It doesn't hurt that you're attractive. You have a great body, too," Mei said, watching him. "Well, being completely honest, that has a lot to do with it. That and I like your approach to life."

Unable to say anything because his brain had shut down completely after being complimented, Ash just kept walking.

Mei hummed musically to herself and turned her face to the path again. Her fingernails lightly grazed back and forth along Ash's forearm, making his skin prickle all over.

***

Walking back into the courtyard at was the center of the rooms they were staying at, Ash couldn't help but grin.

Tala and Moira were once again sparring. Practicing their abilities and sword work.

The most surprising thing, though, was how much Tala had improved. She'd started as a strong swordswoman and had become an equal to Moira at spell work and sword work.

If not perhaps a touch stronger.

The abilities we provided her have shored up any gaps she had. She is… formidable. I've also put together a workup for Moira that would only add a few things to her spell inventory but would more than likely make her much more capable.

"I… did the same for Mei as well. I also included a more useful cultivation ability for her based on her Earth Qi. Thankfully, she won't have to empty her Dantian, but it'll take her time to refine her Qi Sea," Locke said suddenly.

Ok, you really can read my thoughts. Stop hiding it.

"Fine. Yes. Recently I've become able to read your thoughts."

Good. That's… actually a bit easier, if you think about it. I didn't like talking out loud to myself. Sounded like a crazy person.

"For all you know, I'm a figment of your imagination and you are talking to yourself," Locke supplied happily. *"Chosen One."*

Jia and Yue were off talking to one side and seemed amused at Ash's arrival.

Before Ash could ask about it, Jia's face locked into a frozen mask. Her eyes were on a spot behind Ash.

Feeling a sudden itch between his shoulder blades, Ash pushed Mei behind him and turned to face whatever it was Jia had seen.

An older man stood there, his hands held behind his back. He had a congenial smile on his face, but his eyes were ice cold. Cold and lacking anything that could be identified as human.

"Hello young ones," said the older man.

Ash looked to immediately highlight and categorize the man. A small red box greeted him. Rolling out the text, the worst possible scenario seemed to confirm itself.

What would you like your tombstone to say?

"Hello, we were just retiring to our rooms," Ash said, moving backward to the rest of his group. "Gen said he'd be back right about now, so we were going to wait for him."

"Did he now?" said the old man. "Well, I'll just have to make it quick, then. Hand over the Deng girl and I'll leave. Very clean, very simple."

Moira and Tala appeared at Ash's sides. Flanking him, their weapons held loosely in their hands.

"I am afraid we cannot hand you our companion. She is essential to us and our goals. She is providing us with a wealth of information about the Deng clan," Jia said, taking Moira's right as Yue took Tala's left.

"He's a ninth-rank mortal refiner. At least. I would say he is likely stronger than Gen. From what I can tell, however, his Dantian is fractured and delicate. He is in a very similar situation to Gen," Locke provided.

"I don't think we can—"

"Hush, Mei," Ash said, interrupting her before she could suggest something stupid. Like sacrificing herself.

"Mei? Mei Ling of Deng?" the old man asked. Everyone could feel the energy he began to circulate through his meridians.

It was tantamount to loading and chambering a round in a gun.

"Mei Ling, our companion," Ash said. "And Gen will be returning any second. I'd like to see what he does once he finds out about this.

"Remember this moment, senior. This is the moment you can still walk away from this."

Ash activated his toggled abilities and then flexed his hands at his sides.

If this goes off, it'll be fast and brutal. Need to keep moving and keep changing with whatever is happening.

"Oh, I think I'll do just fine," the old man said.

Then he darted forward, lashing out with a strike at Ash's head.

Ducking to one side, Ash didn't dodge in time. The old man was simply too fast. Though instead of striking Ash's skull, he hit him in the shoulder.

Feeling his bones creak with the force of the blow and his arm go numb, Ash fell back two steps.

Bright-blue Essence appeared all around the older man. Wincing in pain, he looked very confused at what had just happened.

Locke! You said his Dantian is cracked. Can I hit it with a Qi attack using my Spiritual Perception?!

Jia moved in, water curling up around her arms as she lashed out with a series of swift attacks.

The older man went to block with one hand and was knocked a single step back.

Looking surprised, he centered himself and stared down at Jia.

Tala stabbed out with her blade, flames licking up around the edges of it. The Rabbit woman herself was a raging inferno, fire wreathing her from head to toe.

Turning his focus to Tala for a second, the old man blocked her sword with his forearm. Stopping it cold in its tracks.

The old man smiled at his block, and then his face turned strange as the fire started to climb up his arm toward his shoulder.

Knocking the blade to the side in an obvious attempt to stop the fire, the man seemed confused as it continued to creep higher.

Mei was working her way around to one side of Ash's view. Then she threw out a hand and closed it.

A crack sounded and the stones around everyone in the courtyard slammed together around the elderly gentleman. The force involved was significant enough to shatter the stones themselves.

Moira waved a hand over the massive impromptu stone tomb, and molten metal began pouring down over the top of it.

Ash hadn't been idle during this time. He'd been moving around behind where he felt the old man would be looking.

There was no way this was over. Power levels varied from cultivator to cultivator.

The problem here was that the elderly man was a mortal refiner. No matter which way one looked at it, a mortal refiner should be able to kill a body refiner with no problem.

Up to this point, Ash had the impression the older man hadn't been given a chance to fully attack. The moment he did, Ash truly believed someone in his group was going to die.

"We cannot fight him one to one—we must continue to keep him unable to attack. That is our opportunity," Jia called out.

Moira and Tala rapidly advanced, putting themselves on either side of the bubbling metallic mountain of paving stones.

Jia and Mei did the same, creating a four-point cardinal around it.

The metal rapidly turned yellow and fell to the sides, the stone it had been covering moving with it.

"Enough of this!" shouted the old man as everything fell down around him, revealing him to be naked but unharmed.

Ash agreed.

Moving forward, Ash punched out at the man's spine. Right behind where his Dantian would be.

Everything came down to this strike, and Ash focused in on it. His entire being, put into a single spike.

Ash launched the entire depth of his Qi Sea in the blow.

A needle-thin stream of Qi hardened to the point of a diamond skewered the old man through his back.

And it slid out the other side of his stomach.

There was no movement, and everyone stood still. The world froze for the moment, it seemed.

Ash retracted his Qi, pulling it back into his hand, and he backed up several steps.

"It's destroyed. This man will never cultivate again, and there is nothing that would ever fix it.

"Even your gifts or an alchemist could not fix this," Locke said. *"You crippled him for life."*

The old man slowly sank to his knees, his hands pressing to his stomach.

"No," he said, his voice soft. Whisper thin. "My Dantian."

Ash blinked once, then came to a slow realization.

This wasn't just a moment the old man would remember going forward. It was one Ash would forever remember as well.

I must remember this moment. And think back on it.

"No. You split my Dantian. It's simply no longer there. It's as if it never were," the old man said, his voice sounding like pure agony.

"You'll remember my warning," Ash said, coming to his decision. "I told you to remember that moment."

"My Dantian," the old man grieved.

"And that moment is long past. This is where you pay for your choices," Ash said. "And where I have to take from you."

"You've taken everything from me!" the old man shouted.

"Not yet," Ash whispered as he glided forward, activating Spring Step. As he stepped up to the old man's back, Ash unsheathed his butterfly sword.

Holding it in his right hand, he used Spring Step again, his shoulder and body flashing.

With a wet squish, the old man's head rolled forward off his neck. The sword had severed it cleanly with one blow.

As arterial spray arced up into the air, the headless body slumped forward into the ground.

"As Master Gen said," Ash said. "It would be a pity to do it, but we do what we must. This is war."

Ash leaned down and wiped the bloody blade against the dead man's clothes.

"And we can't leave someone alive who could speak to what we're doing, and our goals," Ash finished. "Or who my companions are."

"Good. Now let's see if he has anything on his corpse. He won't need it anymore, after all.

"It'll also be a good cultivation tonight. Maybe we'll move up to the peak eighth rank!" Locke said eagerly.

The rest of his group was staring at him. Ash wasn't really sure what to do or say about it.

"Thank you," Mei said, taking shuffling steps up to him. "I know… I know my family is evil. I've seen what they've done and what they've been doing. I know what people see when they look at me.

"Thank you for seeing only me."

Leaning in quickly, Mei kissed Ash on the cheek and then fled away.

Thirty-Two

Gen had been nonplussed to return later in the day to find his disciples had killed someone. Thankfully, Ash had stored the head and the body in his storage ring.

It was morbid and mildly disturbing, but the alternative of leaving a corpse around was worse. Bringing in a middle-aged man, Gen sat him down in front of Ash and Yue.

"Now, you already know why we're here," Gen said to the man, taking a seat halfway between Ash and the new man.

"You're recruiting," said the man without any actual care. "Recruiting cripples and the broken."

"The first part is right," Gen said. Holding a hand out to the man, he made a neutral gesture. "Tell me, if I offered you the chance to take your vengeance out on the Deng clan. Would you?"

"Yes," the man said immediately, finally expressing some emotion. He suddenly looked to be full of fire and rage.

Anger.

"They took everything from me. I'd burn them all. All of them! From elder to infant," hissed the man, foam flecking his lips.

"Yes, I imagined as much," Gen said. From somewhere, he produced a cup that looked to be filled with wine. "Here, take a sip. And as you do, I'd like you to think what you'd give up to take that revenge. We'll give you a minute."

Ash, Yue, and Gen immediately started moving away. Giving the clearly distraught man a chance to get his composure.

"He looks... very angry. Angrier than anyone else," Yue said, her hands pressed to her stomach.

"Yes... he was a rather gifted young man. Talented, strong Qi, signs of extreme brilliance at a very young age.

"He would have easily made it to an Inner Sect elder by now. At the least, if not higher," Gen said. "The Deng family tried to recruit him and he declined, so they killed his family and ended his path of cultivation."

Ash nodded slowly. Locke had already evaluated the man's Dantian.

Much like so many others they'd seen, it was damaged. Damaged, fractured, crumbling, breaking apart.

"I think there's something the Deng family practices that seems to do this type of damage. It's the same thing over and over.

"The same damage, the same problems. Sometimes a little different, sometimes better, sometimes worse—but always the same," Ash said.

"So it would seem," Gen said. "Though thankfully, we have the means to counter it if it should occur again.

"How are you doing on reagents, by the way, Ying Yue?"

"Ah, I've gotten very good at making this medicine now. I don't fail very often anymore. I'll never say no to more ingredients, but we should have more than enough to finish the job. I think.

"I've only been an alchemist for a month or two," Yue said, shrugging her shoulders.

"And you're doing wonderfully," Ash immediately said, wrapping an arm around her. For whatever reason, Ash always felt like he needed to reaffirm Yue and build her confidence up. "Amazingly so. Just because I provided you with the info doesn't take away from your aptitude to apply it."

Yue looked down at her boots, smiling and nodding her head. "Ok."

"Just to make sure," Gen said, getting their attention again. "His problem is the same as all the others?"

"Yeah," Ash confirmed. "It is. That's why it feels like it's an ability the Deng family is using. There hasn't been anything that needed my work.

"For this to keep happening in almost the same way really only leaves that, right?"

"I would imagine so. Ok, let's go take care of him and get him sworn in. After that, we'll break for the day. I think there's only a few more after this that I'll want to recruit.

"We'll have more than enough to challenge the Deng in the Outer Sect, and probably close to enough even for the Inner Sect," Gen said.

Smiling his feral Deng smile, Gen happily moved back to the table.

"I'm exhausted," Yue said, pressing a hand to her brow. "I think I just want to crawl into bed and sleep. How do you do it? Cultivate, train, and do everything else? You never seem to stop."

"Mm. I make time to rest in my schedule," Ash said, arm still around Yue. "If you don't take care of yourself, you'll be no good to anyone else. Me included. So I make sure to force some time into my schedule where I just… sit and recover.

"Sometimes even just lying down helps, even if I don't sleep. Now, let's go solve this guy and get going. We need to practice for the next tournament, and Jia has our next practice set. We won't be doing that as long as we're here."

***

Ash sat in one of the chairs in the courtyard between their rooms. He hadn't done much really, other than constantly assess and recommend treatments for people, but he felt mentally drained.

Listening to the constant stories of cruelty committed by the Deng family had taken a toll on him.

On top of that, Jia was drilling them on how to work together at every level. If they weren't able to physically train, she wanted them mentally going over the scenarios she'd put together for them.

All in all, she was an excellent strategist and planner for them. Ash wasn't going to believe for a second he could compare to her in that regard, and so he wasn't going to bother to try.

He didn't have to lead, anyways. Nor did he want to.

Without his meaning to, Ash's eyes were drawn to the paving stones at the center of the courtyard. The red pool was long since gone. The blocks cleaned and refit by Mei.

It was as if nothing had ever been there.

Other than the rotting corpse of the old man in Ash's storage ring.

There would be no way to dispose of it till they were on the road back to the sect.

I did what I had to do.

He forced my hand.

But I still killed him. Without remorse or a second thought.

Even now, I don't regret his death. But I regret that I was forced to kill him.

I wonder if that's selfish.

"It is. But understandably so," Locke offered. "Eyes up, Jia is on her way to you and she looks… determined."

Ash blinked twice and then looked around.

Everyone was still about what they'd been doing. Except for Jia. She was now on a straight path to where Ash was sitting.

"Let us have that serious match," Jia said. "I would like to know the extent of your capabilities, so I can plan for them."

Ash stared at her evenly. It was an excuse and a poor one. She already knew his capabilities well. She'd seen them many times.

"I don't really see the point in it," Ash said, shrugging. "You're already well aw—"

"Have a serious match with me," Jia said, interrupting him. Her eyes were unyielding, and Ash realized he wasn't going to be able to decline her. Not without making a point of it that was beyond reasonable.

"You're forcing this, then?" Ash asked, hoping that maybe being direct might just poke her hard enough to get her to step back.

Everyone was watching now. The atmosphere had changed. Everyone had eyes on Jia, and she was staring Ash down.

"Yes. I am," she confirmed.

Ash sighed and looked to the ground.

He'd always wondered if Jia could overcome whatever it was that was driving her to this. Her seeking out confrontation to have someone declared a victor in their relationship.

Win or lose, this would change things. And likely it would be permanent.

"Remember this moment, Jia, because this'll be the point you look back to," Ash said, getting to his feet.

"You think you can beat me that easily?" Jia said, her body falling into a neutral posture.

"No. I don't. But you wouldn't hear me if I said it, and you'd argue with me if I said anything else.

"So... we'll do this, as you've asked, and at some point in the future, you'll look back to this," Ash said, "and realize it was exactly what I said, and I never wanted this."

Getting into a defensive stance, Ash activated his abilities one by one. He began to plan out his attacks. His plan for battle.

His goal wasn't to kill her, of course, or to permanently harm her. Which eliminated making anything solid out of his Qi that might harm her.

He'd have to do his best to control the momentum. The flow.

To become a wave in motion. Ash needed to be ready to crash with force, or to recede.

Jia gave her arms a whirl, and Water Essence Qi flowed out rapidly from her hands. Dark-blue power formed and coalesced into large walls of what looked like water.

Question. Do my attacks latch to Essence? If I attack her Essence, can I leech it?

"Ah... no. That's a gap I hadn't thought of. I can fix it, but not for this fight," Locke said.

Great. In other words, if she is able to retain her Qi Sea while utilizing her Essence, it's unlikely we'll be able to beat our way through it.

"Correct. You could always use your own Qi Essence to break through it, but it'd require you attacking her directly. Due to the purity and strength of your Essence, it's likely it could kill her. After putting her abilities together for her, I can honestly say I'm not certain she'd survive a direct hit."

Ash thought quickly. Jia had planned this out, it seemed. Which meant she'd be on the lookout for the other abilities she knew he had.

Not waiting for him to make the first move, Jia drew her right arm around her front. A tidal wave of Essence smashed down toward Ash.

Drawing his Qi through his palm, Ash created an angled and smooth-faced shield. Bracing it to the ground, Ash waited for the impact, coiling himself up.

When the attack struck, Ash moved with the force, activating Spring Step at the same time.

He dove toward Jia. He needed to close the distance and start landing hits. Jia was moving much slower as Ash dipped into his speed.

Her left hand came up two inches at her side, and suddenly the wall of Essence on her left lifted her up into the air, taking her twenty feet up off the ground.

Ash blew through the column of Essence, splattering it outward in an explosion. Turning on his heel, he lashed out with a Spring-Step-enhanced kick to where Jia should have ended up.

Only to kick the same column of Essence he'd gone through after it reformed.

"As her elemental aspect is Water, she can keep it bound together quite tightly. I do not believe she's lost much of her Qi Sea," Locke said.

Ash took several steps backward, knowing Jia was one to counter-attack.

A tendril of Essence smashed down into the spot he'd been in, then immediately flowed back into the wall and reset.

Ash began to slowly pad around in a walk, trying to think of a way through this. The fight hadn't been going on long, but it was fairly obvious to him that his chances of winning were rapidly declining.

A section of the right wall peeled off of itself and splashed down around Jia. It rapidly formed a lake around her, the Essence writhing as it sloshed around.

Needing to know what it did, and figuring he'd only get one chance to test it, Ash leapt forward.

Jia reacted predictably, the wall of Essence moving between himself and her to protect any type of launching attack.

Ash landed a single foot on the lake of Qi and felt his boot stick hard to it.

Damn, it'll lock down my speed. I might have to Spring Step just to get through it, or out of it.

Shaking his foot free, Ash took two steps back and then started throwing out a rapid set of chain-linked Qi chompers.

The glowing balls of Essence sped off toward Jia.

Only to hit the wall she'd kept in front of her and stop dead.

"Need to make sure we can change the targeting of all your attacks to be whatever it hits, rather than whatever it was aimed at," Locke said. *"Probably alter your Thorns as well so that they'll burn whatever the last link available is. In other words, burn the Essence itself, since it can't seem to get back to Jia."*

Ash didn't think Jia knew about his ability to constantly refill his Qi, nor his passive ability to Heal. Which was to his advantage.

Except this was going to be a battle of wills and time. If he could hold out long enough to drag Jia down through persistence, or if she could break him before that happened.

We can win this. It just isn't a guarantee, and it relies on our passives. But that's how the tide goes.

Recede for now, build up our strength, then crash.

"Is that all?" Jia asked suddenly.

Frowning, Ash looked up to Jia's face, and he saw what he'd been afraid of all along.

Disdain.

Condescension over what he'd done so far, his inability to win—and more than likely to her, the apparent eventual win.

Shaking his head, Ash knew his thoughts had been right about her.

After all, he'd been in the same situation she was in when he beat his ex-girlfriend. He'd viewed her differently after that.

Even when she'd called him on it, he hadn't been able to correct his viewpoint quickly enough.

And she'd left him for it. Left him and moved on.

In retrospect, it was all so obvious to Ash. At the time, he'd been blind to it all.

Jia lifted a hand and her Essence began to swirl in front of her.

Then a wall of stone exploded up from the ground. At the same time, trees grew up into wooden barricades, branches shattering through the wall.

A half second later, a wall of fire and metal came to life.

Four walls of elemental Essence had sprung up between Jia and Ash.

"This is over," Mei said, turning her eyes away from the walls. Moving up next to Ash, she took his arm in her own and began escorting him away from the courtyard. "Leave the brute to herself; we should prepare for our trip back."

Yue, Tala, and Moira closed in on Ash as well. Unable to resist them, and honestly not really caring anymore, Ash let the four women corral him. In short order, they had him leaving the courtyard.

"She spent all that time thinking of ways to beat you," Mei said with a frown. "Instead of all the ways she could have improved you or herself."

"She doesn't get it," Yue added. "Oh! I bought a fun little board game I saw two older men playing. After I gave them their medication, I asked if I could purchase it from them. They said they didn't need it anymore.

"Could we play it? Might be fun."

Tala nodded once, her ears bobbing. "Let's do that. It sounds like fun. I've been working on some dice I'd like to show you all as well."

And just like that, Jia was dropped from the conversation. The five of them headed into a room to relax and enjoy themselves.

***

In the following days, it was obvious everyone had decided that Jia was no longer "one of us" and treated her with courtesy, but no warmth.

She'd gone from comrade and strategic leader to little more than someone who gave them the plan to carry out.

They treated her cordially.

And ignored any and every attempt she made to draw them into conversation.

The surprising part was even Gen had noticed. Except that not only had he noticed, he had visibly taken a side.

Ash's.

Jia was being ostracized.

It feels a lot like when we had someone working part time back home. They were on the team, but not really. They weren't there for the long haul. The day-after-day workload.

"Yes, it does appear as if Jia has worn out her welcome in a singular act. She got what she wanted for the most part, and everything that went with it," Locke added. *"To be fair, you warned her off. Practically had a siren going off like it was an air raid.*

"She chose to ignore it and pushed and pushed."

Ash could only nod as he continued deeper into the woods away from their campsite.

He was on a mission.

A mission to dispose of the rotting corpse in his storage ring. With any luck, he could drop the body and be gone before he even got a whiff of it.

He had to do it far enough into the woods that the animals would hopefully take care of it, but close enough that it looked like the man had been dragged off the road.

Stopping in a dimly lit field, Ash sighed and leaned his head back. As he looked up at the star-filled sky, Ash wondered.

"Do you think those stars only exist in this veil?"

"Perhaps a veil is a boundary only on this planet, yet in the universe it might be something more like normal," Ash mused. "Or is it much the same, and each planet has its own veils.

"Veils within veils within veils."

"Those are planets?" asked a subdued voice.

Glancing to his side, Ash found Jia standing there, staring up at the sky.

"Yeah. Each star is actually either a planet or a sun. The much more terrifying aspect is that these are only the ones we can see.

"If we had the right equipment, you'd be able to see that there is literally an untold number of planets out there," Ash said, turning his head back to the night sky.

"With so many planets... should not all of existence be filled with life?"

"One would think so. On my old world, perhaps a planet we're looking at right now, we often wondered about that. Where were other signs of life, and why hadn't they come looking for us. To contact us.

"It's an interesting thought experiment," Ash said. It'd been a while since he'd considered anything outside of what existed in this veil. "Though I don't think this veil will ever reach the level of scientific mastery to reach the stars at the same level.

"Perhaps someone will simply become strong enough to survive in the vacuum of space, but that seems like a one off."

Looking to the field as he finished talking, Ash started to sort through his storage ring to find the elderly man's corpse.

He had other places he'd rather be right now.

"You were right," Jia said into the sudden silence.

"Huh?" Ash mumbled, looking to Jia.

"You were right. It was a moment that would change everything. I did not listen to you," Jia said, her eyes unfocused and staring into the middle distance. "I was so caught up in the idea that you were trying to spare me from losing, that I never considered you were speaking to either end of the fight."

Ash didn't say anything.

There was nothing to say.

"And in that final moment, when I opened my mouth and said what I did, I only did exactly what you said would happen," Jia said. "And now I suffer for my hubris and lack of understanding."

Looking back to the field in front of him, Ash considered dumping the corpse and leaving.

"I do not know how to fix it," Jia said.

Good luck with that.

"To be fair, she can't fix it without someone in particular forgiving her. Visibly. Until such a thing happens, she will be a pariah.

"I would imagine that's why she followed you out into the dead of night. Now isn't it?" Locke said. *"Chosen One."*

Locke wasn't wrong, and unless Ash did something, it'd only get worse. To the point that Jia would leave.

She had been the only one who had comforted him in his distress, in his time of need.

He was being a poor friend.

I'm committing the same mistake from the other way around this time. Have I learned nothing?

"Personally, I forgive you.

"Beyond that, give it time," Ash said. "Be your normal self tomorrow. Try to engage in conversation. It'll take time for them to trust you again, I think. But we'll work—"

Jia was suddenly hugging him tightly. Her face was pressed into his neck.

"Thank you, Ash," she said, sobbing lightly. "I did not realize what I was risking in forcing you. You were right."

Sighing, Ash wrapped his arms around her shoulders and held her.

"I know. But that's how this works, right? A relationship is give and take," Ash said. "You were there for me when I needed you. Gave me all that you could without holding back.

"Fights happen. Just… try not to do something like this again, ok?"

"Mm," she murmured.

Then she surprised him by kissing him. Before he could respond, or even process what had happened, she flew away into the woods.

"That works," Locke said.

Thirty-Three

The weary band trudged through the gates of the sect. Trooping through in the early hours of the morning, they looked more like a bunch of waterlogged sacks of cloth than people.

It'd been raining since the previous day, and they'd decided to press on rather than find shelter. Mostly because they'd heard several strange conversations on the trip back.

Apparently, the start date for the group combat tournament had been moved up. Instead of having more time to prepare for it and learn to fight as a unit, they might only have a few hours.

If what they'd overheard was accurate, the tournament would begin today. If Gen hadn't planned ahead for his compatriot to sign them up regardless of anything, it would be unlikely they'd even be able to participate.

"Rotten scoundrels," Gen complained, his cane tapping with each step. "Dirty filthy mobsters."

"He seems particularly unnerved," Jia said, walking beside Ash.

"Yeah. Definitely so. Not much we can do, I suppose. I say we all collapse and sleep for a few hours before the tournament," Ash said. "What do you think, Jia?"

Since the night in the woods, Ash had been pushing for her involvement in conversations and group decisions.

He engaged her directly and pulled her into almost every subject he thought he could. Trying to get her back to what they all used to be. Before she didn't know what she wanted anymore.

"She still doesn't. At least, not really.

"To be fair, I don't quite understand it myself. It seems like she wants to prove herself by beating you. But I'm not sure if it's beating you, as in Ash, or you as in a Fated One, Chosen One," Locke said.

I suppose there isn't much of a difference, is there?

"Sure there is. One she wants to make her man; the other she wants to defeat. The question is, why does she want to beat you? My own guess, although I'm still new to this culture, is that it has to do with her family," Locke hypothesized.

Certainly not a terrible idea, now is it? She said her family was from the middle realm. That means they're relatively powerful. For her to come down here and slum it, as it were, means she's not just in hiding but possibly disowned.

"...agree. Sleep would be ideal, considering it is likely we will be in combat today," Jia said, her eyes moving to his own.

"Great. Sounds like a plan. Let's just do that then. I'm not even sure Gen will notice us breaking off, so let's just head home," Ash said.

As one, the group looked to Gen. He was still muttering to himself as he clacked his way deeper into the sect.

Turning onto a path that would lead them back to their homes, Ash and company moved through the rain.

"I hate the rain," Tala said, her Rabbit ears curled forward. "It makes my fur coarse and springy."

"You take baths though, don't you?" Yue asked.

"Of course I do. I brush my fur out for that, though, and I'm very careful about it. The rain gives no credence to my desires," Tala said, her mouth in an annoyed frown.

"Take a bath... hmph. Thinks I'm some sort of monster?" she mumbled almost under her breath.

Being right next to her, Ash could actually hear her, though he doubted anyone else could.

Smiling to himself, he shook his head. Tala was the same as ever, but the sharpness of her personality was expected now.

A quirk.

Something that made her—her.

"Should we all be so blessed that you'll be brushing yourself for us?" Ash asked. "Grant everyone at the tournament a good view of your fur in its luxurious state?"

There were some chuckles around him at the prod, and Tala eyed him.

Several seconds passed before she realized there was no heat or malice behind his words, and she smirked at him.

"If only they were so lucky. They're not worthy enough to gaze upon me at my best," Tala said finally.

Even she's starting to realize it.

"Well, not everyone can be as shabbily supreme as myself. I look best in a moth-eaten robe in the back of a crowd.

"Where no one can see me—which means I look my best," Ash said, turning down the street that would lead them to houses one through ten.

"I like the view from behind," Moira said.

"As do I," Mei chimed in. "Though it's equally amusing to compliment him when you can see his face. He blushes."

Tala sniffed, her smirk growing in a wide smile. "This is your comeuppance for mocking my greatness."

"I never said you weren't great, you big, beautiful bunny. I only asked if you would be giving them the full Tala effect," Ash said. Then he waved a hand at the three houses of the others. "Alright. Everyone crash out. Supposedly, the tournament opening is at noon. I'll make sure everyone is up and moving."

The tension that had been gathering around them on the trip back—starting with Jia's ill-advised match—crept back up on them now.

No one was really sure what to think of Jia right now. Despite Ash's best intentions, it was clear no one was willing to immediately forgive her.

Which also meant no one really trusted her, and that would be important for a group battle.

This was probably the worst possible situation for going into such a tournament.

Yue, Mei, and Jia peeled off from the group, heading to their homes.

Moira, Ash, and Tala kept walking. Their house, of course, was at the end of the street.

Getting to the front door, Ash immediately pushed it open and held it aside for Tala and Moira to troop in.

"Drop your clothes at the back door. We'll get them cleaned and dried later," Ash said, closing the door behind him. He immediately started to undress and unload his pack. "I'll take the packs into the ring, so just hand them my way."

"You want me to strip?" Tala asked, her fingers toying with the hem of her tunic.

"Yeah, I do. I don't want massive puddles of water in the house," Ash said, working himself out of his clothes.

Moira handed him her pack and clothes, and then she spread her wings out.

Tala huffed and then proceeded to do the same.

Thinking better of it, Ash just stored the packs and the clothes directly in his ring. "Never mind. I'll just put it all in there. Alright. Going to go hit the sack, see you soon."

Ash ran his hands through his hair as he padded naked to his room.

"I assume you want an alarm set like previously?"

Yes, please.

When he shut the thick, heavy curtains he'd put up in front of his window, his room dropped into pitch blackness. There was nothing he could see at all.

Pulling out a pair of pants from his storage ring, Ash hopped into them and then crawled into his bed.

Before he even settled into his sheets, the door to his bedroom opened and then closed again.

"I appreciate the thought, Moira. But I'm just spent," Ash said, not even opening his eyes.

"It's not Moira," Tala said. "And... I'm not here for that. I wanted to talk to you for a few minutes. If that's ok?"

"Huh? Uh... alright. Sorry," Ash said, sitting up in his bed. Blinking a few times, he rubbed at his heavy eyes. "What's up?"

"I wanted to talk to you about... well... me. The abilities you gave me. Your plans for me.

"What I should expect," Tala said. Her voice drifted closer and closer as she spoke. Then she sat down on the edge of his bed, the bed frame creaking softly.

"Ok? I'm not quite sure what you want to talk about, though. We've already had this discussion, remember?" Ash said. Rubbing at his eyes with one hand he opened them once he'd ground the grit out from the corners.

He could just barely see the outline of Tala's shoulders and ears.

"That's not untrue… I guess… I need—" Tala's head tilted one way and then the other. Then it slowly dipped down, the silhouette of her ears drooping low. "I need reassurance.

"I'm not half as confident as I would like to believe I am. Or as I'd like others to believe I am."

Not… entirely unexpected. Though I never thought she'd admit it.

Reaching out with his right hand, Ash found the top of her head. As gently as he could, he began to pet her, letting his fingers smooth her hair back.

She flinched for a split second, but then she pushed her head up into his hand.

"I know you didn't want this life. I know you didn't ask for it. Nor did you get much of a choice or a chance," Ash said. Carefully, he moved his fingers along the base of her stiff ears, working at the delicate fur there. "And when I chose for you, I picked what I felt was the best option. I didn't think you'd survive if I left you there. I honestly believed you'd be taken by someone with much worse intentions, or just killed.

"And if I took you back without marking you as mine, someone would have taken you from me. I did what I thought was best, even if it was still awful."

Tala's ears twitched at the attention, and she only nodded her head.

"I know. The situation I was in was not… It wasn't good. But what's done is done. You haven't told me what you expect of me.

"What you want from me," Tala said. "You gave me so many abilities. So many ways to fight and to actually win, that I'm a bit confused."

Ash considered her words, dragging his thumb along the edge of her ear.

"That's fair. My needs of you are very simple. Fight with me. Help me. That's it."

"That's… truly it? You don't have any other desires or wishes of me?" Tala asked.

"Well, that's all I'm willing to ask you to do. Anything beyond that would be more of a conversation than anything else," Ash said. "Not an expectation."

"I understand. I'm going to go to bed now," Tala said, standing up.

"Great. I'll see you in the morning," Ash said, lying back down with a yawn.

Tala left his room without another word.

***

Bleary eyed and feeling the lack of sleep, Ash glared up at the noon-day sun above them.

The tournament had indeed been shifted up.

Considerably.

To the point that it was fairly obvious there were even practitioners from the Deng camp who weren't ready for this.

Right now, everything was proceeding as expected. They were taking roll call for everyone there and moving ahead.

Ash and his team were clumped together, with Gen standing behind them. No one was standing near them.

In fact, it was as if they were plague bearers. The next closest group was twenty feet away.

It's fairly obvious no one wants to associate with us. Even the neutral parties who weren't against us before are against us now.

I wonder what changed.

"Everyone on this platform is carrying a Deng identification item. Mei described it as just a token that everyone carried, but she didn't mention the energy it contained.

"I believe they're unaware of it," Locke said. *"Makes it easy for us to identify them, at least."*

"I believe our reinforcements will be arriving tomorrow night," Gen said. "And then… it's just a matter of slowly leeching the strength from the Deng family."

Mei nodded sharply at that.

"Once we break the hold in the Outer Sect, they will have a much harder time in the Inner Sect," she said.

"Yes. Taking away the flow of trained and chosen recruits should hurt them," Gen said as he stabbed his cane into the stones. He was probably about to start grumbling about the fact that they were stalling again when he suddenly stood up straight. "Ah, they're done. Good. I'll go off to my position now. I imagine we'll be in the first match, in the hope that we get eliminated. Be ready."

Ash turned to Jia as Gen stomped off.

"Alright, strategist of mine, what's the plan here?" Ash asked her.

"I… do not know, Ash. Until we know what the first competition will be, I fear I cannot offer any advice," she said, a hand coming up to touch her throat.

"Eh… fair enough. I wonder what—"

A gong sounded from up ahead, and everyone started to push in close to the front.

"Time to find out," Moira said, pressing a hand to Ash's lower back. Then she leaned in and kissed him firmly.

Ash's mind floated away momentarily before he came back to himself.

"For luck," she said, breaking the kiss and pulling away from him with a smile.

Mei eyed him speculatively, as if she were considering doing the same thing. Ash skipped forward to the front of his group, trying to get everyone moving.

"…ser, closer. We'll be discussing the first competition shortly," called an unknown elder.

Getting up close to the people in front of him, Ash got comfortable to wait again.

Mei and Moira suddenly flanked him. Each woman pressed in close and tight to his sides.

"Unsurprising. They're the most forward of your women. Though I'm not sure Yue will ever break out of her worship and move to the bedroom," Locke said.

Shut it.

"Alright, welcome, welcome. The first two teams to compete are Master Gen and Master Deng. That is, the youngest Master Deng," said the elder at the front.

Of course it's us. And of course he has to clarify which one. Most of these masters are all from the Deng family.

"While this is a tournament of groups, it won't be exclusively group fights. With so many teams competing, it is likely this will take some time to have everyone compete."

"First up, Essence utilization and manipulation. Please send your representative to the examination ring, the respective teams to the boxes."

"You have the time it takes for an incense stick to burn."

Turning around where he stood, Ash looked to the rest of his group.

"My Essence is strong, but I'm not completely sold on me being the strongest at its manipulation. Thoughts?" he asked.

Tala immediately shook her head. "Not me."

"Or me," Moira added.

"My control is good, but… I'm not confident," Yue said.

Mei clicked her tongue, her eyes moving from Ash's face to his belt buckle. "The abilities you gave me previously helped me strengthen my Essence, and my control was already quite good. I might be a good candidate."

Jia didn't say anything.

She was well aware that everyone didn't quite trust her yet.

"Jia?" Ash asked, forcing the issue.

"Haaaaaaa," she said, pressing a hand to her brow. "I would elect myself or Mei. Though I think I might edge her out slightly due to the density of my Essence at this time."

Immediately, the ugliness of everyone's opinion was clear. Clear and obvious.

They felt she was right, but they did not like it. Their resistance to the idea had nothing to do with her being right or wrong.

"I would agree," Ash said. "And I'd further put my support behind Jia. Sorry, Mei. Your control is amazing, but I do think Jia's might be just a bit better."

Mei gave him a smile and shrugged her shoulders. "I'll take the compliment for what it is."

"Alright, so I guess we should head over to the ring, and Jia will be taking position for us," Ash said. Indicating a direction with his hand, he waited a second. "Unless someone has something else to offer or suggest?"

Head shakes were all he got in response.

"Then off we go," he said.

Trooping off to the ring, Ash felt his stomach twisting over on itself. The decision had been made, but that didn't make this any easier.

They'd been mostly preparing for group fights or small-scale battles. They hadn't really talked about something like this.

Even Gen hadn't mentioned anything of the sort.

Which meant they were picking things that would skew the results to the Deng family.

In other words, they probably have someone with exceptional control of their Essence.

"*Undeniably. It's what I would suggest we do if the tables were turned. To be quite frank, their tactics are valid. The real problem is we are not them,*" Locke said.

It was a strange and mildly frightening thought.

What would Ash do if he suddenly found that his alliance was in control of the Outer Sect? Would he protect it from outsiders? Would he seek to control it completely?

How far would he go to maintain that control, and what would he do?

What wouldn't he do?

Shit.

As one, his group stepped up to the ring at the same time, each immediately moving into the small outlined "box" they were expected to stand in. It was just a small enclosure of wood that was waist-level high.

Almost like a dugout or a penalty box.

Jia stood with them, looking very unsure of herself.

"Alright, Jia. It's up to you," Ash said. Reaching out, he set a hand down on her shoulder. "I trust you; I believe in you. You can do this."

Jia nodded, still looking a bit lost.

"Ok. You are right. I can do this. I am very capable," Jia said, sounding like she was psyching herself up.

"That you are. So get your ass over there and get to work," Ash said, giving her shoulder a pat. Then, grabbing her, he turned her around to face the middle of the ring and gave her a little shove.

Jia took a stuttering step, then began to walk to the center of the ring.

"You seem to be encouraging us to support her again," Mei said, slipping an arm through Ash's. She drew it close into her side, pressing herself to it deliberately.

"I am. I think... I think Jia doesn't even know what she herself wants. What she did was... insulting, and stupid," Ash said. "But it wasn't meant to be malicious."

Mei sighed, her fingertips starting to brush back and forth along his forearm once more.

"As you like. I'll play nice. Or at least, more so. Though only for you."

"I will gift her with my patience," Tala said, crossing her arms under her breasts.

Yue sniffed once, saying nothing.

Moira didn't seem to care one way or the other.

An elder and a young woman walked out to the center of the ring and began pulling things out of a storage item.

"Oh," Mei said, a frown forming. "It's my cousin. She's actually rather talented at Essence manipulation. One of the best—if not the best."

"I think this will be a stacking or building competition."

"Odd to test someone like that," Tala said, her ears twitching.

"It's… it's a Deng test. It's how we… they… measure control. This is little more than a test that is practiced almost daily for some in the family," Mei said. "This is obviously stacked to the point that it must be obvious to others."

Thirty-Four

Wooden blocks of varying sizes were laid out across the ring. Some were the size of a sofa, others no bigger than a finger.

To Ash it seemed almost like an insane, eclectic mix of things that had no logical sense being together.

"Normally, the goal is to stack a tower as high as you can," Mei murmured. "Though I'm not sure what the plan is here. Many of those blocks are from different households."

"That's... interesting, I suppose," Ash said.

The elder finished with his task and then turned to face the majority of the crowd.

"Today's first task in this challenge is simple. Build the tallest tower you can, using only your Essence. Once the time limit is up, you will have to withdraw your Essence, and we will all see how tall the tower is at the same time.

"And of course, it has to stand on its own."

The elder smiled at the young woman nearby and then looked to Jia.

"Any questions?" he asked.

"Yes. Are we allowed to interfere with the other team's blocks at this time? Or the area around the blocks? Or the area surrounding them? Directly or indirectly?" Jia asked.

The simple fact that she was asking the question was a bit of a slap to the elder's face. It was indirectly reinforcing every way the elder could have overlooked any type of foul, instead putting it out in the open first.

"Ah... no. Neither directly or indirectly may either side affect the other at this juncture," the elder said, his face looking rather stiff.

"I understand. I am ready to compete, then," Jia said, letting her arms hang loosely at her sides.

The elder looked to the other woman one final time.

She gave a small shake of her head.

"As a reminder, your blocks are those on your side of the ring. Do not cross the midpoint line.

"Otherwise... begin!" shouted the elder as he scurried off to one side, getting out of the way.

Jia spun her hands out in front of herself, her Essence splashing out of her palms like a fire hose on full blast.

Moving her body at the same time, Jia did what looked like a slow spin, her arms circling around her and her palms twisting end over end.

"It's almost like a dance," Ash muttered, unable to look away.

"Her control is... very complete," Mei said. "She's using her body to fling her Essence around at the same time."

Now that he looked, he saw Jia really was using herself as a nozzle. With the blocks spread out everywhere around the ring, this actually meant she would be able to gather hers up much more quickly.

Water Essence Qi pooled up into a lake and swarmed over all the blocks on Jia's half of the ring. In no time at all, she had them all flowing towards her. Buoyed and bound by her Essence itself.

"She was the right choice," Yue said. "I haven't forgiven her for being rude to you, but she was the right choice."

A step in the right direction, at least. I'll take it.

"Her heart rate still spikes whenever she looks at you," Locke said. *"Maybe you could take her to bed if you're really looking to change her opinion, Chosen One."*

Ass.

Jia waved an arm and the blocks began to flow to the space directly in front of her.

She quickly began sorting them out visually, moving the larger blocks to one side and the smaller ones to the other.

Mei sighed and pulled at Ash's arm. "I agree with Yue. I'm not quite... over her treatment of a Fated One yet, but she was the right choice."

At least she said yet, rather than not at all.
So that's better than Yue, even.

Jia turned her attention to the pile of larger blocks, and her Essence flowed over it all.

Looking to the Deng woman, Ash raised his eyebrows.

She had literally already built a tower that looked more like a giant pillar. She had clear experience in this, and had built toward something.

Ash wasn't quite sure toward what, but he was fairly certain there was a goal.

He just had to hope Jia had already noticed and was building accordingly.

Turning his attention back to Jia, he frowned. She had formed her large blocks into a column. It was four sided and everything was interlocked surely. The height was already far above and beyond the Deng team's, but it was much thinner.

Jia had just barely finished putting the final pieces on top when someone rang a gong.

"Time is up! Retrieve your Essence and let us see whose tower stands tallest," called the elder.

Jia shook out her hands as her Essence began to rapidly flow back to her. She walked towards Ash and the others.

Her pillar stood tall. Unchanged and exactly as she'd left it.

"I used my Essence to create a lack of air between the pieces," she said.

"Oh, that's actually pretty ingenious. The suction should certainly help keep it all together," Ash said appreciatively.

"I have been experimenting with my Essence and the abilities you gave me. I find that adding or subtracting air in the middle of it can… do some fairly volatile things," Jia said.

"Ah, yeah. You're basically making depth charges, I suppose. That can turn someone into goo pretty fast," Ash said, nodding his head.

"…eam Gen has reached higher in this competition!" called the elder, who was standing next to Jia's tower.

Apparently, they'd missed the measuring entirely.

"They have earned three points for this challenge. One for using all their blocks, one for building a sturdy tower, and one for winning.

"Team Deng has earned two points," said the elder. "The next competition is a defense of the tower!

"Select two members and send them forth. Keep in mind, you cannot use the member who built the tower in this portion."

Everyone turned and looked to one another in Ash's group.

"Who should go?" Mei asked. "It's a defense, so I think I would be rather useful as an Earth Essence user."

That makes sense. She should be able to use the ground quite freely.

Yue coughed and then lifted her hand slightly.

"I think I could support Mei the best. I'd also help offset any problem she'd experience from a direct counter," Yue said.

Ash agreed with that logic as well. Yue could probably support her better than he could.

My limitations seem built into fighting and fighting alone. Defending a location… doesn't seem suitable for me.

"Have you selected your members?" asked the elder, walking up to them.

"Ah… yes. Is there any restriction on weapons?" Ash asked.

"Weapons? Hm. No. Anyone can use any registered weapon. Now hurry up. Send your people to your tower," the elder said, waving a dismissive hand at them.

"Moira, you go with them. We'll keep Tala back just in case there's another event after this," Ash said.

Moira grunted and began marching out into the field.

Mei and Yue looked to Ash for a second longer before they too joined Moira in their march.

"They did not look as angry at me," Jia said, drifting closer to Ash.

"They aren't. They're still mad about how you treated me, but I think your performance helped take that anger away.

"Or at least, some of it," Ash said with a shrug of his shoulders.

"It did. I personally don't care that you treated him rudely, because if the fight had been to the death, Ash would have torn your heart out and given it back to you," Tala said. "The fact that it was just a practice match limited him."

Jia stared at Tala, her eyes widened slightly.

"You… truly believe that?" Jia asked after a second.

"His Essence… or whatever… is rock solid. Could he not have simply formed a bow and arrow and shot you?" Tala asked. "His Essence would have powered through yours and pierced you dead."

"We really should practice doing that," Locke said. *"We've never tried."*

"You can do that?" Jia asked, looking to Ash.

Holding up his right hand, Ash experimented at fashioning an arrow.

Immediately, a barbed arrow appeared in his hand. Handing it to Jia, he then formed a bow with his left hand.

For the string, he did his damnedest to will it to be more flexible.

And a bow was formed, complete with a string that looked like he could pull it.

"It is true. You could have simply killed me. This is as hard as steel," Jia said, tapping the arrow against her palm.

"Little good it does me in a sparring match. Now let's watch the others," Ash said. Reaching out with his right hand, Ash reabsorbed the bow and the arrow, and put his entire focus on Mei.

A man and a woman were facing Yue and Mei. They appeared to be arguing with the elder in between the two groups.

I bet they're arguing about Moira.

A minute later, the elder made a chopping motion with his hand, glaring at the Deng team. Whatever argument that had happened was now over.

"The goal is simple," the elder called, holding up his arms. "Knock over the enemy tower as much as you can. Each team has been awarded one-hundred points. They will lose one for every block lost.

"You have as long as it takes an incense stick to burn again."

Moving to one side, the elder dropped his hands. "Begin!"

Moira's wings burst out and she flapped them powerfully.

Like a white comet, she blew off the ground and barreled headlong for the enemy tower.

The man from the Deng team turned his focus to Moira and began throwing hand signs.

In short order, Fire burst out of his hands as he finished the last sign, a cone of flame splashing out towards Moira.

Banking hard, the Owl woman flew upward and turned out high above the enemies.

"She will work to keep that one busy," Jia said. "Mei will defend against the other Earth user, and Yue will attack."

"We have the upper hand."

"For the time being. Who knows what weapons they'll pull out," Ash muttered.

As if fate had heard him, the woman pulled out several gold-colored balls from her side and tossed them out in front of herself.

Exploding to life, Monsters appeared.

"It is a Giant Flame Bear and two Feral Fire Wolves," Jia said. "Those are… very expensive weapons that only exist for a single use."

"In other words, they really want us gone. They don't want us here at all," Ash said.

"They have no limits to this, it would seem. And this is just the first part of the tournament," Jia said.

Yue and Mei were suddenly tied up with fighting back three monsters and the woman.

Yue began throwing her Essence around. Trees and wood sprouted up from the stones themselves. Branches and bushes grew from nothing and worked to entangle and block their foes.

The two wolves were locked down in the wild growth, the flames around them flaring to life and burning the trap around them as they struggled.

The Bear simply bulled its way through without a problem.

The woman was hurling huge boulders at Jia's tower.

They knew about this. It's why they built a pillar and compacted it so much.

This whole thing has been rigged from the very start.

"*Yes. It has. But that's alright. I do not think this will be a loss. Though I don't think it'll be a win, either.*"

Mei punched upward with one hand, a stone hand shooting up from the ground to send the boulder hurtling away.

Yue was now contending with the Bear, using her abilities to keep it off balance and away from her.

The two Wolves had been strangled to death by burnt trees, their bodies becoming an inferno and turning the trap into a funeral pyre.

A second boulder came, then a third, a sixth, and finally a tenth.

Mei continued to work at deflecting them away, molding the stones to fit her desires and acting like giant hands. She managed to knock a large number of them away, but she didn't block them all.

"Mei Ling, stop this nonsense!" called the woman she was fighting indirectly. "Just let me knock the entire tower down and this'll be over."

"You can rejoin the family! You'd be welcomed back with honor!"

Oh… that's a problem, isn't it?

Mei visibly slowed down at the words.

The woman who had been throwing boulders stood there panting.

"Just let it happen, and you can rejoin the family. Your mother misses you," said the woman.

Building a giant boulder, the woman held it aloft for a second, then flung it at the tower.

Mei instantly threw a hand at it, sending it flying as if it had a rocket strapped to it.

"I know my place, and it is no longer with a family that cast me out. Cast me out like a whipped dog and then tried to snuff me out.

"Were it not for Ash, it is unlikely I'd be here today," Mei said. Looking angry and very much in control of herself, she flung a hand at the other woman. "Come then, child. Let me show you what I've learned since leaving."

Yue was moving away from the bear made out of living fire. Her attacks did little to nothing to the bear, other than keeping it busy.

But she had it locked up. It wasn't going to catch her — nor was she going to break away from it or beat it.

Looking to Moira, Ash watched as she banked around the far side of the Deng tower.

Her sword whipped out and a rod of metal sliced down into the tower, cracking several blocks off from its side near the middle.

There were signs all along the height of it that Moira had made some progress in her attacks, but she hadn't managed a large hit.

A dull gong sounded.

"That's enough!" called the elder.

Before anyone could do anything, Jia flung a giant ball of water at the Bear. Splashing over it and drenching it from toe to ass. The bear was soaked.

Except the ball didn't move. It hovered atop the bear, as if it were a giant snow globe with the bear at its center.

Without air to breathe, and its fire little more than steam, the bear could do nothing.

Then a massive air bubble formed near its head and collapsed. The water exploded, and chunks of bear went out in every direction.

Yue, Mei, and Moira began trooping back to their team. Moira looked somewhat spent, and Mei looked absolutely dead on her feet.

Yue was the only one who looked even moderately alright, but it was clear she was tired as well.

Shuffling over, they collectively found spots in the box.

Yue began pulling out pills from her storage. Several at a time, she put them together into a small pile. Then she held it out to Mei.

Repeating the process, she gave one to Moira, and then did it a third time, only to down the pills herself.

Smart. At least they'll be good to go regardless of whatever else happens.

Ash looked back to the two towers.

Theirs looked like it had lost a good portion of its height. The boulders hadn't needed to strike true—they'd only needed to strike at all.

"Their tower felt as if it had been sealed together with steel," Moira grumbled. "It was like hitting the side of a building."

"I have no doubt that they probably did something to it. It was obvious as soon as the second portion was announced that they knew what it would be long before," Mei said.

Just with a casual visual inspection, it was obvious to Ash his team had suffered more losses than their opponents.

But it wasn't a one-sided stomp. It just wasn't going in their favor was all.

"For what it is worth, I appreciate that you remained with us," Jia said, bowing her head to Mei. "I consider you a companion. And I value your input and presence."

Sighing, Mei pressed a hand to her head. A second ticked by before she lightly dropped the same hand on the back of Jia's shoulder.

"Yes, yes. Come, stand up. I forgive you already. You can help me out later when I ask for a favor. For now, let's see what's going to happen next. If I don't miss my guess, the score will be tied at this point, if we're lucky."

"Though it's equally possible we'll be very far behind if we didn't come close to their own score," Mei said.

"How many tests are there in a single team bracket?" Yue asked.

"Usually there were three in the past," Mei said. "Though I'd say it's pretty obvious at this point that this is anything but the usual. So I can't promise anything."

"Fair. Three. So we just need to win the next one," Yue said.

"Whatever it is," Ash said.

Finally, the elder finished counting and held up a hand.

"The winner is the Deng team. Three points will be awarded to them, and two points to team Gen due to the fact that the number of blocks they lost were within five of the opponent," the elder called.

"Oh, we did better than I thought," Ash said.

"I targeted the smaller blocks," Moira said. "They didn't specify that the smaller blocks would be worth less than the larger blocks."

"Smart woman," Ash said with a grin.

Moira smiled back at him, her wings fluttering on her back.

"The next contest will be a test of Dao!" shouted the elder. "Please send out your final member."

"Huh... guess that's me then. Come on, Tala, you're my weapon this time. Even if all you do is stand there and stare at me, at least I won't be alone."

"Let's give those long legs of yours a quick walk," Ash said, starting to walk out into the ring.

"My long legs?" Tala said, catching up to him.

"You're much taller than the average woman in this veil. And a lot of that is leg," Ash said.

Tala snorted and one of her ears twitched.

"You should feel blessed that you're able to look upon my great beauty. Legs and all."

"I do. That I do," Ash said, coming to a stop in front of the elder.

Let's do this, then.

Thirty-Five

"Come, come," the elder said, waving Ash closer. Not waiting for Ash to arrive, the elder pulled out two five-foot-tall rods from thin air. "You really have no need for your weapon to be here."

"Be that as it may, I'd like her company," Ash said.

The rods were only maybe three inches in diameter and looked to be metallic in nature. On top of that, they looked to be fully engraved on every inch of their surface.

"As you like.

"Each contestant will each take one of these," the elder said, handing one rod to a Deng member Ash didn't know. Then he turned to Ash and simply dropped it on the ground in front of him. "You'll hold one end and place the other into the ground. When I activate them, they will each seek out the other and fire a low-yield beam of Qi from their tops.

"The stronger your Dao, or your knowledge of it, the stronger the beam. Should your beam reach the other's rod, you win.

"And right now, there is no doubt that whoever wins here will win this match."

Of course. Which means this person probably has a great understanding of a Dao. There's no way they'd put someone here otherwise.

"He's actually a mortal refiner," Locke said. "If he's in the Outer Sect, he's a sleeper. He shouldn't be here."

Great.

Ash grimaced and reached down to get the rod.

Flipping it over, he wasn't sure which end was up.

"They're identical."

Grasping one end, Ash plunked the other into the ground and looked back to the elder.

"Ready?" asked the elder.

The Deng family member nodded. Then Ash did as well.

"Then… begin!"

Ash closed his eyes and began to rapidly sink into his Qi Sea.

There, sticking up from the depths, was the golden column that Ash felt was his Dao.

Every time he'd cultivated, he'd let his mind drift toward his Dao.

What he called the Dao of Momentum.

And each time he did cultivate on it, he added a number of bricks, guiding them ever higher toward the top of his Dantian. The roof of the Qi Sea's chamber.

Moving closer to his column, Ash could feel the power radiating off it. Each brick fit and added to the structure.

Which is amusing. Because my Dao is that of momentum. With each brick I add, it'll be that much simpler to add another.

Several bricks formed in thin air and slid into place into the column.

Letting a small piece of his consciousness float up, Ash could feel the beam ejecting from the rod. It was deadlocked in the middle with his opponent's beam.

No, that's not right.

Now that he focused on it, Ash could feel a subtle difference in the beams. Ash's was slowly, in ever-so-minuscule amounts, falling back toward his rod.

He was losing.

Or would lose, that was.

The brief flutter of panic dropped away as Ash smirked to himself.

That is the way of it, though. It's no different than my cultivation technique. Start slow.
Start empty.
Build up strength and continue on, ever and ever.

Letting out a slow breath, he focused on his concept of momentum. So far, he'd been applying it in his mentality.

He'd only touched on it before, but when he thought of his attacks and his abilities, the column felt lacking.

Lacking, but not wrong. It'd just never been applied. Not truly, at least. Or so Ash thought.

And when I truly think on it, is the way I fight even little more than momentum?

I crash or recede. I absorb attacks or return them.

When I take damage, I return part of it to the attacker. I redirect both physical blows and ability attacks.

My attacks become a defense as the Qi I siphon from them returns to be built into my shield, and to heal my wounds.

Rapidly, bricks began to stack up on the column. Slamming into place faster and faster as his thoughts continued along the same track.

Ash imagined how his abilities, his martial arts, and his mentality all could connect easily to be something akin to momentum.

Where with little effort, he could dial the speed of the fight up or down, all on his whim and his desire.

"And that's only the beginning. When we reach peak Body Refining, we'll be able to cleanse ourselves completely of impurities.

"And we can begin building and harnessing our meridians to our needs," Locke said. *"After that, new abilities, new techniques. Molded, harnessed, and built to fit the Dao."*

Ash's mind blanked out for several seconds before he realized what Locke was saying.

His meridians were already flowing to and from a single Dantian. A river in his body that moved according to his will.

And once he reached the top of this stage of his cultivator's path, he would control the momentum of his Qi.

The very blood of his cultivation, his Qi, would be part of his momentum.

His Qi Sea would be the turbine.

A turbine must spin.

As if sensing this thought, his Dantian roiled. The Qi Sea boiled and lapped at the column violently.

The entire vast ocean of Qi began to swirl. Sluggishly, it foamed and frothed, waves being created from the countercurrents it itself was generating.

It was literally fighting itself. Half going one way, half going the opposite.

An ominous creaking noise started to sound from the golden column.

Working quickly, Ash put his entire focus into guiding the Qi Sea. Pushing it all in one direction. Making it all go clockwise at the same time.

Sloshing and throwing Qi around in massive waves, he brought the Sea to heel. As the ocean ceased to churn, stopped throwing rogue waves at the column, and became a giant whirlpool, Ash felt his very soul still.

Slowly, the column was revealed as the center and the focal point of the whirlpool.

Rapidly, the width of the entire column expanded by several feet, bricks practically appearing from thin air. Faster and faster it went, spiraling ever higher.

In no time at all, it reached the highest point, and then kept going.

Higher and higher it went. Reaching ever closer for the ceiling of the Dantian.

"…im alo…" said a faint voice.

"…ver. We ne—"

"No!"

Something sharp and wicked pierced Ash. He felt it when it slipped through his defenses, passed right through his shield, and spit his Dantian on a thin skewer of Essence.

His eyes snapped open, and he was face to face with the Deng elder. A palm was pressed to Ash's middle, and there was no hiding what the man had just done.

Or had tried to do.

Yue had spent considerable time strengthening everyone's Dantians. Giving them a daily regimen of medicine made to directly build up the toughness of their cores.

So that if the Deng family tried something like this, it'd fail outright. Or so the hope was.

Rather than reveal that it hadn't worked, Ash knocked the elder's hand away and stumbled backward.

Tala was on him in an instant. It was obvious she'd been trying to fight off the elder, who was considerably stronger than her.

The elder's eyes followed Ash as he moved. As if weighing whether he should do more.

Not waiting to find out what he'd do, Ash immediately began limping back towards his team, Tala aiding him directly.

As he did so, Ash realized the atmosphere had changed. Changed and become a hellscape.

Cultivators were battling with others all over the yard.

His team was hunkered down behind a half shield of Water Essence. All over the place, the Deng clan was attacking anyone who wasn't part of them.

"It would seem they don't care about the results. This feels like it was little more than a distraction to bring you and your friends out," Locke said. *"That or they didn't want to slow down whatever they were planning, and this was just an option to draw someone else out of more importance."*

Whatever. Either way I feel like we miscalculated here.

"Yes. Yes, we did. To be fair, this feels reckless and aggressive. It lacks planning and finesse."

Watching as a Deng clan member literally stabbed an unaffiliated cultivator through the chest, Ash couldn't help but agree.

Emphatically so.

"Is he watching?" Ash asked, leaning heavily into Tala's side. "Elder Deng."

Tala snatched a look over her shoulder. "No."

Ash gently pushed Tala away and started sprinting for his team. Seeing him coming, Jia opened a small hole in her screen for himself and Tala to blow through.

"What do we do?" Jia asked him when he got to her.

"We get the fuck out," Ash said back. "Gen is going to start gathering our forces, I imagine, and get working on this.

"The best thing we can do is get out of the way."

"I don't really see that as an option," Mei said.

"I have an option, but... it'll be strange," Ash said.

"I think strange is a valid option right now," Yue said.

All around them, the Essence bubble shuddered. More and more unaffiliated cultivators were escaping or dying.

Leaving Deng clan members able to turn their attention to Ash and his team.

"Fine, ok. We're going to go into my storage ring," Ash said.

"What? Storage items do not work like that," Jia countered.

"I'll keep an eye out here. Once it's clear, we can discuss options. And if you so desire, I can bring you all back when you decide its time," Locke promised.

"Mine does. Time to go — hold on everyone," Ash said.

Mentally gathering everyone up, including Jia's Essence, Ash transported them all into the ring.

And to the Hall.

Great. Time to answer a lot of questions.

***

"It would seem the vast majority of the combatants are gone. The only people left are the dead, dying, or crippled," Locke said.

Ash lifted his head up from his arms and blinked several times.

He'd been dozing lightly at a table in the middle of the library hall.

Everyone else had been exploring the Hall or the contents of his storage ring. Since technically, it all ended up here.

Moira and Tala were talking quietly not far away. Mei and Jia were sitting at the table he was at, reading books.

"She's still at the medicine stall, right where you left her," Locke said before Ash could even wonder about Yue.

She had apparently spent the entire time at the stall and with its inventory. With any luck, she'd been refining medicine and making more pills.

We're gonna need anything she can make. I hope she's been productive.

Standing up slowly, Ash stretched his back one way and then the other.

"Alright, I'm going to go see what's in store for us in the square. I can't sense anything out there that would be problematic," Ash said. He wasn't about to share Locke's existence with them.

At least, not yet. Locke felt like something even beyond what a "Fated One" would have, and he wasn't about to talk about it right now.

"I'll go with you," Mei said, bouncing to her feet. "I can build fortifications quickly if I need to."

True. Earth Essence users would have that in their repertoire, wouldn't they?

"Alright. Let's go then. We'll be back shortly if it looks fine," Ash said, looking to Jia.

"Okay. A question before you go — is there a time dilation here? Should I expect you back immediately, or add time?" Jia asked.

That's… an interesting question. Can we time dilate this place?

"It… is possible. It'd require much more Essence than we've been gathering. Much, much more. Though we could alter the flow eventually," Locke confirmed.

Alter the flow.

Ash paused in mid thought, his eyes moving to the middle distance.

"Well?" Jia asked.

Shaken from his contemplation, Ash shook his head. "No. No time dilation. Sorry."

Transfer us over.

A flash of light and Ash was standing in the square. Except it felt more like a butcher's shop.

It smelled of blood and guts. The sweet, sickly odor of copper.

He could practically taste it.

Looking around, he saw the smell and taste matched the reality. There were corpses, body parts, people bleeding out all over the place.

"Looks clear," Ash said. "Start building a place for us to lie low. Preferably underground, if it's doable. I'm going to start sorting out the living from the dead. Maybe we can make some friends."

Can you relay my voice to the Hall?

"Easily."

Great. I'm going to speak now.

"The square is clear, but there's a lot of wounded. I'm bringing everyone over. Start sorting out the living and the dead. Yue, you're playing medic. Start feeding everyone medicinal pills.

"If we end up healing a Deng family member, we'll just put them somewhere safe for a time. Maybe we can make some converts out of them," Ash said.

"Message relayed. They appear to be readying themselves," Locke said.

Give 'em a minute, then bring them over.

Also… uh… can you put a green marker over everyone who's alive?

Actually, put a red marker over everyone who is alive and close to death.

Oh! Let's make it so that if they're in danger of dying, make it a square, and if they're a Deng family member make it a bright red. Everyone else a bright blue.

Everyone who isn't in a life-threatening situation, make them stars. Red and blue accordingly.

"Done. Anything else?"

Can you provide me with arrows to who's going to die first? By your own estimations.

Green arrows flashed into Ash's view, guiding him onward.

After following an indicator, Ash found himself standing over a young woman. With a bright-red square.

She was unconscious, her skin as pale as paper.

I guess I get to decide how to handle it much earlier than I expected.

There was a large pool of blood around her. It looked as if something had blown through her chest. Going in one side and exiting the other.

"We can secure her with your leeching abilities. Tap her three times. It'll be enough to keep her from generating Qi, but not enough to kill her.

"Then you can just tie her up like a normal human as the pills do their job," Locke offered up.

Sighing, Ash realized it was the best idea at this moment. Running his hands along the woman's body, he quickly emptied her of anything that might help her or aid her in escaping.

Pulling out a small, circular token, Ash paused.

It was a smooth metal slug, without any type of identification.

"That's the Deng power source I keep sensing. It's coming from that."

Huh. Alright. We'll keep this one just in case.

Ash pocketed the slug.

Pulling a pill from his storage, he pushed it into the woman's mouth, then tapped her three times on the shoulder.

Do I have time to drop this one off before going for the next one?

"Yes. Or so I estimate."

Ash attached the chains to his belt and hefted the woman up over his shoulder. Turning to find Mei, he was surprised to see her standing still, staring down into the ground.

Shifting the woman around on his shoulder a bit, Ash started making his way to Mei.

The arrow that was still pointing to the woman bounced around from her to someone else a few times.

Then it settled in another direction entirely. As if the woman Ash was carrying was no longer in immediate danger.

Mei glanced up at him as he approached, her eyes moving to the woman on his shoulder.

"Cheating on me already? I haven't even had the pleasure of knowing you in bed," Mei said, the corner of her mouth curving up. She held one hand open and pointing toward the ground as she spoke.

Whatever she was doing, it was happening beneath the ground, out of sight.

"Uh huh. She was dying, and she's apparently a family member of yours. I've already got her stabilized. Need to tie her up and put her somewhere. She won't be harming anyone or doing anything for a bit. She looks like the one from the first test."

"I suppose I can forgive you for that. Let's see who it is," Mei said. "Turn around for me so I can get a look. At her as well."

Snorting at the flirting, Ash turned around so Mei could see the woman.

"Surprising," Mei said after a second. "And a loss for the Deng family. I won't bother you with her name since you'll probably forget it. But it is indeed the one Jia fought against in the Essence competition. If we can convert her, or at least keep her from doing anything more, it would help us greatly."

Jia, Moira, Tala, and Yue popped into existence. Almost immediately, they began fanning out. Checking people for signs of life, then moving on or starting to treat them.

Mei rolled a hand and then snapped her fingers.

A rectangle opened up in the ground and yawned into an open doorway below.

"There. That should work. It's deep enough that we can't be attacked directly, and built in such a way that people won't be able to understand it from above," Mei said. "I'll take her. You get back to work."

"Right, just bind her with rope or something of that nature. She'll be as weak as a citizen."

Ash handed over the woman to Mei and then turned to the square.

There was bloody work to do.

Thirty-Six

It took what was probably close to two hours, but the square was cleared. Deng family members were healed, drained of Qi, and tied up.

Those who had no Deng affiliation were healed and enlisted to help with the square's cleanup process.

Jia clapped her hands together, and Water Essence washed her hands clean.

"What do we do now? We have not heard from Gen, and there is no… word. Of anything," Jia said.

"I'm not sure. Part of me thinks we should just stay put. There isn't much we can do against elders and masters," Ash said with a sigh. "We'd just get killed."

Moira folded her arms in front of herself and nodded her head.

"It's true. We're not at their power level. We'd be little more than a strike or two if they decided we shouldn't be there.

"We can't really impact this battle any more than we have," Moira said.

True. Other than getting Gen an army to fight the Deng with, there isn't much we can do against those higher-leveled individuals.

"We should attack the Outer Sect Deng clan house," Mei said. "There is much to take there, and it would only be guarded by those able to handle body refiners. Anyone above that would be sent to fight.

"It's also a fallback point. A stronghold. They would be that much worse off if we took it and they needed it."

Jia's eyebrows went up, and Yue looked interested.

"It's not as if we can do anything more here," Yue said. "We've secured the area, provided shelter for the wounded, and secured the enemy combatants. Anything we could fight against, they could as well."

"That and if something comes to wipe out this location, there is likely little we could add," Tala said. "We'd just be killed with the rest."

"Accurate," Locke said.

"And you think we can get in? And win?" Ash asked.

"Yes. The defenses aren't complicated. Most of the problem is the security there. I do strongly believe it'll be gone, though," Mei said.

"The alternative is to sit here with nothing to do and hope we are not attacked," Jia said. "I think it would be good to strike them there. If they were hoping to use it as a defensive location or a storehouse to rearm, it would be good to take it."

Ash looked to Mei.

"Lead on, then. We're in your care," he said.

Without hesitation, Mei turned on her heel and started leading them deeper into the sect. Everyone else fell into a wedge formation behind her.

Ash put himself in the rear since he could react faster than anyone else. Moira and Tala flanked him a step ahead, though still next to him.

"This is a good moment to remind you she was given a chance to betray us, and she did not," Moira murmured softly. Her lips practically brushed his ear as she did it, ensuring no one would hear it but him. "She is loyal to you, and I think it wouldn't be a bad idea to consider tying her to us more closely."

Ash blinked at the unsaid words.

There wasn't much more he could do to tie her to himself, other than marrying her or pledging a blood oath with her.

"She's also very polite to me, and she treats me as an equal despite my status," Moira continued. "Think on it. You're destined to have more than one woman in your life—it's just a matter of time. Better to pick now, before you are forced."

Moira then kissed his ear and followed it up with a small nip of her teeth against his ear lobe. "And we're visiting the Hall tonight. Alone. I'm tired of sleeping by myself."

Then she withdrew, the warmth on his ear fading quickly.

Though Ash certainly felt warm everywhere else.

"I tend to agree with her. Though I personally would take Yue to my bed first, rather than Mei."

"Mei I would take after that," Locke offered helpfully. *"I think I'd leave Jia to herself. She won't be ready until she unwinds whatever problem she has with her family.*

"As for Tala, I'd wait for her to make the move. I don't think that'll be long after you bed your second woman, though. She won't want to be much further behind than that."

Why do you seem to think this is a competition? It's my life! This isn't some dating show where I just hump my way to victory.

"Isn't it, though? Whatever woman becomes your primary wife will have infinitely more power than whoever is last.

"They're not wrong in calling you a Fated One, Chosen One. You're destined to leave a mark."

Whatever.

Ash ignored Locke entirely and focused on keeping an active watch on their surroundings. This was the worst possible time to let himself be distracted.

The sect was under what seemed like a siege.

After what felt like ten minutes and a number of turns, they stood in front of a warehouse.

One that seemed shoved back into the depths of the Outer Sect and long forsaken.

"Yes. This is it. There's a small door in the floor inside the warehouse. One must know it's there to be able to get in," Mei said. "I don't believe they would have changed anything here, as they're not aware I know.

"My aunt told me about several locations like this. If she were to admit it to others, she would be heavily punished. I cannot imagine she'd be willing to take a hit like that to her image."

"In other words, in being selfish and fearing repercussions, you know where several safe houses and storage areas are," Jia summed up.

"Yes, and isn't that grand?" Mei said with a smile as she opened the warehouse door. "Everyone in. I can't open the door if this is open."

Once everyone got inside, Mei shut the door and turned to the wall adjacent to the entry.

"It's a false wall," she said. Reaching up, she began pushing on the bricks one at a time. "Auntie said one of these would give way and allow it to open."

"This one," Locke said, highlighting one brick in particular. *"It has a faint Deng power signature to it. I think it won't open without one of those tokens."*

Pulling out the Deng token, Ash reached up and started tapping bricks with it. He wasn't going to go straight to the right brick. He had to make it seem like he was searching blindly.

"You have a Deng coin," Mei said, eying him and pausing in her search.

"Took it from the Essence girl. I figured why not, might come in handy," Ash said. Then he tapped the slug to the brick Locke had told him was the right one.

A small pop and the crackle of static electricity provided the noticeable clue that something had happened.

"Ah, the token must be required," Jia said. "Your aunt must have thought since she did not include that piece of information, she could keep you from snooping."

Mei frowned and then pushed on the wall near the corner. It slid into itself as if it were on wheels. "I did try. Twice. So I suppose she wasn't wrong in not telling me about it.

"I thought the Deng coin was just a way to identify members."

"It's a power source," Ash said, pocketing the coin. "I can sense them on people."

Mei walked into the cutout in the wall and vanished.

"Oh, that's how you identified who was in the Deng family," Yue said, following Mei. "That makes sense."

"Let us be silent. We have no idea who waits below for us," Jia advised.

One by one, everyone went into the hidden passage, following Mei down into the darkness.

"No guards," Mei said as they passed out of an antechamber and entered a hallway. At the end of the hallway, two doors looked like they went in different directions.

Moving to a small pedestal off to one side at the starting point of the hallway, Mei rotated the small statue that sat atop it.

There was a soft pop as it settled into a new position, and Ash had the sense that a number of nasty things had just been deactivated.

"Traps are on, though," Mei said. "That means if someone is home, they are no stronger than we are."

"Will deactivating the traps signify we are here?" Jia asked.

"Possibly. If they're paying attention. Unlikely though," Mei said. Turning, she waved a hand at the door they'd passed through.

A massive earthen wall appeared that must have been ten feet deep.

"That'll keep anyone out that doesn't belong, and give us a moment to decide what to do if someone stronger shows up," Mei said. "Otherwise... what's our plan?"

"Do you know the layout? Can we just go to the vault, then burn everything down after we've robbed them blind?" Yue asked.

"I don't. I'm sorry," Mei apologized with a shrug.

"You have done enough, Mei. We would have had no plan at all without you," Jia said, dismissing the problem.

"I would recommend we split into two groups. Three and three. Myself, Mei, and Yue as the first. Between us three, I know we have enough storage space to clean out anything we encounter.

"The second would of course be Ash, Tala, and Moira," Jia said, looking to the rest of the group. "I doubt there is anyone here who could stand up to either three of us. And if there is, we can double back and find the other group simply enough. This is a safe house, not a maze."

Yue nodded her head, quickly followed by Mei doing the same.

"As you like," Ash said. Then he gestured at the hallway and the two paths ahead of them. "I'll take the left, then. You can have the right side."

All three women looked askance at him.

"No reason," he said to the unspoken question. Which wasn't quite true. It was just that this reasoning wouldn't make sense to anyone.

Always clear dungeons left to right, and make sure everything is checked. This is no different.

Work it one side to the other, make sure it's all clear, and move on.

Mei's face pinched together in clear worry.

"Be safe, Ash. Without our Fated One, I don't think we'd last long," she said.

"I'll do my best to remain safe. Promise," Ash said, waving a hand at her. With Moira and Tala in tow, Ash opened the left-hand door and went in.

As they worked their way down the hall, Ash found himself looking around cautiously. He had the distinct feeling the Essence around them was changing.

Changing in a strange way. It almost felt oily, in a way.

Hey, Locke, is there something different here?

"Nothing that's showing up to what I can see or scan. Your companions seem unaffected," Locke said.

Frowning, Ash nodded and continued. Maybe it was just his nerves, after all.

There was an all-out war going on. Ash couldn't do much on the front line, but if he could deny the enemy a fallback point and resources, then he'd be pulling his own weight.

"Taking the square, recovering allies, and taking prisoners will help in its own way," Locke said.

Ash grimaced. His thoughts must have been circling around that point if Locke wanted to comment on it.

Grasping the handle on the door in front of him, he began to slowly open it.

Admittedly, I just hate feeling like a lump of nothing.

"Furthest thing from it, but that all plays into why you don't try very hard."

Ash was about to argue with him, except that when he got a look into the room—it was full.

From wall to wall, floor to ceiling, there was what Ash could only think of as loot.

Spirit stones, gold coins, potions, treasures, medicinal pill bottles, dried resources, and a whole lot of stuff Ash couldn't identify.

"This is… a lot," Ash said.

"Yes. I would say that in taking this, we really will cause them no small amount of distress," Moira said. "How quickly can you pick all this up?"

Ash bit his lip and then started to try and load everything into his storage space as quickly as he could. He worked his way around the room, taking piles of things at a time.

"Sorry, it isn't meant to take groups of items."

"Ash, there's a door over here," Tala said, interrupting his work.

"Ok. Is there something different about it?" he asked, unsure of the point. With a flick of his hand, a small mound of spirit stones vanished.

"It's hidden. Built into the floor itself," Tala continued.

Looking over to her, he saw her standing over what looked like normal stone. She was tapping at it with a foot.

"You can tell?" he asked her.

"I can hear someone down there," she said. "Curses and shouting."

Moira came over and smashed a hand down into the stones. Liquid Metal Essence poured out of her hand and flowed around the stones. It began to seep through cracks and gaps that Ash couldn't see but were clearly there.

"Found it," Moira said. She clenched her other hand. There was a clack, and the stones began to shift around, sliding into themselves.

An entry began to reveal itself, and inside of it steps led down into the dark.

"Cursing and shouting, you said?" Ash asked.

"Yes. A lot. And a lot of just screaming," Tala said. "Screaming full of pain and anger."

"Right. So… a prisoner. Let's go see who they have chained up," Ash said.

Taking the lead, he began walking down the steps and into the darkness below.

With each step he took, it felt like the Essence around him grew more and more putrid. Foul.

It was like he was walking through a dump on a hot day.

Then the stink hit him. A rancid, foul smell that reminded him of his Black Day. It had the same awful sick odor to it that would haunt his memories forever.

"Behind that door," Tala said, gesturing at the solid wooden door that had appeared in front of them out of the gloom. It had metal bands running along the top, the middle, and the bottom.

It was very clearly reinforced.

Whatever or whoever was down here, they weren't just being punished but locked away at the same time.

Shrieks and gibbering words without meaning could be heard through the thick door and walls.

It was the sound of madness.

"I think this is actually a bad idea," Ash said when they stepped up to the door. "Suddenly I'd very much rather leave this door closed."

"I would as well," Moira said, and Tala agreed with a nod of her head.

"Right, we're gone then," Ash said, and turned around.

"Ashley?" shouted the voice from inside the cell. "Ashley Sheng!?"

"Identified. The occupant of the cell is Jing Sheng," Locke said. *"And I do not think opening the door is a good idea, either. It would be best to leave. Immediately."*

"ASHLEY SHENG!" shouted the voice. Then there was a change in the air.

The dark Essence thickened. It began to creep and crawl into the cell. Through the walls and the door itself. As if nothing could stand in its way.

"ASHLEY!" the voice shouted again.

Then everything shook, and the door melted away into black goo.

Thirty-Seven

Jing stood in the middle of the cell.

His face was a black mask of what looked like blood and Black Day filth. Open wounds bled and oozed. It looked like he'd been worked over for a long time.

His eyes looked haunted, each ringed with a black circle. The whites of his eyes were solid black as well—as if he wasn't even human anymore.

It wasn't just his face, though.

His torso, his arms, his hands—everything Ash could see of Jing—indicated he had taken a severe beating. One so bad it was amazing he was standing.

"Hello... brother," Jing said, a smile spreading across his face. Several of his teeth were missing. "I've been here for so long. What day is it? I don't know anymore.

"I tried counting. But they punished me for it. Punished me for everything. Punished me for taking my punishment badly."

Jing's eyes unfocused as he stared at the space between himself and Ash.

"They fed me Black Day filth for meals. Made me eat it when I refused. But... you know what? After a while, it wasn't so bad. It gave me strength.

"Gave me power," Jing said. "The last one they sent to punish me didn't leave alive. I beat her, had her, then ate part of her while she lived. Then I tore out her heart and held it up for her to see."

Ash followed Jing's gaze as it moved to a corner.

A naked and very abused female corpse lay there. It looked as if it'd been there for a bit. This wasn't something that had happened recently.

"They stopped feeding me after that. So I've been eating her. She doesn't mind."

"She didn't mind at all," Jing said, then looked to Ash.

As if a switch had been flicked, the man Ash had known as Jing was replaced by a frightening black shadow of death.

"You did this. This is all your fault, Ashley. All your fault!" Jing shouted. Then he shot forward. "I was the son first. I was the brother. You're at fault!"

Ash had been ready for something like this, though. Triggering his Spring Step, Ash flew up the steps behind himself.

But Jing was there already, practically on top of him.

As they dashed up the stairs, Jing started to throw punches at Ash.

Deflecting them away and countering as best as he could, Ash placed most of his focus on getting out of the stairwell and away from his friends.

He wasn't sure he could take Jing with their help in a short battle. Not without one of them getting hurt. Or so Ash gauged from what he was feeling from Jing.

And he wasn't about to risk their lives for a fight he was sure he could win if he got into an open space.

Tapping his hands to his waist as he cleared the stairs, Ash turned and fled down the hallway.

"We can't siphon any Essence from him. It's all corrupted. Corrupted and very poisonous," Locke said. *"We're lucky his Essence has no ability to break into our Dantian. Otherwise, we would be no more."*

What?

"He can't subsume us with his poison because we have no elemental affinity. Otherwise, we would be dead already."

He's that deadly!?

"Very."

Ash panicked for a second as he saw the Earthen wall Mei had built up ahead of him.

Clapping his hands together, he formed a wedge of his Essence and bulldozed through the construct.

Hitting it at full speed, Ash only lost a fraction of his momentum as he burst up into the warehouse.

It was all Jing needed to land a strike between Ash's shoulder blades.

Instantly, it felt as if his skin was on fire. Burning and itching like acid had been dropped on it.

Shooting out of the warehouse, Ash turned around mid-stride.

Jing was on him, throwing a heavy kick towards his middle.

Ash deflected the strike away with his leg and threw a counter-punch as he circled to Jing's side.

Turning it aside as if he saw it coming, Jing snarled at Ash and lashed out with a thick, shadowy saber made of pure black Essence.

Not wanting to even touch it, Ash ducked low and began speeding away again.

"You're heading for the Inner-Sect. I strongly advise not moving in that direction. The Essence waves coming from there are still very violent. It is likely the battle continues."

Good. Maybe I can get Jing to go after someone else and they can deal with him for me.

Ash hunkered low, activating Spring Step every time his feet touched the ground.

Except Jing was on him. He was only three steps away and matching him on speed.

Leaping upward with an explosive burst of Essence, Ash began to practically jump from building to building, flashing forward.

Reaching down into himself, he began to press on his Dantian. On the swirling maelstrom of his Qi Sea. Each and every time he landed, he activated Spring Step and shoved on the circling mass of Qi in his Dantian.

His meridians flared and stretched each time, Qi racing throughout his body as he pushed himself harder and harder.

Feeling the momentum in his movements with every beat of his heart when he hit the ground, and the massive flow of Qi, Ash watched as his golden column flared to life.

It exploded into a golden pillar of light and filled the space from where it stood to the ceiling of his Dantian, then stopped dead.

As it happened, he felt something inside himself *pop* and fall away.

The next time he activated Spring Step, Ash felt himself practically vanish with the speed he launched off with.

Glancing over his shoulder, he saw Jing start to barely fall behind.

"ASHLEY! I WILL CATCH YOU!" Jing screeched at the top of his lungs.

Disappearing from view in a puff of black smoke, Jing appeared right behind him.

"His power just increased," Locke said.

No shit!

Gritting his teeth, Ash looked ahead and strove to get to the middle of the Inner-Sect.

He could actually see the disturbance now with his eyes. Essence and Qi flashed with explosive force ahead of himself. It was clear there were a number of cultivators locked in a heated battle up there.

Pushing on his Dantian, Ash felt his heart shudder. His body wouldn't be able to keep up with something like this for much longer.

Landing in the midst of what looked like a mad melee of older men, Ash ran straight into a pack of Deng masters and elders.

They saw him at the same time and looked rather confused.

Ash could imagine it from their point of view. An Outer Sect nobody landing amongst what could only be described as a bloodbath between mortal and spirit refiners.

Bracing himself to be struck during the maneuver, Ash got low and then sprang up and over the Deng group.

Before he'd cleared the front line, Jing appeared. Like a predator sighting prey, Jing lashed out at all the Deng clan members in front of him.

Each time his hands, feet, or weapon landed on one of them, they shrieked in pain. Flesh and limbs came away from the exchange with black smoke roiling off them.

Ash landed behind the group and began sprinting wide around, trying to get away from the whole situation.

Those Deng cultivators who were mortal refiners died within seconds of Jing touching them. Their Qi literally turned on them, becoming pitch black and devouring them.

Seeing someone he recognized as not a Deng affiliate, Ash waved him down.

"Get everyone out from here! That's a monster that kills by touch. We have two safe havens in the Outer Sect," Ash told him as he passed by. "It might be time for a strategic retreat."

The older cultivator looked to the situation Ash had pointed out.

By now, more and more Deng clan members were getting involved. Some splitting off from their fights with other masters to help out.

Realizing something was happening that was outside of their expectation, the elder nodded. Lifting his arm, he fell back toward the Outer Sect. More and more, Gen's allies, unaffiliated cultivators, and those who simply opposed the Deng, were leaving the square.

Getting into a reasonable spot, Ash got low to the ground and tried to calm his racing heart. His body was beaten and tired, but this wasn't over.

Jing was a whirlwind of anger and death. Everything and anything he got a hold of suffered for it.

"We can't win," Locke said suddenly.

What?

"We can't win. There is little we can do to stop him. And with every life he's taking, I sense a strong upswell in his power.

"He is much like you in that he gains power from those he kills."

Great. Any ideas, then? If we can't beat him in a straight-out fight, I'd love to hear any other options.

"You could put him in the Hall. It'd make it off limits, and I strongly believe there's a good chance he'll corrupt it with his Essence," Locke said.

Pass. Not a great solution because it doesn't really solve the problem. I'd still have to let him out eventually or risk you and the Hall.

When he hit me, did it have any effect on him? Did it burn him?

"Yes, but only marginally. It did nothing to him."

Ash stood up, having gotten his breathing under control. His options felt beyond limited, and he lacked any way to actually make this work.

It felt like the only thing he could do was try to make Jing leave. Except nothing mattered to him. He had betrayed his sister and tried to rob Ash directly.

There wasn't anything that could—

Mother Far!

He always was a mother's boy. Far would be a trigger for him.

Did Mei ever mention where the Deng family head is?

"Middle realm. They're a low-tier family there," Locke said.

That's the plan, then. Try to convince him somehow that the Deng family is after Mother Far, and the only way to stop them is to go after the head.

"To be honest, it's already likely they are indeed after Far. They may not have acted yet because they're not sure who's behind you."

Ash blinked and felt his heart quail. Locke was right, of course.

"Jing!" Ash shouted.

Wrapping his hand around a Deng woman's throat, Jing looked to Ash.

"Wait a moment, brother—I'll take your life shortly," he said, then closed his hand. The woman who had been struggling up to that moment withered, turned black, and collapsed to the ground.

"It can't wait, Jing. The Deng clan head is after Mother Far," Ash said, and put his entire belief of this statement behind it. Because he did truly believe they were probably targeting the Sheng family.

"What!?" Jing said, taking a step toward Ash. His brawl with the Deng family was forgotten.

"The clan head of the Deng family. He was making plans to go after Mother Far. Because they thought you were lying about what you knew.

"So they're going after her, and he's the only one who can take back that attack," Ash said.

Jing stood frozen to the ground, shivering from head to toe.

"You know this? You believe it?" Jing asked.

"I do believe it. It's what they would do. Just look at what they did to you."

"Imagine them doing that to Mother Far," Ash said.

Jing snorted, black mist exhaling from his nose. He was clearly contemplating what to do. How to respond.

Even in his rage and madness, he was still Far's son.

"Where is he?" he asked finally.

"I don't know. I only know the Deng family is from the middle realm," Ash said honestly.

Jing stared at Ash for several long seconds.

Then he vanished, as if he'd never been there. In his place was a black fog. One that held the very essence of death and pain.

It swarmed over the remaining Deng members, blocking them from view. Screams, shouts, and the occasional Qi explosion were all Ash could hear and see.

Then Jing, a living cloud of evil, sped off into the sky. Vanishing out of sight.

All he left behind were the corpses of all the Deng clan that'd been standing there only moments before.

"I pity you, Chosen One. It would seem the ploy worked, but what if he finds out you lied? I think the rage he has will be entirely directed at you, then," Locke said.

Yeah... probably. Take it as we go.

"More Deng clan members are coming. They are all very much stronger than you."

Right, uh, time to go then. Let's head back to the warehouse and finishing cleaning it out, then go to where we put the wounded.

"A wise course of action, Chosen One. Though... I fear this isn't the end of this problem. Either the Deng family will win, and you and yours will be hunted and executed, or Gen and his followers will win, and the sect will be very bad off for its loses.

"This is a no-win situation, really."

Yeah, I know. But this is where we'll stay.

So let's do what we can.

Epilogue

Gen eased himself down into a chair across from Ash and smiled at him.

Half of his face was a mask of burnt skin, and one ear looked as if it might be lost entirely if he didn't take some time to have it checked.

"So... you tended to the wounded, took prisoners, ransacked their holding here, and then led a shadow monster into their ranks causing excessive losses," said his master.

"Yes, Master Gen. That's what we did," Ash said.

"Hm. I'd like a more thorough accounting. To really understand all that happened. But that can wait for another time. When we're not struggling to put the sect back together.

"And speaking of that, the sect leader will want to see you soon, I imagine. It is by no small means that it is our faction alone he still leads," Gen said.

It'd been several days since Ash had last seen Jing.

Since then, they'd remained in the Outer Sect, acting as a controlling force. Supplies were waylaid that were intended for the Deng members, and Gen and his allies had a fallback point to rest and restock.

It'd been a battle of attrition in the end. Little had happened outside of daily battles until the Deng clan members who remained had all surrendered or fled.

"We're at his disposal," Ash said.

"No... not everyone else. Just you, Ash. I'm afraid you'll not be able to hide some of what you can do after this.

"It's too obvious," Gen said with a shrug. "For what it's worth, I trust the sect leader to keep it secret. Though if he does, he won't be able to do much to give you anything in the way of assistance.

"Anonymity does limit his capabilities, after all."

Ash didn't really care, and he shrugged his shoulders.

"I have what I need. I don't think there is much he could offer or do for me that I would want right now," Ash said honestly.

Gen reached up and ran a finger along the edge of his burned skin.

"Yes, I can imagine," Gen said. "So, what is your plan then? My understanding was you were wanting to take vengeance on the Deng clan. As far as they're concerned in the sect, that is done and taken care of.

"They no longer exist here. Though their allies remain."

Letting his eyes drop to the floor, Ash wasn't quite sure how to respond. He really didn't know what he wanted to do right now.

"I think... I want to get into the Inner Sect. Lie low. Gain more power," Ash said after a minute of self-reflection. "Sure, I have many gifts and things available to me, but I don't have the power to protect myself. At least, not completely. I need time to develop."

Nodding, Gen pressed a hand to his chin.

"That's a fairly wise outlook on the whole situation. That isn't exactly quick, though. It'll take time."

"Yeah, well, I have that," Ash said. "My biggest issue right now is just... being left alone, I think."

Gen chuckled at that.

"Yes. So it would seem. I don't think this is the end of your troubles, though. Just because the Deng have left doesn't mean you are any more well liked or respected.

"If anything, in doing what you did, all the other families in the sect — other clans — will look to you and try to determine what you are. What you're doing.

"I would wager that your life is going to be the furthest thing from peaceful. Though... at least it will be relatively safe here," Gen said. "Relatively."

Ash closed his eyes and pressed his hands to his forehead.

"He's not wrong. But at least we have a place to hang our hat, so to speak. This isn't a bad place to build our strength, Chosen One."

"I'll leave you to your thoughts. The sect leader will probably ask to see you tomorrow, if I don't miss my guess.

"You should rest; you look tired," Gen said.

Ash pulled his hands away from his face, except Gen was already gone. He was quiet, very quiet. And his ability to vanish without a sound was getting better.

It only took about ten seconds before someone walked in. Ash knew everyone else was outside and probably wanted to talk to him about various things.

Though he hadn't expected Jia to be the first one in.

"I wish to speak," Jia said, standing in front of Ash. Her hands were twisting into each other, her fingers locked tight. "About… what all happened and me."

"Alright," Ash said, looking up at the woman. This really didn't feel like the time or place, but he wouldn't look a gift horse in the mouth.

The sooner he could settle Jia back into place, the better.

"I wanted to be defeated by you," she said. "I wanted you to beat me black and blue. To crush me as if I were not a threat."

Blinking, Ash raised his eyebrows at that. He wasn't quite sure what to say.

"I wanted that, because then I could validate… what I was thinking. That I was not wrong in my actions," Jia said. "You know I ran away from my family. I spoke of it once."

"Yeah," Ash said.

"I did so because they wished to marry me off once I reached a certain point in my cultivator's path.

"They wanted me to stop so I would not eventually grow stronger than the man I would be given to.

"Instead, I ran away, and here I am," Jia said. "And you… changed the rules for me. I am very strong, now. If I am able to continue this way, I can challenge for the leadership of my clan.

"Except… I do not wish to."

"Uh huh," Ash said, still confused.

"I wish to remain here. With you. And if you were able to defeat me, then remaining here made sense. I did not have to leave because you were stronger than me."

"And when I couldn't instantly beat you, you felt… scared?"

Jia's brows bunched up, and then she nodded once. "Yes. That would be accurate."

"I was. But no longer. I understand… myself now… or at least more so."

"That's good."

"Though, I have another problem," Jia said with a sad smile.

"Alright?" Ash was barely able to keep up right now, and he wasn't sure he wanted a surprise of bad news at the moment.

"I received a letter from my cousin. She was my one friend at home."

"She visited me once in Xing City," Jia said with a sigh.

"Apparently, my location has been discovered. It is very likely that in the next six months, I will have someone try to come and claim me," Jia said. "And I would ask for your assistance in this matter."

Jia suddenly clenched her hands into her clothes and bent down toward him at the waist.

"I need your help, Ashley Sheng. Please assist me in breaking free of my family. I think they will send a peak mortal refiner to fetch me," she said.

A peak mortal refiner? What the hell am I supposed to do against that?

"It is my older brother, and I desperately hope we can do this without killing or permanently harming him," Jia asked, her head dipping lower still.

Great. Ok.

Ash leaned back into his chair with a sigh.

"Yeah. I get it. I'll do everything I can to help, Jia. Family counts, after all. One way or the other," Ash said.

And that leads me back to the other problem.

Where are you, Trav, and how do I find you?

"Then… thank you, Ash. I am in your debt," Jia said, standing up. "If you do not mind, I would like to start paying that back.

"Would you be willing to have dinner with me?"

"Rather forward of her. Good for her," Locke said. *"Let's say yes."*

Ash smiled and set his chin in his hand.

"Why not," he said.

"Good. I will let Yue and Mei know that I have secured you for myself, so they may need to alter their plans.

"Tala and Moira have already agreed to watch the houses," Jia said, giving him a bright and wide smile. "And I know just where to take you to hide from prying eyes."

"Very forward of her. Hm. Maybe she finally figured out what she wanted, after all," Locke said. *"You."*

Thank you, dear reader!

I'm hopeful you enjoyed reading Cultivating Chaos. Please consider leaving a review, commentary, or messages. Feedback is imperative to an author's growth.

And if you enjoyed Ash's travels through the Veils, be sure to check out the other novels in the VeilVerse:

Asgard Awakening: Blaise Corvin

Oh, and of course, positive reviews never hurt. So do be a friend and go add a review.

Feel free to drop me a line at: WilliamDArand@gmail.com

Join my mailing list for book updates: William D. Arand Newsletter

Keep up to date—Facebook: https://www.facebook.com/WilliamDArand
Patreon: https://www.patreon.com/WilliamDArand
Blog: http://williamdarand.blogspot.com/
Harem Lit Group: https://www.facebook.com/groups/haremlit/
LitRPG Group: https://www.facebook.com/groups/LitRPGsociety/

If you enjoyed this book, try out the books of some of my close friends. I can heartily recommend them.

Blaise Corvin- A close and dear friend of mine. He's been there for me since I was nothing but a rookie with a single book to my name. He told me from the start that it was clear I had talent and had to keep writing. His background in European martial arts creates an accurate and detail driven action segments as well as his world building.

https://www.amazon.com/Blaise-Corvin/e/B01LYK8VG5

John Van Stry- John was an author I read, and re-read, and re-read again, before I was an author. In a world of books written for everything except harems, I found that not only did I truly enjoy his writing, but his concepts as well.
In discovering he was an indie author, I realized that there was nothing separating me from being just like him. I attribute him as an influence in my own work.
He now has two pen names, and both are great.

https://www.amazon.com/John-Van-Stry/e/B004U7JY8I

Jan Stryvant-

https://www.amazon.com/Jan-Stryvant/e/B06ZY7L62L

Daniel Schinhofen- Daniel was another one of those early adopters of my work who encouraged and pushed me along. He's almost as introverted as I am, so we get along famously. He recently released a new book, and by all accounts including mine, is a well written author with interesting storylines.

https://www.amazon.com/Daniel-Schinhofen/e/B01LXQWPZA

CPSIA information can be obtained
at www.ICGtesting.com
Printed in the USA
LVHW032244191218
601160LV00017B/703/P